Praise for

When the Heart Cries

"As a native of Lancaster County, born and raised among Amish and Mennonite neighbors, I began reading *When the Heart Cries* with some trepidation. My concerns were quickly put aside: Cindy Woodsmall's research is thorough, and Hannah Lapp's Amish voice rings true. Her story is both touching and tragic, yet hope shines through every page-turning chapter. A moving and meaningful first novel."

—LIZ CURTIS HIGGS, best-selling author
of *Grace in Thine Eyes*

"Reaching deep into the heart of the reader, Cindy Woodsmall pens a beautifully lyrical story in her debut novel, *When the Heart Cries.* She paints a vivid backdrop of Amish and Mennonite cultures with fascinating detail and memorable clarity. Fans of this genre will be thrilled to discover this new author, and I look forward to the next book in the Sisters of the Quilt series."

—TAMERA ALEXANDER, best-selling author of *Rekindled*

"What a vibrant, strong, emotional story! *When the Heart Cries* will grip you and not let go, I promise. Highly recommended!"

—GAYLE ROPER, author of *Allah's Fire*
and the Seaside Seasons series

"*When the Heart Cries* is a story of tragedy and strength when an Amish girl's life is struck with the horror of reality. A powerful first novel."

—DIANN MILLS, author of *Leather and Lace*
and *When the Lion Roars*

"*When the Heart Cries* is a compelling and moving beginning to what promises to be a great new series. Cindy Woodsmall's characters wrapped themselves around my heart and wouldn't let go."

—DEBORAH RANEY, author of *A Vow to Cherish* and *Remember to Forget*

When *the* Heart Cries

A NOVEL

Cindy Woodsmall

Sisters of the Quilt, Book One

WaterBrook Press

When the Heart Cries
Published by WaterBrook Press
12265 Oracle Boulevard, Suite 200
Colorado Springs, Colorado 80921

The characters and events in this book are fictional, and any resemblance to actual persons or events is coincidental.

Mass Market ISBN 978-1-60142-711-3
Trade Paperback ISBN 978-1-4000-7292-7
eBook ISBN 978-0-307-44627-5

Published in the United States by WaterBrook Multnomah, an imprint of the Crown Publishing Group, a division of Random House LLC, New York, a Penguin Random House Company.

The Library of Congress cataloged the trade paperback edition as follows:
Woodsmall, Cindy.
When the heart cries : a novel / Cindy Woodsmall. — 1st ed.
p. cm. — (Sisters of the quilt ; bk. 1)
ISBN-13: 978-1-4000-7292-7
ISBN-10: 1-4000-7292-1
1. Amish—Fiction. I. Title. II. Series: Woodsmall, Cindy. Sisters of the quilt ; bk. 1.
PS3623.O678W47 2006
813'.6—dc22

2006011000

Printed in the United States of America
2014—First Mass Market Edition

10 9 8 7 6 5 4 3 2 1

To the one man I never wanted to live my life without,
my staunchest supporter, my closest friend: my husband.
With you, life is more than I ever thought possible. Thank you.

To my two oldest sons, who believed in me.
You sacrificed your personal time to help with the needs of the household
and took great care of your younger brother so I could write. Thank you.
You also have my gratitude for keeping my computers and Internet in good
running order in spite of my best attempts at sabotage.

To my youngest son, the radiant energy to each day.
You never doubted I could do this.
When I needed humor in this story, your imagination came to the rescue.
May you one day write the stories of your heart.

To my new daughter-in-law, who has helped in hundreds of various ways.
I'm so thankful you're now a permanent part of our lives.

And above all, to God,
whose patience, love, and forgiveness make
every relationship in my life possible.
May I hear and respond to You and no other.

In loving memory of my mother,
whose inner character always strengthens me
and continues to make its mark on her descendants.

And to all daughters who navigate this ever-changing world,
trying to find who they really are as a child of the King.

Acknowledgments

I'd like to give a very special thanks to three women without whom this book and its sequels would not be possible: Miriam Flaud, my dear Old Order Amish friend, who opened her home, her family life, and her heart to this writing endeavor; Linda Wertz, who knows the Amish community well and opened doors for me, chauffeured me tirelessly whenever I landed in Pennsylvania, and never questioned if it would all be worth it; and Kathy Ide, editor, mentor, and friend. You in no way doubted that I could do this, even though you saw the roughest drafts of them all.

I'd like to thank everyone who had a hand in making sure all fictional patients responded in ways that were medically accurate: Rebecca T. Slagle, BSN, MN, neonatal nurse practitioner; Kim Pace, RN, BSN, manager, NICU/Nursery, Northeast GA Medical Center; Jeffry J. Bizon, MD, OB/GYN; Terri Driesel, physical therapist; Elizabeth Curtis, RN.

Thank you to my critique partner, Marci Burke, whose fast-paced imagination, problem-solving skills, and faithful diligence can get any author out of a writer's block and back to work long before he or she is ready!

To Kathy Port, Kathy Bizon, Lori Petroni, and others who offered prayers and bits of time and creativity to various aspects of this project.

Thank you to Karen Kingsbury, who found time to reach out to me, even with a husband, six children, and a writing career.

Thanks to Deborah Raney, whose critiques, brainstorming, and encouragements are too numerous to list.

Thank you to Shannon Hill, who believed in this work from the moment she read the first chapter. I'm so grateful for the privilege of working with you.

And to all the staff at WaterBrook Press. You're absolutely amazing!

1

Hannah Lapp covered the basket of freshly gathered eggs with her hand, glanced behind her, and bolted down the dirt road. Early morning light filtered through the broad leaves of the great oaks as she ran toward her hopes...and her fears.

A mixed fragrance of light fog, soil, garden vegetables, and jasmine drifted through the air. Hannah adored nature's varying scents. When she topped the knoll and was far enough away that her father couldn't spot her, she turned, taking in the view behind her. Her family's gray stone farmhouse was perched amid rolling acreage. Seventeen years ago she'd been born in that house.

She closed her eyes, breaking the visual connection to home. Her Amish heritage was hundreds of years old, but her heart yearned to be as modern as personal computers and the Internet. Freedom beckoned to her, but so did her relatives.

Some days the desire to break from her family's confinements sneaked up on her. There was a life out there—one that had elbowroom—and it called to her. She took another long look at her homestead before traipsing onward. Paul would be at the end of her one-mile jaunt. Joy quickened her pace. Her journey passed rapidly as she listened to birds singing their morning songs and counted fence posts.

As she topped the hill, a baritone voice sang an unfamiliar tune. The melody was coming from the barn. She headed for the cattle gate at the back of the pastureland that was lined by the dirt road. Beyond the barn sat Paul's grandmother's house, and past that was the paved road used by the English in their cars.

Paul used the cars of the English. Hannah's lips curved into a smile. More accurately, he drove a rattletrap of an old truck. Even though his order of Mennonites was very conservative, much more so than many of the Mennonite groups, they didn't hesitate to use electricity and vehicles. Still, his sect believed in cape dresses and prayer *Kapps* for the women. Surely there was nothing wrong with her caring for Paul since the Amish didn't consider anyone from his order as being an *Englischer* or fancy.

As Hannah opened the cattle gate, Paul appeared in the double-wide doorway to the barn. His head was hatless, a condition frowned upon by her bishop, revealing hair the color of ripe hay glistening under the sun. His blue eyes showed up in Hannah's dreams regularly.

He came toward her, carrying a pitchfork, a frown creasing his brow. "Hannah Lapp, what are you doing, stealing away at this time of day? The whole of Perry County will hear thunder roar when your father finds out." He stopped, jammed the pitchfork into the ground, and stared at her.

The seriousness in his features made Hannah's heart pound in her chest. She wondered if she'd overstepped her boundaries. "It's your last day here for the summer." She held up the basket of eggs. "I thought you and your grandmother might like a special breakfast."

He wiped his brow, his stern gaze never leaving her face. "Gram's awful mean this morning."

"Worse than yesterday?"

He nodded. *"Ya."* A hint of a smile touched his lips. He often teased her about the word she used so much, threatening to tell everyone at the university about that word and the girl who used it. He knew her Pennsylvania Dutch pronunciation of the word as "jah" was correct, but that didn't stop him from ribbing her about it. As the slight smile turned into a broad grin, it erased all seriousness from his face.

Hannah clutched an egg, reared back, and mimicked throwing it at him.

A deep chuckle rumbled through the air. "Can't hit anything if you don't release it…or in your case, even if you do."

His laughter warmed Hannah's insides. She placed the egg back in the basket, huffed mockingly, and turned to cross the lawn toward the house.

This would be Paul's fourth year to return to college. Once again he'd be leaving her throughout fall, winter, and spring—with letters being their sole communication. Even that limited connection had to come through his grandmother's mailbox. Hannah's father would end their friendship with no apologies if he ever learned of it.

Paul covered the space between them, lifted the basket from her hands, and smiled down at her. "So, won't your family be missing you this morning? Or should I expect your father's horse and buggy to come charging into my grandmother's drive at any moment?"

"My *Daed* would not cause a spectacle like that." Hannah licked her lips, thirsty after hurrying the mile to get there. "I arranged with my sister to do my chores this morning."

"Then who will do her chores?"

"Sarah's off this morning 'cause it's her afternoon to sell produce at Miller's Roadside Stand. I paid her to do my chores. So it all works out, *ya*?"

"You paid her. Was that necessary?"

Hannah shrugged. "I'm not her favorite person. But let's not talk about that. She was willing to work out a deal, and here I am."

Paul opened the screen door to his grandmother's back porch. "I just hope Sarah doesn't say anything to your father."

"There's nothing for her to say. As far as she knows, Gram told me to be here to work." Hannah paused, grasping one side of the basket Paul held. "Besides, even *Daed* tries to remember it's my *rumschpringe*."

He released the basket to her. "But extra freedoms don't hold a lot of meaning for your father, do they?"

She refused the disrespectful sigh that begged to be let loose. Her father could be exasperating at times. "The traditional rules keep him a bit subdued. It wouldn't do to have the bishop discover he's not following our traditions."

Hannah opened the door to the house, but Paul placed his arm across the doorframe in front of her, stopping her in her tracks.

He bent close. Hannah kept her focus straight ahead.

"Look at me, Hannah." The soft rumble of his words against her ear made a tingle run through her. The aroma that she'd come to recognize as easily as the man himself filled her. His scent had come to make her think of integrity, and it made her long to draw closer to him.

Several seconds passed before she managed to lift her gaze to meet his. His lips were pressed together in a smile, but his blue eyes held a look she didn't understand.

"I've been aching to talk to you before I return to college. There are some things I just can't write in a letter. If you hadn't come today, I was planning to knock on your door this afternoon." A light sigh escaped his lips. "But the problems that would have caused would have prevented us from getting to speak."

"Paul!" a shaky voice screeched out. The slow thump of a cane against the wooden floor announced that his grandmother was only a few steps from seeing them.

Hannah took a step backward, thinking she'd die of embarrassment if anyone saw her this close to Paul.

He straightened, putting even more distance between them. "Promise me we'll get time alone today. I need to talk with you before I leave."

Hannah stared into his eyes, promising him anything. "I give you my word," she breathed.

He lowered his hand from the doorframe. "Gram, Hannah's here."

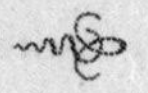

From the berry patch, Paul heard the familiar chime of the sitting room's clock. It rang out five times, but Paul needed no reminder of the hour. He was more than ready to see Hannah for a second time today and before he left for the fall semester.

He dumped the handful of blueberries into the half-full galvanized bucket. He straightened the kinks out of his back and studied the horizon for a glimpse of Hannah. The moment they had washed the last breakfast dish, Hannah had scurried home, hoping no one had missed her. So they hadn't managed to find a moment for private conversation. He turned his attention back to the almost-bare bushes, glad he'd bought two pints of blueberries from Lee McNabb's Farmers' Market yesterday.

He'd had more than enough of treating Hannah as if she were only a friend when he was in love with her. If she were a few years older, he'd have shared how he felt long before now. But even if he told her and she felt the same way, she wasn't the only one who would have to continue keeping their relationship hidden. If he wanted to keep her out of trouble with her father and even her community, he couldn't afford to tell anyone about her. He had too many distant relatives in Owl's Perch who could ruin their future by getting talk started.

Assuming she was interested in a future with him.

As Paul stood at the picnic table, adding the purchased berries to those he'd picked, he saw Hannah topping the hillock of the dirt road. The sight of her caused his pulse to race.

Most of her beautiful chestnut-colored hair was hidden by the prayer *Kapp.* Her brown dress, thick with pleats, came far below her knees and was covered by a full-length black apron. The Amish aimed to be plain in every possible way, from their eighth-grade education to the strict codes of their clothing. A smile tugged at his lips. Hannah had the heart of a lioness and the gentleness of a kitten. Keeping her ordinary was a feat that couldn't be accomplished by a set of rules—even the laws of the *Ordnung.*

She spotted him and waved. He returned her greeting and set down the bucket. His entire being reacted to her: his heart pounded, his palms sweated, and his thoughts became jumbled. But what kept him returning to Owl's Perch each summer wasn't his physical attraction to her. There was something between them that he didn't understand, but he knew it was hard to come by in a guy-girl relationship. With her as his wife and his degree in social work, there was no telling what the two of them could accomplish. He and Hannah both wanted to make a difference in the lives of others—especially children. What better way than to become a lifelong team, even though Hannah was just now learning how to pray and trust God. Until recently, for her everything had been a matter of adherence to rules.

Paul watched her every move as she opened the back gate and crossed the field. As he unlatched the cattle opening to the front of the pasture, loving words rose in his throat and all but forced their way out of his mouth. But, as always, his lack of confidence and his respect for her more stoic ways kept the words unspoken.

"Hi." She handed him the cloth-covered bundle she'd been carrying.

He raised the bundle to his face and breathed in the aroma of fresh-baked bread. "Mmm."

She gave him a challenging grin. "So, who do you think made that bread?"

"You." He spoke with absolute confidence.

Her hands settled on her hips. "There are four bread makers in my home. How can you tell whether I made it?"

"When you've made the dough, the loaf has a hint of blaze within it, as if you put part of your soul in it."

Hannah laughed. "You talk foolishness, no?"

"I'm serious, Hannah." He inhaled the scent of the cloth-wrapped loaf again. "If you breathe deeply, you'll smell the heat." He held the bread toward her face. "Just like the fire in you, Lion-heart."

She clicked her tongue, warning him he was edging toward impropriety. He lowered the loaf and gazed into her eyes, not wanting to disrupt the power of the feelings that ran between them. To him, Hannah possessed all the courage, control, and nobility associated with lions. The term fit perfectly, even if its use did embarrass her.

"Wait here." Paul strode to the back door, grasping the handle to the bucket of blueberries on the way. He marched across the porch and into the kitchen. After setting the pail and the loaf of bread on the table, he hollered, "Gram."

Finding her in the living room reading her Bible, he stepped to the round mahogany end table next to her. "Hannah's here. We're going for a walk." He took one of the walkie-talkie radios off the table and turned it on. "If you need anything, just push this button." He pointed to the knob with the musical note on it. "If you buzz us, we'll come back pronto." He set the radio on the table and attached the matching one to his belt loop.

His grandmother's eyes searched his face.

Paul raised an eyebrow. "Please try not to need anything." He kissed her on the head.

"I'll give you fifteen minutes, young man. Then I'm pushing that button. Young people don't require any more time than that."

"Come on, Gram. Hannah and I need some uninterrupted time to talk."

Soft wrinkles creased her face as she studied him. "I'll give you twenty. After that, whatever needs to be said can be said on the back porch or in the kitchen. And no back talk or I'll drive to her parents' place myself."

Paul sighed. "Yes ma'am." He hurried to the back door. Gram never allowed him to feel like an adult. When he was with his parents in Maryland, they gave him a lot more freedom than his gram did, and at the university he had freedom galore. He didn't need it there.

He checked his pocket for the gift box and bounded out the back door.

Hannah stood on a knoll, staring across the green pastures at the grazing herd as the breeze fluttered through her skirts and played with the strings of the *Kapp* on her head. He'd love to have a photo of that. Any photo of Hannah would be nice.

He came up to her and held out his hand. For the first time, she placed her hand in his.

They jogged across the field and into the shade of the woods. When they came to a bridge that stretched across the creek, they slowed. Hannah peeled off her slip-on shoes and sat on the edge of the wooden planks. Her feet dangled high above the water.

Paul shook off his sandals and sat beside her.

For a moment no words were spoken. The sounds of the water babbling, some birds chirping, and an occasional cow mooing filled the air.

Ignoring the nervousness that clawed at his gut, Paul covered her hand with his. "It gets harder to leave every year." He drew her hand to his lips and kissed it.

She gawked at him, as if she hadn't ever expected him to kiss her. He leaned in closer, hoping to kiss her cheek.

Clearing her throat, she pulled away from him. "I think it would be best if we go back now." She stood.

"But..." Paul jumped up. "I...I'm not finished with what I wanted to say. I want to talk about us."

She picked up her shoes. "Don't ask to see my heart and then return to your girls on campus." Without looking at him, she stuffed a foot into each shoe. "I may not be educated like them, but I'm nobody's fool, Paul

Waddell. I've heard stories of what it's like out there, and I don't appreciate this. We're better friends than this." Brushing her hands against her apron, she lifted her gaze to him.

Uncertainty roiled inside him, making his stomach hurt. He slid his feet into his sandals. Was he ruining the very friendship he cherished above everything else in his life? "I do not have a girl on campus, and I never have. There's no one for me but you...if you'd care to be called my girl."

She stared at him for a moment. "What are you saying?" Her hoarse whisper etched itself into his soul.

Paul moved in closer. "I'm saying I want us to have a future...together." He reached into his pocket and pulled out a long, thin, gold-colored box. "This is for you."

Hannah shook her head. "I can't take that."

"All this time we've been friends, and you can't take a simple gift?" He held it out for her, hoping she'd accept it. "It's what we've done together, working for Gram along with making goods to sell at McNabb's Farmers' Market."

She lifted the box from his hands and held it while questions remained in her eyes.

Paul dared to touch her cheek with his fingers. "Hannah, you are all my thoughts and hopes."

She stared at him, her breathing rapid.

"We'll have to wait at least a year, but..." Paul stared at his feet, kicked a patch of moss, and tried not to mumble. "Hannah Lapp, will you marry me?"

She didn't utter a sound or even twitch a foot. He raised his eyes. Her face had disbelief written across it. "But...my family... I...I... It'll be hard enough on *Mamm* if I don't join the faith, but her heart will break if I move out of Owl's Perch."

Paul rubbed the back of his neck. Winning the approval of her family was an uphill battle, one he had to win or her heart would rend in two. He gazed into her eyes, hoping to assure her that he'd do his best.

They both knew that if she married him, it would affect her relationship with her family for the rest of her life. Since she hadn't been baptized into the Amish faith, she wouldn't be shunned if she chose to marry a Mennonite. But her father wouldn't allow an outside influence to enter his home any more than he would allow electricity. When she was permitted to have a rare visit, she would not be allowed to enter the house. Things weren't that way in every Amish family, but that didn't help Hannah's situation.

The key to winning over her father, Paul hoped, was patience and timing. As much as he wished for the right words to soothe Hannah's concerns, he didn't have all the answers.

As if absorbing and accepting the truth of his feelings for her, a slow smile erased her distress. She managed a nod.

"Is that a yes?" He clasped his hands over hers, which were still holding the unopened box.

"Yes," she whispered.

"Hannah, I can't believe this. I mean...I didn't think... You keep a man guessing, that's for sure."

She angled her head. "Would you have me be bold, like those girls I hear about among the English?"

Paul squeezed her hands. "I'll never be interested in anyone but you." He reached for her face. His fingers lightly trailed down the sides of her cheeks. "You're so beautiful."

Hannah backed away, sputtering. "Beauty is vanity, and I'll thank you not to put any stock in it."

Paul laughed. "Oh, you are beautiful, but that's not why I'm interested. Why, I could find lots of beautiful girls if that's what mattered to me."

She studied him for a moment before she chuckled. "Listen to your boldness. Why, I should have thrown that egg at you this morning."

Paul laughed. "Too late." He pointed to the gift. "Open the present."

With her cheeks covered in a blush, Hannah removed the golden ribbon wrapped around the small box. She lifted the lid and pulled out a thin book, about two inches by three inches. Her brows knitted slightly as she opened the book to a page of columns and numbers.

"The card I had you sign last week wasn't for Gram's tax purposes. It was for our savings account." He pointed to the bottom number in one of the columns. "With all our work over the summers, this is what we've earned so far to sponsor that little girl in Thailand."

The joy-filled surprise in her eyes made every drop of sweat worth it. "You've saved that much?"

"*We've* saved it. We planted that huge garden beside Gram's every spring for three years. We sold the vegetables and bought the supplies for canning. I may be the one who got stuck with the handyman jobs of roofing and such, but you sewed all those doodads—from dolls to comforters. It took both of us to earn this money. Thanks to our efforts, some young Thai girl will go to live at House of Grace instead of being sold into slavery. She'll get clothes, food, and an education."

Hannah ran her fingers over the columns of numbers. "Who would have thought that with a little hard work we could do so much for someone?"

"God, I suspect." He desperately wanted to kiss her. Instead, he held his hand out for the book. "I want to show you something else."

Hannah gave him the book, and he flipped the page. "This section shows a portion of money I've set aside in a separate account." He pointed to the right spot. "This is for our living expenses."

Hannah's attention moved from the book to him. "But you're the only one who's been putting money into the living expenses part, right?"

Paul nodded, unsure what she was getting at.

She scrunched her brows. "Then how do you have so much already?"

"I've been aiming at this for years."

She seemed too surprised to respond. He kissed her on the forehead and was taken aback by the softness of her skin. The longer he stood so close to her, the stronger the need to kiss her lips became. But he was afraid she might not appreciate that move. "As soon as I graduate, I'll work for your father all summer without charging him. During that time, I hope to get his blessing to marry you."

Hannah rubbed her throat, concern flashing in her eyes. "And if he doesn't approve?"

"He will, Hannah, even if we need to wait an extra year or two." Paul bent and planted a kiss on her cheek. Her soft skin smelled sweet, like honey and cinnamon. "Your folks will come around."

A shadow seemed to cross her features. She picked up the side of her apron and tucked the gift box, ribbon, and book into the hidden pocket inside her pinafore. "If anyone can win over my family and community, it'll be you." Lifting her chin and squaring her shoulders, she giggled. *"Ya?"*

"Ya." Paul nodded and smiled.

The two-way radio beeped at him, and Gram's voice muttered his name.

"Come on." He held out his hand. "We'd better get back before Gram ruins my plans to win your father's approval."

Hannah put her hand in his, and they hurried toward his grandmother's house. "My heart is fluttering."

Paul paused, tightening his hand around hers. "I love you, Hannah Lapp."

She lowered her head, staring at their clasped hands. "I love you too."

Carrying the bucket of blueberries, Hannah locked the back cattle gate and waved her last farewell to Paul. As she headed for home, her heart was soaring higher than the jets she'd seen streak across the sky. Wherever those people were going couldn't be as exciting as where her dreams were taking her.

What a remarkable man, to be willing to work for her father in order to win his approval, to wait patiently to win her family over. Her heart thumped with excitement, and laughter welled up within her.

She moved the thin metal handle on the bucket of blueberries to her other hand and wiped a bead of sweat off her neck. Paul had spent time on a hot August afternoon picking berries for her family, and he'd get no credit for the kind deed. It was just like him to work hard for others and be thankful if he'd managed to be of help. She couldn't believe such a wonderful man considered it a privilege to marry her.

Since his dream was to become a social worker and for them to be foster parents, perhaps she could do him justice even though she had only an eighth-grade education. She loved children. And she knew how to run a household and how to turn a profit doing ordinary things like canning, sewing, and cleaning. The English girls at his college might have their education, but Hannah was determined to outshine all of them when it came to being a perfect wife for Paul and a wonderful mother to their children.

She touched her *Kapp,* proud that Paul found her ways pleasing. Oh, there were so many things she wanted to ask him, so many conversations they could have now that she knew he loved her. She looked forward to his letters more than ever. This time, there was no question that the sea of girls out there held no interest for him.

At the sound of car tires crunching against the pebbles on the dirt road behind her, she stepped to the far shoulder. Was it really possible that Paul had asked her to marry him? The tiny bubble of doubt burst as she slid her hand under her apron and felt the leather book in the hidden pocket. He'd put her name on all his hard-earned money. He trusted her with his heart, his dreams, and his earnings. He'd win her parents' approval. She knew he would.

Realizing the car she'd heard hadn't passed her yet and assuming the driver wanted more space, she stepped farther to the side of the road. It was just a one-lane country road, used mainly by horses and buggies. She refrained from looking over her shoulder, even though the smell of the acrid fumes from the growling engine grew stronger.

The car pulled up beside her. "Excuse me," a man said.

Hannah stopped and turned. She saw a sleek car that looked different from anything she'd ever seen. Shifting her gaze to the driver, she supposed he wasn't even as old as Paul, although she couldn't see much of his face. He had a beard that looked a couple of days old, and he wore a baseball cap and sunglasses.

"Can you tell me how to get to Duncannon?"

Studying the countryside, she thought of the route the hired drivers always took when chauffeuring her and her family toward Duncannon. Hannah pointed down the road in the direction his car was headed. "Keep going until you come to a four-way stop. Take a left. You'll go quite a piece until you come to another stop sign. Turn left again. Then keep going, and you'll start seeing signs that show how to get to Duncannon."

The man frowned and shook his head. After turning off the car engine, he opened the door. As he got out, he looked behind him at the long dirt road. Then he turned back. "How far until I reach a paved road?"

"About a mile."

The man smiled and eyed her from head to toe. "Right after that one farmhouse?"

Feeling pinpricks of discomfort, Hannah smoothed her skirt with her free hand and swallowed hard. He wasn't as unfamiliar with these roads as he'd made himself sound at first. Hoping he'd get in his car and leave, she started walking.

The man grabbed her arm. "No need to run off."

She fought against the sense of panic, jerked her arm free of his grip, and ran.

Two large hands hit her back, pushing her hard. She went sprawling across the gravel road. Her blueberries tumbled in every direction as the bucket flew from her hand. Hannah tried to stand up, but another forceful push to her back sent her careening again. She pulled herself to her knees, trying to gain her balance. As she scrambled to her feet, she realized her palms were bleeding.

She glanced back at the stranger. Although most of his face was hidden behind his sunglasses, beard, and hat, she saw him smirk as he reached for her. *Run, Hannah! Run!* her mind screamed, but she couldn't move.

The man grabbed her by the thick apron straps that crisscrossed her back. He lifted her body slightly, dragged her to his car, spun her around to face him, and tossed her across the seat like a rag doll. Grabbing her by the pinafore, he shoved her farther into the car. The back of her head hit the door on the other side. Her vision blurred.

The man climbed on top of her. Hannah pushed against his face and body, but he didn't budge. She flailed at him, but he didn't flinch. He repositioned his body, jerking at her skirts.

What was happening?

Tears streamed down Hannah's cheeks. Shadows swirled from within, as if she were being buried under layers of suffocating soil. Fear and anger joined forces within her, altering, shifting who she was, how she thought about life.

When she no longer felt like Hannah Lapp, his weight lifted, and he pulled her out of the car. He dragged her several feet in front of the vehicle, then flung her to the road like a filthy rag.

Only vaguely aware of her surroundings, she heard his car engine roar. Confusion lifted. She knew he intended to run over her. Crawling on her hands and knees, she moved out from in front of his car. Her dress tangled around her knees, and she couldn't move any farther. She pulled herself upright. Gravel spewed from the tires. As he passed her, he flung the car door open, hitting her with it. She flew forward and landed hard on the ground as his car sped off.

Gasping for air, she spotted the shiny silver pail lying near the ditch. On her hands and knees, she grabbed the bucket and tried to gather its spilled contents. Her body screamed out in pain with every movement, but *Daed* would be furious if she wasted the produce. She swiped at her tears, desperate to find all the berries. Clawing at the road, sifting through dirt and pebbles, she searched for the fruit, dropping each berry into the bucket. Dragging her apron across her eyes, she cleared the tears away. She looked in the pail. It contained mostly gravel and clods of earth with a few bruised and torn berries.

After staggering to her feet, she turned in one direction and then the other. Confused, she stood in the middle of the familiar road. Which way was home? She had to get home.

Her *Mamm* would know what to do.

The scent of freshly baked bread wafted through the evening air, guiding her in the right direction.

2

Afraid the man might return, Hannah hurried along the road toward home, faltering with every step. When her house came into sight, a bit of relief nipped at the corners of her panicked soul. She stumbled across a patch of grass, dropping the bucket of ravaged blueberries.

As she ran across the dirt driveway, the heel of her shoe caught on the ripped hem of her long brown skirt. She went sprawling across dirt and gravel, scraping more flesh off her palms and forearms. Getting to her feet, she reached to adjust her *Kapp* and realized it was missing. Bands of hair had fallen loose from the regulated bun.

Forbidden.

A painful shudder ran through her. She placed her bleeding palms over her skirts, bent over, and threw up. Shaking so hard it frightened her, she wiped her mouth with her apron. The scorching sun and miserable August heat made staying on her feet even harder.

Surely her mother would make sense of this nightmare. Hannah's eyes searched from one end of the property to the other, covering the yard, barns, and garden. She finally spotted her, carrying an armful of sweet corn.

Mamm's smile faded when she caught sight of Hannah. The husked corn fell to the ground, rolling in every direction. She gathered her long skirts and ran to her daughter. The odd sight of *Mamm* letting go of everything and running added to Hannah's nausea.

Mamm wrapped a consoling arm around her.

"Oh, *Mamm,* there was this horrible man." The words stammered from her lips in Pennsylvania Dutch. "He...he pulled me into his car."

She stepped back, resisting her daughter's embrace. Pulling Hannah's chin level with her own, she gazed into her face. Her mother's eyes, which had always embodied gentleness and control, grew strange and unfamiliar. The color drained from her face, like apple cider spilling out of an upturned Mason jar. *Mamm* shrieked at the top of her lungs.

Horror ripped through Hannah. Confusion once again churned inside her soul. She had never heard her mother scream before. Ever.

"Zeb!" *Mamm's* high-pitched voice rang throughout the farm. "Zeb!" She elongated the word, sending it once again across the peaceful grounds.

Her father sprinted from the garden, dropping the hoe from his hand.

Chills ran up and down Hannah's body. The familiar sight of her father in his black trousers, brown shirt, suspenders, and straw hat looked real enough. Then why did she feel so detached from her body? Her siblings seemed to float from the corners of the property to see what was going on.

Her father waved a hand at them without slowing his pace. "Tend to your chores." They slid out of sight.

Daed didn't slow until his hand was under his wife's forearm, supporting her. "*Was iss letz?*" he asked, using the only language they spoke among themselves. Hannah was relieved they had their own language. If that horrid man was lurking in the woods, he wouldn't know what was being said. Her father looked at her fallen hair and torn clothing.

"My Hannah." *Mamm's* ruddy hand pointed a shaky finger in her daughter's face. "She's been attacked!" A moan escaped her lips.

Nausea churned in the pit of Hannah's stomach at the guttural sound. Suddenly she wished she hadn't told. Her mother clung to her father, screaming in agony as if God Himself had pronounced a curse upon the Lapp family. *Mamm* released her grip, doubled over in pain, and collapsed. *Daed* clutched her, keeping her from falling to the ground. He lifted her and carried her in his arms.

He looked at both of the females with equal concern and confusion in his gray blue eyes. "Are you in need of a doctor?"

Hannah stared at the limp body in her father's arms. That couldn't really be her mother. This woman seemed too tired to walk, and yet she continued to tug at her father's shirt, mumbling nonsense about Hannah's future.

"I'm speaking to you, child." *Daed's* tone remained even. His calmness seemed out of place.

He shifted the woman in his arms while keeping his focus on Hannah. "Luke and Levi are gone for the evening. Do ya need your sister to go to Mrs. Waddell's for help?" His words came out slow and purposeful.

Hannah looked toward the road. That man might be out there, creeping around. If everything happening was real and her sister did go for help… "No. I…I don't need a doctor." She stared at her palms, wondering how she'd ever heal from such gashes. Lowering her hands, she focused on her father.

The taut lines in his face showed more stress than his voice. "Can you get some water for you and your mother?"

Hannah nodded and then watched her father stride toward the wooden bench that sat a stone's throw behind their home, under the broad, heavily leafed limbs of the beech tree.

Disoriented and dreamlike, Hannah moved to the pump and wrapped a corner of her apron over her right hand so she could cushion the cuts from the pump handle. She took the tin cup from the wooden bucket. Lifting and lowering the pump handle soon produced a trickle of water. When the cup was filled, she trudged up the slope to her mother, who was being held upright on the seat by her father. He was patting her hand and telling her to trust God. Hannah thrust the cup toward her parents. Her father took the drink and held it to *Mamm's* lips, insisting she swallow.

Hannah turned away and gazed at the scenes playing out across the yard as if she were watching life in slow motion. Her fifteen-year-old sister, Sarah, appeared to be purposely distracting their younger siblings by taking them to the pond. Lifting Rebecca onto her hip, Sarah carried the three-year-old across the road. Samuel ran ahead and grabbed a fishing pole that was propped against a tree. Twelve-year-old Esther opened the gate and waited for the brood to enter the pasture before fastening the lock.

Hannah turned her focus back to her parents. Her father was still holding the cup of water to *Mamm's* lips. Hannah waited, feeling nearly invisible, wishing she truly were.

Daed talked in soft tones, assuring his wife everything was fine. When her mother stopped mumbling gibberish, his attention moved to Hannah. "Have you caused more trouble than you should have, child?"

"I…I…" The pain in her chest grew. It was an unfamiliar, sickening feeling. Unlike the times when she'd skinned her knee as a child or baked a bad batch of bread, this pain was being intensified by the very people who had comforted her through the other bad things.

The frustration on his face eased, and the gentleness she knew so well softened his features. "Tell me of this thing that's happened."

She tried to comply but found embarrassment so thick that it made speaking impossible.

"You can always tell your father what's going on. How else can I guide the household?" His slow, patient manner reminded her of the closeness they had shared—before she changed from being his little girl to a nearly grown woman.

Hannah swallowed hard and willed herself to obey. She managed to release pieces of information between her sobbing and stammering. Tears filled her father's eyes and burned a trail down his weathered face. He pulled his arm from her mother, making sure she was steady enough not to keel over.

He eased to his feet and placed his hands on her shoulders. "'Tis not right, Hannah," he whispered. "What happened to you should happen to no one." Her father enfolded her in his arms. She could smell the familiar mixture of garden soil and hard work. But his embrace didn't carry the same warmth it had yesterday. Oddly, his touch, which had always held pleasant fellowship, disgusted her.

"The unmentionable has happened to you."

She pushed free of his embrace. "I don't understand."

The horrid noise of her father fighting to keep control of his emotions filled the air. "You were forced to do the unmentionable," he whispered hoarsely. "You were…raped. And that is illegal, even among the English."

She covered her face with her apron and wailed. Unable to keep herself upright any longer, she sank to her knees on the cool grass and rested her forehead against the earth.

Within moments, her mother's arms enfolded her. She nuzzled her chin against Hannah's shoulder, rocking back and forth. The two cried bitterly.

Guilt bore down on Hannah, blame so heavy that no amount of tears would ever wash it away. But she couldn't pinpoint why she felt in the wrong. As Hannah gained some control and sat up, anger burned even more than the guilt. "It's not right, *Mamm*. It's not right."

Her mother's swollen eyelids closed slowly as she nodded. "I know."

"Then let's do something about it." The words hurled out, vengeful and desperate.

A pair of strong hands wrapped around her upper arms and raised her to her feet. She found herself staring into her father's eyes.

"You're upset. You can't really mean that." He released her.

Hannah staggered backward.

His eyes misted. "You know we must let God take vengeance, not man."

The throbbing in her temples matched the ache in her abdomen and

the rending of her heart. "If we don't tell someone...maybe the police..."
—she searched for words amid the confusion that screamed inside her head—"he could do this again to someone else, no?"

The shoulders of the stout man she'd always trusted slumped. "Ruth, please try to talk some sense into her."

Rising from the ground, *Mamm* took hold of her husband's arm to support her shaking body. "We live a simple life, Hannah, as God commanded." The quaking of her voice made her words hard to understand. "You know our ways do not allow us to defend ourselves. Besides, without phones or cars, we would have no way to get help if we provoked this man. What would we do if he...brought trouble? It is best to leave things in the Lord's hands."

"But—"

"Look around you, daughter." Her father made a sweep with his hand in the air. Hannah viewed the rolling landscape, cattle, outbuildings, and her house. At the pond across the road, her brother and sisters sat on the pier, dangling their bare feet in the water. "Peace reigns here. You cannot destroy that just because you want vengeance. I understand how you feel. I do. But we must leave this alone and move forward."

"*Daed*, please—"

"I'm sorry you don't understand, Hannah, but I must do what is best for the family and the community." He patted *Mamm's* arm. "Ruth, you must calm yourself. Your daughter is upset, and rightly so, but we will take good care of her. She is safe, and we'll put this behind us. Now take her inside and prepare a bath for her. Then she can go to bed for the evening. Sarah will tend to the young children for tonight." When he folded his arms across his chest, Hannah knew the conversation was over.

Hannah sat on the stool in the bathroom, struggling not to cry as *Mamm* connected a hose to fill the large tin tub. The hose ran from the window behind the kitchen sink—the only source of heated water—along the side of the house and through the bathroom window. Trying to block out the vision of what had taken place less than an hour before, Hannah watched her mother pour vinegar and Epsom salts under the running water.

"You'll be fine," *Mamm* cooed with a shaky voice. "Fervent prayers and a few days of time will get this behind you, *ya*?"

Unable to share her feelings, Hannah nodded.

Her mother stirred the water with her hand. "It's not in your father's ways to use a doctor, but if you need one after a few days of rest, he'll take you."

Hannah tried to stop herself from shaking. Her father had said she was safe. But she didn't feel safe.

Laying the hose in the galvanized tub, her mother's hands still trembled. She dried them on her apron. "I'll grind some lobelia seeds for your pain."

Hannah gasped for air. "Yes, I'm sure that will help." A sharp pain stabbed her throat. Had she not just lied? She shook her head, burying the guilt.

Mamm squirted some liquid soap under the hose. "I'll fetch your gown and a towel." She left the room.

Hannah sat on a stool beside the tub and stared at the bubbles as the horror of the attack played out in her mind. The suds burst and disappeared, much like the innocent life she'd known before today.

Her heart ached to talk to Paul. He was good at explaining things to her, at making life take on joy and hope. But what would he think of her now? Unable to imagine sharing such a horridly embarrassing thing with him, she pushed aside thoughts of getting comfort from him. Instead she tried to visualize him pleased with her—as he'd been when she had agreed to marry him. It was a vain effort, for every time she tried to see Paul smiling, all she saw was that man dragging her into his car.

"Hannah." Her father's deep voice rumbled through the washroom.

Unsure of which images flashing in front of her were real, she blinked. "Yes?" she whispered.

"Take this." He held out a small piece of brown paper folded in half with a powdery substance in the crease. Her mother thrust a mug in front of her. But Hannah's arms remained limp by her side, refusing to respond.

Mamm lowered the cup. "I told you she didn't hear me when I was talking to her. I tried for three or four minutes to get her to hear me. Look at her, Zeb. What are we going to do?"

Her father held the folded paper filled with crushed lobelia seeds between his thumb and forefinger. "Open your mouth, child." Hannah obeyed. Her father dumped the medicine on her tongue. Her mother held the cup to Hannah's lips. Hannah swallowed, her throat burning at the invasion.

"She'll be fine." *Daed* placed his hands firmly on Hannah's shoulders. "Won't you?"

Wondering if her father really believed that, she nodded.

Mamm broke into fresh tears and ran from the room. *Daed* stared after her. "Go ahead and take your bath." Without another glance in her direction, he pulled the door closed behind him.

Forcing her body to do as her father had told her, Hannah rose from the stool and locked the door. Her arms and legs felt heavy, as if each were carrying a bucket of feed. She pulled off her filthy, torn clothing. After she slid into the tub of warm water, she buried her face in a towel and sobbed quietly.

A tap on the door interrupted her weeping.

"Hannah?" *Mamm* called through the door. "Are you okay?"

Hannah lowered the thick towel from her face. She kept her eyes shut tight, afraid if she opened them, she might discover she was in that car again. "*Ya.*" Her voice sounded feeble in her ears.

"You've been in there for two hours." Her voice sounded scratchy. "The water must be cold."

Hannah had only been in the bath for a few minutes. She forced her eyes open. The room was dark. How could that be?

She stood and wrapped her aching, dripping body in a towel. Climbing out of the tub, she realized how cool the water had become. She dried off, then grabbed the matches from the shelf to light the kerosene lamp. Her hands were still trembling as she lit a match and placed the flame against the wick. As the blaze lit the room, odd shapes took form. Everything looked unfamiliar. She'd helped do laundry in this room every winter since she was three, but the wooden shelves, pegs, and basket for dirty clothes appeared foreign.

Hannah slid into her nightgown and wrapped a shawl over her shoulders. Paul must be at his parents' place by now. Maybe *Daed* would let her go to Mrs. Waddell's and call him, just this once. She wouldn't tell Paul what had happened, but she was desperate to hear his voice. He'd tell her of his love and the wonderful future they would have together.

But if she asked permission to call him, her father would know of their friendship. If he learned of the relationship this way, it would be much harder for Paul to earn *Daed's* approval later on. And then the monster—that awful, nasty man—would have ruined everything.

An odd, prickly sensation ran through her chest, making breathing difficult. She removed the wooden peg lock and opened the door. Her mother stood just outside, in the small back entryway where boots and coats lined the walls. A shadowy glow from the lamp fell across *Mamm's* stricken face. Resisting the urge to fall into her mother's arms and cry, Hannah remained at a distance.

Her father entered from the kitchen, carrying a small jar of salve. His medium-sized frame appeared large when encircled by the shadows from the lamplight. "Your younger siblings are asleep. You will get some peace and quiet tonight." He smiled, obviously trying to sound like his normal self. "See, all is well," he assured her, though his confidence seemed forced. But there was something different in her father's voice, something suggesting an edgy coldness he'd never had before.

She handed her father the lamp and followed her mother into the kitchen. Stiff and shaky as a new colt, Hannah made her way to one of the benches that sat on each side of the kitchen table. The familiar rich wood brought no warmth to her tonight. Too weak and dizzy to talk, she sat in silence, hoping with every blink of her eyes that she would awaken from this horrible nightmare.

Her father set the lamp on a nearby shelf and paused in the doorway. "I've been thinking. It is best that you not speak of this to anyone, including your brothers and sisters. They only need to know that you fell on your way home and your mother thought you were more injured than you are." He paused. "Everything I just said is true, no?"

She didn't want anyone to know what had really happened, including herself. She silently begged God to let her die. She couldn't handle this. Incapable of responding, Hannah lowered her eyes.

Mamm shuffled to the gas stove and removed the lid of a simmering pot. "I prepared some broth and rice while you were in the bath. It'll make you feel better." Her mother's jerky movements and quivering voice made Hannah think *Mamm* might start screaming again.

Hannah glanced at her father, wordlessly asking permission to turn down the offer. The muscles in his face appeared taut as he stepped closer to her. Lifting the edge of the shawl that had fallen off her shoulder, he nuzzled it against her neck. The movement was comforting, causing Hannah to think she might survive the night yet. Then he leaned close and whispered, "Do as your mother says."

The shaking that had subsided returned with a vengeance.

Her father knelt in front of her. "She needs to know you'll be fine," he whispered before turning her hands over and gently rubbing some salve on her wounds.

Closing her eyes tight against the onslaught of nausea, Hannah realized her father's desire to prove to *Mamm* that Hannah was fine outweighed everything else.

She gulped. The hard, dry swallow was followed by an intense desire to flee the house and seek refuge at Mrs. Waddell's. Fear grew until it seemed to form its own silhouette. The thought of going to Mrs. Waddell's was ridiculous. Hannah couldn't go anywhere. *He* might be out there waiting for her.

Hannah hung the shawl on a wooden peg and silently padded to the foot of the bed. Moonbeams cast a silvery glow across the room, revealing the two double beds with her three younger sisters in them. The wonderful scent of air-dried sheets brought no comfort as she slid between them.

Sarah roused. "You okay?" Her slow speech and groggy voice felt like a slap across Hannah's bruised heart. How could she have been sleeping peacefully while Hannah's world was crashing down around her?

Loneliness filled Hannah, smothering her just as that man's body had. "*Ya.* Go back to sleep."

Sarah turned her back to Hannah and snuggled against the pillow beneath her head. Soon Hannah heard the deep breaths of her sisters sleeping all around her. *Mamm* was still downstairs, talking to *Daed.* The whispers of her mother's stress settled over the night. Her scratchy voice mingled with *Daed's* muted tones.

Hannah curled into a ball and buried her face in the pillow, afraid to make any noise.

3

Paul sat at the desk in his bedroom, writing a letter to Hannah. Yesterday evening when he got home, his parents had all seven of his high-school classmates waiting to see him. A huge meal had been spread out on picnic tables in his backyard, and his sister and her family were there. Since the parents of his graduating class had pulled their kids from the local public school in seventh grade and had begun their own school in a garage-turned-classroom, the eight of them stayed in contact with each other regularly. Marcus, his closest friend, was there too. He was the only one at the get-together who wasn't Mennonite, but Marcus wasn't one to ever feel out of place. He and Paul had been neighbors and good friends most of their lives, and now they were college roommates. Without Marcus's influence over Paul's parents, Paul might not have been allowed to further his education, since most of his sect didn't believe in going on to college.

The only disappointing part of the evening was that Hannah was not by his side. As he wrote to her about the party, he assured her there would be plenty more gatherings that she would be a part of. It was easier to write to her now that he knew how she felt about him, now that they had plans to marry.

A knock at the bedroom door made him lay down his pen and turn the top page of his letter facedown. "Come in."

The door eased open just enough to reveal Carol's upper body. Paul rocked back in his seat, facing the doorway. "I thought you and William had plans with your boys tonight."

His sister was seven years older than he, and her face seemed to be quickly becoming identical to their mother's. "I was hoping I could talk you into joining us for the evening. We're going to the Senators' game." She looked at the stack of papers on the desk.

Paul laid his hand on top of the letter. Hannah would love to see a minor-league baseball game. Snacks at the stadium and the entertainment between each inning would be treats for her. "I have some things I need to get done today, packing and such. I have to leave tomorrow afternoon since classes start on Tuesday. I need time to apply for jobs and get settled in before Tuesday."

Carol huffed. "You cut your time with us shorter every summer."

Paul rose from the desk, guilt nipping at him. "There's just not enough time to spread around. It's nothing personal."

She pushed the door open farther, and Paul saw Dorcas standing behind her. She was one of his seven classmates and the daughter of his mother's best friend.

Looking at the lace on her dress, he felt his face flush. His sister was up to something, and he didn't need his bachelor's degree to figure it out. He wanted to shoot an angry look toward Carol, but Dorcas would see it. He didn't want to hurt the girl's feelings. She was a nice-enough person, he guessed. But Paul had seen enough of her selfish side over the years to make him wonder if she was truly as manipulative as she sometimes appeared.

Carol's eyebrows rose, warning him to behave.

Paul willed himself to smile at Dorcas. "Did you sleep in after our late-night gathering?"

Dorcas's green eyes fastened on him as they'd done for as long as he could remember. "My sister piled on my head at eleven o'clock, calling me Rip Van Winkle. You?"

"I awoke before the sun rose."

An awkward silence fell between them. Every possible topic had been discussed at length last night as his company had talked and laughed until after two in the morning. The only subject that hadn't come up was Hannah. Every once in a while over the past few years, he had mentioned to Carol that he was interested in someone—usually whenever she started pushing Dorcas on him. His know-it-all sister had accused him of having his eye on Gram's Amish helper. Paul hadn't denied or confirmed her suspicions. But he trusted that Carol had never said a word to his parents about why he was willing to spend his summers helping Gram while doing odd jobs for her neighbors.

Carol edged to the side of his bed and took a T-shirt from a clean but crumpled pile. She shook it out and folded it. "We'll help you get ready and pack tomorrow if you'll go out with us tonight."

Paul shook his head. "I can handle it. You guys have fun."

After placing the folded shirt on the bed, Carol moved to his desk. "Are you making a list of things to do?" Her fingertips grasped the corner of Paul's letter.

Paul placed his palm over the paper. He gave a firm look to his sister, hoping she'd realize that he was an adult with a right to his privacy.

Concern shone in her eyes. "Please don't tell me you're still infatuated with that Amish girl." She said the words "Amish girl" as if Hannah were inferior.

Dorcas gasped. Paul looked back to the doorway where she was standing. She looked hurt. Was it possible she still hoped that Paul would take an interest in her? Her attention moved to the letter in his hand before she turned her head. But she remained there, listening.

"You're out of line, Carol. And I'd appreciate it if you wouldn't say the word *Amish* as though they're dirt."

Carol sighed. "Look, I have nothing against them. But if you're planning on courting one of them and bringing her out from her people, I'm warning you, it'll never work."

He stood and placed his hands on Carol's shoulders and forced a gentle tone. "She and I both hold to God's truth. He'll give our relationship strength to work through our differences."

Carol eased onto the bed, freeing herself from his tender grip. She grabbed the folded shirt and squeezed it to her chest. "Is it that Hannah something-or-other?"

Hoping he wasn't making a mistake in admitting it, Paul nodded.

"Paul, the Amish aren't like us. They're legalistic beyond reason. I mean, we live without television and radios, but that's nothing compared to the Old Order Amish restrictions. She'll continue in her ways, even if she's physically removed from her people."

Paul scoffed. "Hannah will find whatever freedoms she thinks are the right ones, given time."

Carol stood, facing him. "You're being naive. She could never be comfortable outside the ways she's been taught. It's the same as you getting comfortable wearing a dress and a *Kapp*." She tossed the shirt on the bed. "Everything that girl's been taught she learned from the Amish, including her schoolteacher—someone with only an eighth-grade Amish education herself. Even those who leave almost always go back."

Paul crouched beside his bed and grabbed a duffel bag from under it. "You're exaggerating, and you know it."

Carol stepped back, giving him room to get the bag out. "Paul, for goodness sake, think this through. If she marries outside her faith, it'll break her parents' hearts, ruin all fellowship with her siblings, and bring embarrassment to her whole family."

He pulled the bag out and stood.

At the bedroom doorway, Dorcas tapped the wooden frame with her fingernails, drawing their attention. "I'm sure Paul knows what he's doing."

"But...," Carol sputtered.

Dorcas tilted her head and gave a slight shrug. "You've already shared your opinion, Carol. It's time to let it go."

Carol stood motionless, other than blinking a few times.

The right words were leaving Dorcas's mouth, and Paul appreciated it, but something about the way she looked hinted that she wasn't saying what she really thought. Putting an end to the game playing from both of them, Paul decided to disclose his secret. "I'm not going to change my mind about Hannah. I've already asked her to marry me."

Carol's eyes opened wide. "You what?"

Paul glanced at Dorcas's blank face, then returned his focus to Carol. "I need you both to keep this between us. I'm hoping I can win her family's approval before they find out."

Carol's eyes narrowed. "Marry her? You can't possibly believe you love this girl."

"Oh, Paul," Dorcas whispered, as if he'd just shared terrifying news.

"This is ridiculous." Carol grabbed several pages of the letter and shook them.

With a gentleness he didn't feel, he wrapped his fingers over the rumpled pages in Carol's hand. "Let go of it." His calm tone belied how much anger was rising within him. When she hesitated, Paul spoke slowly and purposefully. "Now, Carol."

She released her grip on the pages. "You have no idea what it takes to make a marriage work. It's like..." She paused, clearly trying to think of the perfect allegory. "It's like using your truck to carry a dozen people to a formal wedding."

"You're comparing Hannah to my truck?" In spite of his best effort, sarcasm oozed from his words.

"What I mean is that Hannah was built for one kind of life. Changing her will cause serious problems, not just to her but to her family. And you. Not to mention your children. Can't you see that?"

"I know this isn't what you want for me, Carol. But you're gonna have to trust me on this."

Her shoulders slumped. "This conversation isn't over."

Paul kissed her on the cheek. "Of course not." He smiled down at her. "I know what I'm asking of my family and friends—and hers. But the only life I want is with her." Paul laid the pages against his chest and smoothed some of the wrinkles from them.

Carol rolled her eyes. "You always were melodramatic."

He placed the letter back on his desk and chuckled. "Levelheadedness must make room for love, or we have no need of living sensibly. For without true affection, practicality has nothing to protect." He grabbed his bag and unzipped it.

An obviously forced but peacemaking smile crossed his sister's face. "Spare me your philosophical ramblings." She tapped the papers on Paul's desk. "So, can you pull yourself away long enough to watch a Senators' game with us? I'll still help you pack tomorrow."

Paul was glad he'd been so bold as to tell them of his plans. They'd both accepted the news better than he'd thought possible. Maybe now his sister would recognize that he would never be more than cordial friends with Dorcas.

From the doorway, Dorcas pointed to his clothes on the bed. "We might even swipe an iron over one or two things." She giggled. "You know my motto: putting off work until tomorrow can make today a ton of fun."

Paul tossed the travel bag onto the bed. "I guess a night at City Island would be a nice distraction."

4

Bristly heat and sweat roused Hannah to consciousness. She pushed the sheet away from her face and half opened her eyes, checking the clock. Streams of sunlight filtered in around the green shades. The room was sweltering as the cool morning air gave way to the scorching heat of late summer. Unsure why she was still in bed, confusion swirled for a moment before the all-too-familiar images hurled against her. How many days had passed since the attack—two, maybe three?

She lay motionless, searching for a ray of hope that would bring comfort, but she couldn't find one.

Nausea rose. Desperate for some cooler air, she darted down the steps and out the front door. She hurried to the beech tree, hoping to go unnoticed by her family. A cool breeze stirred the air.

"Hannah."

The sound made her jolt. Looking in the direction of the voice, she saw her twenty-year-old brother, Luke, striding across the yard toward her. Her body tensed, making her injuries hurt even more. Standing in the yard in her nightgown, she could easily imagine what words of correction her eldest brother would have.

Luke came to a halt in front of her. He held a galvanized bucket in one hand; with the other, he hooked his thumb through a brown suspender. Compassion shone in his brown eyes. "Are you still feeling poorly this morning?" He gestured to her gown. "I suppose that's a foolish question. *Daed* said you lost a whole pail of berries the other day. He had me scavenging the countryside this morning to replace them, but it's so late in the season, I'm surprised you found a bucketful when you did." He set the almost-empty container on the ground.

Hannah tried to say something, but the words wouldn't come.

Luke smiled. "Cat got your tongue?"

Determined to give an answer, she found her voice. "It was a nice try." She stared at the pitiful pile of blueberries lying in the same bucket that had been brimming with them before…

Luke gently took her hands, facing the palms up. *"Ach, wie entsetzlich."* He raised his eyes to hers. "Are your knees this bad?"

She cleared her throat, surprised to find that the simple action helped her gain control of her emotions. "I'm fine, Luke."

Her brother tilted his head, a dozen questions reflected in his eyes. He nodded and released her hands. "I'm sorry you got hurt."

Knowing nothing else to say, she left without answering him. If she could see through the fog that covered her mind, maybe she could make some sense of what had happened and figure out how to fix it. But clear thought seemed impossible.

She walked barefoot across the thick grass, eased open the screen door, and stepped inside. Hoping to avoid seeing anyone else, she paused to listen. She heard her youngest sister, Rebecca, in the kitchen with their mother and Esther. By the sound of things, they were busy canning. Somehow Hannah's bolt outside had escaped her mother's notice.

Or maybe her mother was unwilling to face her.

Too weak and drained to work through any more thoughts, she tiptoed upstairs and crawled back into bed. She covered her head with the lightweight sheet.

The rumbling of an English vehicle startled Hannah from her sleep. A sense of panic rose within her as the engine noise grew louder and then stopped right outside her window. The acrid smell of exhaust fumes drifted through the open window and past the closed blind. Visions of her attacker loomed in her mind's eye.

Shaking, Hannah rose from the bed. Barely able to breathe, she forced herself to take a quick peek out the side of the drawn shade. Relief flooded her. It was only Mr. Carlisle in his refrigerated truck. He was here to get the milk. He always came between two and three in the afternoon.

He stepped out of his truck, talking to her father. As Mr. Carlisle leaned against his truck, he looked up at her bedroom window. She jumped back as if she'd touched a fire. Could he tell what had happened just by looking at her? She crawled between the sheets and buried her head again.

Moments later a rapping on the bedroom door seemed to shoot through Hannah's last nerve. She lay still, with her head under the covers. She heard the door open and tried not to budge so whoever it was would go away and leave her alone.

"Mr. Carlisle stopped by." Her mother's reassuring voice worked its way through Hannah's mind. *Mamm* sat on the side of the bed. "It's almost suppertime. You've got to eat. You can't hide forever."

Hannah squeezed her eyes tighter. It couldn't be suppertime. Hadn't Mr. Carlisle just left? Something odd was happening. Time kept jumping—as if it were no longer bound by any rules.

A clinking metallic sound, like an eating utensil against a plate, filled the silence. "You haven't eaten anything in two days, Hannah. I peeled and chopped the fruit for you." She patted Hannah's leg through the bedcovers. "Come on, child. Sit up and eat."

Hannah remained quiet, hoping her mother would give up and go away.

"Now." *Mamm* tugged at the covers over Hannah's head. At first Hannah resisted, but out of dread that her mother might call *Daed,* she let go of the sheets.

"That's my girl." *Mamm's* soft hands caressed Hannah's cheeks, brushing wisps of curly hair from her face. "I know this is hard. But it's time to push against how you feel and do what's necessary. Do you understand?"

Fresh tears slid from the corners of Hannah's eyes. She nodded.

"Good. Now, dry your eyes." Her mother lifted the bowl of fruit. "Sit up and eat."

Hannah sat up and took the plate of fruit her mother held toward her. *Mamm* rose and grabbed a hairbrush from the nightstand. With the fork, Hannah stabbed a piece of green fruit. *Mamm* ran the brush through Hannah's long curls. The soothing strokes of the brush and the delicious medley of fruits provided a welcome relief from the isolation of the last... She didn't know how much time had passed.

Her mother worked on Hannah's untamed curls without complaint. She twisted Hannah's hair into a bun and pinned it. She then placed the translucent white *Kapp* over her head and fastened it to her hair with straight pins.

Mamm laid the brush on the side table. "Slip into your clothes and sit with us in the yard. There's a cool breeze. It's enough to refresh anybody's soul."

Hannah didn't want to, but to refuse would cause more problems than it would solve. "What has *Daed* told everyone?"

Pushing the sheet off Hannah's legs, *Mamm* seemed unable to look her in the eyes. "As little as possible. They think a car hit you and the fall caused the gashes on your hands." She took a blue dress off its hook and laid it on the bed. "He wasn't going to say that much. But you've holed up in this room so long, they knew you hadn't just fallen on your way home. If you don't get out of bed and return to normal chores, they aren't going to accept that story either."

Her mother turned to leave. "We need you, Hannah." She faced

Hannah squarely this time, her brown eyes filled with sorrow. "The house never runs as well without you." She gave her daughter a forced smile.

When *Mamm* pulled the door closed behind her, Hannah sank back onto the bed. Is this what her life would be like from now on? Pretending she was fine in order to hide the truth of the unmentionable from her siblings, and hiding from her parents the fact that she was going insane? She stared at the floor, trying to gain enough strength to go downstairs and pretend.

Ten minutes later Hannah stood at the back door, running her hands around her waist to verify that she'd pinned her apron securely. She peered through the screen, watching her family. *Mamm* and *Daed* sat on the bench, watching the children. The younger ones were catching fireflies in the open field while the older ones helped them place the bugs in a jar. Hannah tried to take a breath, but a stabbing pain in her chest stopped it short.

As she pushed the door open, the squeaky noise drew her parents' attention. Willing herself to walk, she started across the lawn. Her chest ached. Her skin felt as if someone were peeling it off. But worse, here in the open she had no ability to silence her thoughts. She came to a halt in front of her father, her gaze fixed on the ground, her arms limp at her sides.

Mamm rose from the bench. Her fingers cupped Hannah's face, and she kissed her on the cheek. "I'll fetch us some lemonade."

"Dankes," Hannah whispered.

Daed patted the empty spot beside him. "Come and we'll talk."

Hannah eased onto the far end of the bench.

With both feet planted on the soft earth, her father placed his hands on his knees and straightened his back. "God will get us through this, Hannah. Our ways are not easy, but they are right." Her father removed his straw hat and lowered his head. "I'm not yet sure what's the right thing to do between you and the bishop."

Hot pain shot through her chest. She lifted her head and stared into her father's eyes. "What do you mean?"

He turned toward the fields. "I should inform him of what happened so he can make a ruling of what needs to be done."

Swallowing hard, she willed herself not to cry. "*Daed,* no, please. No one can know."

His sigh assured her he understood her feelings. "I'm not saying I'm going to tell him. I haven't decided yet. To keep this from the bishop is wrong. He's our spiritual leader. He can't guide us properly if we keep secrets from him." His jaw clenched as he stood. "Because this is so uncommon, if we share it, he's likely to seek counsel from the church leaders, maybe even from the head of each household. Then it'll be impossible to keep it from spreading to our whole community and beyond. That'll mean the news will reach any prospective beaus." He glanced at her, sorrow filling his eyes. "And that will ruin your chance of ever having a family of your own. You've lost your virtue, child, and there's nothing anyone can do about it."

As she stared at the bend in the dirt road that led to Mrs. Waddell's, guilt threatened to swallow her. Maybe God had allowed this attack so she wouldn't leave the community He'd placed her in. Who was she to consider changing God's plan for her life?

Guilt gave way to anger at the injustice of her situation. How could she *not* want to get away from this place?

She stood. Like nectar to a bee, her bed called to her. But she couldn't continue to give in to the urge to bury herself in it. She had duties, responsibilities. "I should take a loaf of bread to Mrs. Waddell," she said, dreading even that chore.

"No," he said, his voice gruff. "You're not to return there for now.

Luke or Levi will take Sarah back and forth to help the elderly lady until she can hire someone else."

Hannah turned to look at her father. He seemed to expect her to plead for the right to work at Mrs. Waddell's, but she had no energy to walk on eggshells while she argued with him. The set of his jaw was a clear indication that his patience with her was used up.

He stared at her, as if reminding her of his rights as head of the household. "You must help out around here. Your family needs you."

Numb, she trudged toward the house.

5

The round-faced clock that hung on the wall behind the professor's head showed that class should have been over ten minutes ago. Nonetheless, the man droned on, making Paul later for work by the minute.

School had been back in session for three weeks, and he missed Hannah so badly he couldn't sleep at night or concentrate during the day. If a letter would arrive, maybe that would take some of the edge off his misery. Letters from Hannah were always slow in coming, but it'd been weeks since he'd left.

Writing to him was problematic. She had to have time alone to secretly pen him a note. Then she had to get it to his gram's place so she could mail it without Hannah's family getting wind of it. Even though he often went up to six weeks without hearing from her, he'd never gotten used to it.

Scribbling notes as quickly as he could, Paul tried not to think about the interview he had coming up this afternoon. He was hoping to land an internship as a caseworker with social services. If he landed this position, he would get enough training so that he could find a job closer to Owl's Perch after he graduated. If he found a job near Owl's Perch, he could juggle working for Hannah's father and for social services.

His boss at the tire store wouldn't be too thrilled when he arrived late. He'd be even angrier when Paul requested time off during the middle of his shift to go on his interview.

His part-time job at the retail tire store came with long hours and unfriendly co-workers. But it was his own fault. Instead of putting in his job applications in May for the fall, he'd hightailed it to his gram's place the day school was out so he could see Hannah. And he hadn't returned to campus until the weekend before classes began. Now he'd spend the entire school year paying the price for his impatience.

Paul sighed and glanced at the clock again. As usual he was half paying attention to the teacher and half missing Hannah. A long-distance relationship was one thing, but no communication other than letters was almost unbearable, especially since it was so long between letters.

A few students slipped out the side door. Paul wanted to follow them, but he needed the details of the next project due for class, and this teacher didn't pass out info sheets, post assignments on the Web, or write lists on the white board. He gave all pertinent instruction orally, once, as if the students' presence at the end of class was part of the project itself. Paul drew a ragged breath and began to pack his book bag as he listened to the teacher's last few recommendations regarding the assignment. As more students slipped out, the professor glanced at his watch and dismissed the class.

Slinging the strap of his backpack over one shoulder, Paul merged into the flow of human traffic. The past month had dispelled any question of how crazy his senior year would be. He wished he'd known four years ago how to plan his required course hours. He should have taken extra classes early on to give himself more time for his most important classes now. He had to graduate this spring.

It would be easier if he could stay in school one extra semester. But he couldn't do that. He'd promised Hannah they'd be together by summer. Besides, his heart was set on being with her come mid-May. *Graduation.* What a liberating word. Right now, however, graduation seemed a decade away.

He ran through the corridors, out the main doorway, and across the parking lot. Jerking open the unlocked truck door, he tossed his backpack to the passenger side and dug into his jeans pocket for his keys.

They weren't there. He tapped the outside of the pockets in his jacket and on the back of his pants.

Couldn't *something* go right? One thing? Anything?

He stifled the urge to let an angry scream ring out across the parking lot. Leaning across the bench seat, he grabbed his backpack and searched its array of small pockets. Life had been like this since he'd arrived on campus. Murphy's Law was working overtime for him, and he wished it would just go to work for somebody else.

Unable to find his keys, Paul climbed into his truck. *God, am I off track? Is this not where I'm supposed to be? Or is this just a part of learning patience?*

Paul wrapped his fingers around the top of the steering wheel and leaned his forehead against the backs of his hands. Visions of Hannah flooded his thoughts. *I miss her so badly, Father. I…I didn't think it would be this tough.* How many times over the past month had he fought the desire to forget school and go be with her?

He lifted his head and squared his shoulders. This was no time to think about quitting school. If life wanted a battle, he'd fight. And he'd win. Because to lose would hurt his and Hannah's future, and there was no way he was going to allow that to happen. No way on earth.

His stomach grumbled, and suddenly he remembered where his keys were. He jumped out of his truck and ran across the parking lot, back inside the building, to the closest vending machine. He grabbed his keys off the top of the red appliance. All this trouble and he hadn't even gotten a pack of crackers from the antiquated junk-food source. It wouldn't take his crumpled dollar, and he had no change.

Running back across the parking lot, Paul was glad his job was only a few minutes away.

Soon he pulled into the parking lot of the tire store and ran inside.

"Waddell."

Paul stopped midstride. There was no denying that crotchety, booming voice bellowing out his last name as if it were a curse word. He turned. "Sir?"

"You're late. Again." Kyle Brown's face turned a deeper shade of purple than normal.

"Yes sir. I'm sorry. Class was—"

"Give it a rest, Waddell. I don't care what was going on at that place you call a learning institute. Seems to me you college boys can't even tell time."

Paul hated this place. But life was expensive. "I'll come in early and stay late on Saturday to make up for it."

"You better believe you will." The man wiped his hands on a filthy rag and shoved it back into his pocket. "But that don't change the fact that the guys in the pit can't begin lunch shifts until there's a fourth person here. Three men've been waiting on you so somebody can go eat." He glanced at his watch. "At two thirty in the afternoon."

"I'm sorry, sir."

Mr. Brown clapped his hands. "Well, what are you waitin' for? Get to work."

"Yes, I'll do that, sir. But first...I need to tell you that I have to be somewhere at four. I told Mr. Banks about it when—"

"Well, Mr. Banks ain't runnin' this department. I am. If you leave before the last customer is taken care of, don't bother coming back. We'll mail you your check along with an 'adios, amigo' card."

Paul nodded. He'd explained his scheduling issues to Mr. Banks. The owner had assured him it could all be worked out. But obviously Kyle Brown didn't care what his boss had agreed to.

If Paul got this internship, he'd be doing his dream job with child services part-time during the week, but he could work here on days he wasn't a caseworker and all day on Saturdays. Jobs with decent hours that didn't make him work on Sundays were hard to come by. He had to keep this one.

6

Luke clomped up the steps of the old farmhouse. He looked into his parents' bedroom and found what he was searching for: Hannah. She sat on a low-rise stool with her back to him, sewing. He tapped on the open door.

Hannah jerked as if he'd startled her, but she didn't turn to see who had knocked. *"Kumm uff rei."*

Doing as she bid, Luke entered the room.

He was still baffled as to why his mother had made him move the sewing machine out of the kitchen and into his parents' bedroom yesterday. Every Amish home in his community had the sewing machine in front of a set of windows in the main part of the house, either the kitchen or the sitting room. It was what the district leaders had agreed upon, long before either Luke or Hannah was born. The bishop's job was to help keep conformity inside and outside each home to squelch man's natural bent toward competition.

So why had his mother insisted that he move it upstairs? He wasn't at all sure the church leaders would approve. But when he had turned questioningly to his father, his *Daed* had waved a hand in the air and barked at him to do as his mother told him. It had cost Luke the better part of the afternoon to disconnect, move, and then reconnect the machine, the automobile battery, and the converter to the upstairs.

Realizing Hannah wasn't going to stop sewing, he spoke over the whir of the machine. "I'm not sure if you heard, but there's a singing tonight. The bishop's gonna be gone tomorrow, so he moved it to tonight instead of Sunday. Don't know if that's ever happened before. But I'd be glad to take you." He crossed the room to stand beside her.

Accelerating the speed of the machine, she continued to run a pair of broadcloth trousers under the needle. "You've talked me into all the singings I ever care to attend."

With his middle finger and thumb, Luke lightly thumped her shoulder—half joking and half in frustration. "You beat all. Everybody that's not married likes the singings. It's the only way to really get to know someone."

The machine stopped its annoying hum, leaving the soft ticking of the wall clock as the only sound in the room. His sister shifted her focus and stared up at him. The circles under her eyes and her pale skin revealed exhaustion, although she'd done very little work of late. For reasons that made no sense to him, she was being allowed to do nothing but sew clothes for the family in a private room. She wasn't even responsible for juggling any cooking and childcare duties while she sewed. That was even stranger than moving the old Singer.

Hannah scowled. "I have no desire to be driven home from the singing by some...man...in hopes of us finding interest in each other."

Luke grasped a straight pin out of an overstuffed, tomato-shaped cushion and plunged it in and out, over and over. His sister had always had a mind of her own, one that didn't follow all the beliefs of the Old Ways, but she'd never been rude before. He decided, for both their sakes, to keep his tongue in check with her.

"I didn't tell ya that the bishop said the singing won't last long tonight. If you don't come, Mary won't either. She'll think it's too brazen to be seen alone with me at my parents' place on a singin' night. Plus, she's afraid if we're together without you, it'll cause rumors to spread that we're a couple." Luke shrugged. "She's not ready for that. You know Mary gets miserably embarrassed if she thinks people are talking about her."

He picked up one of Samuel's newly made shirts and tried to poke his pinky through a fresh-sewn buttonhole. Hannah hadn't done a good job of cutting the hole inside her stitching. "I was hoping to take Mary for a walk across our land tonight after the singing. I want to show her where *Daed* and I are considering building me a harness shop. If you'll come too, no one will think anything about us all going to the pond and millin' about since the three of us are seen together all the time."

Surely his sister understood what he was unable to speak of freely. If he could get Mary to see how stable his future was and if she cared for him as he hoped, they would become promised to each other by the night's end.

Hannah, seeing the mistake with the buttonhole, held her hand out for the shirt. "If you want to walk the property with Mary, just do so."

He passed her the shirt, holding on to part of it to help keep her attention. He boldly stared into her eyes.

Hannah released the shirt, leaving it dangling from Luke's hand to the floor. Her head lowered as if she were too weary to continue holding it up. "I...I...can't."

Disappointment formed a knot in Luke's chest. He dropped the shirt on the floor and grabbed his suspenders, squeezing them tight. "Your company for the night doesn't have to include a guy from the singing. It can be just us three."

Hannah didn't answer. She left the shirt on the floor and began sewing on the trousers again, ignoring Luke altogether.

If he told their father about Hannah's disinterest in being courted by any Amish men, *Daed* would set her straight quick. A *rumschpringe* was for finding an Amish mate, nothing else. Luke had plenty of suspicions about why Hannah found such great joy in working for the elderly woman down the road. But he hadn't shared his thoughts with their father. *Daed* had a strong opinion about his kids not turning to the Mennonite ways.

Luke hoped his sister's desire to spend time at the Waddell place had nothing to do with any of the English farm hands or Mrs. Waddell's grandson, whatever his name was. The grandson was from a very conservative Mennonite family, but they weren't in fellowship with the Old Order Amish. "*Daed* still doesn't know that Mary and I have been bringing you home from the singings."

A look of defiance came over her face. She lifted her hand, showing an inch of space between her index finger and her thumb. "I have about this much freedom under our bishop, and only because it's my time of *rumschpringe.* Singings and buggy courting are a private thing. Don't take that away from me, Luke."

"But, Hannah, you ain't using your freedom to find a mate. You're just pretending to. It's not right."

Her eyes grew cold and hard. "It'd be best not to talk to me of what's right. Not now. Maybe not ever." She turned away from him and pressed the pedal on the old Singer.

Laying the trousers aside, Hannah rose from the stool and crossed to the far window. She watched Luke amble toward the barn to hitch the horse to the buggy. He and Mary would fritter the night away, laughing and having their mock arguments. Not long ago the three of them had delighted in playing board games and strolling in the cool of the evening. Now all she felt was indifference and bitterness. Where had her love for life and for her family gone?

Her dear friend Mary always listened whenever Hannah was chafing against the strict conformity demanded among the People. But even with Mary, Hannah didn't share too much. If Mary's parents knew Hannah questioned the authority of the bishop, preachers, and even the *Ordnung,* they'd never let Mary see her.

But those irritations didn't compare to the resentment and vengeance that warred in her soul of late. What seemed like years ago she used to dream of Mary and Luke remaining close to her even if she didn't join the faith. Now nothing seemed possible. Hannah no longer shared kindred thoughts with anyone—Luke, Mary, or even herself. Paul had loved her energy and sense of humor, but she didn't possess that now. She'd become an empty kerosene lamp, the outward part of no use without its fuel.

Yet, in spite of every gloomy thought moving within her, she felt a lingering trace of optimism that when she heard from Paul, her once-hopeful soul would return, and life would again have purpose. The haunting question of why Paul hadn't written made a shudder run through her body.

For several nights now, her father had been pacing the floors hours before the four o'clock milking. And she knew why. He still hadn't decided whether to tell the bishop what had happened to his daughter. If he did, all power to have final say over her life would be removed from him. If the bishop chose to tell certain ones in the community about the incident, the news would eventually get back to Paul since he had distant cousins who lived in Owl's Perch.

Glancing at the shiny, gold-trimmed clock, Hannah took a deep, miserable breath. Paul had promised to send her a letter within two days after he left. Although she couldn't manage to keep track of the days, *Mamm* had told her it had been more than three weeks since that day on the road.

Sarah had ridden the mile to Mrs. Waddell's with their brother Levi. Surely Sarah would bring a letter for her today. Hannah had spent quite a bit of time patiently reasoning with Sarah to convince her to bring home any letters without telling *Mamm* or *Daed.* Her sister had finally agreed.

Hannah sighed and shuffled to the machine. Bending to grab the shirt off the floor, she spotted several folded papers sticking out from between the bottom of the dresser and the last drawer—as if someone had hidden them under a drawer and they had worked their way out. A closer look said it was probably a letter. Without hesitation, she eased the papers out of their half-hidden spot.

Paul sat in his apartment with his open books spread across the small desk as he studied for another psychology test. The place was quiet since his roommates were all out enjoying the evening with a group of girls. The alarm on his watch sent out an elf-sized rendition of reveille. He pushed a button, silencing the tinny music. It was four o'clock and finally past all chance that his grandmother was still down for a nap. Now he could call her. Of course his true goal was to speak with Hannah.

If they could instant message each other, e-mail, or talk on the phone, their separation would be much easier to deal with. Conversing only through letters in this day and age felt like trying to send for help by carrier pigeon. His chance of catching Hannah was minimal since her scheduled time at Gram's was a bit irregular, shifting as the needs of the Lapp household altered. But it was worth trying, repeatedly.

He picked up the cordless and punched in Gram's number.

The phone was on its tenth ring when the slow, rustling noise told him his grandmother had picked up.

"Hi, Gram. It's Paul. How are you feeling today?"

They spoke of the weather, her aching joints, and how often she'd walked to the pond to feed the fish. Paul had to ease into the subject of

Hannah, or his gram might get defensive. In the past she'd minced no words explaining her feelings about him and Hannah. She wavered between accepting the ever-growing friendship between her Mennonite grandson and her favorite Amish girl and detesting the heartache that lay ahead for both of them—whether the relationship lasted or not.

"Gram, I haven't gotten any letters from you."

"More to the point, no letters from Hannah." Her tone sounded cheerful. That was good. "Sarah's been comin' here in her stead. I'd like to say she's been doing Hannah's job, but that'd be a lie."

That piece of news bothered him. He hoped his extra time with Hannah the day he left hadn't caused her to get into trouble. Then again, whenever life became hectic at the Lapp household, they kept Hannah at home and sent Sarah in her place.

"I can let you talk to Sarah next time she comes," Gram said with a bit of mischief in her voice.

Paul chuckled. This was the grandmother he'd known growing up—before the aches and pains of old age made her irritable with life and everyone around her. "You offer that every time the Lapps send her. Why can't you do that when Hannah's there?"

"Because ya need no encouragement when it comes to her." Silence filled the line for a moment. "Paul, are ya sure you're doing the right thing…for Hannah's sake?"

The concern in her voice echoed his own anxiety. But his grandmother had no idea how far he'd let his feelings for Hannah take him. She only knew they cared for each other. There was no way she could miss that.

"She's of courting age, Paul. She needs to be going out with her own kind. Is she doing that? Or is she waiting for you?"

Jealousy and guilt nibbled at his conscience. He couldn't bear to think of her seeing anyone else. That was why he had asked her to marry him before he left—that and his concern that she might join the church this spring if he didn't give her another option.

"Paul." His grandmother's firm tone brought his thoughts up short.

"Yes ma'am."

The line fell silent again. He had no desire to try to answer her question. Fact was, he had no answer that she'd care to hear.

"There's no sense in you looking for letters from Hannah or sending any here for her, not for a while. Sarah says it'll be weeks before Hannah returns. In the meantime, you'd better think this through. Let this space clear your thoughts." She worded it as a suggestion, but her tone made it more of an order, one he'd better follow if he didn't want the wrong people to learn of this relationship.

"Were you able to give her the letter I sent?"

"I haven't received any mail from you since you left for school last."

"You must have. I sent a manila envelope with a letter to you and a thick white envelope inside it for Hannah."

"I'd remember a letter from you, Paul, and it ain't arrived. Just as well. I think it's best if you two stop conversing for a spell. I let things get out of hand over the summer."

Keeping his voice respectful, Paul said, "I'm not a child, Gram."

"No, you ain't. But she is."

"You and Grandpa were eighteen when you married."

"Our parents approved of us seeing each other from the get-go. If Hannah's father weren't so stubborn about his kids remainin' Amish and staying in his district..." Gram paused.

Paul wondered why Gram, who had nothing to do with the Amish community aside from Hannah working for her, seemed to think she knew how Zeb Lapp felt. "But—"

"But," Gram interrupted. "But Hannah's father will not spare the rod on her if he gets wind of this, and you know it. Now, no more talk. You'd best spend your time looking at the realistic aspects of this relationship instead of letter writin' and callin' and such."

Paul's temper threatened to get the best of him. "I need to go, Gram. I'll call you in a few days." He hung up the phone.

Irritation pulsed through him. Still, Gram had made some good points. Hannah was young. But she was mature enough to make lifelong decisions.

Wasn't she?

He glanced at the psychology books spread out over the desk. He was torn between his desperation to make a connection with Hannah and the nagging feeling that maybe his grandmother was right.

But where was the letter he'd written, the one in which he'd shared openly about his love for her? If a letter from him never arrived, what would she think of his commitment to her?

He could try to circumvent his grandmother's wishes and drive to Owl's Perch to see Hannah. But that could prove detrimental to their future relationship and get Hannah in a lot of trouble.

Paul's only option was to give his grandmother time to change her mind about allowing Hannah and him to communicate through her address.

Her heart pounding, Hannah unfolded the letter. The top page had a watercolor painting of a sunset on a beach. She shifted to the second page, where large handwriting in the salutation said, "Dearest One." Refusing to give in to defeat just yet, she flipped to the last page. It was another beach scene but from a bird's-eye view. She flipped back to the second page to find the closing: "With all my love, Zabeth."

Disappointment drained what little strength Hannah had. She sat on the side of the bed, holding the letter in her lap. Her momentary hope that Paul had written to her and that somehow, through the mystical way of love, the letter had found its way to her was gone. It was a childish dream, without merit or good sense. As she adjusted to the fresh setback, a new thought worked its way to the front of her mind: who was Zabeth, and was that even an Amish name?

If it was, she'd never heard of it. Dozens of questions floated through her mind. She wondered who "Dearest One" was, why the letter had been stuffed under a drawer, and if the written words might hold any clues as to why she hadn't heard from Paul. As she sat there, the questions grew and so did a desire for answers.

Rising, Hannah hid the letter behind her. After bolting the door, she returned to the bed and unfolded the letter.

Dearest One,

It has been too long since we've seen, spoken to, or written to each other. I pray you will set aside your shame of me and find it within yourself to return a letter.

When we were but youth, I made my choices and you made yours. Now we are fast approaching old age, and I need no one's judgment—every day of my life I've paid the price for my decisions. But surely, as I deal with this horrid illness, our separation need not go any further.

I'm your twin. We shared our mother's womb. And once we shared a love so deep we could each feel what the other one felt before any words were spoken. Perhaps the need to break that connection is why you moved away from Ohio and joined the Amish in Pennsylvania.

The shunning of the past two and a half decades has been bitter. When it is my time to die, I do not wish to leave you behind with acrimony in your heart against me.

With all my love,
Zabeth

Like hornets buzzing in panic during late fall, Hannah's thoughts zipped around furiously without landing anywhere.

Who is "Dearest One"?

She flipped to the backside of each page, looking for a clue. There was none, not even a date anywhere on the letter, so it could be really old, although it didn't appear to be.

She glanced back to the closing of the letter. Zabeth sounded like a woman's name. Skimming the note for any hints of whom it was to, Hannah paused at the word *Ohio.* Her father had a few distant relatives in Ohio, but he didn't have a sister. Most of his brothers lived outside Lancaster, where his parents were buried.

She'd been told her grandparents *Daadi* John and *Mammi* Martha had moved to Lancaster several generations ago. So whoever Zabeth was, she—or he—had probably been a sibling to one of Hannah's grandparents.

In spite of her disappointment, the few moments of reading the letter had given Hannah's raging emotions a welcome distraction. But her attention wasn't drawn away for long, especially over something that went back to her grandparents' youth.

Deciding that the letter was none of her business and not of interest anyway, she put it back where she'd gotten it—careful to hide it better this time. But one nagging thought kept coming at her as she headed for bed. Would she one day send a letter begging her siblings to write to her?

7

Luke positioned the harness over the gentle mare's muzzle, then slid the bit into her mouth before placing the bridle around her head. He connected metal fasteners, leather straps, and leads from the horse to the courting buggy. Blue skies and wispy clouds filled the late-September sky. It was perfect weather for an outing. Since there'd been church last Sunday, no services would be held tomorrow.

As he hooked the shafts from the buggy to the mare, he wiped his sweaty palms on his trousers, hoping he didn't look as nervous as he felt. He'd been courting Mary Yoder for nearly five months. Tonight, after the singing, he was going to ask her to marry him. He hoped she was willing to do all that it would take for them to wed.

He threw the leather straps across the horse's backside and pulled its tail through the loose restraints. He remembered the first time he had worked up the nerve to ask Mary if he could take her home after one of the singings. He'd spent hours that day polishing his buggy to a shine and grooming the mare in preparation. He grinned as he looked at the buggy and horse he'd readied for tonight. He didn't feel any less nervous now than he had then.

In spite of Hannah's attitude about the singings, he thought the ritual was a good setup. All those of courting age within the community gathered in a barn and sang a cappella for hours. One or two of the older singles would start the hymn at a faster pace than used during church times. And even though the bishop and some of the parents were always there, plenty of laughter and quick-witted humor rang out during the singings. Sometimes words were altered to make the serious lyrics come to life with youthful glee. As long as the songs stayed respectful, the bishop allowed it.

Young people could get to know each other better during a ride or two home, without anyone committing to a relationship. If they weren't compatible, no one's feelings got hurt. The man didn't have to take a girl home again if he didn't want to. The girls never had to accept a ride from anyone.

This was one area that parents didn't get involved in, not even with a suggestion. The bishop saw to that. He said God was responsible for putting young people together, not man.

In his years of going to singings, Luke had taken several girls home. But Mary was the only one he'd ever truly courted, the only one he made a point of seeing at times other than during a ride home from the gathering. Now they ducked her parents' eyes and went out every chance they got.

Her decision to marry him would mean she was ready to give up her time of extra freedoms and submit to the *Ordnung,* the written and unwritten rules of the People. Luke never doubted that she would give up those things. He just wasn't confident she was ready to do so now. If they planned to marry next fall, Mary would have to start going through instruction by springtime.

He'd chosen to be baptized into the church a year and a half ago. According to the *Ordnung,* he could only marry a baptized member.

Luke pulled his handkerchief from his pocket and gave the leather seats one last cleaning.

Sometimes, after an evening of a cappella hymns, Mary liked to try her hand at driving the buggy. He considered himself a liberal man, and he enjoyed occasionally letting her take the reins. His father would scowl at a woman driving when a man was in the buggy, but Luke saw things differently. When Mary grasped the reins, her greenish blue eyes reflected both excitement and insecurity. She even talked to the horse to get it to behave. Luke never conceded whether he thought the horse understood her. But Mary was awfully cute working her way through her fears and making the horse do her bidding. As the only girl among the ten siblings, Mary'd had little opportunity to drive a buggy at home.

After tucking the bandanna into his pocket, he climbed into the buggy and sat on the leather seat. He stared at the house and thought about Hannah. Something was wrong with her, seriously wrong. She hadn't been the same since the night she had fallen nearly a month ago. She barely ate, talked, or worked. *Daed* had even allowed her to stay home from church since the incident and to get out of the work gathering at the Millers' yesterday.

Worse than all that, Hannah had no spunk lately. Why, she hadn't baked him a cake or even fetched him some cool water when he was working in the fields. He flicked the reins and clicked his tongue. *Wunnerlich.* That's what it was. *Strange.*

Too tormented to do any more work and too anxious to sleep, Hannah lay on her bed, listening for the sound of a horse's hoofs, while daylight still streamed in her window. She felt a little sorry she hadn't gone to the singing with Luke. Some fun time with Mary might have helped Hannah's sanity return. But she was still waiting to hear from Paul. Her chest ached with worry that when Sarah returned, she might not have a letter with her.

Thoughts of the letter from Zabeth came and went. Asking her parents about it was not an option. When Hannah was very young, they'd made their position clear: if a topic was approachable, they'd bring it up during mealtime. If they didn't bring it up, their children weren't to do so.

But what if her parents had lost the letter and then forgotten it? Hannah sighed. That was silly. People didn't just forget such important—

She bolted upright.

Paul's gift! The small leather book. Hannah rubbed her forehead, desperate for a moment of clarity. Where was it? When had she last seen it?

Feeling dizzy, she sprinted down the stairs, grasping the handrail firmly. "*Mamm?*" She hurried through the living room and into the kitchen. "*Mamm?*"

"In the laundry room."

Barely recognizing her mother's scratchy and tired voice, Hannah came to an abrupt halt when she arrived at the doorway. Huge stacks of dirty clothes were shoved into a corner, covered with a sheet. Clean, wet clothes sat in a pile in the large galvanized tub. "Why are you doing laundry this close to nightfall?"

Her mother turned and smiled. "Oh, Hannah, it's good to see you downstairs again." *Mamm* looked about the room. "We aren't managing things very well without you." She whispered the words as if *Daed* wouldn't figure out how poorly Hannah was doing if *Mamm* didn't tell him.

"I had a small leather book in my apron—"

"Today?" *Mamm's* brows furrowed.

"No. When…" Hannah searched for the right words.

Her mother lifted an armful of dirty clothes and tossed them into one of the smaller galvanized tubs. "You mean the last day you worked for Mrs. Waddell?"

Blinking back her resentment, Hannah realized how comfortable her mother had become with that awful night. "Yes. I had a small book in the hidden pocket. Have you seen it?"

Studying her daughter, *Mamm* pushed the tub of dirty clothes into the corner. "I never saw it. But the clothes you had on were burned the next day."

Burned?

Hannah dashed out the side door and across the back field. Clawing through cold ashes and soot in the barrel where they burned trash, she found no shreds of clothing.

It was Esther's job to burn trash. Maybe she had found the book and put it away somewhere. Looking across the yards and gardens, Hannah soon spotted her sister picking lettuce in the garden.

"Esther, can you come here, please?"

Leaving the small basket, Esther strolled toward Hannah, wiping the dirt from her hands on her black apron. "Feeling better?"

Hannah shook her head. "My clothes you were told to burn, you know the ones?"

Esther nodded.

"There was a small leather book in the hidden pocket of my apron. Tell me you have it."

Esther shrugged. "I can't tell ya that. I would have brought it to ya had I found something." Still rubbing dirt off her hands, Esther huffed. "I can tell ya that I'm tired of doing my chores and yours. So is Sarah, and now she's having to work for Mrs. Waddell too. You ought not do us this way."

Ignoring her sister's irritation, Hannah got down on her hands and knees, searching the grassy grounds near the barrel. "Is there any way the book might have fallen out of the pocket?"

"Don't see how. *Daed* had your clothes all bundled up when he gave them to me. I unfolded them over the barrel so they'd burn more thoroughly. I know how to do my jobs, Hannah." Esther put her hands on her hips. "And yours too, now."

Unwilling to give up hope, Hannah continued hunting for the missing item until the newly healed skin from the gashes turned raw. It was no use. The book was nowhere to be found. Why had she stayed in bed like a fool and let the gift Paul had given her come to ruin?

Her bitter disappointment jolted to a halt when she heard hoof steps. Standing, she saw Levi and Sarah riding bareback together. The horse ambled toward the barn. Hannah sprinted in that direction.

Levi paused while his sister slid off the back of the chestnut horse. Sarah thrust an envelope toward Hannah. "I don't see how you put up with working for Mrs. Waddell. She's the crankiest woman I've ever dealt with. According to her, I didn't do one thing right all day."

Hannah took the envelope and pressed it to her chest. "Thank you, Sarah. Thank you." Feeling waves of joy, Hannah beelined to the side yard, ripping open the letter. But it wasn't a letter. It was a card with a scene of a white-steepled church sitting among autumn trees with leaves of gold, red, and yellow. That was odd. Since the People rotated homes for their services rather than use church buildings, it didn't seem likely Paul would send her a note like this. She flipped open the card.

Dear Hannah,

I'm sorry to hear you aren't well. I find it even more distressing that you won't be returning to work for me. We have an arrangement. I will be in especially deep need when the holidays come. You must speak to your father about this, or I will.

Sincerely,
Mrs. Waddell

Hannah ran inside, searching for Sarah. She found her in the laundry room with *Mamm*. "This is it?" She waved the card in her sister's face. "This is all you came back with?"

"It is." Sarah lifted a galvanized tub filled with clean, wet clothes. "Would you have me write the letter myself that you want so badly?"

Hannah stared at Sarah. Then she glanced at her mother, aware of how much she had just revealed.

Her mother sighed, seemingly unaware of the new piece of Hannah's life she'd just learned. "All right, girls. That's enough. You'd do well to remember your quiet upbringing and the teachings to hold your tongue, before your father uses his strap."

Sarah set the cumbersome tub on the floor. "I've been doing Hannah's chores for nigh on four weeks now. That Mrs. Waddell is as harsh as the cold winter's wind in January. And then my sister comes fussing at me about things I have no control over."

Nearly four weeks? Was that possible? Surely Sarah was exaggerating. There was no way nearly a month had passed.

"Silence." The thunderous voice filled the room. All three women turned, wide eyed, to face Zeb Lapp. "Sarah," he snapped, "are you complaining?" His voice was loud enough to be heard into tomorrow. "Has your older sister not always carried more than her fair share in this house? Yet now that she's been feeling poorly, you whine like a feeble cat."

He turned his focus on Hannah. "And you. Did I not tell you to start pulling your weight around here? Look at your mother. She's worn ragged. Life on this farm must have everyone's full strength for each and every day. Have you become lazy like the fancy folks who can't get meals on the table even when the expensive stores do most of the cooking for them?"

He raised a finger and pointed at Sarah. "Hannah's not the one who told you to do her chores. I am! How dare you grumble! If I hear one more word, I'll take you to the smokehouse and teach you a lesson you won't soon forget. Do you hear me?"

Hannah wondered how they could not hear him. His face was red, and his throat would hurt from screaming when his temper settled. But she refused to apologize. She was sorry for lots of things, but snipping at Sarah was not one of them. And she'd not lie about it, whether she was made to go to the smokehouse or not.

Sarah lowered her head, seemingly unable to look at anyone. She was trembling so hard Hannah thought she might pass out. "I was wrong. I beg your forgiveness."

Waving his hands in the air, their father continued. "When I see the fruit of your words, then we'll talk of forgiveness. Now, leave the clean laundry there. There's no sense in hanging it out to dry at nearly dusk. We're getting behind on more important things than laundry. We didn't harvest near enough potatoes for a full day's work."

He took a long, deep breath. "Sarah, gather your siblings. All of you go help Levi sort today's potatoes and get the bins cleaned out for tomorrow's digging."

"Yes, *Daed*." Sarah headed for the door without lifting her head.

"And remember my warnings, Sarah." Her father's booming voice made *Mamm* jump. "Do not let the youngsters out of your sight. No one is to go near that road without one of your older brothers."

Sarah scurried off.

Hannah wondered what good a pacifist brother would do. What would Levi do if something awful happened to one of his sisters? Stand there and politely ask the person to go away? Panic roiled within her, but she held her tongue and started for the door.

Her father glowered at her. "Samuel's been out of pants that fit him for far too long. Have you finished sewing for the day?"

She'd been so distracted by the letter from Zabeth, the realization she'd lost the bankbook, and the disappointment of another day without a letter from Paul that she'd forgotten her goal for today. "No, *Daed*. I'll go do that."

"The three of us need to talk but not now. There's work to be done."

Dreading the idea of anything her father might say to her, Hannah nodded compliantly before she scurried through the living room and up the steps.

Luke watched all the young people making their way out of the Stoltzfuses' barn and to the buggies. He felt sad for some of the young men who'd come to the singing hoping to find a girl but were leaving alone. Some twenty-odd years ago a slew of boys had been born into the community. That was a great blessing to all the men who needed strong hands to help run the family farms. But now, when it came time to find wives for them all, the gender imbalance was a problem. Having so many males in each household also made it difficult for parents to uphold the long-standing tradition of offering their sons housing and land when they married.

Mary climbed into Luke's buggy, not pausing a bit to see who was getting into the other buggies. Luke smiled at her and took hold of the reins with a wink.

She folded her hands in her lap. "The air is so refreshing tonight. The first comfortable evening for months, *ya*?"

Nodding to Mary, Luke mumbled softly to the horse. *"Kumm zerick."* The horse began backing up. *"Gut."* The mare stopped. Luke clicked his tongue, and the buggy lurched forward.

Only the silvery glow of the moon gave them light to see by. Looking at a sea of open buggies with single occupants, he mumbled, "So many of the young men go home alone."

Sighing, Mary stared at her folded hands. "I heard the Miller twins are going to Mennonite singings."

The horse's hoofs clopped against the paved road. "If word of that gets back to their *Mamm,* they won't be doing it for long."

The local parents preferred their children to stay within the district to marry, though they'd bend in that area if need be. However, flirting with the Mennonite ways was equal to treason in the hearts of lots of Amish folk. Many respected their Mennonite neighbors, but they didn't want to lose their children to them. Luke's own father was the most determined on the issue of any man he'd ever met. None of Zeb Lapp's children would turn from the Old Order ways. None.

Mary shook her head. "Those Mennonite girls would do well to catch one of the Miller twins. Can't say I like their sense of modesty, though. The lightweight material they use and the few pleats they put in show off their figures much more than we're allowed. Have you noticed?"

Luke pulled the left rein, causing the horse to turn onto Newberry Road. "I'd best not be admitting to noticing such a thing even if I did."

Mary laughed gently and shoved her elbow into his side. "Your cousin Elizabeth thinks we should make our clothing by their pattern and material. Though it doesn't much matter what any of us think. Bishop Eli said it's not the right way to dress, and he gets final say."

Coming to a stop sign, Luke pulled back the reins. "I was hoping not to take you straight home tonight. Do you mind if we ride slow and talk for a while?"

Mary shifted in her seat, facing him a little more. "I don't mind."

When they turned onto a gravel road, Luke slowed the horse. He would have liked to stop the buggy entirely so they could talk without having to speak above the clopping horse hoofs and the grinding gravel under the wheels. But if someone saw them parked, he wouldn't be abstaining from the appearance of evil as he'd agreed to do when he joined the church.

As the horse plodded along, Luke grasped both leads in one fist. Then he reached for Mary's hand. She jumped with a start and jerked from him. Luke's heart sank.

She giggled. "Ya caught me by surprise, Luke. I wasn't expecting…"

Luke took the reins with both hands again. Mary reached out and enfolded her soft, delicate fingers over his. They lowered their entwined hands onto the seat. Her touch made him think the horse and carriage would float through the sky like a hot-air balloon. "I care for you ever so much."

She gazed at the scenery to the right side of the buggy, away from him. A few agonizing moments later she turned and faced him. "I feel the same way."

"Does your father know who's bringing you home from the singings?"

"I don't think so. But he's in a much better mood since he knows I'm going to the singings regularly and not fritterin' my Saturday nights away among the English."

Heat ran up the back of Luke's neck. "He's just glad you're not using any more of your *rumschpringe* to slip into town and date English boys." His words came out angry, and he immediately regretted them.

"Like you didn't mix among those English girls while you were deciding where you'd spend your future. You even kissed one or two if the rumors have any truth to them." In spite of her words, Mary's face reflected peaceful acceptance of his running-around time.

Swallowing hard, Luke once again wished he'd never gone out with those English girls. He couldn't tell Mary that he had just used them to boost his ego. It was fun to cross the forbidden border and go out with a few English girls. But soon enough he'd realized he didn't like the non-Amish women, not one of them. They were nice enough and all, but he just didn't have enough in common with them. They wanted to talk about television, music, movies, and computer games. His idea of a good conversation was about last week's softball game in the Millers' mowed field, but the English girls never knew the people he was talking about. It wasn't just that; it was everything. There was a wall between him and those fancy girls, a wall he decided he didn't want to tear down.

His father would be furious if he learned that Luke hadn't used his *rumschpringe* for its real purpose of finding an Amish mate. Nonetheless, that time of being free from the usual constraints had caused him to know without any doubt that he'd rather live the strict, simple life of his forefathers.

The swift clomping of a faster buggy came up behind them, the driver clearly wanting to pass Luke's slow pace. Glad for the few minutes of distraction, Luke pulled the right lead, making the horse move as far off the shoulder as it could.

While waiting for the buggy to pass, he wondered about Mary's days of extra freedoms. Had she cared for some English boy before Luke had started bringing her home from the singings? Even now, with her beside him, annoyance ripped at his insides as he thought of his sweet Mary spending time with those conceited, worldly young men.

He knew Mary would eventually choose to join the church, but left on her own, she might wait a few more years. She, like Hannah, enjoyed having some freedoms from her parents' watchful eyes. Wondering what indiscretions Mary would confess to her mother before her baptism, he gripped the reins until his hands tingled with numbness. There were worse things than what could be expressed through a confession. What if she had given part of her heart away, a part he'd never own? That would haunt him the rest of his days, whether she was his wife or not.

Mary nudged him. When he glanced at her, she tilted her head toward the buggy that was beside them. He turned to look. Matthew Esh had slowed his carriage. He was riding alone, obviously milling about, wasting time. Luke had done a fair amount of that himself before he had a girl to spend time with.

Luke smiled back. "Fine evening for a buggy ride, *ya*?"

Matthew pulled back on the reins, keeping his horse at an even pace with Luke's. "'Tis that. I thought maybe your horse had gone lame you were goin' so slow."

Luke shook his head. "It's a good night for riding and talking." He winked at Mary, then turned back to Matthew. "But not to you."

Matthew's laughter filled the cool night air. "I'll not be insulted by honesty. Is Hannah not gonna come to any of the singings?"

Trying to think how to be honest and yet not say too much, Luke answered, "She's mostly staying around the house."

A look of concern flickered across Matthew's face. "That could be *gut* news, I s'pose."

"Could be." Luke shrugged.

"*Gut* evening to ya now." Matthew clicked his tongue, and the spirited horse took off.

The leather seat moaned as Mary leaned in close. "There aren't enough girls for all the men in our community as it is. Hannah shouldn't be holing up at home, making herself unavailable."

Slapping the reins against the horse's backside, Luke looked straight ahead. "Is that how you feel as well?"

In his peripheral vision he saw her chin tilt up, but she didn't respond. Sometimes she and Hannah were too alike for his tastes. He hated when Hannah pulled that chin-tilting silent routine. "Mary Yoder, if you want to drive this buggy, you'll answer me." He held the reins toward her.

She smiled victoriously and took them from his hand. Her body tensed with excitement and nervousness. "I can do this, right?"

Luke leaned back, enjoying her pleasure. "You always do, panicky as it makes you."

She moved her head from side to side. "It always makes my shoulders hurt."

Luke dared to place his hands on her shoulders and rub gently. "That's because you get so uptight. The mare is old and well mannered. Just relax."

Mary fidgeted with the reins, looking as if she might bolt from the buggy if the horse so much as swooshed its tail.

"All right, now you'd better start talking to me, or I'll take the reins away." As she briefly glanced his way, he smiled. "Spill it, Mary Yoder."

"Druwwel," she muttered.

Luke leaned forward, feigning innocence. "Trouble? Me?"

"No, the horse," Mary teased.

Bending close to her ear, he whispered, "You made a deal."

"All right. Give a girl a chance to think." She turned the horse and buggy onto a small path.

He breathed in the fragrance of freshly cut hay, the last for the season. His nervousness evaporated under the spell of Mary Yoder. She had a wonderful way of making him fall in love with life all over again every time they were together.

She continued out the small path and stopped under a huge tree at the back of the Knepps' place. "Do you mind?"

Mind? She had to be kidding. "You did the stopping, not me. If someone sees us, I'm pleading innocent."

She shook her head at him, but her giggles let him know she wasn't the least bit put out. Wrapping the reins around the short metal post on the dash in front of them, she sat on the edge of the seat. She began looping the reins in her fingers. "When I was enjoying my freedoms, I learned things I didn't know and experienced things that will be forbidden when I join the church."

Feeling anxious, Luke pressed. "What have you experienced?"

"Well, one night I went out to eat at a restaurant with Ina, and I wore a silky red dress that showed my knees."

He could easily accept that she'd dressed that way once. And he wasn't surprised she considered it a great freedom to go to an eatery. If he had nine brothers to help cook and wash for, he'd have made eating out one of his first thrills too. Mary hadn't hidden the fact that she was fond of Ina, the English girl whose parents owned the music store where Mary worked. Being employed there would be forbidden when she joined the church.

Luke removed his hat and held it for a moment to help cover his fears. "That can't be all you've done with your freedom."

Brushing a gnat away from her face, she continued. "Another time I bought a bathing suit and went swimming in Ina's pool. It's in her backyard. We swam until past midnight. I'll never forget that."

Feeling naked without his hat, Luke placed it firmly on his head. "Just the two of you?"

"Oh no. There were a dozen girls there. We laughed about silly things until my sides hurt."

Luke raised an eyebrow. "Only girls?"

"Luke Lapp, are you edging toward asking if I went swimming with boys?"

He gazed into her eyes, determined to confront the things on his mind. "It crossed my mind."

"I would never…" She scowled at him. "You know, if I weren't so fond of you, I'd get out of this buggy and walk home."

A goofy smile etched itself on his face, and he was powerless to erase it. "How fond?"

"Luke!"

Confident this was the door he was looking for, he became serious. "Fond enough to be baptized into the church this spring, published next October, and married by early winter during the wedding season?"

Her face went blank. Luke couldn't tell what she was thinking. Soon her greenish blue eyes danced with laughter. "Are you asking 'cause you're curious or because you'd like to be the one I'm published with?"

"You got somebody else in mind?"

She giggled and huffed at the same time. "Answer my question before you go asking more things."

Doing his best not to lose his nerve, he took a deep breath. "I'm asking because I can't imagine there being a better wife in the whole world than you."

The words were barely out of his mouth when Mary flung her arms around his neck. "Oh, Luke, when you started taking me home from the singings, I was sure it was just because Hannah and I are such good friends. As I grew to love you, I was afraid you didn't return those feelings."

Joy turning flips within his chest, he held her tight. Slowly he backed away and bent to kiss her on the lips.

She put her hands against his chest and pushed against him. "There'll be no lip kissing until we're married."

His jaws ached from the huge smile on his face. "And is this a new rule?"

She planted a kiss on his cheek. "That's the first kiss I've given any young man who wasn't a brother."

"Ah, so you kiss *old* men, is that it?" The buggy shook as Luke laughed.

Mary lifted one of the dangling reins from its resting post and playfully smacked him with it. Luke wrapped her delicate face in the palms of his hands. "I'm so proud of who you are. I...I wish I could give you the same gift of not having kissed anyone else."

Her playfulness stopped cold. She released the leather strap. "Luke, I remember the day you joined the church. Although you didn't say the words, I knew your time among the English had brought you nothing but grief in your soul. I forgave you that very day, knowing even then that I'd marry you in a minute if you asked. Now, we'll talk no more of it. Ever."

Feeling warm and blessed, he kissed her on the cheek. Luke wanted to marry her immediately and not wait until harvest season was over next fall. But Amish life didn't work that way. He puffed out his chest, a silly move that might be deemed prideful and sinful if certain ones within the community saw it. "I didn't realize I was such a fine catch as to have Mary Yoder willing to marry me back when she was but fifteen years old."

She slapped his hat off.

"Mary!" Luke grabbed his hat off the floor of the buggy, wanting ever so much to tickle her rib cage. "That's not proper."

She clicked her tongue at him. The buggy jolted forward as the horse began walking. They broke into laughter.

"You'd better take the reins and drive, Mary."

"Not me. I've had enough driving for one night."

The horse kept plodding forward, though neither one took the reins. They laughed and joked, but each refused to be the one to give in. The horse continued onward, leaving the small path and ambling straight across the three-way, unpaved intersection. When the horse came to the edge of the ditch on the far side of the road, it stopped. Luke and Mary stared at each other, laughing.

Out of the pitch blackness, rays of car lights crossed the top of the hill. Luke grabbed for the reins, but they wouldn't loosen from the post. Standing, he reached for the reins closer to the horse's backside.

The lights blinded him.

Mary screamed.

8

Hannah folded the clothes she'd sewn for Samuel and laid them on *Mamm's* dresser. Through the open windows, she heard people moving downstairs. The back screen door creaked open and then slammed. She recognized the heavy, paced footsteps that entered the home as her father's.

He'd been in the barn for well over two hours, and from the sounds of it, he'd returned without any of her siblings. He must be ready for that private talk he'd mentioned earlier. Hannah eased down the steps. Halfway down the stairs she heard a few whispery words from her mother, and Hannah stopped cold to listen.

"Zeb, I can't stand seeing you like this. I know I agreed to your terms when we married, but it's been twenty-four years, and I've changed my mind."

In an effort to hear the whispers of her parents, Hannah stilled her breathing.

"It's not *your* mind you want to change, Ruth. It's mine. You're not seein' how dangerous this is. Zabeth destroyed the roots of an entire family. I had to move hundreds of miles just to get some peace. She was the cause of an early grave for both my parents. If we aren't careful..."

His voice lowered, and Hannah couldn't hear his words for several long moments. Was it possible that her father and Zabeth were the twins she'd read about in that letter? Something about that idea tasted delicious—as if there was a depth to her father she hadn't known existed.

Even if *Daed* and Zabeth were just siblings and not twins, Hannah had an aunt on her father's side—an aunt none of *Daed's* brothers ever spoke of when they came to visit. Her uncles didn't come from Lancaster often, not even once every few years. Stranger than that, her family never, ever went to visit them. *Daed* said they couldn't leave the farm long enough to make the trip to his brothers' homes. The dairy cows had to be milked twice a day—no exceptions. But inwardly Hannah questioned that excuse. Other dairy farmers hired workers and went on trips.

Her mother's coarse whisper interrupted her thoughts. "Zeb, you don't think Zabeth would show up and try—"

"I don't know, Ruth." *Daed* sounded upset and confused. A wave of compassion ran through Hannah before her father's voice rose. "But I won't stand for Zabeth's rebellious influence coming into our home, especially with what's going on with Hannah. We've got to remain in unity."

His voice lowered, so Hannah couldn't hear anything else. Maybe the letter said more than she realized. She tiptoed back up the steps to her parents' bedroom. She eased the bottom dresser drawer out of its track and set it to the side. The gas-powered pole lamp cast more shadows than actual light. She ran her hands across the wooden runner. Feeling something made of paper that was thinner than the letter, she pulled it out. An empty envelope. Surely it went with the letter she'd read earlier. She held it up, allowing the lamplight to catch the letters so she could read what it said.

It was addressed to her father. The return address had only one name: Bender. That was an Amish last name. Still, she supposed it could belong to someone not Amish. The street address: 4201 Hanover Place, Winding Creek, Ohio. A warm, relaxing feeling ran through Hannah.

"Hannah?" *Daed* called from the foot of the steps, his voice void of the intensity of a few moments before.

Hannah hid the envelope behind her and hurried to the top of the steps. "Yes, *Daed*." Her voice trembled, threatening to betray her.

He motioned for her to follow him.

"I'll be right there." Without waiting for him to order otherwise, she hurried back into her parents' room and put the envelope back in its hiding place. After she slid the drawer back in as quietly as possible, she turned off the gas pole lamp.

With her chest pounding, she made her way down the steps and into the kitchen.

Her father waved toward the refrigerator before taking his spot at the head of the table. In hurried movements, *Mamm* grabbed a glass and poured him some cold lemonade. Hannah walked to the far side of the table and took a seat. Once the drink was in her father's hand, her mother's motions slowed, and she eased into a chair adjacent to his. The women sat in silence while he sipped his cool drink, the furrow never leaving his brow.

The kerosene lamp sputtered, needing to be refilled. Even in the dim, wavering glow, her father looked weary. Another round of guilt assaulted Hannah. He, too, was getting behind because of the disruption she'd caused. Added to that, there was a stress in her home she'd never known before. She had no idea whether it was because of the new rules concerning the road and her younger siblings needing to be watched closely or because Hannah wasn't pulling her load or because of hidden stress brought on by her mystery aunt. But the whole family seemed to be suffering under some unspoken, unbearable burden.

Finally he placed the empty glass on the wooden table and removed his straw hat. "The bishop came by today when I was in the potato field. He was checking to see if we were doing all right."

Hannah's breath caught in her chest. The flame of the lamp spit and dimmed, barely staying lit as the last of the fuel on the wick burned. Bishop Eli checking on a family usually meant he had concerns that someone in the family was moving toward needing a correction. That could mean her father would be questioned in depth by the church leaders. She always thought the bishop's visits were nothing more than a spying mission, but her father considered them a worthy part of staying submissive and humble under a higher authority.

Mamm leaned toward her husband. *"Was denkscht?"*

Hannah also wondered what her father thought. They both waited on the head of the household to answer the burning question.

"He wants to know why Hannah missed two church services and the work frolic and why she wasn't in the field working with me."

A look of concern shrouded *Mamm*. "What did you say?"

"I told him the truth. I said that Hannah's behavior had nothing to do with rebellion and that all my children were obedient and respectful."

"Ya. Gut." Her mother breathed a sigh of relief. The ticktock of the living room clock kept a steady rhythm through the quiet house as the three of them sat in silence.

In spite of her upbringing, Hannah wanted to protest this game. Her father was always telling the truth and yet not. It was enough to drive her mad. Why couldn't he tell the bishop that it was none of his concern what Hannah was or wasn't doing with her time? She wasn't a baptized member of the church. The bishop had only a certain amount of say over the young adults who hadn't yet submitted to the *Ordnung*. So he used his power on the ones who had been baptized—the parents—knowing that few young people were willing to cause trouble for their *Mamm* or *Daed*, even if they disagreed with the views of the church on a particular matter.

Mamm rose and pulled a full kerosene lamp out of the pantry. She set it on the table and lit it just as the other lamp went out.

Her father folded his hands and rested them on the table. "I told him that if I had anything I thought needed sharing, I'd come to him right quick like. I just ain't decided whether this unmentionable should be told or not. It's not like there are rules concerning it. Still, I'm wonderin' if it might be best to go ahead and tell him and let him decide what the right thing is."

Hannah stood. "*Daed,* I think this needs to stay just with us three. You said so yourself the night I was…the night I came home."

His hand came down on the table hard. "Do not try to confuse me, Hannah. I am trying to do what's right. Have you no sense of respect for my position or the bishop's?"

Her chest tightened, and her heartbeat seemed to speed up something horrible. Breathing became difficult, and she bolted outside.

The cool night air brought no relief. She glanced toward the barn with its kerosene lights glowing through the windows. Her siblings were still working, trying to make up for her lack.

Somewhere in the not-too-far distance, a long, continuous car horn pierced the quietness of the night.

An awful noise rang through the air, waking Luke. He tried to open his eyes. Piercing pain ran up Luke's right arm and down his back. Where was he? And why did he hurt so badly? Forcing his eyes open, he gazed at a dark sky filled with brilliant stars and a sliver of the new moon. He was lying on damp grass, but why? And what was that ear-piercing sound?

He rolled to his side and pushed against the dewy grass, but only one arm was able to help him; the other hung limp with excruciating pain. As he staggered to his feet, pieces of what had happened came to him. He spun, looking across the open field where he'd landed. He didn't see Mary. Blinking, he turned his attention to the buggy—some thirty feet away. Pain beyond anything he'd ever experienced throbbed through his head and down his right arm and back. He didn't care. He had to find her.

A car with its headlights on was smashed against the open-top carriage. The impact must have thrown him. Maybe it threw Mary too.

Cringing in agony, Luke strode toward the car. "Mary! Mary!" If he could stop that deafening noise, she might be able to hear him. Scanning the surrounding area through his blurred vision, he stumbled across the open field and toward the road. As he got closer, the car lights silhouetted his overturned buggy. Pain disappeared as panic struck him. With his long legs, he straddled the barbed-wire fence and then brought his back leg over. While trying to gain his balance, he fell into the ditch on the other side.

"Mary! Where are you?" He dragged himself to his feet. The horse was on its side, thrashing and whinnying. Even with the aid of the car lights, he couldn't find Mary. For the first time in his life he ached to lift a heartfelt prayer, a plea from his soul to God. Suddenly he realized he didn't know how to pray, other than the standard rote prayers from the *Christenpflicht.*

O Lord God, heavenly Father, bless us with these Thy gifts, which we shall... The memorized words flooded his thoughts. Pushing past the ceremonial jargon that filled his mind, he tried to think of a more-applicable prayer. He couldn't. Never in his life had he used anything but the rote prayers. He needed real help, and he needed a real God to hear him. Now.

Luke looked toward heaven. "God, please." Shame swallowed him. How dare he think he had the right to lift his head toward heaven and speak so honestly to the Lord of all?

He glanced at what was left of the upended carriage. His legs buckled. He landed on his knees. "Please, Father, if You will, help us."

Warm chills ran through his body, sort of like the ones he felt when Mary touched him, but these were stronger, more...

He looked at the deep purple sky with glittering white stars and a tiny, crescent-shaped moon.

A strong desire to release the mare flowed over him. With renewed strength, he stumbled to his feet and made his way to the horse. In the twin streams of light from the car, Luke witnessed terror in the animal's bulging eyes. Based on the stride marks in the soft dirt and torn-up grasses of the shallow ditch, she'd worked hard to try to stand. She had gashes where the shafts of the buggy had gouged her flanks when it was pushed forward by the impact of the car.

"Easy, Old Bess, easy. *Begreiflich, alt Gaul. Langsam un begreiflich.*" Luke murmured idle phrases as he used his able hand to unfasten the leather straps from the shafts. Gently pulling on the reins, Luke guided and cajoled her until she finally stood. Old Bess tossed her head toward the sky and took off.

Luke ran to the car. In the driver's seat he found a man slumped over the steering wheel. "Mister?" The man didn't answer. Luke reached in and eased the man off the wheel. The deafening noise stopped.

A moment later Luke thought he heard a soft moan coming from the other side of the buggy. "Mary?" He headed toward the sound. When he reached the far side of the carriage, which the car lights didn't illuminate, he saw Mary's body pinned under it. He realized the horse had been jerking the buggy back and forth while Mary was pinned under it. What a strange thing that he had felt so strongly about releasing the horse before doing anything else.

Luke grabbed the sides of the carriage. Pain seared through him, and he fell to his knees. His right arm had no strength. Furthermore, it seemed to be draining his whole being of its power.

Staggering to his feet, he tried to think. The overturned buggy was angled toward the downward slope of the ditch, causing leverage and gravity to work against him. He squatted, placing his left shoulder under the side of the coach, and pushed with all the strength he could muster. The carriage didn't budge. He was too weak to lift the weight off Mary.

Mary moaned. "Luke."

He turned to see her reaching for him. He knelt, brushing back the tall grasses around her face. "Hold on. I'll get help."

He studied the fields and roads. The accident had occurred so far away from any main streets, no one would have seen or heard the collision. And no one would miss them for hours.

A gentle brush against his leg jolted his attention back to Mary. "Listen to me." Her faint voice brought tears to his eyes. He bent closer, and she reached for his face. "I have loved you for as long as I can remember, Luke. We would have made a *gut* family, *ya*?"

"Mary, don't talk like that. We *will* make a *gut* family. You'll see. I…" Luke wanted to promise her she'd live and all would be set right, but he knew better than to cross that line. It wasn't within his power to make such things happen.

Caressing his face, she whispered, "Don't you ever forget, you're the best catch around. You'll find someone else."

"No. Do you hear me? I said no!"

Her hand fell from his face, and her eyes closed. He clasped her hand in his. It felt lifeless and cold.

"Mary?" He patted her cheek. She gave no response. He tried again. "Mary!"

He rested her hand across her chest. Swaying, he stood. After stumbling back to the car, he pushed on the steering wheel, hunting for the horn. When he shoved the silver metal piece, that awful noise blasted through the still night again. On the floorboard he spied a tiny blue telephone. After placing the man's limp body against the horn, Luke headed for the passenger side. As he rounded the back of the car, he wondered if he would be able to figure out how to use the device. He'd seen people use cell phones but had never tried one. He'd only used a corded touch-tone twice in his life.

After opening the car door, he grabbed the phone. He moved in front of the headlights and pressed the thing to his ear. No dial tone. He remembered the day a couple of local firefighters had come to his school and, among other things, said that in an emergency a person needed to get to a phone and dial 911. He pushed those numbers. Each time he pressed a button, an odd electronic sound chirped. But no sound came out of the earpiece.

He gazed across the field, screaming, "Somebody help us. Please."

Looking back at the cell phone, Luke saw the light on the screen go out. He put the device to his ear. Still no sound. He punched the buttons again. The numbers illuminated. Now the screen read 911911. He pressed every button, but nothing helped.

Luke tossed the phone onto the car seat. He stumbled back to Mary and sat on the dirt beside her. When he touched her face, it still held a bit of warmth. Stretching out his legs, he lifted her head and placed it on his lap. Feeling helpless, he brushed wisps of hair from her face. "I don't know what to do, Mary. I'm so sorry."

Drops of blood fell onto Mary's head from somewhere. Luke wiped them off with the palm of his hand. When he looked at his right arm, he saw blood dripping out of the cuff of his long-sleeved jacket. Leaning back, he lay down on the gravelly area. Darkness pulled in on him, and he was unable to resist it. As he closed his eyes, something resembling sleep took over. He could still hear the horn blasting. Maybe someone would come searching for the source of that awful racket.

Drifting into a place he couldn't pull out of, Luke heard sirens. Car doors slammed. Two voices—a man and a woman—began talking. Luke tried to rouse himself. He ached to yell, "Over here! Come help my beloved Mary!" But no matter how much desire welled up within him, something kept pulling him deeper into nothingness.

"We've got a bleeder," a woman shouted. He heard the sound of scissors working against fabric, then felt his jacket being pulled from his shoulder.

No. Not me. No.

"Male. Approximately twenty years of age."

My Mary. Please, save Mary. Can't you see her?

"It looks like a bone from a compound fracture has nicked the artery in the right arm."

An awesome feeling, which went beyond the rules of the *Ordnung,* called to him.

Through the silence that continued to envelop him, he heard the faint sound of the woman's voice.

"I can't find a pulse."

9

The Lapp house was silent, with everyone asleep, as Hannah crept to a straight-backed chair on the porch, next to the open front door. If she saw car lights, she'd be in the house with the door locked before the driver could spot her. In spite of her fears, the cool air and the night sky with its shiny jewels staring down ministered to her bruised heart.

For the second time that day, she listened for the sound of hoofbeats against the hard-packed dirt road. The sirens she'd heard earlier bothered her. She knew worry was a sin, but Luke didn't usually stay out this late. It was past eleven. He'd need to be up milking the cows before he knew it.

The cool air made her shiver. She wrapped the shawl tighter around her. No doubt she wasn't the only one in love. Luke probably fell just short of worshiping Mary. With love like that, he'd draw plenty of strength to sustain him through his workday tomorrow, no matter how little sleep he got.

In spite of not hearing from Paul, she had begun to feel her sanity trickling back. Although the moments were rare, they brought enough relief to comfort her. She had to find her way out of this embarrassing, angry, painful fog she was living in.

Having a shunned aunt in Ohio made her curious if her aunt ever felt some of the same things she did. Somehow that thought helped her, and she began to wonder what her aunt was like.

A single moving light on the road caught her attention, and she quickly dismissed her daydreams. The glow was coming from a kerosene lantern on an open buggy. A tiny laugh escaped her. The horse was trotting at an incredible gait. After whiling away the hours with Mary, Luke was trying to make double time coming home.

As the courting buggy came closer, Hannah could see it wasn't being pulled by their old mare. She stood and walked to the edge of the porch. When the carriage came into clear sight, she recognized its occupant.

Matthew Esh.

Concern slid up her spine. Why was he heading away from his home and at such a speed at this time of night?

Matthew stopped the buggy and gave his warm smile. "You're up awful late."

"I was hoping Luke would be home before now."

"Ah." Matthew propped his foot on the side of the cart. "I saw *Mr. Lapp* and *Miss Yoder* a good bit earlier. They were moseying 'round outside our district."

His jovial tone caught Hannah off guard, and she laughed. Only the English called each other by such titles. Amish students called even their teachers by their first names. But their relaxed ways about names didn't apply when they were talking to or about the English.

Matthew's horse snorted, drawing Hannah's attention to the gorgeous creature pulling the cart. "You got a new horse, *ya*?"

"I bought him at auction last week, thinkin' I could turn a profit. I already sold him to the wealthy folks in Virginia that my brother is building cabinets for. I'm gonna take him to the new owners as soon as the Sabbath is over."

Hannah couldn't remember ever seeing such a fine horse. Its body was lean and sinewy. The reddish brown color shimmered even under the cover of night. When Hannah touched its shoulder, she realized she'd come off the porch and was standing beside Matthew's buggy. She lowered her hand, wondering afresh about her sanity.

Matthew leaned forward. "He's mesmerizing, no?" The lilt in Matthew's whisper made her lift her gaze. He held his index finger to his lips. "But if ya say I boasted about the horse, I'll have to deny it."

Hannah bit her bottom lip and refused the smile that wanted to be expressed. "Does the new courting buggy go with the horse?"

"Yep. I refinished it myself. Those Virginia people want it as a treat for their fancy inn. The stallion was a racetrack runner, ran well for many years."

Moving to the front of the horse, Hannah caressed its muzzle. "He's gorgeous."

The horse whinnied and tossed his head high in the air.

Matthew chuckled. "I think he agrees with you. But I didn't know you cared anything for horses."

"Some things are too striking not to notice. What's his name?"

"Vento Delicato. It's Italian for 'gentle wind.' With a track record like his, I'd think they could have named him better."

Hannah murmured to the horse. "Gentle Wind's not such a bad name."

Vento Delicato lowered his head and allowed her to stroke his face.

Matthew propped his elbow on his knee. "If you don't mind me saying, you're looking a bit down in the mouth these days, Hannah."

She hated that "if you don't mind me saying" phrase. When someone said that, a body might as well brace itself to mind whatever was about to be said. Even so, it was wrong of her to carry her sadness for the world to see.

"I…I was…under the weather. I'm feeling better. Thanks."

Matthew slid forward on the seat. "He won't get your hands dirty. I spent too much time grooming him before the singing tonight. I got all the loose hair off him I could so it wouldn't fly off and cling to a girl's good dre—"

Hannah knew the rest of the sentence. He'd hoped to take a girl home from the singing. More than ever before, she realized the pain of Matthew's disappointment. Leaving the singings alone time after time had to hurt deeply, causing loneliness to grow unchecked.

Hannah looked down at her clothing. Surprise reverberated through her. She was in her nightgown! Modest as it was, going from her neck to her ankles and down to her elbows, it was still improper. She glanced up at Matthew.

His familiar lopsided grin brought back memories of their school days and softball games. He'd graduated two years before Hannah. But because he'd had to repeat a grade when he was very young, he was three years older than she.

He pointed at her and then the horse. "Obviously one of you is too gussied up for the occasion."

Suppressing a smile, Hannah mocked, "Are ya saying I'm not dressed well enough to be standing beside your horse?"

"If the brand-new horseshoe fits, Hannah Lapp..."

Quiet snickers erupted from both of them.

"Would you like to see how smooth his gait is? It's like riding on a fast-moving cloud."

Hannah glanced down at her attire. "I'd better not."

"If you're worried that I'll think this means something, don't be. It doesn't take a genius to figure out that you're more interested in my horse than any single guy around here."

She studied him.

He shrugged. "At least you picked the finest horse."

His relaxed posture and easy talk were refreshing after the misery of the past few weeks. She had a strong hankering to climb into the carriage and see what this horse could do. But first she'd need to change out of her nightgown.

"Can you wait a minute?"

Matthew held up his hand. "Just a dart down the private path on the other side of the barn. It'll take less than five minutes." He spread his fingers apart, signaling five. "If ya go change, you'll likely wake someone, and then you'll never get a chance to see how riding with this race-winning stallion feels."

The horse bobbed its head up and down. Matthew motioned toward Vento. "See, even he agrees."

Hannah glanced back at her lifeless house. Everyone was sound asleep, and they'd be back awful quick like. Vento stomped his foot and shook his mane as if telling her to give him a try. Eager to give life another chance, Hannah clutched her shawl with one hand. "Let's see how this gentle wind rides." Grabbing the buggy handle, Hannah pulled herself aboard.

Matthew gave the signal, and the stallion took off. The force of the forward movement made them fall back against the seat. Their laughter erupted, and the negative thoughts that had haunted her for a month finally gave way to positive ones.

Surely Paul would write her soon. He had to be terribly swamped at school. He'd told her they only had to get through this year, and then he'd work for her father until they had his blessing. She took a deep cleansing breath. Paul had no way of knowing her world had been shattered, and he couldn't be held responsible for being busy with his last year of schooling and... What did he call that other thing? Oh yes, internship. He was also busy doing that.

The wheels to the carriage left the ground as they rolled over an in-ground rock. Hannah grabbed the seat on each side of her. Both she and Matthew burst out laughing. Feeling exhilarated, she sensed faith in the future beginning to stir within her.

Sarah stood on her tiptoes, peering out the bedroom window as her sister climbed into a buggy with a man. All Sarah could see of the driver was the top of his straw hat.

Hannah Lapp, you're a liar.

Hannah had everyone doing all her work because she was too tired. Sarah clenched her fists so tight her arms tingled with numbness. She'd spent all day at that awful Mrs. Waddell's, and for what? So Hannah could traipse around the countryside at all hours in her nightdress? The bishop would hear about this.

The congregation was told regularly not to cause trouble by confronting someone. If there was a questionable issue, it was to be brought to the bishop, and he'd sort things out. If need be, he'd do it without ever saying who told him. And he could approach people confidentially. If they repented, no one else even need know about the event.

Then again, maybe she didn't want to keep this quiet. It irked her to no end how Hannah always managed to sponge up everyone's admiration; *Daed, Mamm,* and even Luke seemed to think she was some kind of Amish superhero or something. Levi wasn't as bad about it as everyone else, but even he thought Hannah could bake, sew, and take care of the young'uns better than she could, which just plain out wasn't true.

It would serve her sister right if they all knew the real Hannah. Why, if *Daed* and *Mamm* knew their daughter was gadding about like this, Sarah would never again have to hear her father say that she needed to be more like Hannah.

A shudder of excitement ran through her. Maybe this was more than just a way to open her parents' eyes. Maybe it was what Sarah had been looking for ever since Jacob Yoder had taken to noticing Hannah over her. Why, Sarah'd had her eye on Jacob for more than a year, but of late the only Lapp he ever noticed at the meeting place was Hannah.

Sarah figured that whenever her sister went to Mary's house, she was warming herself up to Jacob. The very thought made Sarah so mad she sometimes thought she hated her own sister. She'd told Hannah a long time ago how she felt about Jacob. Hannah had given her word she wasn't interested in him. But Sarah wasn't a fool. Jacob hadn't shifted his attention to Hannah for no reason. His interest in her would end quickly if he knew about tonight.

Still, Sarah couldn't be the one to tell him. He might take offense, saying she was a tattletale. There had to be a way for her parents—and Jacob Yoder—to know about this without anyone thinking less of her for it.

Hearing the sound of buggy wheels against the road, Sarah realized they'd returned. Wanting accurate details, Sarah took notice of everything she could. She had never seen a horse like that within her community, nor had she seen that courting gig. It wasn't either Old Order Amish or Old Order Mennonite. As a matter of fact, it looked like some type of commercial rig, used for touristy stuff. If that was true, the driver probably wasn't Amish or Mennonite. He was more than likely English. Oh, this was getting better and better. But why would an English boy be out at this time of night?

She watched Hannah climb out of the buggy. Her sister must've made some English friends from the hired workers Mrs. Waddell took on during the summer months. This man probably drove a tourist buggy for a living and wore that straw hat to make himself look more authentic for his customers.

Sarah would bet this wasn't the first time Hannah had pulled such a stunt. No wonder her sister was always looking for mail to come to Mrs. Waddell's. She had an English beau she needed to hear from in order to make her sneaky plans. Sarah huffed. Hannah out taking rides and whooping it up with a man while pretending to be sick. Sarah would get her back just as soon as she could speak with the bishop without anyone else knowing. If telling the bishop didn't get this piece of news to her parents and Jacob Yoder, she would figure out another way. She was sick of playing second best to the likes of such a liar as her sister.

10

Morning light filtered through the bedroom windows as Hannah made her and Sarah's bed. Careful not to wake her two youngest sisters, Hannah slipped into her day clothes.

The aroma of bacon and sausage wafting through the house smelled inviting. In spite of the minor nausea that still clung to her these days, a bit of hunger gnawed at her stomach. Maybe, somehow, she'd survived the worst and things would get better from here.

She tiptoed down the stairs, hoping to find Luke before her mother realized she was up. Hannah had no doubts that if Luke had managed to propose, Mary had accepted.

Hannah also knew it was time to try to resume her full set of chores and make up for the difficulties she had caused her family. She scurried out the side door and headed for the barn. Sucking in a lungful of clean, brisk air, she resolved to hold on to those refreshing feelings that had come to her last night.

As she traipsed up the hill toward the milking barn, she spotted Old Bess, one of Luke's mares, standing outside the fence. *How did she get out?* Hoping that in his tired state Luke hadn't left the gate open, she sprinted across the yards to the pasture gate. It was latched securely.

She glanced across the meadows, looking for something that would make sense of this strange occurrence. Finding nothing out of the ordinary apart from the horse outside its fence, she grabbed a rope harness off the fence post and eased toward the mare. "Where's your master this fine morning?" As Hannah slid the rope around its neck, she noticed that the horse's left side was covered in dried mud. Puzzled, she led the limping mare toward the barn.

As she entered the open doorway into the barn, she saw her father toss a sack of feed onto his shoulder. But Luke was nowhere in sight. *Daed* glanced her way and paused. A smile worked its way across his weary face. "I'm glad to see you up and ready to help with chores. Do you know where Luke is?"

Hannah twisted the horse's lead rope as if she were wringing out wet laundry. "He's not here?"

He tossed the feed sack onto the ground and stood it on end. "He must be around here somewhere. He wouldn't leave before milking." He pulled a pocketknife from his trousers, opened it, and jabbed it into the feed sack.

Levi stepped out of a stall, looking more like his older brother as each day brought Levi closer to his nineteenth birthday. He hung the pitchfork in its place on the barn wall, and strolled to Hannah. "Where'd you find Old Bess?"

"She was outside the fence."

Levi's eyes skimmed over the horse. A frown knitted his brows as he rubbed the matted dirt that covered the mare's girth and belly. The horse whinnied and stepped back from him. "*Daed!* She's got gashes."

Dropping the knife and letting the sack of feed fall over, *Daed* tore out of the milking barn. Levi and Hannah followed him. He ran to the carriage house and flung open the door. When he turned back to face Levi and Hannah, the concern in his eyes made her cringe. "Luke's buggy is missing."

Quick, repetitive sounds of a horse's hoofs made the three of them turn toward the driveway. A horse and rider came sprinting toward the barn. Matthew Esh brought Vento up short a few feet from them. His hat was missing, and his face was rigid. "Zeb," he said in a breathless voice, "is Luke here?"

Daed shook his head. "His buggy ain't here either, but his horse is. And it's injured."

Matthew squirmed in his saddle. "Someone from the hospital came to Bishop Eli's place this morning. Said there are two unidentified young people in the hospital. They're sending out word to all the surrounding districts."

Daed lowered his head and moaned.

Matthew shielded his eyes from the first rays of the day. "I saw Luke and Mary last night. They were headin' toward the very area where the accident took place."

Daed grabbed Levi's arm, his eyes wide and his face drained of color. "Hitch up two horses and two buggies. I'll get your mother and the children."

Levi took off running toward the barn, and her father ran down the drive and into the house. Hannah stood there, frozen, unable to move or even think.

Matthew dug his heels into Vento's sides and charged to the back door of Hannah's house. He slid off the horse and knocked on the screen door. "Zeb, I got an idea that will save some time."

"Tell."

"If I ride straight to the bishop's house and have him send one van here and one to the Yoders, it'll save at least an hour, probably more."

"Yes. Yes. That's sound thinking. We'll get everyone ready. Hurry, young man, hurry."

Hannah held her baby brother Samuel's tender hand in hers, reassured by the comfort of it. All eight Lapps stood in their front yard, watching billows of dust follow a large car down the dirt road. *Mamm* had her wedding travel bag by her side, the closest thing to a suitcase she owned. If Luke was staying at the hospital, so would she.

The van slowed, then came to a stop. A petite woman in bright pink pants and a matching top stepped out of the vehicle. "I'm Kelsey Morgan." She held out her hand to *Daed.* "I'm Hank Carlisle's daughter and a nurse at Hershey Medical Center."

Daed released his suspender and held out his hand. "I'm Zeb Lapp. This is my family."

Ms. Morgan shook his hand. "You believe your son may have been in the accident last night?"

His cheeks flushed. "Our oldest did not come home last night. He's never done that before."

The woman pulled a picture out of her pocket and showed it to him. "Is this your son?"

He grimaced. "It is."

"He's in the intensive care unit at our hospital. It's not the closest hospital, but it's where he needed to be for the type of injuries he sustained. If you'll load your family members into the vehicle, I'll take you all there." She opened the passenger-side door and then climbed behind the wheel.

Without delay or questions, *Mamm* and *Daed* collected their brood. As he lifted the children into the van, she operated the seat belt buckles for them.

Hannah stood near the open van door, peering inside. The interior smelled of dyed leather and a sickeningly sweet air freshener. The odor caused her stomach to roil. At the sight of the long bench seat, she began to shake as visions of being thrown into her attacker's car pelted her. She stumbled backward. The day of the unmentionable flooded her mind in horrid, living color.

"Get in, Hannah." *Mamm* pointed to an empty seat.

Gasping for air, Hannah backed farther away. "I can't."

"You're safe, Hannah. Trust me and get in, please," her father reasoned.

Hannah shook her head. She could hear the sound of each breath that she forced through her lungs.

The nurse climbed out of the van and came around to their side of the vehicle. "Does she have asthma?"

Mamm reached for Hannah. "No, she's just a bit spooked at the car."

Avoiding her mother's grasp, Hannah turned away. The nurse stood directly in front of her, compassion in her eyes. "Honey, you'll be safe in the vehicle. I promise." Her golden voice washed over Hannah. "Normally this isn't how the hospital handles these situations. But my dad feels strong ties with the Amish in these parts. So when he heard that some local Amish were taken by helicopter to the hospital where I work, he asked me to come here personally and try to help. Surely after I've traveled all this way, you'll let me help, won't you?"

Hannah stared at the woman, unable to speak or even nod.

She gave a warm, endearing smile. "Your brother gained consciousness for a few minutes a couple of times. He was anxious and confused. He needs his family around him."

Hannah gazed into the woman's eyes and caught a glimpse of unspoken truth about Luke's situation. A different type of panic ran down Hannah's spine. "And Mary?"

The nurse took a deep breath. "I'm not at liberty to say anything about her except that she was brought to our facility by helicopter. Another van is taking her family to the hospital."

Nightmarish memories warred within Hannah. Setting her will against her emotions, she cleared her throat and forced herself to step into the van.

Ignoring her pounding heart and the nausea, Hannah gazed out the car window and tried to focus on the scenery. Gentle hills and farmlands whizzed by. After forty-five minutes of back roads, the view outside changed from rolling acreage to a wide, flat river. Brown rapids and white foam seemed to be racing the van. The sun's brilliance sparkled against the rippling water as if starlight had been captured and brought to earth. The first bit of fall color nipped at the leaves on some of the sprawling oaks along the riverbank. She closed her eyes, tuning out the ever-changing scenery and hoping the sick feeling would go away.

When the van pulled into a parking space and the engine cut off, Hannah exited as quickly as she could, the rest of her family following.

A noise ripped through the air as if it were destroying the vast parking area. The air around them seemed to vibrate from the sound. With Samuel holding Sarah's hand and Rebecca sitting on Hannah's hip, all nine of them made their way across the acrid-smelling lot. A few moments later Hannah saw the source of the racket: a helicopter landing near the far end of the hospital. The same helicopter, she guessed, that had brought Luke and Mary here.

Somewhere a siren shrieked and a car horn blasted. Those noises, mixed with the busyness of cars coming in and out of the lot, assaulted her nerves.

Rebecca wailed. Hannah hugged her close and snuggled against her soft neck. "Sh, little one. It's all right."

In spite of Samuel being seven years old, Sarah lifted him into her arms and kissed his cheek. "The English must search for ways to make noise. No?" Samuel bobbed his head in agreement, and his baby-fine, straight, blond hair moved with the wind.

The worst of the summer heat was over at home, but here it seemed to radiate from the blacktop.

They followed Ms. Morgan to a square, brownish building. Two large sliding-glass doors opened without so much as a touch.

The city smells disappeared along with the heat as they entered. The room they stepped into was three times as large as any barn Hannah had ever been in. She had visited the doctor near her home a few times in her life, but she'd never been to a hospital. She blinked, trying to take it all in. The lobby wasn't cold, menacing, or intimidating, as Hannah had expected. Dozens of beautiful chairs sat near small tables. Lamps and plant stands with various types of foliage were scattered throughout the room, giving the place a peaceful feeling.

They turned right, walking past a hexagon-shaped oak desk with a sign above it that said Information. *Daed's* focus stayed straight on where they were going, unlike his children, who gaped at everything around them. Regardless of the nice setting, Hannah was sure Luke and Mary ached to be home, where a breeze coming through an open window gave more refreshment than air from a machine.

Ms. Morgan took a sharp right. The Lapps followed her. After a couple of yards she turned right again and then stopped outside an elevator door. Ms. Morgan pushed a large button with an arrow pointing up on it. "After you speak with a doctor, you'll need to return to this floor and fill out some paperwork."

"I'd like to see Luke before we see the doctor," *Daed* said as the doors opened.

Once they all squeezed in, Ms. Morgan pushed another button, and the doors slid shut. "We'll find a quiet place on the second floor for you to talk with the doctor. After he explains things, you may see Luke."

Daed removed his hat and fidgeted with it. "We don't have insurance."

Ms. Morgan nodded. "Luke and Mary came in under emergency status. Care is guaranteed, but there are still forms to fill out."

Hannah listened to the nervous murmuring of her family as they all waited in a conference room behind closed doors. Her mother paced the floor, bouncing a whimpering Rebecca on her hip. Her father appeared calm, sitting in a chair with his hands propped on the large table. But he kept squeezing his fists so tight they turned white. Then he'd release them and do it again. Tiny dots of sweat covered his forehead.

Levi and Sarah sat quietly with their hands folded in their laps. Samuel bounced on Esther's knee, eating peanuts that a hospital worker had bought for him from a vending machine.

The oversized wooden door opened. A man in his late twenties entered. He glanced about the room and gave a smile. "I'm Dr. Greenfield." He took a seat across from *Daed. Mamm* passed Rebecca to Hannah and sat in the chair next to her husband. The young doctor pulled an ink pen from his shirt pocket. "Mr. and Mrs. Lapp?"

Her parents nodded, looking too emotional to try to speak.

Dr. Greenfield slid his hands into the pockets of his lab coat. "Your son is in serious but stable condition. He has a concussion, but that is mild and temporary. Our main concern is the injury to his arm. We had to operate on it. There was a slight nick on an artery, and the blood flow wasn't sufficient to give the hand and lower arm the circulation they needed. We repaired the artery, and things look good right now. The next few days will let us know how well his lower arm and hand will heal. We'll need to watch him closely during that time. He's in ICU, so he'll get the medical care he needs."

Daed's eyes narrowed. "You said he had a concussion."

The doctor gave a slight nod. "We are closely monitoring his condition, but there's every indication that his head will be fine."

He squeezed his hands into fists again. "Is there a chance he could lose his arm?"

A grimace caused lines across the man's face. "Yes. But we hope that won't be necessary. Right now everything appears to be healing. There's no damage to any tendons or ligaments, which means if his arm and hand do well over the next twenty-four to forty-eight hours, he won't have any lingering issues to deal with—except needing as little stress as possible and getting plenty of rest for three to four weeks."

Swallowing hard and hoping she wasn't about to upset her family further, Hannah spoke. "What about Mary?"

The doctor gave her a friendly smile. "I'm sorry, but I can't tell you about a patient who isn't a family member. The Yoders arrived a few minutes after you, and they're currently meeting with Mary's doctor. They can share with you any information they wish."

He turned back to her father. "Two adults at a time are allowed in ICU, but no one under twelve is admitted unless circumstances dictate. With supervision, the younger children can stay in here or go to a waiting room. There's a cafeteria downstairs. If you'll go to the nurses' station, they'll show you to Luke's room."

Her mother took a deep breath. "Thank you."

Daed nodded. "Yes, thank you."

"Glad to help." Dr. Greenfield left.

Mamm straightened her pinafore. She turned, eying each of her children to make sure they were ready to cope with what faced them without drawing undue attention.

In a quiet, stoic manner they filed out of the room.

For the first time in months, maybe years, Hannah felt her own ideas and desires fade. All that mattered was that Luke and Mary get well.

11

"Hannah." Her father's voice cracked a bit as he called to her from the doorway of the hospital waiting room.

"Yes sir." Hannah rose and placed little Rebecca in Sarah's lap.

"You go in next. Then you can get Sarah, Esther, and Levi ready to see Luke. I'll find a pay phone and call the Bylers to let our community know how things stand."

"Yes sir." Hannah hoped the Bylers would be close enough to hear their phone. It was located in a shanty at the end of their long lane and used mainly for business purposes. They had an answering machine inside the shanty, but days passed without them remembering to check it. After thinking about it, Hannah was sure her father would call Mr. Carlisle if he couldn't reach the Bylers. Mr. Carlisle would see to it that the community was informed of what was going on.

Leaving Sarah to watch over their three youngest siblings, Hannah walked through the door and down the ICU corridor. As she made her way along the hallway, she saw Jacob Yoder leaving ICU and heading for the waiting room. The young man looked pale and shaken. But Sarah was here; she'd be pleased to keep him company. Hannah dipped her head low, avoiding eye contact just as she'd promised Sarah she'd do. But a quick glance up said he never even saw her.

Hannah nodded at a nurse who glanced up from her station. Coming to a halt outside Luke's room, she saw her brother through the sliding glass entryway. She froze.

He lay in the bed with his eyes closed. His right arm and hand were bandaged. Restraints held both arms to the metal sides of the bed. A bag containing some type of amber liquid and a bag of what had to be blood dripped into different tubes attached to his good arm by needles. Strange machines were connected to him and to various boxes she'd heard the nurse call *monitors.*

Her mother sat in an upright recliner beside the bed, staring at Luke. The expression on her face spoke of despair and hopelessness. Determined to help as best she could, Hannah stepped into the room and eased into the small chair beside her mother. "It's okay, *Mamm.* Luke and Mary are gonna be all right. You just wait and see."

Although Hannah hadn't gone in to see Mary yet, she'd overheard Becky Yoder tell all she knew of her daughter's injuries. Poor Mary. She'd suffered a right femur fracture, a right dislocated shoulder, and a left subdural hematoma. The doctors had said that with physical therapy Mary's leg and shoulder weren't a concern. But she could have problems with her memory, speech, and coordination because of the head injury that required surgery to relieve the buildup of blood against her brain. She might not remember her family or friends. She might need to learn how to brush her teeth, feed herself, walk, and get dressed all over again. She'd also need months of physical therapy for the injuries to her shoulder and leg.

Becky said her daughter's heartbeat had been so weak at the scene of the accident that the medic thought she didn't have a pulse. Hannah wondered just how close to dying Mary had come.

Guilt nibbled at Hannah, for even with the grief of this situation, she was finding this world of medicine fascinating.

Hours dragged by as Hannah and her family took turns watching Luke breathe. Various nurses and doctors came by and explained all sorts of medical issues that were hard to keep up with.

The younger kids were miserable camping out in the waiting room, and *Daed* was fed up with just waiting for Luke to awaken. He'd mumbled something a few hours earlier about the rest of the potatoes having to be harvested before the weather turned.

While Hannah sat in Luke's room, both sets of parents gathered in a conference room to discuss who would stay at the hospital and who would return to the farm. Hannah knew the heads of the households wanted to get as much of their families as possible back home. Not only was there plenty that needed to be done, but the contact with such worldliness through the televisions and some of the people was not something either man wanted his children exposed to. And meals at the cafeteria were expensive for an entire family. Besides, it made no sense for two entire families to hold a vigil here.

"Hannah." Her mother motioned for her to leave Luke's room and come with her. Hannah followed her out of the ICU area and into a secluded hallway. Her mother turned to her. "Your father came to me about this and then talked to Becky and John Yoder. We think the best place for you to be is here. Becky and I will stay as well."

The sadness in her mother's eyes and voice hurt, and Hannah couldn't answer.

Mamm glanced down the hallway. "John and Becky would like you here in case Mary wakes up. If you tell her she's safe and everything is okay, that will settle the matter." She smiled, but it never entered her eyes. "Won't it?"

Hannah nodded. Mary did trust her. There had been a time when Mary wouldn't believe she was safe from a storm or an imaginary monster unless Hannah told her so. But that was years ago, back when Mary was a child.

Hannah was also fairly sure of what her mother wasn't saying. If Mary never woke, or if she woke with some of the problems the doctor had mentioned, Hannah could be a comfort to Becky.

Mamm took Hannah by the hand. "The man driving the car that ran into Luke and Mary showed up here at the hospital."

Hannah hadn't expected this. "Why?"

"He's in the conference room with your *Daed*, John, and Becky. He's so sorry for the accident, Hannah." Her voice cracked, and she fought to control her emotions. "It ain't his fault. He wasn't speeding. He just topped the hill as the buggy was crossing the road. He and his wife have both offered to come work for us awhile. I think it'll do the poor man some good to know he's helping those he hurt, even if it wasn't on purpose. And with their help, we won't be short-handed if you stay here." She paused, searching her daughter's face. "Besides, your *Daed* says that you're doing better here than at the farm and that maybe you need some time away."

Hannah swallowed. "I'd be happy to stay here with Luke and Mary. I'm learning bits and pieces about medical stuff, and it's fascinating."

Their conversation paused as they waited on a man to pass them in the hallway. Hannah hated the reason they were at this place, but there was so much to learn around here. When no one saw her, she'd managed to read a few lines from a novel that someone had left in a waiting room and had flipped through a few psychology magazines.

Her mother smiled. "I've always said you'd make a good midwife one day, Hannah. Now, go on back in with Luke."

An hour later *Mamm* came into Luke's room, explaining that John Yoder and *Daed* had found lodging near the hospital for the three of them who were staying. Two drivers had arrived, and everyone else was downstairs loading up to leave.

Mamm, Becky, and Hannah went down to say good-bye to their families. Mary's father promised to return in a few days. In the meantime, Becky was to call him at the Bylers' house with updates at a preset time each evening. In what seemed like a blur, Hannah stood in front of the hospital waving good-bye to most of her family.

How did life change so quickly?

Luke couldn't manage to open his eyes, but he felt a peacefulness in his heart that he'd never known existed. The God who dictated the strict ways of the *Ordnung* had another side to Him. Based on what Luke's heart felt, it was a gentle, listening, loving side. One that was quick to warm Luke's being and build hope during desperate times.

He heard Hannah near him, singing a hymn from the *Ausbund.* He pushed against the weight that tried to force his eyes shut and caught a glimpse of his sister.

Hannah smiled. "Hi, Luke."

Where was he? His eyes closed and refused to open again, but he didn't give in to the pull of sleep.

An image of Mary broke through his murky thoughts. He tried to focus while his sister explained to him where he was, where Mary was, and why. Hannah's always gentle voice now irritated him. He wanted to get up and demand that someone take him to see Mary. Now! But no matter how hard he fought against the engulfing grogginess, he couldn't break free.

In addition to his sister's voice, he could hear other strange noises. There was a whooshing sound that reminded him of the diesel-powered milkers used on the dairy cows, rhythmic beeps like he'd never heard before, and the faint hum of some machine. Something under his nose was blowing cold air up his nostrils, but beyond that he detected a smell like the chemical his *Mamm* used to clean the floors. He ached from the top of his head down to his lower back, but his eyes refused to open, and his body occasionally jerked against its imprisonment. Unable to fight any longer, he allowed himself to sink back into that restful place.

Sitting in the recliner beside Luke's bed, Hannah hurt for both Luke and Mary. She closed her eyes. With them in such a bad way, it was only the beginning of difficult times.

In spite of her concerns, sleepiness nipped at her. While she relaxed, an idea flowed into her mind.

A quilt.

With Mary having months of recuperation ahead and Hannah intending to spend as many of those hours with her dear friend as she could, it seemed a good time to start a quilt for Luke and Mary. If her friend awoke with problems remembering her life, it could serve to tie Mary to her past and to her future as they worked on the squares together. Thoughts of gathering materials and designing a special pattern brought a sense of peace, causing Hannah to close her eyes and lean back in the recliner.

"Wh-where's Mary?" Luke's scratchy voice shot through her.

Hannah jumped to her feet, startled. Breathless, she grasped his hand. "Luke, you're awake."

He stared at her, confusion radiating from his eyes. "Is…Mary…alive?"

"Yes. She's in a room down the hall."

A nervous chill ran through her. A nurse had said that when Luke woke, no one was to tell him any more than Mary was alive and resting. Desperate not to utter the wrong thing, Hannah motioned toward the door. "I...I'll tell *Mamm* and the nurses that you're awake."

As nurses flitted in and out of Luke's room, *Mamm* sat in the cushioned chair, keeping her show of emotion to a minimum. But the light in her eyes helped to ease Hannah's heartache.

Luke was awake, absorbing his new surroundings with a mixture of thankfulness and frustration. In spite of his numerous attempts to see Mary, the staff had refused. Dr. Greenfield was concerned that the stress might slow Luke's progress. Sometime after she was removed from life support—if all went well—Luke would be allowed to see her.

On Mary's third day after her surgery, the doctor would run tests to see what was going on inside her skull. If there were signs of healing and no pools or clots of blood, the staff would begin the process of waking her and might remove the ventilator.

Hannah's heart turned a flip every time she thought about the doctor's words. They were so noncommittal. *If* Mary responded well, she *should* be able to breathe on her own. Recovery seemed so tentative, so faltering. The possibilities made Hannah feel panicky. But quiet misery seemed the only way to respond as the waiting went on and on.

Paul walked beside his supervisor as they strode down the corridor of the family-services department. Connie, a thirty-something mother of three children, was his mentor in this learning process. She had blond hair and wore slacks with tailored jackets whenever Paul saw her, which hadn't been often since he'd begun working here only a week ago. After this initial two-week training period, Paul would work here two days a week.

Thankfully, his immediate boss at the tire store hadn't had the last word about Paul getting fired if he left work early to go to the interview for this job. Mr. Banks stepped in and told Kyle that Paul having flexibility with his work schedule was part of the store's agreement when Paul was hired. Kyle seemed to quietly seethe over the reminder of that piece of news, but he'd stopped breathing threats at Paul.

"You studied my notes last night?" Connie flipped open the thick file and skimmed the first page, checking to see if Paul had initialed it.

"Yes ma'am." The case in question involved the Holmes family—mother, father, and four children, including a teenage daughter named Kirsten, who had shown a tendency to throw fits at her family while in the yard where neighbors could see her. She also had a penchant for hysteria while standing on her property. When Kirsten ran away from home, the police brought her back and contacted social services.

After the initial home visit, the caseworker determined the situation to be detrimental for all the children. An uncle who lived with the family had a history of alcohol abuse and violence. The parents had been ordered to attend counseling sessions, which, according to the report, they had been doing faithfully. Today's session would include Kirsten. *This should be interesting,* Paul thought.

"Any questions?" his supervisor asked.

"Yeah. What's the status on the uncle?"

Connie closed the file. "Both parents have sworn that he is not allowed back into their home."

"What will happen if Kirsten runs away again?"

"Well, there are a couple of ways this could be handled, but I'd suggest we do another in-home visit and interview the other kids to see if something is going on that shouldn't be."

Approaching a closed door, Connie put her hand on the doorknob and turned to Paul. "Now, Kirsten is dramatic. She's quite good at putting on a show. I can guarantee she's going to cry and try to throw blame on everyone but herself. Her dramatic ways are not necessarily an indicator of what's really taking place inside the home. There's plenty of blame to go around, but our job is to help this family function as a unit, not to take sides."

Paul nodded. "I'll do my best to remain objective."

The third day after Mary's surgery finally arrived. Her test results had indicated that the area inside her skull where surgery had been performed was healing better than the doctors had expected. The medicines that were keeping her in a coma had been reduced a few hours ago. Mary's doctor, Dr. Hill—a man much older and rounder than Dr. Greenfield—predicted that Mary should be awake by nightfall.

Still feeling as if her mind and heart were shrouded in a thick fog, Hannah sat by Mary's bed on one side while Becky sat on the other. *Mamm* hadn't left Luke's room all day. He'd been moved out of ICU and onto the fifth floor. The hardest part of the last few days had been dealing with Luke, even though the doctor kept him mildly sedated. When Luke was awake, he was irritable and constantly demanded to see Mary. Then the sedatives would take over, and he'd drift back off to sleep.

Hannah believed Dr. Greenfield was right; Luke didn't need to see Mary like this. Becky had agreed to visit Luke here and there, knowing he'd come closer to believing Mary was doing well if her mother wasn't staying by her side every second. Hannah admired Becky for being willing to leave her daughter for periods of time to help Luke stay calm.

The past few days had taxed everyone's strength, although no physical work was required. Hannah, *Mamm,* and Becky took turns sitting with Luke and Mary, returning to the hotel for catnaps and grabbing quick bites of food in the cafeteria. A lot of Old Order Amish folk—some relatives, some not—had come from all over Pennsylvania, Ohio, and Indiana, many hiring drivers to bring them, to visit and offer support. Those who could donated money for the mounting hospital bills. Even though they wanted to return to the farm with the young ones, *Mamm,* Becky, and Hannah were far from feeling lonely with all the Amish folks who came. From what Hannah was told, only one of Mary's aunts didn't come to visit, the one who was expecting twins in February and lived in Ohio. Her husband came by train, traveling with relatives and friends.

In his phone calls with *Mamm, Daed* told her about the dozens of Amish men and boys who were pitching in with the farming. Several brought their wives to help with the cooking and such at both the Yoder and Lapp homes. The community support given during this time did Hannah's heart good. Her people were kind and generous. Somehow, because of her vehement desire to marry outside her community, she'd forgotten the many blessings of being Amish.

Her *Mamm* said that their English neighbors had been stopping by and offering to help too. People were putting their heads and money together to design a harness shop and an attached apartment as a surprise for Luke and Mary. Hannah hoped they could get that built. That would be a wonderful gift for her friend.

Singing a made-up song from their childhood, Hannah glanced at Becky, whose eyes were glued to her daughter. Mary's limp, lifeless body had been moved into what the nurse called a semi-Fowler's position, with the head of the hospital bed at a forty-five-degree angle.

The minutes droned into hours as Hannah sat beside Mary's bed, softly singing and rehashing old memories. For now, Becky was in Luke's room, trying to convince him that Mary was fine. Hannah squeezed

Mary's hand. "Remember the day we found that litter of abandoned kittens in your *Daed's* old tool shed?" A soft laugh escaped Hannah. "It took us days to convince our mothers those poor things really were abandoned." Hannah ran her fingers up and down Mary's arm. "When they finally believed us, they gave us milk for them and let us use eyedroppers to feed them. We held those tiny kittens and fed them every hour like we'd die if one of them didn't make it." Hannah clicked her tongue in disgust. "They aren't worth the milk we put into their stomachs. They turned out to be mean old rascals that killed every decent cat your *Daed* had in his barn. But they lived."

Hannah laughed. "How about when we were thirteen and worked all fall collecting and sewing comforters for the Mission House? Oh, Mary, we were such a determined pair of girls about everything, remember?"

Whenever there was an occasional slight shifting of Mary's fingers or toes, Hannah whispered to her friend where she was and why. The staff came in and out a lot, though they didn't seem to be particularly concerned.

The ventilator was set to breathe for Mary only when she didn't breathe for herself. Hopefully, Mary's own respiratory system would take over as soon as the medicine-induced paralysis had completely lifted. Hannah listened to the machine force air into Mary's lungs. It happened more times than she thought it should.

Come on, Mary, breathe. Just breathe.

A white form crossed the doorway. Hannah's gaze moved from Mary to see Dr. Greenfield.

"Patience." He smiled. "Her slowness to wake is well within normal."

Hannah forced a smile, glad that Dr. Greenfield was around. He stepped farther into the room and adjusted something on Mary's IV bag. Without saying a word, Becky slipped into the room and took a seat beside her daughter's bed. Mary's eyelids twitched, and her legs shifted. She turned her head, as if trying to free herself of the contraption that covered her mouth. She coughed and pulled against her restraints. A long, loud shrill began.

Dr. Greenfield pushed a button on the ventilator, turning off the alarm. He moved to the bedside and checked Mary's pupils. "This is all perfectly normal," he assured Hannah and Becky. "Dr. Hill began making his rounds a little while ago. He'll be in soon." He turned and walked out the door.

As the hours wore on, Mary looked less and less like a corpse, though Hannah would be hard pressed to say why.

Mary's legs shifted, and Hannah leaned near her ear. "Mary, you were in an accident. We're at the hospital, and you're safe. The odd feeling in your throat is a tube that's helping you breathe. A machine is breathing for you some of the time. Don't fight it. Just relax. Luke is down the hall, waiting to hear that you're awake. When he woke, he felt very much like you do, and he's doing really good now."

Hannah talked on, repeating herself over and over. It seemed that Becky found talking impossible right now. A few times she'd tried speaking to her daughter, but she had choked on the words and returned to silence. Whenever Hannah paused in singing or talking, Mary pulled her head to the side, trying to free herself of the tube attached to her face, pulling against the restraints and coughing.

Becky's face drained of all color before she motioned to the doorway and then left.

Tears spilled down Hannah's cheeks. "There are communities across several states pulling for you, Mary. Luke needs you." She lifted her friend's hand to her cheek and caressed it. "I need you." Hannah swallowed, determined to keep the conversation hopeful. "I...I have a plan for us to work on a special quilt. But it'll take both of us to make this patchwork come true."

When Dr. Hill and a nurse entered the room, Hannah stopped talking.

Mary turned her head, pulling against the tubing going down her throat. Her wrists tugged at the restraints. Hannah grasped her friend's hand. "Easy now, *Liewi.* I'm still here. The doctor is here too. Everything will be fine."

Reading over the chart in his hand, he said, "Her oxygen rate is good, and it's been stable for some time now. She hasn't relied on the ventilator for two hours." He passed the chart to the nurse and moved to the far side of the bed. "Mary, we're going to remove the machine that's breathing for you. It might feel like we've taken your breath away for a few seconds, but don't panic or be frightened. Just relax, and you'll soon be breathing on your own."

Wishing Becky hadn't just gone to see Luke, Hannah laid her hand over Mary's and repeated in Pennsylvania Dutch what the doctor had said. As Dr. Hill worked on Mary, making her cough, Hannah closed her eyes tight and kept talking to Mary, assuring her she was fine. Hannah shivered when she heard a suctioning noise, but she refused to open her eyes. She muttered and sang to Mary, hoping her voice didn't betray how scared she was.

Someone touched Hannah's shoulder. "She's breathing on her own," Dr. Hill said. "The tubes have been removed."

Hannah opened her eyes. The contraption that had been taped over Mary's mouth was gone. A nurse was placing a thin tube under Mary's nose. Mary managed to open her bleary eyes and focus on Hannah. Elation soared through Hannah's soul, and her lips parted in a wide grin.

"Ah, a smile," Dr. Greenfield teased her. "That alone was worth altering my rounds for."

Hannah beamed at him. Until this moment, she hadn't realized he'd come into the room too. "Thank you." She looked at Dr. Hill. "Thank both of you for everything. I should go tell her *Mamm.*"

Dr. Hill grunted. "You stay here and help her remain calm. A nurse will see to that."

"Th-h-h-h," Mary barely got the sound out before she started coughing.

A nurse grabbed the container of ice water and a cup off the nightstand. She filled the cup and placed a straw in it. Hannah placed the straw in Mary's mouth and held the drink for her.

After several difficult swallows, Mary tried to speak again. "L-l-l-l-l…Luke?"

Chills ran over Hannah's body. Mary remembered!

As soon as the medical personnel left the room, Hannah started talking to Mary about Luke and their future and the beautiful children they would be blessed with. She told her about her plan for the two of them to make a special quilt together.

It wasn't always easy to understand Mary. Her words were a bit jumbled, her memory blank about some things, and her voice hoarse. But she appeared to remember all the important things in life: her childhood, her love for Luke, and her faith in God.

Hannah was thrilled.

12

Luke stifled a moan as he eased his body into the wheelchair his sister was holding steady. It was nearly midnight. *Mamm* and Becky had gone to the hotel for the night.

He looked straight ahead as Hannah wheeled him onto the elevator, off at the second floor, and toward Mary's room. He didn't care what the doctor said; he had to see Mary. He heard Hannah take a nervous breath as she pushed his wheelchair past the nurses' station on the way to Mary's room.

A plump, dark-haired nurse glanced up from her work. "Fifteen minutes maximum."

Luke lifted his good hand in acknowledgment. "Thank you."

Hannah bent down to his ear. "I feel much better now that we have permission." She stopped his chair outside Mary's room. "Luke, they've shaved her head. They had to. She had a lot of gashes that needed tending to besides where they performed surgery."

"I'll be fine. Let's go on in."

Hannah opened the door and wheeled him inside.

Mary was white as a sheet and gaunt. How much weight had she lost since Sunday night? She looked frail and helpless. Her bald head had a huge white patch taped to the side and several smaller patches showing through her white prayer *Kapp*.

Hannah wheeled him closer to the bed and squatted beside him. "Dr. Hill said she will probably get to leave ICU within the next day or so."

Luke's hands began to shake. How had this happened to them? They'd been so happy, laughing and teasing, and then…

Miserable guilt bore down on him until he thought he might pass out. His breath came in short, wheezing spurts. As he searched through his feelings for something that made this bearable, an idea came to him. Maybe it wasn't his fault. Finally he was able to catch a breath.

But then whose fault was it? He stared at poor Mary while he tumbled that thought around and around. He wouldn't have been near the Knepps' place if…

Not comfortable with where his thoughts were taking him, Luke resisted.

A few moments later the blame pointed its finger again, and this time he didn't resist. If Hannah had gone with them to the singing as he'd begged her to, they would have been at the farm, and this would have never happened. He sat there, staring at his sleeping fiancée, wondering why Hannah hadn't joined them that night.

"She's doing very well, Luke. Really," Hannah whispered.

Luke studied his girl. His throat constricted, and his eyes burned with threatening tears. Mary's best friend had put them out there on that road. Why did his sister have to be so stubborn?

A dark-haired nurse entered the room with a full IV bag. As she quietly changed the bag, Mary woke. When she saw him, excitement shone in her eyes for an instant before dread took over. She touched her bald head around the edges of her *Kapp,* looking painfully embarrassed.

The nurse lowered Mary's bed and then the rail between Luke and Mary.

He reached for her, and his fingers enveloped her fragile hand. He knew the anguish of having her head shaved would haunt her for years to come. "You're alive. Don't you dare think anything else matters." His voice broke as he fought to not cry.

Mary wept. "Oh, L-l-luke," she said in her faltering, broken speech, "I 'idn't want you to 'ee me like 'is."

How can she think that matters?

The nurse cleared her throat. "I'll be back in fifteen minutes."

"Me too." Hannah followed the nurse out of the room.

Luke lifted Mary's hand, caressing the smooth skin. "Your hair will grow back, sweetheart."

She cradled his hand in hers. "I 'on't 'emember what 'appened." Her voice sounded as if she had laryngitis.

"It's sort of hazy for me too."

Relief that he'd understood her reflected in her eyes.

He glanced at the machines still attached to her, pumping pure air and keeping track of her heart rate and such. "How are you feeling?"

"S-s-scared."

Luke kissed Mary's hand. The feel of her warm skin against his lips broke through his resolve. He choked on his tears. "I've been so worried." He buried his face against her shoulder.

She leaned her cheek against the top of his head. "I 'on't know what I'd do without Hannah. She..."

When he looked up, he realized Mary was trying to speak, but her thoughts wouldn't form into words. He began to see her need to keep Hannah close. If anyone could speak for Mary, understand her without words being spoken, it would be his sister.

But Mary didn't know what Luke knew.

Setting the blame aside, Luke reached for her. After awkward hugs and sputtering words of thankfulness that they were both alive, Luke lifted his head and touched her angelic face. "You do remember agreeing to marry me, right?"

"M–m–maybe." Playfulness entered her eyes, filling him with thankfulness. "I 'member you s-s-saying s-s-something about yard work not bein' w–w–women's w-w-work."

Luke laughed. "But yard work *is* women's work. You've known that since before you were born, I s'pect. There might even be an edict from the bishop on the matter."

Mary smiled. "Is n–n–not."

"So, in order to marry you, I have to agree to do what everyone in our community considers a woman's job?"

She nodded.

"Done," Luke quipped.

Mary laughed and then moaned from pain. "Should've m-m-made a harder 'argain."

Luke tried to clarify her sentence. "Oh, I think you drive a plenty hard bargain, don't you?"

She nodded.

Luke kissed her fingertips. "You can have anything I'm capable of giving. Just name it."

She eased her hand from his, placed her fingers over her lips, and kissed them. Then, shaking, she laid her fingers on Luke's lips. He kissed her fingers, reveling in how much that simple touch felt as if his lips had touched hers.

Mary smiled. "I…m–m-marry you n–n–no m-m-matter what."

His throat constricted, and he couldn't answer for several moments. She leaned back against the bed while he smothered her hand in kisses. Her eyes closed, and she drifted off to sleep.

Tomorrow he'd explain to her that he was being released from the hospital soon and had promised his mother he'd follow the doctor's orders by going home and resting. The doctor assured Luke if he didn't follow his advice, he'd be in no shape to help Mary in the months to come.

Hannah paced the corridor near Mary's room, basking in the joy of her friend's recovery as well as her brother's. There was no denying the light in Mary's eyes the moment she saw Luke.

Her heart fluttered a bit. There was something so precious, so strengthening about the kind of love that ran between a man and a woman who wanted to marry. Love that strong would endure a lot and come back even stronger. A fresh ache to see Paul stole some of her excitement for Luke and Mary.

Her thoughts jumped to the long road of recovery that lay before the two. Mary's journey would be a particularly difficult one, but Hannah intended to be by her side every minute that Mary needed her.

Determined to settle her emotions, Hannah stopped pacing and eased into a chair. She leaned her head back against the wall and tried to quiet her mind. If only there was some way she could communicate with Paul, some way to get a letter to him…

She gasped. *There is!*

Why hadn't she thought of this before? If she could get her hands on some paper, she could write Paul a letter and mail it from here. If he received the letter before Mary was discharged, maybe he could sneak in a visit with her at the hospital.

She jumped to her feet and glanced at the clock over the nurses' station. She had seven minutes before she'd have to take Luke back to his room. The gift shop would have paper and pens. Her mother had left her money for food. If she skipped breakfast, maybe lunch too, she'd have enough to buy paper, envelopes, and stamps.

She dashed for the elevators. Once inside she pushed the *L* for lobby. When the doors opened, she scurried to the gift shop. Disappointment filled her when she saw that it was closed. But the sign on the door said it would open again at nine the next morning.

For a moment she considered calling Paul. That thought faded as quickly as it came. His phone number at the apartment wasn't listed under his name. She knew his best friend's name was Marcus King, but the phone wasn't in Marcus's name either. She didn't know Ryan's or Taylor's last name. Paul had written down the number for her once, but it was taped to the underside of a drawer at home.

She'd just have to wait until tomorrow and mail him a letter.

The nagging question of why she hadn't heard from him ruffled her elation. Maybe he was sorry he'd asked her to marry him. He did wait until the last day to ask. That could mean it was a spur-of-the-moment idea. But no. The savings book proved he'd been planning this for years. Then again, maybe his years of planning referred simply to sponsoring a little Thai girl. She couldn't remember exactly how the conversation had gone.

She did remember two columns of figures in the book he'd given her. But since it had been burned along with her clothes from that day—

A bolt of excitement shot through her. Memories of that day were no longer a mass of confusion. She knew what had taken place between her and Paul. She could think.

Yes. She remembered.

She balled her hands into fists that hung by her side, refusing to show her emotions to anyone in the lobby.

Through the bars of the gift shop, she saw the selection of writing items. No stationery but plenty of greeting cards. In the morning, when the store opened, she would go in, make her purchase, and write to him. Her family had passed through Harrisburg, the city that shared part of the name of his college, on the drive to the hospital. If Paul got her note in time, it'd take him less than an hour to drive to Hershey. Then she would finally know what was really going on with him.

Doubts jerked her emotions. Part of her feared what the truth might be.

But determination won out over her concerns. Whatever was going on with Paul, it was time she found out.

13

Pushing her disappointment aside, Hannah tried not to think about the five days that had passed since she had written to Paul. She hadn't heard anything from him, and Mary would be discharged tomorrow. Hannah stepped inside the physical-therapy room, awed at the amount and variety of equipment. She was here to learn the workout routines her friend would need to do over the next weeks and months.

It was an interesting place. Three patients, all in different areas of the room, worked with their own personal physical therapists. A man dressed in shorts and a sleeveless shirt pushed against some type of cushioned armrest thing. The pulleys lifted a stack of thin, oblong items that, based on the strain on the man's arms, she assumed had to be weights. In the middle of the floor was a short set of stairs that had steps on each side so a person could walk up one side and down the other. Huge rubber balls, each taller than her youngest sister, rested against the walls. Scattered throughout the room were treadmills, stacks of towels, jump ropes, rods that looked like broom handles, and an array of things she didn't recognize.

Hannah waited by the door, hoping to spot Mary's physical therapist. Desiree, who looked barely old enough to be done with her schooling, had come to Mary's room daily and worked with her, lifting and rotating her limbs, even before she was brought out of the coma. She was energetic and friendly, but she gave Mary very little slack when it came to the workout.

Desiree came waltzing out of an office with her jet-black ponytail banded carelessly on her head. She had on a burgundy hospital uniform.

She spotted Hannah and headed toward her. "Hi. Glad to see you found the place." She held out her hand.

Hannah shook her hand. "Good morning."

Desiree glanced at her watch. "You're right on time. But I need to speak with someone before we get started. Okay?"

"Sure." Hannah waited at the entrance of the workout room while the physical therapist walked over to a middle-aged man wearing a similar uniform.

The young woman didn't seem miffed that John and Becky Yoder had decided that once their daughter was discharged from the hospital, she wouldn't return here or go anywhere else for physical therapy. One of the many discoveries Hannah had made while staying at the hospital was the rights of all Americans to certain health-related freedoms. Not only was health care provided for Luke and Mary before the hospital knew who they were or if the bill would ever be paid, but they also had the right to refuse medical help—no matter how a doctor, nurse, or the entire medical staff felt. Even the most educated had to yield to the individual's rights.

Desiree motioned for Hannah to follow her. "Let me grab Mary's chart, and we'll get started." She sauntered into a small office and over to a stack of clipboards that were lying on a well-organized desk.

Hannah waited by the office door, marveling at the many health-related books lining the shelves.

Sifting through the clipboards, Desiree picked one out. "I'll teach you what she needs to do on a daily basis. The routine will change as the days and weeks pass, but we'll cover that too. I'll send home all sorts of information you can use for reference."

She walked to the stack of towels. "Our first goal is to get a good range of motion back into Mary's injured shoulder." She grabbed a folded towel and passed it to Hannah. "Let's sit on the floor and work from there."

While showing Hannah the workout routine, Desiree shared her medical knowledge. Each thing she explained caused a sense of excitement in Hannah unlike anything she'd ever experienced. The young woman explained things about the muscular, pulmonary, cardiac, and vascular systems, as well as various symptoms to watch for. As their two-hour time slot drew to a close, Hannah had a long list of health-related facts. She knew more than she ever could have imagined, but her appetite for medical knowledge gnawed at her to learn more.

"Okay." Desiree gathered into one pile the workout routine charts that were spread over the floor. "Tomorrow I'll teach you about gait training, where she'll learn to use a walker for short periods of time. But she won't be ready for that for another month. I'll also show you how to use a rolling walker and a quad cane." She rose to her feet. "When we've covered everything, I'll attach my card to the stuff I'm sending home with you so you can call me if you have any questions."

Taking one last look at the chart in her hand, Hannah passed it to Desiree. "It's fascinating."

Desiree nodded. "I think so. And I think you'll do well with Mary. You picked up on everything quickly. Next on your to-do list is learning how to check Mary's blood pressure and heart rate. Someone will work with you on that later this afternoon."

Wow. Hannah wished she had more time to learn.

Paul parked his car in the lot behind his apartment and headed up the curved sidewalk. Exhaustion covered him, just like the gloomy, starless canopy overhead. He needed sleep. So far today he'd accomplished getting through his classes, working all afternoon at the tire store, and studying for hours at the library—all on about four hours of sleep. His bed was calling to him.

As he passed the student mailboxes, he had a fleeting thought of picking up his mail. *I'll do it tomorrow...or the next day.*

He used to check his mailbox every day, eagerly anticipating a letter from Hannah. But since Gram had put her foot down on passing letters to him, there was no way he was going to hear from Hannah anytime soon. With that possibility gone, he felt no reason to check except to occasionally keep up with bills. Since he'd always intercepted the mail, his roommates never went to the mailbox.

He placed his key into the apartment lock and slipped inside. After pulling off his shoes, he shoved them against the wall. Using the only light on in the place, a dim one in the hallway, he made his way to his and Marcus's room. He dropped his heavy book bag in a corner and sprawled across his twin bed. He would get ready for bed in a few minutes. Right now he had no energy for anything but to lie there.

Paul dozed in and out but never really fell asleep. He eased his feet to the side of the bed and rubbed his face. Perhaps if he changed out of his street clothes, he'd sleep better. As he stood, his keys fell to the floor. In one slow swoop, he picked them up and tossed them onto the nightstand. The small, gold mailbox key on the chain reflected the hallway light. The desire to check his mailbox returned. Ignoring it, he shook his head and made his way into the bathroom.

He brushed his teeth and peeled down to his boxers. Then he crept back to his bed and pulled down the covers. As he slid between the sheets, the nagging desire to look in his mailbox persisted. Finally giving in to the craving, Paul pulled on a pair of jeans, grasped the key, and headed outside.

His bare feet tingled as he crossed the cold concrete sidewalk. Under the glow of a streetlamp, he opened his box and pulled out a few items. A green flier advertising a sale on tires made him snort. Beneath that, he noticed a couple of bills, a coupon ad, and a note-sized envelope. He tucked the miscellaneous items under his arm and turned the envelope address side up.

His heart lurched. The return address belonged to his grandmother, but the handwriting was Hannah's. He tore it open while dashing back to his apartment. In spite of the solitude of the campus this late at night, the privacy of his bedroom was the only place to read Hannah's letters.

After flipping on the reading lamp, he sat on the side of the bed.

Paul,

My brother Luke and my dear friend Mary have been in an accident. I'm staying at Hershey Medical Center. If you get this letter in time and wish to speak with me, do come. Mary's room is on the second floor.

Hannah

If he wished to speak to her? Of course he wanted to speak to her. He wanted it so badly he had to squelch his feelings of joy in light of her reason for being at Hershey. He said a prayer for Luke and Mary, and then he checked out the postmark on the letter. Hannah had mailed it five days ago. It had probably been in his mailbox for two or three days. In spite of hoping Luke and Mary were well on their way to being released, he also hoped they were still at HMC.

He skimmed the brief note again. Excited as he was at the prospect of seeing Hannah, the coolness of her note gave him pause. She was not one to indulge in giddy romantic nonsense, so her letters never contained words of endearment or had a flirtatious tone. But this one made him flinch. They were engaged, for Pete's sake, yet she mentioned nothing about missing him or wanting to see him. It was more like an invitation offered out of protocol, because she was now in the vicinity, rather than an opportunity she hoped he didn't miss.

Reading the message again, he decided he was being self-centered. She'd managed to mail him a note. What more should he expect in such a traumatic situation?

Scurrying around like a maniac, Paul wrote Marcus a brief note and headed out the door.

The thirty-minute ride to Hershey was not a pleasant one. His thoughts and desires pulled him in ten different directions for every minute he drove. He wished he didn't have to be separated from Hannah like this, but he had to get his bachelor's degree under his belt. Frustration with Gram hounded him. But what if she was right? His family wouldn't have as many qualms about Hannah as hers would about him, but they'd have plenty of reservations.

His thoughts zipped in every direction, but when he pulled into the parking lot of the hospital, he knew one thing for sure: he had no answers, only desire.

While jogging across the lot and through the main entrance, he formed a plan. He'd check each waiting room on the second floor and hopefully catch a glimpse of Hannah without being spotted by any of her family. That would be far preferable to asking at a nurses' station about Luke Lapp or Mary Yoder. The fewer people who knew of his visit, the safer his and Hannah's secret connection would be.

When the elevator doors opened at the second floor and he stepped into the hallway, Paul realized he was on the ICU floor. It must have been a bad accident. Striding down the long corridor, he checked the first waiting room. She wasn't there. After searching the last wing of the unit, he gave up and went to the nurses' station.

"Excuse me."

A plump, dark-haired nurse looked up from the papers on the desk in front of her. "Visiting hours are over, sir."

"I'm looking for Luke Lapp."

"He was removed from ICU four days ago. I heard he was released from the hospital two days later."

Paul rubbed his forehead, chastising himself for not checking his mailbox sooner.

A half smile graced her lips. "I take it that wasn't the answer you were looking for."

Paul tried to hide his mounting disappointment. "Is Mary Yoder still here?"

A buzzer went off, and the nurse jumped to her feet and hustled down the hallway. Without slowing, she turned toward Paul. "She's been released from ICU. If she's still a patient here, she'll be on the fifth floor. But their visiting hours are over too."

"Thank you," he called after her.

The woman waved as she disappeared inside a cubicle.

Paul strode to the elevators, clinging to a draining hope that Hannah might still be at the hospital.

Just as he'd done on the second floor, he walked the corridors, looking and listening for any sign of Hannah. When he heard a man's voice with a distinctly Amish way of turning a phrase, he slowed his pace. He peered into the waiting area from an angle that wouldn't catch the attention of whoever was in the room.

Excitement pumped through his veins. There she was, his beautiful Hannah, sitting and talking to an Amish man. She laughed in that friendly, shy way of hers. Leaning her head toward him, she spoke softly. "I wouldn't confess this to a relative, and you'd better not either. But as a friend, I'm telling you, I did."

Friend? This guy wasn't a relative?

In an instant, insecurity took over. Jealousy reared up. His Hannah was sitting directly beside some young man, talking nonchalantly and chuckling. Paul's view only gave him a profile of Hannah and her *friend.* Their legs were stretched out side by side, their feet propped in a chair across from them.

He'd never seen Hannah in her own world, but this was not how he'd always envisioned her. To him, she had seemed reserved. He'd assumed she would have a backward way about her when it came to men, even among her people.

The man, who looked to be about Paul's age, pushed against her feet with his. "Ya did not."

Hannah laughed. "Why, Matthew Esh, how would you know? Were you there?"

"Ya know I weren't. But I've knowed ya since before ya could walk. I know ya like nobody else, Hannah Lapp. If anyone could tell when you're lyin', it'd be me. So tell the truth. It ain't true, is it?"

Paul's breath shortened. Who was this Matthew fellow who claimed to know his Hannah unlike anyone else?

Hannah bit her bottom lip and tilted her head. "If you're so sure I'm lying, then you don't need me to tell you anything."

Matthew chuckled, plunking his feet onto the floor. "This round of the game ain't over, but I better be headin' out. The driver said he'd be leaving his party at twelve, and I'm to meet 'im out the main entrance at quarter after." He rose. "Tell Mary that when she's settled at home and up to havin' company, I'll pay her a visit."

Hannah stood. "I'll tell her. It was nice of you to go out of your way to come here."

Matthew straightened his hat. Paul darted quietly down the hallway and around a corner where he couldn't be seen by the two leaving the waiting room. From his hiding place, Paul watched Hannah and Matthew stroll to the elevator, where she bid him good-bye. As she turned to come back down the hallway, Paul stepped out from the corner and called her name.

She wheeled around so fast she almost lost her balance. Her face flushed. Her movements froze. Guilt and embarrassment seemed to flood her entire being. "Paul." Her voice was a hoarse whisper, but there was no smile, no sign that he was welcome.

He glanced down each hallway. They needed someplace where they could talk in private. "Let's go back to that waiting room you just came from."

Without any show of emotion, Hannah moved back to the quiet space. Paul followed. Something hung between them, but he had no idea what it was. They stood in the small room, staring at each other. The unspoken friction whispered words of disbelief in his heart. They'd been so close, so sure of things just a month ago.

Paul cleared his throat. "Are Luke and Mary going to be all right?"

She lowered her head and fidgeted with her apron. "Luke's been released. It looks like he'll completely recover. Mary will be released tomorrow. The doctors suggested she stay a few days to a week longer, but she and her parents signed an AMA form."

"AMA?" Paul asked.

"Against Medical Advice. Her parents insist she's well enough to go home." Hannah shrugged. "I'm not sure she is, but they didn't ask me. She's got a long way to go—if she *ever* gets her full strength and agility back."

Hannah sounded as though she'd learned a lot during her stay here. Her speech patterns were even smoother, more scholarly than before. She'd always hungered to learn, and he'd shared books with her for years—books that had to stay at Gram's.

"What happened?"

Hannah wiped her palms down the front of her pinafore. "They were riding in a buggy when a car hit them. They both came close to dying. Mary can't talk very well. She has too many injuries to even try walking just yet."

"I'm so sorry."

Hannah cleared her throat. "They are mending."

"I'm glad."

Paul studied her, but she never looked at him. He knew the rigid upbringing that took place under Zeb Lapp. She fell into guilt far too effortlessly. The side effect was that she thought everything that went wrong was a direct result of her not handling something right. She probably considered herself at fault for Luke and Mary's accident, even though she had nothing to do with it. Her tendency toward guilt bothered him greatly. But he was confident that, given time and freedom, she'd overcome this trait.

Then again, perhaps what he was seeing written on her face had nothing to do with her oversensitivity to her self-accusing nature. Maybe it had more to do with Matthew. As much as he hated to ask her, they had to clear the air. He stared at the floor while shifting from one foot to the other. He shoved his hands into his pockets. "So, who is Matthew Esh?"

When Hannah didn't answer, he lifted his gaze. She stared at a blank television screen in the corner of the room. "He is the man you just saw leave."

"Yes, but..." Never in all their years as friends had he seen such a look in her eyes. It was an odd mixture of things, maybe embarrassment and... and...something else.

Father, help me. Help us. Please.

Her hands fluttered to her head, feeling for wisps of misplaced hair and making sure her *Kapp* was in place. "You sent no letter."

It was a statement that seemed to hold no irritation or worry. Was that supposed to explain who Matthew was?

"I did, but..." He stepped closer to her. She didn't look up at him. "I don't understand why, but it never arrived at Gram's. Before I could send another one, Gram decided we needed to think about our relationship for a while before she'd let us pass letters through her."

She lifted her gaze. To his surprise, anger blazed in her eyes. "So, now that you've had time to think about our relationship, what have you decided?"

"Hannah." Paul touched her arm. "What is going on with you?"

Her eyes clouded with tears. She gasped for air and backed away from him. As she lifted a hand to wipe a tear off her face, something on her palm caught Paul's attention.

He grasped her hand and turned it palm side up, seeing long, raised areas of pink tissue. "You have scars. What happened to you?"

Her face and lips grew pale. She eased into the closest chair.

She took a deep breath and straightened her back. With her shoulders squared with resolve, she gazed up into his eyes, her eyes brimming with tears. "Let me go." The hoarse whisper in her voice made Hannah sound old and tired.

Physical pain shot through him. "You're not making any sense, Hannah."

She grabbed some tissues out of a box on a coffee table. "Trust me. You don't want to wait...for the likes of me."

For the *likes* of her? Another inkling of suspicion concerning her faithfulness to him rose within his heart. "What are you talking about?"

"I...I..." Tears choked her, and she could say no more.

Paul sat beside her, determined to figure her out. "Hannah, close your eyes and take a deep breath." He gave her a moment to do so. "Now, let one thing come forward in your mind. Don't try to tie it all in. Just stick to one issue, and with your eyes closed, tell me."

She swiped a Kleenex over her cheeks and nodded, as if he'd given her a task she could manage. "The bankbook is missing." She opened her eyes, absent-mindedly tracing the scars on her right palm with her left forefinger. "I'm not sure what happened to it. I…I…" She turned ashen again.

He placed his hand on her back. "It's okay. The bank doesn't even use those kinds of books anymore. They haven't for decades. I got that one from a friend who works there and had a few books still stashed in his desk."

"It must've been in my pocket when *Daed* burned my clothes."

Paul removed his hand. "Burned them? Gram said you'd been sick. Were you so sick that they thought your clothes needed burning?"

Hannah's eyes carried uncertainty. She fled to the other side of the room and stared at the beige wall.

He understood a little more now. To Hannah, losing the gift was probably unforgivable. Still, her reaction seemed too much for just a lost bankbook. He sighed. Perhaps getting to the bottom of all that was on her mind wasn't possible with the time constraints they had to deal with.

She sniffled.

Walking up behind her, he grabbed some tissues and passed them over her shoulder. He longed to share consoling words with her, but one thing stood in his way. "Do you care for someone else?"

She turned to face him, indignation burning in her eyes. "No!" She sidestepped him and walked across the room, sobbing into the tissue. "Never!"

Her reaction worked the doubts and fears right out of him. He walked to the corner of the small room and placed his hands on her shoulders. "Then nothing else can stand in our way. I promise you that, Hannah."

She turned to face him. "You don't understand."

"Then tell me."

A look of terror came over her. Clearly she was fighting to gain control of her emotions. Coughing and gasping, she whispered, "The…the day…you left…"

Her face was white, humiliation carved in her features. Seeing her like this cut him to the core. All he wanted was to remove whatever was bothering her. But how?

He touched her *Kapp* and ran a finger along one of the ties. He did his best to smile. "Hannah Lapp, we can do this. But you have to trust me."

She studied him through teary eyes. "Oh, Paul." She lowered her forehead onto his chest. "The day you left…a car…with a man…he…it…knocked me…"

The power of her words hit him so hard he couldn't move. He heard her fighting for air. "You were sideswiped by a car?" He felt her head nod. He took her by the shoulders and put some space between them. "Did your father contact the police?"

She shook her head. "I…I asked him to."

Just then a nurse came into the waiting area. "Hannah, Mary's mother called. She was unable to sleep and is on her way back here. She said you can take the shuttle back to the hotel and get some sleep."

"Okay. Thank you." She sighed as the nurse left the room. "She'll be here within ten minutes."

He wasn't concerned with Mary's mother arriving. He wondered if the anxiety of that incident was what had made her so sick that her father had thought it best to burn her clothes. Rage at the idiot driver and anger that no one had stood up for Hannah made him understand a little better Hannah's wild emotions. She'd been traumatized that day. Obviously, that's where the scars on her hands had come from. He wrapped his arms around her, resigned that there was nothing he could do about the incident now.

Her body was stiff, yet he could feel her tremble.

"We need to look ahead, not behind." He kissed the top of her head through her *Kapp*. "I'll love you forever, Hannah."

A moment later he felt her take a deep breath. She wrapped her arms around him. Her embrace filled him with renewed commitment.

The frailty of her feminine frame became clear in that moment. She wasn't just a stalwart, stoic, good-natured worker. She was also a girl, overwhelmed by the odds against them.

She embraced him tighter. "It's been dreadful since the moment you left."

If Hannah, his queen of understatements, used the word *dreadful*, he knew things had been horrendous. He held her, not sure he'd ever know the full extent of what had gone wrong since he'd left. For now, it was enough to know that in eight months, he'd be finished with school and living within a mile of her. As soon as possible they'd get married, and no one would ever keep them apart again.

When her tears finally began to subside, Paul led Hannah to a chair and sat beside her.

He glanced at the clock. Their conversation, with all its patchwork exchanges, had taken over an hour. And he still felt she was keeping something from him, though he couldn't imagine what or why. Still, with their time running out, and since there was little chance they'd be able to communicate again in the near future, he had to bring their time to a close on a positive note.

"Hannah."

She looked up at him.

He opened her hand and kissed her scarred palm. "Conversations make a relationship strong. Unfortunately, they won't be a part of our relationship for a while. But we can clear away whatever weeds grow during this time if we hang tough and faithful"—he winked—"until May."

She offered a slight grin. "Don't you dare start that winking business with me, Paul Waddell."

He chuckled. He'd winked at her years ago and made her so angry she wouldn't speak to him for weeks. There was a scripture in the Old Testament about it, but he figured her real problem was that winks went hand in hand with flirting, and it seemed to unnerve her to think of him winking so easily at girls.

He squeezed her hand. "Eight months, Hannah. No problem for us, right?"

Hannah drew a ragged breath. "*Ya.* I'll be busy helping Mary with her physical therapy for that long at least." She finally gave him a little smile. "And Mary and I have plans to make a quilt I've been designing in my mind. I'm going to call it a 'Past and Future' quilt, and it's going to have a diamond-in-the-square design."

Paul brushed her cheek with the back of his fingers, glad to see a spark of pleasure in her eyes. "And in the meantime, I'll be busy working toward our future together."

For a brief moment she closed her eyes and leaned her cheek against his fingers. Then she stood. "I've got to get out front before Mary's mother arrives. After Mary is released, I'll be living at her grandmother's house for a while, helping Mary get her strength and agility back."

"At Mary's grandmother's? Why?"

"Her parents' house is narrow, with two large flights of steps and two single steps. She'll be in a wheelchair, so that won't do. Her grandmother's house has two stories, but everything we need is on one very wide level. Mary's mother has her other children to tend to. And her grandmother can't lift Mary, so she'll move in with Becky for a while, giving Mary and me a house to ourselves." Hannah smiled. "Besides, Mary wanted me to stay by her side, and she could ask for the moon right now, and her parents would find a way to get it for her."

Hannah stared at him. The look in her eyes said she loved him. "It was so good to see you."

Paul rose, wishing they had more time. "You must never forget how much I love you." He'd expected her to nod and turn to leave, but she put her hands on his waist and drew him close.

A nurse peeked into the room. "Mary's mother just stepped off the elevator." She sang the words like a friendly warning.

Hannah jolted and released him. Without another word, Paul disappeared down the hallway just as Becky rounded the corner.

14

A sigh escaped Hannah's lips. Darkness seemed to surround her like billows of toxic fumes. She hadn't come clean with Paul. What would happen if he figured out that she was keeping secrets from him?

If that unmentionable night wasn't so humiliating, she might find the courage to tell him. But which was worse—Paul knowing nothing, leaving her to pretend she was fine, or his knowing the truth? She ached for the peace and freedom that would come only if there were no secrets between them. But there was no way to know if he could handle finding out about the rape unless she told him about it.

I wish I could just vanish for a while and hide out while I think this through. Maybe go to Ohio. How hard would it be to find Aunt Zabeth?

But then Paul came back to mind, and the thought of fleeing to Ohio lost all its luster. He'd looked so good last night, his touch making life seem worth its troubles. She wished that she hadn't cried through most of his visit. The nightmare of her attack had to be put behind her, or it was going to ruin everything.

After being pulled one way and then the other, in a moment of clarity she realized a truth. Carrying the weight of silence was certainly not the worst thing that could happen. The worst tragedy of all would be to lose Paul.

Hannah leaned against the windowsill of Mary's fifth-floor room. The fresh rays of daylight filtered through the glass as Mary slept fitfully. Becky was down in billing, taking care of whatever it was that needed taking care of in order for Mary to leave the hospital today.

The door to the room opened. Dr. Greenfield stepped inside, holding two plastic foam cups on top of a large hardback book. Hannah had to smile. Their friendship was fleeting and sometimes awkward, but he seemed to be a truly genuine person.

He shoved the door closed with his foot. "I was hoping for a minute with you before Mary's release." He held the book toward her.

Hannah took the cup closest to her, surveying its steaming contents. "Hot chocolate?"

"You're too young for coffee." He smiled, lifting the cup of coffee to his lips with one hand and holding the book toward her with the other. "This is for you. It's about anatomy and how the body works. I think your family will allow you to have this since, among other things, it explains what to expect during a woman's recuperation from a subdural hematoma. I think you'll find it quite helpful as you work with Mary."

She grasped the book and opened it. An outline of a human body stared back at her. Dr. Greenfield reached across and turned a clear page, laying it on top of the nondescript image. The clear page revealed the vital organs and the veins and arteries running throughout the body. Beside the organs were lines with numbers.

"Ach, wie wunderbaar."

"Excuse me?"

Hannah looked up, embarrassed at her lack of manners. "Forgive me. I...I said it's wonderful."

He beamed at her. "It's an overlay. There are several of them." He turned to another page. "This one shows the respiratory system." He flipped a few more pages and then stopped at solid white ones covered in typed print. "This part explains what you're looking at."

Hannah slid her hand over the silky page. "This is amazing." She looked up. "Thank you."

Dr. Greenfield nodded. "You're welcome." He took a pen from his pocket and held his hand out for the book. She passed it to him. He wrote on the inside of the back cover. "I know getting to a phone is problematic for you. Nonetheless, if you ever need anything, this is the number for my answering service. Just tell them who you are, and they'll reach me. It might be a few hours before I get the message, depending on where I am and what I'm doing at the time. But I promise I'll return your call ASAP."

She watched him write in her new book and had to squelch the desire to tell him not to. Books were too special to be written in. "ASAP?"

"As soon as possible."

Hannah grinned. "Ah." She was going to miss talking with someone as good-humored and open-minded as Dr. Greenfield.

He closed the book and handed it to her. "The nurse will be in shortly to change Mary's bandage. Then she'll be released. You should already have all the instructions for her care, but if you have any questions, don't hesitate to call the number the nurse gave you." He strode out the door.

She opened her new book and began devouring the pages.

A crackling noise made her stop reading and look up. Edie Walls, one of the young nurses, stood there with a cup pressed against her lips. She lowered the cup, crunching on ice. "Sorry. Didn't mean to disturb you." She set the cup on the side table. "Ice chips. It's the best thing I've found for morning sickness." She opened a drawer in the table beside the bed and pulled out a roll of gauze and tape. "Morning sickness is a stupid thing to call it, though. When I was pregnant with my first child, I only felt nauseated in the evening. With this one, I'm sick all day every day. And then I'm so tired."

Nausea and tiredness. Hannah had felt that way for weeks. But there were so many odors around here, and she hadn't slept decently in forever, and—

"But that's not the worst part." Edie unrolled a long piece of gauze. "Why, my emotions are such a roller-coaster ride, they're driving me nuts."

Blood rushed to Hannah's temple. Was that the reason her feelings were going in every direction at once?

No, it couldn't be.

Pregnant? Surely that couldn't be the reason for the feelings of nausea and sickness. She was just stressed and—

Edie pulled a pair of scissors from her pocket. "The first time I was pregnant, I couldn't stand the idea of eating anything those first few weeks."

The book fell from Hannah's hand. Her arms and legs felt too heavy for her body.

From the outermost part of her peripheral vision, blackness closed in. It gradually blocked out the room as well as Edie.

Hannah felt Edie's hand under her forearm. Edie was saying something, but Hannah couldn't make out her words.

God! The words screamed inside her. *Please. Please. Noooooooo.* Her heart raced as the continual cry rang out in her soul.

It couldn't be.

It couldn't.

"Hannah? Can you hear me?" Edie took her by the shoulders and eased her to the floor. "Hannah, lie back. Help is on the way."

Edie held Hannah's ankles, keeping her feet and legs slightly elevated. Some sense of reality flowed back into her. Terror and chills ran throughout her body. Fighting to gain control, she jerked her feet loose and sat up.

"I...I'm fine." She wasn't. But no one could help her. Hannah turned, placing her hands on the seat of the chair behind her, and pushed herself upright. On wavering legs, she made her way to the door.

In the hallway a woman took her by the arm and spoke to her. Hannah couldn't make out what she said. Pulling free, she ran to the stairwell. The door closed behind her, thudding loudly. She flew down one flight of steps before stopping. She leaned against the wall, gasping for air.

A moment later the stairwell door above her burst open, and Edie barged in. When she spotted Hannah, she scurried down the steps. The blank look on her face said that she had no idea what to do or say.

Hannah's vision blurred as someone else clomped down the steps.

"What happened?"

With her back against the wall, Hannah slid to a sitting position on the cold tile floor. She wrapped her arms around her knees and buried her face. A pair of large hands took one of her arms and held it. Velcro ripped, her arm was covered with a band, and the strap was tightened. It loosened. Stayed loose for a while. Then tightened again.

"What happened right before she began blacking out?" The voice sounded like Dr. Greenfield's but different…sterner. She didn't want to see him.

Then again, who better? But how would she ever explain…

"We were talking," Edie said. "That's all."

"About?"

Hannah's chin was gently lifted and the back of her head pressed against the wall. She felt what had to be a stethoscope roam over her chest.

"Can't hear much of anything through all these layers of clothes," the man mumbled.

"Actually, now that I think about it, I was doing all the talking. I was telling her about being pregnant and how ice chips help me feel less nauseated."

Determined to get out of there, Hannah pushed the hand holding the stethoscope away from her. She ripped the Velcro loose from its grip and slid the cuff off her arm. Bracing herself against the wall, she tried to stand. A strong hand helped her to her feet.

"Let's get you to the ER, Hannah." Dr. Greenfield placed his hand under her forearm, steadying her.

She shook her head, desperate to get away. "I'm fine. I need air. That's all." She pulled away from his grip. "Leave me alone. Please."

With his hand under her arm, supporting her, Dr. Greenfield led Hannah outdoors like a child. The cool fall air, mixed with the smells of automobiles, whipped against her face. She eased her arm out of his grip and followed the sidewalk away from the hospital to a private nook between two wings of the building. Shaking, without any power to stop, Hannah sat on a gray stone bench that doubled as a retaining wall for plants.

Dr. Greenfield sat beside her and took her wrist, pressing his fingers against her pulse. "I'd really like you to be checked out."

She barely shook her head and managed a whisper. "No."

Patches of puffy clouds moved across the sky, transforming shapes as quickly and easily as life altered. If she really was pregnant, Paul must never find out. *Never.* Maybe she wasn't. Maybe what happened to her wasn't how women got pregnant. How would she know? The subject was forbidden.

She hated that man. Hated him. Images of slashing a knife across his belly flooded her. But the fury would do her no good. She was powerless on all sides. She didn't know who he was.

Dr. Greenfield placed his forearms on his legs and leaned forward, his gaze never leaving her face.

Hannah swallowed. She had to know if she might be pregnant. And she had no one better to ask. "The Amish don't talk about...certain things."

"I'll talk to you about anything you want to know."

She shifted, turning away slightly. There was no way she could ask him this. "Never mind."

"Hannah, Edie says she was telling you about her pregnancy. Is there something about that conversation that caused your reaction?"

Hannah shrugged and gave a slight nod.

"Is that a yes?"

She nodded.

"Are you pregnant?"

Hannah closed her eyes. "I…I don't know."

Dr. Greenfield's face didn't change a bit. "But there's a chance you're pregnant—is that it?"

"I…I don't know."

"You don't know if you're pregnant, or you don't know how someone gets that way?"

Hannah could feel her cheeks burning.

"I'm going to take a shot in the dark here and tell you how a woman conceives." With a voice as kind and gentle as she'd ever heard, he told her all she needed to know.

It made perfect sense. She lived on a farm, for heaven's sake, with livestock that were bred. But somehow understanding how women became pregnant had eluded her. Feelings of embarrassment were so thick she thought her heart would stop beating right then.

She cleared her throat. "And if…if someone is…overpowered…forced to…can she still get pregnant?"

"Hannah, if this happened to you, you need to see a doctor and the police."

"No." Her voice shook.

He drew a deep breath. "Yes, a woman can conceive a child even then."

She rose. "Mary's probably been released by now. Her mother will be searching for me. Thank you, Dr. Greenfield." She eased one foot in front of the other, taking several shaky steps.

"Hannah, wait." In one quick movement, he stood in front of her. "What can I do to help you? What will you let me do?"

The compassion in his voice touched a place deep inside her. She stared at the stethoscope dangling around his neck. "There's nothing to do." Her jaws ached. Her eyes burned. Why couldn't the earth just open and swallow her? "Who knows? Maybe I'm jumping to conclusions."

"It's possible. Trauma causes a woman's body to do odd things: feel nauseated, skip cycles, have panic attacks. It can even result in chemical changes in the brain that can send a person into severe depression. But if you're having those symptoms and pregnancy isn't the cause..."

She touched the sides of her *Kapp,* making sure it was in place.

"Hannah, I know a woman doctor who works exclusively with females. She's gentle and understanding. She can at least confirm whether or not you're—"

"Please don't," Hannah interrupted him. "I'm going home and pray for the best."

Dr. Greenfield put one hand on her shoulder, gazing into her eyes. "I'm so sorry."

"Hannah!" *Daed's* voice made her jump. Dr. Greenfield immediately removed his hand and pulled away from her.

She turned toward the voice and saw her father standing at the T in the sidewalk, the bishop right beside him. The looks on their faces were a mixture of bewilderment and accusation. Dr. Greenfield leaned in close behind her. "We aren't finished talking yet, Hannah."

Her father's brows knitted. "Come, child. Now."

Dr. Greenfield stepped forward, looking her in the face. "You don't have to, Hannah. You can stay here, and we can get you some help."

She knew the word *we* meant other doctors, the system, even the police. But she couldn't for one moment imagine them all examining her and asking questions. She needed to go home, to wait and find out if she truly was pregnant.

"Now, Hannah." Her father removed his hat and squeezed the brim, avoiding the doctor's eyes.

"Your daughter and I are in the middle of a private conversation," Dr. Greenfield retorted. "She has rights among the English."

She shook her head at him. He was only making things worse.

Her father and the bishop gave a nod of grudging acceptance and strode past them into the hospital. They weren't going to argue; to cause conflict was against their rules and their ways.

Dr. Greenfield turned to face her. "Are you sure going back is the right thing to do?"

She nodded. "My family will do more for me than your whole staff can."

"Hannah, please. We could—"

She held up her hand. "No more."

"If you'll work with me, we can find all sorts of ways to help you. There are programs for rape victims, homes for unwed mothers, adoption agencies, and clinics that can offer you other…options."

She closed her eyes, knowing that none of those things would help her if Paul found out. "I'm going home, Dr. Greenfield."

"But, Hannah, you must be seen by a physician."

She crossed her arms against the nip in the air.

He rubbed his forehead, looking resigned but not pleased. "You have my phone number in the book. If you need me for anything, Hannah, please call me." He pulled a card from his wallet and held it out to her. "This is my private cell phone number."

She studied his face. "I'm glad we met, and I'll always remember the nice English doctor at this hospital. But I won't be seeing you again."

15

Hannah opened the potbellied stove and stirred the coals with the poker. Mary, sitting in her wheelchair by the window, kept a watchful eye on the driveway, waiting for Luke to arrive.

She and Mary were living in the Yoders' *Daadi Haus*—Mary's grandmother's home. *Mammi* Annie, Mary's grandmother, had moved into the main house, a stone's throw away, with Mary's parents and brothers. The *Daadi Haus* was small, but the rooms were able to accommodate Mary's wheelchair. The home had indoor plumbing and a bathroom off the bedroom that the two girls shared. It was a good setup, except that Hannah had to put forth extra effort to avoid Sarah's beloved Jacob. Mary's brother lived next door with his parents, so keeping her distance from him was a bit tricky, especially when he came to visit his sister. But Hannah thought she was managing that quite well and Sarah should be pleased.

Between working with Mary several times a day on her physical therapy and using the kitchen and laundry room of the *Daadi Haus* to help Becky with the laundry, baking, and canning needs of the main house, Hannah felt as if the three weeks since they'd left the hospital had flown by.

As time allowed, she and Mary worked on the "Past and Future" quilt. While Luke visited, Hannah made herself scarce by digging around in Mary's grandmother's attic for scraps of material from doll clothing she and Mary had sewn when they were young. She found the first apron they'd ever made and even pieces of a doll's blanket they'd sewn.

Luke.

He hadn't said anything unkind to Hannah, but he seemed a little angrier with her with each visit. Between Hannah disappearing to the attic when he came in and Luke keeping his visits short, they'd not talked about whatever was bothering him. She figured he was just grumpy from still being on certain medicines and from worrying about what Mary was going through.

But his visits did give her time to search for material. She didn't want just any fabric; it had to tie into Mary's or Luke's life. *Mammi* Annie had spread the word to the women of the community about what Hannah was doing. Pieces of material were coming to Hannah and Mary with notes on them as to how they were a part of Mary's or Luke's past.

At this rate, the past side of the quilt would not lack for fabric. Now if she could figure out how to acquire plenty of material for the future side, the rest of her plan would come together.

Neither her father nor the bishop had mentioned the incident with Dr. Greenfield. She was sure the event had looked lustful to them. Hannah refused to think about that day. She had become quite adept at tuning out things she didn't want to think about, but the change didn't feel like a victory.

She set the pressing iron facedown on the stove and removed the handle. Hopefully no one would catch her ironing on a Sunday. She grabbed a split log from the woodbin beside the stove and tossed it onto the glowing embers. After closing the small metal door, she placed a few bricks on the back part of the flat stove and dusted off her hands with her apron.

The house was especially quiet today. At nearly lunchtime, only she and Mary remained on the property. It was a no-church Sunday, so Mary's family would spend the day out visiting, repaying folks—through words and homemade goodies—for the kindness they'd shown during this ordeal. In addition to helping Mary's father with his farm during the weeks following the accident, their Amish neighbors had built a harness shop with attached living quarters for Luke and Mary after they were wed.

Placing Mary's cotton head scarf over the towel that lay on the ironing table, Hannah smoothed it as straight as possible with her fingers. Today held the promise of rekindling some of life's joy. She would witness Mary seeing the harness shop for the first time. Mary wasn't even aware that a living area above the shop had been built for them. From what John Yoder had told Hannah, Luke and Mary shouldn't outgrow the small home until their third baby arrived. Hannah couldn't wait to see Mary's face when she saw her future home.

After slipping the handle back onto the pressing iron, Hannah lifted the iron from the stove and worked the wrinkles out of the scarf. In spite of the nervous edge she felt concerning today's trip, Hannah was confident that Mary had enough strength to endure the five-mile ride one way, though she would probably need a nap before heading back. But Mary needed to see firsthand the progress that had been made toward her future. Besides, Luke would no doubt mollycoddle Mary every step of the way.

Hannah had to admit that her excitement wasn't entirely on Mary's behalf. The way Luke described the location of the shop made it sound as if it bordered Gram's property and was in clear sight of her house. If that was true, surely Hannah could steal a visit to see her sometime today. She missed the elderly woman more than she'd expected to, and the need to see her grew with each passing day.

Shifting her wheelchair slightly, Mary turned from the window. "Has Luke shown you this shop he's so excited about?"

"I haven't stepped foot off this farm since we arrived here from the hospital," Hannah said. She hoped her voice didn't give away that there were troubled waters between her and Luke. She didn't know what the problems were, but with secrets to keep hidden, silence was Hannah's safest harbor. When May came, Paul would begin trying to win the approval of her family. In the meantime she needed to keep as much peace as possible between her and her family and the community.

When the wrinkles were gone, Hannah flapped the material in the air to cool it. She looked forward to seeing her home again and getting out of this place for a bit. Mary's progress had been better than Hannah could have imagined, but helping Mary maneuver to the bathroom at all hours of the night and day was taxing.

Hannah crossed the room to Mary and tied the purple scarf over her head, being careful to cover the blond peach fuzz but not to bind the cloth around her skull too tightly.

Mary was healing quickly. Hannah hadn't needed to call the doctor's office once, even though the bishop had approved the Yoders having a telephone installed only sixty feet from the house. Mary's father and brothers had built a phone shanty—a wooden booth with windows. The phone company had come out and installed a black, push-button wall phone.

Mary lifted her *Kapp* off her lap and handed it to Hannah. "Getting me ready would be easier if we didn't need to attach the prayer covering to the bald-head covering."

Hannah took several straight pins from her pinafore and clenched them between her teeth, removing one at a time as she attached the *Kapp* to the head wrap. "Even the community's most beloved princess must wear her prayer veil." Hannah kissed Mary on the forehead.

Mary ran her hands over her scarf and *Kapp*. "I'm going to do you a favor and not tell the bishop how cheeky you can get. Calling a dedicated Plain woman a princess..." She turned to face the window, keeping a sharp lookout for Luke.

Hannah sat on the arm of the couch right behind her. It felt good to hear Mary tease her. The fear that had threatened to take over Mary, the panic that wouldn't let Hannah out of her sight, had slowly been replaced by a fragile peace as the People surrounded Mary with love.

The sounds of horse's hoofs and grinding gravel drew Hannah out of her musings.

Mary's pale face lit up. "He's here. Grab the blankets and wheel me outside."

Hannah seized the stack of folded blankets off the couch and laid them in Mary's lap. Grabbing their shawls off the coatrack, she mentally ran through her to-do list for today's outing.

Mary pounded the arms of her wheelchair. "Come on. Come on. What's taking you so long?" Her jesting made Hannah's day.

She wheeled her friend toward the doorway. "If you had half this much enthusiasm for your therapy, I wouldn't have to argue with you about it every day."

Mary scrunched her shoulders. "It's a dreadful routine, and you know it."

Before Hannah reached the door, Luke tapped and then eased it open. He scanned Hannah disapprovingly before absorbing Mary like rain after a drought. "You're looking mighty healthy today." He strode inside. "Here, let me take those for you." He lifted the blankets from her lap. "She'll need some heated bricks for her feet."

Hannah wrapped the shawl around Mary's shoulders. Then, like a maid, she shuffled off to the kitchen to finish her chores. While Luke took the blankets and Mary to the buggy, Hannah packed the bricks in old towels and finished gathering the picnic items.

As she hurried through the house, she made a quick visual inspection of all the kerosene lamps, making sure they were out. Satisfied that everything was in order, Hannah pushed through the door.

Luke loomed in front of her. "I'll take that."

His voice was demanding, and Hannah knew that saying "thank you" was inappropriate. He lifted the basket from her.

Hannah drew a deep breath to steady her hurt feelings. "She hasn't heard one word about the apartment that's been built for both of you. I can't wait to see her face. Mary's been through so much, and I—"

Resentment entered Luke's eyes, startling Hannah. "I think you've done more than enough."

He spoke as if correcting a dog, but why?

Luke pointed his finger at her. "If it wasn't for you, she wouldn't have been through so much, now, would she?" He turned his back on her and marched to the waiting buggy.

Stunned, Hannah was unable to move. What could she have possibly done to make life harder on Mary? With her knees shaking, she stood on the porch watching Luke tenderly place the heated bricks under Mary's feet and wrap her in blanket after blanket.

When Luke began to shut the door on the buggy, Mary held up her hand, and Luke stopped. "Tell Hannah to come on. I'm eager to be on our way."

"Hannah will go another time. She needs to stay here." Luke's face became like granite as he faced her. "Isn't that right, Sister?"

How can Mary miss the venom in his voice?

With heaviness bearing down on her, Hannah slowly walked to Mary's side. "I think I'll rest while you're gone."

Compassion filled Mary's eyes. "You deserve time to rest. I keep you up all night, and then I sleep during the day while you help *Mamm*. But I'm disappointed you aren't coming. Are you sure you don't feel up to it?"

Hannah nodded. "I'm sure." She tucked a slipping blanket corner around Mary's back and closed the carriage door. As Luke made his way around the back, Hannah followed him. "What have I done?" she whispered.

He turned to face her. "It was your fault we were out near the Knepps' place."

"My fault?"

"Oh, don't act so innocent. I begged you to go with us to the singing so Mary would feel comfortable returning to our farm afterward. You knew she wouldn't come with just me. I needed you to go with us. But you didn't *feel* like it."

Hannah shook her head. "I…I remember you and I had some sharp words, but I…I don't recall… My mind was so cluttered from—"

"Yeah, you took a spill on the side of the road and cut your hands and knees. Somehow that stole your memory, your ability to work, and your loyalty to your family." He glared at her. "Yet look at all that's happened to Mary, and she's bounced back."

"Luke, I'm…I'm sorry. I never meant—"

He strode to the driver's side and climbed inside.

She watched the buggy pull away with the people she loved leaving her behind.

16

A cold wind whipped through Hannah's skirts and shawl, but the temperature in her heart seemed even colder. Her jaws ached as tears threatened to form. Disappointment worked its way through her. She'd really wanted to see the harness shop and Luke and Mary's future home, not to mention the joy on Mary's face as she took it all in for the first time.

A calf in the barn bawled for its mother. Hannah trudged across the back field to the barn.

My fault? How could he think that? Was it true? She remembered so little of those dark times following the attack.

She pulled the barn door open just far enough to slip inside. The place was warm and smelled of sweet feed and calf starter. She took a few steps toward the calf pen, and another familiar scent filled her nostrils: fresh cow manure.

The calf stuck its head through the split-rail pen, begging to be touched. Hannah patted the cowlick in the center of its forehead. The calf's tongue looked like saltwater taffy being pulled and stretched as the calf lapped at her clothing. It butted its head against her arm as if she had milk for the needy thing. "Sorry, fella. You're plain outta luck."

Hannah stepped back and folded her arms across her chest, tucking her shawl around her. Streams of sunlight caused dancing dust particles from the hay to look like shiny flecks of gold. She and Luke used to pretend the floating bits of dirt were tiny people and that if they could catch them and immerse them in water, they'd grow into life-sized children. They'd spent hours trying to create people from suspended pieces of hay dust.

Now Luke hated her. And she couldn't fully remember what he was talking about. She didn't doubt his account of what had happened. She'd never had much desire to attend the singings for appearance' sake. She was sure that during those most confusing days of her life, she'd refused to go anywhere with anyone.

Desperate for a place to hide and think, she climbed the ladder to the hayloft. She clambered over the mounds of loose hay and opened the hayloft door. Another blast of cold air stung her cheeks. Brown leaves swirled in the wind, falling from the trees like rain. She wrapped the shawl around her and tried to find solace in the beauty of the earth. Most of the trees had lost their leaves, and they stood with gray branches reaching out and upward. Brown fields lay resting for the season. Brilliant blue skies carried such a variety of clouds—thick mounting ones, wispy ones, thin-lined ones.

She wondered if her Aunt Zabeth had once loved her father the way Hannah loved Luke. She bet Zabeth would understand how badly she hurt, how isolated her life had become. Hannah wondered what her aunt had done that caused her to be shunned. Whatever it was, she never repented, because the letter said she was still under the ban.

A flock of twelve or more purple finches gathered under the sweet gum tree, enjoying the seeds that had fallen.

She looked out at the land and drew a deep breath. God had done a magnificent job with creation. Warmth spread throughout her body, and in spite of the stabbing pains from Luke's accusation, peace flooded her.

I know the plans I have for you…

She'd heard this verse during a church service, and it had struck her as powerful even then. But today, as she stood in a hayloft alone and unsure of her future, it meant hope. Hannah knelt and closed her eyes. "God, I know so little… I understand almost nothing." Chills covered her body. "You are my God, whether I understand You or not. I choose You."

Thoughts from every corner of her life assailed her. She saw herself sitting in various homes, barns, and workshops for preaching services, hearing strong messages against sin. A snapshot of her father kissing her fingers the time they got mashed in the buggy door made her smile even now. It had amazed her that day how a tiny kiss truly made the pain disappear. Visions of Paul laughing with her over the years and aching with her when she cried on his shoulder at the hospital filled her with fresh turmoil.

Faster and faster, images flew through her mind—arguments with sisters, cooking in a hot kitchen, and respect for the Old Ways even though much about those ways stirred doubt within her. Then the puzzle pieces of her life took an ominous turn, and she could barely see a clear picture of anything in her mind's eye. Luke and Mary's buggy accident. Luke's anger.

The attack.

That was the real reason she'd had nothing to say to God for two months.

She shifted off of her knees and sat. Life didn't make sense. Parts of it were so beautiful, so touching, that a moment of it brought her strength that could last for years and could only have come from God. But what about the other part, the part that was so wretched with ugliness it stole her desire to live?

It didn't make sense that God willed both. Maybe it never would make sense.

Hannah struggled day in and day out with blind acceptance of everything that happened in life. If God put a person where he or she was supposed to stay, then how did the Pilgrims come to America? How did the Amish cross an ocean to get free of the Church of England?

If authority couldn't sometimes be ignored, there would be no Old Ways to cling to. So who got to decide when it was time to stand against authority and when it was time to submit?

She sighed, not knowing the answers to any of that.

The tugging question in her heart right now seemed to be if she trusted God to be her strength and guiding force, whether she understood things or not.

Pulling her knees to her chin, she wrapped the shawl around them and closed her eyes, sifting through more of her thoughts. "God, I…I can't accept that the attack was Your will. I can't." Oddly, fresh peace flooded her, as if God understood her feelings.

"Hannah!"

The shout startled her so badly she screamed. Her eyes flew open, and she jumped to her feet. On the ground, some fifteen feet below, Matthew stood, looking up at her.

"Matthew Esh, scare a girl to death, why don't ya!" But seeing his friendly face quickly removed her frustration.

The gleam in Matthew's eyes, which defined him more than any other trait, didn't falter for a moment. "Well, it's not like I weren't calling to ya," he said, pointing to the ridge where Esh land met Yoder ground, "from the moment I recognized it was you sittin' up here. I been wantin' to see how you're doin'. Everybody's so wrapped up in Luke and Mary, pampering them like—" He stopped cold. "I mean, they've had it rough and all, but…" Matthew grabbed his suspenders and kicked a rock.

He had a good heart, one that didn't want to say anything negative. Sometimes, in his honesty, things slipped out anyway. But with no one home, they needed to find a better time to visit.

"I think we'd better talk later, Matthew." She enjoyed his company. He often reminded her of Paul with his sense of humor and work ethic.

And he reminded her of the best parts of Luke, with his sincerity and dedication to the Old Ways and his family.

"Aw, come on. It's important."

Seeing the disappointment in his eyes, she relented. "Well, if you're needing to talk, come on up."

A wind gust zipped through the barn and right through Hannah's clothing. She pulled on the handles to the double doors of the hayloft and bolted them shut.

The ladder creaked, and soon Matthew's black winter hat peeked through the small entrance. "Can't say I ever climbed into a haymow to talk to a girl before."

"Did too." Hannah eased onto a mound of hay and stretched out her legs, thankful for a break from the seriousness of her life.

Matthew mocked a scowl at her as he finished climbing into the loft. "Liar."

Hannah laughed. They'd get in ever so much trouble if the adults knew how they threw such an ugly word around like it was nothing. His playfulness reminded her so much of Luke…before the buggy accident.

Wrapping her cloak tighter around herself, Hannah clenched her jaw in feigned annoyance. "You told me about it yourself."

Matthew slid off his jacket and threw it on her lap before he fell back on the hay beside her. She coughed at the spray of dust he caused, then realized he'd probably planned that little dust-scattering move. She waved her hand through the air, clearing it some so she could breathe. He stretched out his long legs, obviously unperturbed at her reaction.

Glad for the extra warmth, she spread his jacket over her lap.

"Prove it." Matthew picked up a long straw and stuck it between his teeth.

"Got to that point of the game already?" Hannah took the straw from his mouth and tossed it into his lap.

He shrugged and grabbed another straw. "I got somethin' I want to tell ya. But first, you have to prove your claim."

Curiosity grabbed her attention. "Motty Ball."

"Climbing a haymow to talk to a cat doesn't count."

Hannah buried her cold hands under the jacket. "Motty Ball is a female, and that's what you said. So, what's this news?"

Matthew's eyes danced with mischief. "I met somebody."

"Old Order Amish?" Her automatic question bothered her. Was she that much of a hypocrite that Matthew had to find an Amish girl but she could be engaged to a Mennonite?

Matthew laced his fingers together and tucked them behind his head, looking quite pleased with himself. "Of course."

A chorus of relief sang within her. "Who?"

"Won't say. Not yet."

"For tradition's sake—keeping the relationship a secret until you're published?" She was too excited to drop the subject easily.

"Nah. That's silly stuff for old women and childish girls. It's 'cause I don't know yet how she feels about me."

"Oh." Her excitement ended abruptly. She would hurt all over if Matthew fell for someone who didn't return his feelings.

Looking at courting from this viewpoint, she saw some of her father's concerns. Suddenly she couldn't find fault with him for taking it so seriously.

"Come on, Matthew. You gotta tell me."

Matthew picked up a straw and twirled it. "If you can figure out the riddle, you'll know. But you can't tell nobody." He placed the straw between his teeth. "Now, pay attention 'cause I'm only going to say it once." He shifted his feet and leaned back in a relaxed manner. "She comes and she goes almost daily...by driver. In thick snow, she'll stay. Her name is said like it's one letter. She's not yet been allowed to take her vows, but she's been old enough for several years."

Hannah shook her head. "Not allowed to take her vows yet? I never heard of such a thing. Matthew, are you playing games with me?"

He smiled. "It's the honest-to-heaven's truth. And if I told you more, you'd get more confused. She's as unique as an Amish community has ever knowed."

Hannah sat there, dumbfounded. "If she comes and goes by driver, then she's not from this district."

Matthew smiled broadly. "Not yet."

His confidence was disconcerting. He was missing a huge part of the chain of command: the girl's father. The bishop of each district would easily agree to let any Amish of good standing move to a different district. But a girl's father—well, that put a whole new spin on the issue.

Matthew squared his shoulders. "That's all I'm saying. Either you're as smart as I think you are and can figure it out, or you won't know."

"Well, I'll know when you get published."

Matthew laughed loud and strong. "She ain't even gone for a buggy ride with me yet." He shrugged, clearly having a moment of insecurity. "But when I met her, there was something between us, Hannah. Ya know?"

She wanted to argue that his feelings were too much too soon, but she of all people couldn't argue that point. She'd fallen for Paul as hard and as quickly as a tree felled for firewood. "Yeah, I know." The dreamy look in his eyes made Hannah ache to see this work out for him.

His riddle was quite a puzzle. A girl of age but not yet allowed to take her vows. Strange. Her name sounds like one letter. Hmm. This would take some considering.

Ready for a little childlike reprieve after weeks of hard labor, she reached for the straw dangling from his lips. He threw his hand up, deflecting hers. A scuffling match ensued as she tried to grab the straw and he tried to keep her from getting it.

"Schick dich, Hannah. *Schick dich."* He grabbed a fistful of hay and rubbed it on her head. *"Du bischt Druwwel."*

She stood and threw his jacket to the foot of the ladder.

"Dankes, Hannah."

Hannah curtsied. "You're welcome."

"What'd you do that for?"

Feigning innocence, she said, "It flew there all by itself."

"Aha! Proof! You are a liar!" He squared his shoulders in triumph, clearly certain he'd won this round of the game.

"Hello!" A deep voice boomed through the air.

Hannah stopped dead as if the breath had been knocked out of her. That was the bishop's voice.

Matthew tilted his head, studying her. "It's okay, Hannah. We've done nothing wrong." He put both feet on the ladder and began his descent. He stopped on the third rung. "Perhaps one day the lot will fall to me, and I'll become a bishop." The words came out but a whisper so the bishop could not hear him. "Maybe then you will behave around me, *ya*?" He smiled and straightened his hat before he climbed down the ladder.

His humor did nothing to settle the terror that ran through Hannah's body. There were so many levels on which she feared the bishop. She wanted to be all that he and her parents wanted. She really did. It just never seemed to work out that way, no matter how hard she tried. The bishop would call her mind-set sin. Dr. Greenfield would probably call it free will.

She called it utter confusion.

She peered through the hole to the ground floor. The bishop handed Matthew his jacket, then looked up into the loft. Her hands fluttered over her apron, trying to free it of loose hay. She reached for her *Kapp.* It was askew, one side nearly touching her shoulder and her hair pulling free of its restraints.

The bishop's austere glare bored into Hannah, and guilt hounded her—guilt for every ungodly thought she'd ever had. The bishop rubbed the palms of his hands together, making a noise like sandpaper against wood. "I came to see John Yoder. I take it no one is home but the two of you."

Matthew glanced up at her, and she knew he was just realizing that himself.

The bishop cleared his throat. "I think it's time you go home, Matthew. Hannah, I'm sure there are better ways to spend the Lord's Sabbath than this. Tell Mary's father I came by to see him and I'll catch up with him later in the week."

The two men disappeared from her tiny square view from the hayloft. With a heavy heart she made her way down the ladder.

17

Hannah stirred the chocolate frosting with all the strength she could muster. An electric mixer would be awfully nice on days like this. Her arms were weary from having washed clothes all morning. She had always known that a lot of jobs fell to Mary as the only daughter among ten children, but she hadn't realized the full magnitude of her workload. Thankfully, four of Mary's brothers were married and had homes of their own now. So Becky, *Mammi* Annie, and Hannah had only six males to look after. The responsibilities had been minimal when Mary first returned from the hospital, but as more and more Amish women went back to their homes, both Hannah's and Becky's workloads increased.

Hannah placed a layer of cake on a plate and began frosting it with a dinner knife. She had done mounds of laundry today, including a full tub of towels. Of all the items that had to be run through the gas-powered agitator, worked through the hand-cranked dry wringer to squish the soap out, rinsed by hand in a tub of clear water, and worked through the wringer again, towels were the most tiring. They got quite heavy as she dunked them in the rinse water and lifted them in the air, repeating the process over and over until the soap was out. Of course, boys' and men's shirts, of which there was no shortage in the Yoder household, were no picnic. They weren't heavy to rinse, but the wringer broke the buttons easily. At least at this stage of Mary's recuperation, she was well enough to sew buttons back on.

Hannah positioned the second layer of cake on top of the frosted one and dropped a large dollop of icing on it. As she smoothed it around the top and over the sides, she let her mind wander. A few more weeks had swept by as she'd stayed busy helping Mary regain her strength and the Yoders run their household.

There was one benefit to all the jobs and concentration: it helped time pass as she dreamed of seeing Paul again. Going without letters had been harder than she'd imagined. But with a little less than six weeks until Christmas, she'd almost made it through the arctic wasteland of time. A sense of well-being washed over her. She had set her will, defied her emotions, and carried out her responsibilities.

But Hannah didn't understand Gram's ridiculous edict that she and Paul could not write to each other. For the thousandth time, she wondered if there was some other way to pass letters back and forth without her family finding out.

With the aid of her walker, Mary shuffled into the kitchen. A patchwork potholder she had been sewing was scrunched between her palm and the handle of the walker. "I'm afraid the entire wedding season will pass by before I'm strong enough to attend any of them."

Hannah set the frosting to the side. She pulled a golden brown loaf of bread from the gas stove and set the pan on a baker's rack to cool. She put another pan of unbaked bread in the oven and closed the door. "Every bride and groom has come to see you before the wedding, no?"

Pinching off a bit of a freshly iced cake, Mary nodded, then popped the chunk of cake into her mouth. "Mmm, *vat's* awful *goot.*"

"Molmumumpm," Hannah mocked jovially. "How can I understand that garbled talk? Neither English nor Pennsylvania Dutch. Shame on you." Hannah cut the cake where Mary had pinched off a piece and set the slice on a plate on the table. "You've had plenty of nutrition. It's time for some much-needed calories." She grabbed a fork out of a drawer and laid it beside the plate.

Mary eased into the chair. "I came out to help, but, as usual, I sit and take it easy while you work."

Hannah grabbed a glass and filled it with milk, then placed it in front of Mary. "You're doing just as you should."

Mary took several long gulps of milk before setting the glass on the table. "I'll make all this up to you someday, Hannah. You'll see."

Hannah lifted the kettle of boiling water off the stove and poured the steaming liquid into a cup that held a tea bag and the last of the honey they had from the Esh farm. "What I see is my friend being strong enough to want to do things but too weak to do them just yet, no?"

Mary sighed. "It's frustrating. I lie in bed dreaming of doing things, and as soon as I stand, all my strength is gone."

"It will return."

"But I slept for days after my outing with Luke."

"I know. When you start getting your strength, it'll come quick like." Hannah set the hot drink in front of Mary. "The womenfolk will be here soon with their quilting items in tow. I want all of us to work on your quilt, and they want to come and lift your spirits. But if you get tired during the gathering, you say so, and I'll cart you off to bed."

Mary frowned. "I'm to go to bed while everyone else gets to work on the quilt you designed for me?"

Hannah opened the stove, checking the next batch of bread. She closed the oven, then turned to dump the other loaf onto a rack so it could finish cooling without getting soggy. "You'll do as your body asks."

Mary took another bite of cake. "You've done a wonderful job planning and gathering fabric for our quilt." She paused, her eyes studying Hannah with a depth of caring that only Mary had for her. "Hannah, I'm not so weak or confused from the medicines that I haven't noticed how sad you've been. I vainly assumed my injuries were the reason. But something much deeper is going on with you. It haunts your sleep and brings tears to your eyes when you think no one sees. If everyone wasn't so concerned over me and Luke, they'd be sick with worry about you. Can you tell me what's going on?"

Hannah scraped the last of the frosting out of the bowl and swirled it onto the cake, wondering if Mary was strong enough to hear the full, horrendous story. Although Hannah had to keep her and Paul's relationship a secret even from her best friend, she had always shared everything else with Mary.

The explanation of her unhappiness would be a painful shock for Mary. On one hand, Hannah wanted to spare Mary the ugly truth; on the other, she ached to talk to her, was desperate to share with someone the burden that ate away at her night and day. With her living here, her parents seemed to have forgotten the whole thing had ever happened.

Hannah gave a smile that had to look fake in spite of her best effort.

Mary's eyes brimmed with pools of water. "Something awful is wrong, and I'm so sorry. I feel so selfish, beaming about the new apartment and shop." Using the table as support, Mary stood. Her cool, soft hands pressed against Hannah's arm. *"Mei liewe, liewe Bobbeli, was iss es?"*

Dear, dear baby. The term of endearment would have caused giggles if the situation weren't so filled with misery.

Dread swamped Hannah. How could she talk about the attack when Mary knew little to nothing about what Dr. Greenfield called sex? For Hannah, getting the explanation past her lips would be tough enough if Mary already fully understood the concepts.

Hannah placed the spreading knife on a plate. She turned and faced her friend. So much love and compassion shone in Mary's eyes.

She swallowed. *"Du kannscht net saage..."*

Mary shook her head. "I won't, dear Hannah. You know I'll not tell a soul."

Hannah's knees shook so hard that she plunked into a kitchen chair. Mary sat beside her, holding her hands. Hannah swallowed. "A few weeks before your accident—"

A swift rap at the door startled both of them. Mary engulfed Hannah in a hug. "It's probably just *Mamm* dropping some sewing stuff off early, and I forgot to unlock the door. I'll ask her to give us some more time."

Hannah squeezed Mary gingerly before letting her go. As Mary shuffled to the door using her walker, Hannah rinsed her face at the sink, still debating how much to share with Mary. She could just tell her about Paul and how hard it was being separated from him. Was it safe for her friend's health to tell her any more than that? Could she handle even that much? It had taken Mary a week of extra rest to recoup from her visit to the harness shop, and Luke hadn't even allowed her to climb the steps to get a gander at their future home. She was more frail than she knew.

Mary opened the front door, then turned to look at Hannah. The crestfallen expression on her face said it all; they'd lost track of time. The women had arrived for the quilting.

"Are you all right, Mary?" Naomi Esh looked past her, searching for Hannah. Behind Naomi stood Deborah Miller and Grace Hostetler, all of them looking concerned.

Hannah stepped forward, placing her hands on Mary's shoulders. "She's fine. *Kumm uff rei,*" Hannah added, showing them in. Hannah helped Mary take a few steps backward with the aid of the walker, making room for the women and all their sewing goods to enter the room. Maybe this interruption was for the best. Mary's sudden inquisitiveness had caught Hannah off guard. Hannah needed time to weigh her words, to decide what Mary could handle.

The women cleared the food off the kitchen table and scrubbed the surface clean before spreading the partially finished "Past and Future" quilt across the table.

Mary remained near the front door, leaning on Hannah. "It's always about me. I'm so sorry." Her body shook like a newborn calf.

"Sh, *Liewi.* Sh." Hannah forced a smile, hoping it looked genuine. "It's a day we've looked forward to, no?"

Mary laid her head on Hannah's shoulder and wept. Beyond any question, Hannah knew that her friend was not strong or well enough to deal with the truth of what had taken place in her life. Just the idea that Hannah was unhappy had caused Mary to tremble and quake.

More women arrived, including Mary's mother and grandmother. When they saw Mary weeping in Hannah's arms, anxiety filled Becky's eyes. *Mammi* Annie frowned in concern. Hannah nodded to assure both women that Mary would be fine in a few minutes. Becky helped *Mammi* Annie move into the room and get seated.

Sarah bounded through the door next, chattering as only fifteen-year-old girls can, with no regard to the somber mood of the room. Hannah's sister didn't even speak to her. Then again, maybe she was giving her and Mary some privacy.

A quick glance outside informed Hannah that her *Mamm* hadn't come. Sarah had apparently hitched a ride with Edna Smucker, their closest Amish neighbor, who was walking toward the house with a small stack of already-sewn quilt patches.

"Kumm," Hannah whispered to Mary. Leaving the walker behind, she led Mary to the best seat at the table, the one near the wood stove, so she wouldn't need to shift out of the way as people milled about.

Mary wiped at her eyes, her hands still trembling. As she sank into the seat, she clung to Hannah's hand like a frightened child.

Hannah kissed her on the cheek and whispered, "Don't let my girlhood silliness upset you. This season of life will change soon enough, no?"

"Ehrlich?" Mary asked, her hushed voice unheard by the babbling women busily spreading the quilt background over the table.

Hannah drew a deep breath. No, it wasn't honest, but it was the truth condensed into something Mary could handle. Hannah would move beyond this spell and be happy. All she needed was Paul close by. *"Ya."* Hannah patted Mary's shoulder. *"Ya."*

The women talked as they laid small pieces of fabric over the off-white background. Each one seemed keenly aware of Mary's fretfulness but acted nonchalant and oblivious.

Hannah lifted two pieces of cloth off the table, a deep purple and a gorgeous magenta. She held them in front of Mary. "Impatiens wait to be designed into this quilt by the best among us at sewing flowers." She lowered the material in front of Mary. It was well known that Mary could outdo any seamstress when it came to designing flowers into quilts. As Mary's hands went toward the material Hannah held, she withdrew the squares and held them toward Becky.

The whole room, including Mary, broke into laughter. Although Becky Yoder was good at sewing all sorts of items from nature, she had often complained that she couldn't sew a flower to save her life but her daughter could do it in her sleep.

Mary laughed. "I thought you wanted impatiens, not blobs."

Becky mockingly wagged her finger in her daughter's face. "Not one of my children has suffered yet due to my lack of skill."

Ah, the mantra of every mother alive: for her children not to suffer because of what she lacked. Hannah cleared her throat, drawing everyone's attention. "That might be taking it a bit far, don't you think?" She peered at Mary, whose face was brightening by the moment.

Mary nodded. "When Robert lay under that blanket you made for him, he thought one of your flowers was a monster about to smother him in his sleep."

As laughter filled the room, Hannah returned to the stove to check the loaf of bread she'd forgotten. Becky wasn't nearly as bad at sewing flowers as she took ribbing for. She loved the teasing, egged it on most times. She often said that she considered a sense of humor about oneself to be nourishing to the soul and to the souls of others as well.

Hannah pulled the bread pan from the oven and, with great theatrics, turned it toward the women. Their hoots and cackles made the room vibrate. Her loaf of bread was burned all around the edges and gave off a horrible aroma. "It seems one of you could have noticed the scent of burned bread before now."

Naomi, with splayed fingers, waved her hand like a Victorian lady, then placed it over her heart. "It's an aroma we didn't recognize, having never burned bread in our lives."

Fresh roars of laughter filled the home. Every woman had burned foods while baking. The day was too filled with juggling babies, food preparation, and side businesses to keep up with everything perfectly.

Hannah carried the pan toward the doorway. Becky hurried to open the door for her. As Hannah stepped outside, she whispered, "I may take a few moments for myself while Mary's distracted. Do you mind?"

"No, child." Becky looked lovingly at Hannah. "Annie and I will tend to lunch." Becky closed the door, keeping the brisk wind out of the house.

The cold air almost took Hannah's breath away. She should have thought to get her shawl. Hurrying to the edge of the yard, she dumped the pan over, emptying it of the smoldering bread.

She stood straight, gazing over the brown lands of late fall. The husbands of the lighthearted quilters were out hunting pheasant and quail today, hoping to bring home some good birds before Thanksgiving next week. A few of the menfolk had managed to kill wild turkeys a couple of weeks back, but that season was closed now, so the other men were aiming for something less weighty.

The strength and pleasure of the women who loved, laughed, gave birth, served their families as well as their community, and finally died having tried to fulfill God's call on their lives warmed Hannah like nothing else. The tenderness of those who had known her all her life—who knew her mother, grandmother, and even her great-grandmother—melted the edges of ice that had formed around her heart.

Hannah walked toward Becky Yoder's home. She could at least wash a few dishes for Becky while the women quilted.

18

Sarah's hopes of seeing Jacob had taken a hard blow the moment she learned that all the Yoder men had gone hunting today. She'd spent weeks looking forward to catching a few words with him today even if she had to mill about the property half the day to see him.

What a miserable disappointment.

She wondered how many times Hannah had made ways to see Jacob without any of the Yoders realizing it. When the sewing needle pricked Sarah's index finger, she yelped. A few of the women tittered with laughter. Mary barely glanced up. Her reaction stung Sarah deeply. It didn't seem to matter at all to Mary that years ago, before Mary and Hannah began school, Mary had been Sarah's best friend, not Hannah's. Everyone in this room spoke highly of Hannah, even Grace Hostetler. Clearly Grace's husband, Bishop Eli, had not yet shared with her the information Sarah had given him about Hannah's midnight ride in her nightgown. If these women knew the truth about her sister's indiscretions, Hannah wouldn't be the queen bee around here. Sarah put her finger in her mouth to keep blood from staining the quilt.

Mary passed her a handkerchief, which Sarah quickly wrapped around her wound. When Mary rose from her chair, Grace bounded to fetch the walker.

"Dankes." Clutching the handgrips, Mary shuffled away from the table. "Come with me to the bathroom, Sarah. I've got just the thing for that finger."

Surprised and a bit honored, Sarah followed Mary, trying to think of something she could say that would impress the girl and make them close friends again.

Mary opened the mirrored medicine cabinet. She pulled out a box of Band-Aids and then turned on the faucet. "Hold it under the water for a minute."

Sarah removed the handkerchief and stuck her finger under the stream. "*Daed* finally got our plumbing all straight."

Mary squeezed Sarah's finger, expressing a few drops of blood. "I bet that makes life a lot easier, especially with Hannah here all the time."

Ire ignited in Sarah's chest. Why did everyone talk as if Hannah were everything and Sarah nothing? "Hannah's not all that great, you know."

Mary turned off the water. "That little prick should be all cleaned out now." She pointed to the cabinet under the sink. "Clean washrags are under there, but you'll have to get one yourself. I can't bend that low yet."

"I'll do it." Sarah grabbed a rag and dried her wet hand.

Mary's lack of response to her comment about Hannah was a clear indicator of her loyalties. If she only knew the truth. "Since you two are best friends and all, I'm sure Hannah's told you she's been running off with some *Englischer* during the night." Sarah gave her sweetest grin, hoping she'd worded that piece of news in a way that sounded upright and innocent.

Mary peeled the Band-Aid out of its paper wrapper. "This should keep your finger from bleeding on the fabric."

Sarah huffed. "I guess she didn't mention it to you after all. But it's true. I saw her myself." She glanced in the shaving mirror, pretending to make sure her blond locks were safely tucked inside her *Kapp*. "You know, *Daed* and the bishop saw her with an English doctor at the hospital. In his arms in broad daylight! I overheard *Daed* telling *Mamm* about it. He's fit to be tied."

Grasping the walker tightly, Mary shot Sarah an angry look in the mirror. "Why are you telling me this?"

"Since you're her best friend, I thought you'd want to help keep her on the straight and narrow. It'd be a shame if she—"

"Who else have you told these things to?"

Sarah bristled. "Look, you can keep secrets for her if you want, but I'm not going to. She can't pretend to be something she's not."

"Oh, really?" Mary's voice quavered like a pot of simmering stew. "Isn't that precisely what you're doing? Trying to make me think you're telling me something for Hannah's sake when you're simply doing it out of spite. Though why you would want to harm your own sister is beyond me." Trembling, Mary grasped the walker and shuffled out the door.

Sarah followed her to the bedroom. Concern for how badly Mary was shaking made Sarah fear for what she'd begun. She hadn't meant to upset Mary, but it was only right that the girl see Hannah for who she really was.

Mary sat on the side of the bed, her breathing labored. "Did you"—Mary took a quick breath, her speech coming in gasps—"approach Hannah...before spreading your version of...whatever it is you're talking about?"

Mary's accusation stung, but Sarah wasn't ready to give up. "Hannah has been far too preoccupied with herself to be approached about anything."

Mary glared at Sarah. "What a *deerich* girl you are. What a foolish, foolish girl." Her eyes rolled back, and she fell over limp on the bed.

"Mary!" Sarah screamed.

Within seconds, a herd of women raced into the bedroom.

Becky grabbed her daughter's head, obviously searching for signs of alertness. "Mary!" There was no response. "Go get Hannah. She's outside somewhere. Hurry."

Confused and frightened, Sarah ran out of the bedroom and through the front door. "Hannah! Hannah!" She dashed toward the road, skimming the lands for her sister. Oh, why had she tried to win Mary's approval by sharing her secret? She should have known it was a pointless venture. Mary was now Hannah's close friend, and nothing she could say would change that. Hearing the truth about her wouldn't easily dissuade the loyal girl.

When the women learned she was the reason Mary had gotten upset, they'd wag their tongues about Hannah's mean little sister for years to come. She searched her mind for ways to avoid the scolding she was in for.

As she ran past the Yoders' home, she saw Hannah coming out the front door, looking relaxed and carefree, wiping her hands on her apron.

"Hannah," she shrieked, "Mary's having a spell of some sort. She collapsed. *Dabber schpring!*"

Even before Sarah finished screaming, Hannah was bolting up the driveway toward the *Daadi Haus.*

Hannah barreled through the side door, out of breath after her short sprint.

Grace pointed to the bedroom. *"Kammer."*

Upon entering the small room, Hannah found the rest of the women hovering around the bed. "What happened?"

The terror in Becky's eyes made Hannah's knees nearly buckle. *"Ich kann net saage."*

She couldn't say?

Hannah grabbed the blood-pressure cuff and stethoscope out of the dresser in a far corner of the room. If Becky didn't know what was wrong, then Mary must have been more stressed by thoughts of the secret Hannah had never shared than she had realized.

As Hannah came to the edge of the bed, the women cleared the way for her. Mary's face was flushed, but she looked coherent, even a bit annoyed. Hannah passed the items in her hand to Grace.

"Deerich," Mary mumbled.

"*Liewe* Mary, you're not foolish at all. Now just relax." Placing her hand behind Mary's back, Hannah eased her forward and removed the pillows that were propping her up. She helped Mary slide downward in the bed, the loving hands of several women easing her into a flat position.

Hannah placed the pillows under Mary's feet. "Close your eyes. Take slow, deep breaths. Everything will be just fine." She retrieved the blood-pressure cuff and stethoscope from Grace. Hannah cooed in her most consoling voice while wrapping the cuff around Mary's arm. Hannah pumped the rubber bulb on the blood-pressure cuff. After the appropriate number of pumps, she stopped to read the gauge; it said 112/71, normal for Mary. Hannah loosened the cuff and let it hang. She tossed the stethoscope onto the bed and took Mary's wrist, checking her pulse.

Mary motioned with one hand. *"Du muscht verschteh."*

"I do understand. Shush now. I need to think." Counting the beats for thirty seconds and then doubling that number, she came up with 134 beats per minute. That was high, definitely worth calling about. "Sarah?"

Sarah edged forward. *"Ya?"*

"There's a little pamphlet in the top drawer of the dresser. Could you get it, please?"

She scurried to do Hannah's bidding.

"A nurse's direct line is written on there. Take the pamphlet to the phone shanty and dial that number. Tell whoever answers who you are and what's going on. I'll come to the shanty before the nurse gets on the line."

"Deerich." Mary raised herself up on her elbows and glared at Sarah. *"Die entsetzlich Druwwel Du duscht."*

"Mary," Hannah whispered, "lie back. You're talking nonsense. Sarah hasn't brought any awful trouble to me." Hannah glanced at Sarah. The girl looked stricken with worry. "It's okay, Sarah. Just go call that number. I'll be there in a few minutes. I want to check her blood pressure and pulse one more time first."

Sarah darted out of the room.

"Hannah." Mary pulled at her arm, nodding at the women in the room and then toward the door.

Clearly Mary wanted to speak to Hannah alone. It seemed rude and bold, but Hannah wasn't about to argue. "Becky, I think some homemade chicken soup would do her a world of good."

The women all filed out of the room with a new mission, to pull together a batch of soup as quickly as they could. As the last woman to leave, Edna closed the door behind her.

Hannah tightened the dangling blood-pressure cuff and put the stethoscope on Mary's antecubital as she'd been taught. "Mary, what happened to you?"

Mary's greenish blue eyes were wide open, her pupils dilated. "Sarah told me some things. Dreadful things. Hannah, I believe your sister is betraying you to the community, and you'll end up paying for it for years to come. You've got to stop her. You've got to."

Hannah's heart raced, battling between compassion for her younger sister, who often spoke first and thought second, and wrath at Sarah's lack of tongue control. But what had the girl told Mary about her? What did she know that could hurt her so badly? Had Mrs. Waddell told her about Hannah's relationship with Paul? Or had she overheard their parents talking about the unmentionable?

When she got another normal reading on Mary's blood pressure, she took off the stethoscope. "What did Sarah tell you?" she asked, her voice trembling.

"She said you were in the arms of some doctor and that she saw you in your nightgown taking a midnight ride with a man."

A slap across the face couldn't have hurt any worse. Hannah forced a smile. "Little sisters do that sometimes—tattle in hopes of causing trouble. Since you don't have any sisters, you just didn't know." Hannah patted her leg. "I need to get to that phone and see if the nurse agrees with my thoughts. Rest now. I'll be back soon."

When Hannah walked out of the bedroom, Becky met her. "Do you think she needs a doctor?"

Hannah fought against her indignation at Sarah and tried to find a gentle tone to answer her. "I'm not sure, but I think she's fine, just a bit weak."

Becky grasped Hannah's hand. "I'll go sit with her."

Hannah nodded and whisked out the side door and down the driveway toward the phone shanty. Thoughts of striking Sarah roiled through her. What had the girl been thinking, sharing such idle gossip? Their father must have said something about the doctor, probably not with the intention of Sarah or any other sibling hearing him. Hannah squeezed her fists.

Father God, help me see beyond my fury.

She glanced at the sky. Gray clouds hung low, and the scent of snow hung on the air. It would be Christmastime soon, and Hannah would see Paul. Thankful for that refreshing thought, she drew a deep breath.

As she watched the movement of wisps of clouds, she thought of Vento. Matthew had been right; the stallion's gait was as smooth as the clouds he'd compared the horse to.

Sudden concern lurched within her heart. *Matthew.* If Sarah's gossip got to the ears of Matthew's prospective girl, it would end things between them for sure.

Through the windows of the small shanty, Hannah saw Sarah holding the phone to her ear. Hannah opened the door.

Sarah lowered the mouthpiece. "I'm still on hold. How's Mary?"

"What did you say to her?" Hannah seethed.

"I-I…" Sarah stammered, looking like a frightened little girl.

"Out with it, Sarah. What did you tell Mary about the buggy ride?"

She gritted her teeth, making that "tcht" noise she was famous for. "I told her the truth. That you were out with some *Englischer* in the middle of the night in your nightgown."

An Englischer? Anger at her sister took a backseat to the relief that poured over Hannah. Sarah had no idea the driver was Matthew. "We were gone for five minutes. How much fuss have you caused over this?"

Sarah's right cheek twitched. "Five minutes, nothing! I saw you. You were gone over half an hour."

Hannah glared at her. "Liar!"

A distant voice spoke through the earpiece. Sarah thrust the phone at Hannah. As she skirted around Hannah to leave the shanty, their backs raised like two cats in a fight.

The woman on the phone spoke again. Hannah raised the receiver to her ear. "Yes, this is Hannah Lapp. I'm calling about Mary Yoder. She was in ICU six weeks ago with a head injury."

"Hold, please."

She wasn't going to let any damage between her and Sarah distract her. Only two things were important right now: making sure Mary was fine and getting word to Matthew to tell no one that he was the driver of the buggy that night. But how could she manage to speak to him privately?

19

Hannah hung up the phone, relieved that the nurse believed Mary was probably fine, just too weak to deal with visitors and activity. She needed solitude, good meals, and lots of sleep.

Hannah finished jotting down the nurse's instructions so she wouldn't forget anything. She needed to keep tabs on Mary's blood pressure and heart rate over the next few days. Help her pace herself, allowing for physical therapy but no more sewingfests. Mary needed lots of water, and Hannah was to start pushing the extra calories, as she'd done earlier with the cake. A brisk wind could topple Mary right over these days.

As she left the phone shanty, Hannah's focus was on alleviating the concerns of everyone who was worried about Mary and then figuring out a way to talk to Matthew. But how? It wasn't like she had any real reason for visiting him.

She ran up the small hill to the *Daadi Haus.* Concerned faces met her as she entered. How had she managed to get this role of being the medically knowledgeable one? She was too young for all these mothers and grandmothers to look at her with such hopeful confidence. Hannah smiled as warmly as she could manage. "The nurse thinks she's fine, just a bit weak with so much going on. She's to sleep, eat, rest, and not have much company or excitement for a few more weeks, maybe longer."

Nods of agreement made a round through the room.

Becky came out of the bedroom. "She's asleep now, but she was asking for you." She pulled the door closed behind her. "What did the nurse say?"

"Basically that we're too wild of a group for a fragile young woman on the mend." Hannah flashed a broad smile, hoping no one saw past it to her anger at Sarah.

The women busied themselves putting all the sewing stuff that wasn't theirs back in its out-of-the-way spot in the living room. Then they streamed out the door, bidding good-bye to her, Becky, and Mary's grandmother Annie. Sarah passed her sister without a word.

Edna gave Hannah a quick hug. "We'll spread the word that Mary shouldn't have visitors. As soon as she's up to it, let everyone know."

Hannah patted Edna's back, assuring her that she'd keep the women informed of Mary's progress. As she watched her sister climb into Edna's buggy, Hannah wondered what meanspirited things Sarah would say about her on the ride home.

Naomi Esh paused in front of Hannah, carrying a large basket filled with sewing supplies. "I'm a stone's throw from here. If you think of anything I could do for Mary, the Yoders, or you, just holler."

Still trying to come up with a way to talk to Matthew, Hannah said, "That basket looks awful heavy."

Naomi let out a sigh. "Matthew drove me here. But since our get-together broke up earlier than expected, looks like I'll have to walk back home with this load."

Hannah glanced into the kitchen, where Mary's mother and grandmother were tidying up. "I'd be happy to walk with you while Mary sleeps." It would be considerably out of anyone's way to drive Naomi home following the roads that made a huge square to get to the Esh place. But it was a fairly short trip to march across the back fields where the two properties met.

"You have plenty to do here. I can manage."

Hannah's heart fell for an instant. Then she perked up. "I used the last of the honey in Mary's tea tonic this morning. If I walk with you now, I could bring some back with me."

Naomi held the basket out to her. *"Kumm."*

The two women walked in silence across the open fields from the Yoder place to Esh land. Unable to think of anything but what Sarah's gossip could do to Matthew's future, Hannah only managed nods and grunts at Naomi's attempts at conversation. Finally Naomi stopped talking, and they walked in silence.

As the chilly air whipped around her and her temper began to calm a bit, Hannah grew cold. She had, once again, forgotten to grab her shawl. Pulling the basket closer, she was struck so hard by a new thought that she had to fight for her footing.

If by some chance she was pregnant and Matthew's name got out to the community as the one Hannah was with in her nightgown, he might as well dig a grave for his chances of finding a wife anywhere in these parts. Her steps quickened as that worry took root.

"Give an older woman a break, Hannah. I can't go at that pace."

Chafing, Hannah slowed. She wasn't pregnant. She couldn't be. Conceiving that monster's child was more than she could cope with. It was all she could do to keep the rape a secret from Paul. How would she conceal a pregnancy? And what would she do with a baby? She shuddered.

Just don't think about that. It's not true. It's not.

The internal pep talk worked, as it had for well over a month, and her fears calmed to a bearable state.

Naomi and Hannah left the rough terrain of the fields and stepped onto a horse-trodden path. They crossed the driveway and soon were walking into the Esh home. Hannah had been there several times before, had sat on the front porch on many a no-church Sunday. Although the layout of the place was somewhat different from her own home, it was similar in many respects, such as the color of the sofa and the type of clock on the wall. If she weren't so livid with Sarah and so tired of Luke being angry with her, the scene might have made her homesick.

Hannah set the basket on the table as Naomi walked to the bottom of the stairs. "Peter? David?"

Loud, awkwardly rhythmic clomps echoed against the stairway. "They're at the Millers' place, *Mamm,* pluckin' feathers off today's hunt."

At the top of the twisting stairway, through the red cherry balusters, Hannah saw Matthew's feet, one with a sock on and one with both a sock and a shoe.

He hobbled down another step, gripping the rail, keeping his socked foot elevated. "Whatcha need?"

His legs came into full view as he hopped on one foot past the walled section of the winding stairwell. When he reached the midpoint landing, his face lit up. "Hannah. Hey."

She pointed to the foot he was keeping off the ground. "What happened?"

A corner of his mouth rose, and his eyes twinkled. "I fell…in more ways than one." He jerked his eyebrows up and down quickly.

Naomi waved her hand in the air. "I don't want to know about all this." She scurried up the steps and past her son. "Hannah needs honey. Go to the storage room and find her a couple of quart jars, will you?"

"Sure thing, *Mamm.*" Using the railing, Matthew limped down the last ten steps.

Hannah pointed at his hurt foot. "When? Where?"

He motioned toward the corner. "Guess."

Hannah turned to see what he was pointing at and spotted a pair of crutches. "There's no time for games, Matthew. We need to talk." She grabbed the crutches and handed them to him.

"Aw, come on, Hannah." He paused, gripping the handles of the crutches and studying her. "Okay, short version. But you're ruinin' the fun." He clunked the props this way and that until he was finally headed in the right direction.

Hannah fell in behind Matthew as they maneuvered at a snail's pace through the house toward the storage room that had once been a small back porch. He angled his head, talking over his shoulder. "When I took Peter and David to school a week ago Monday, I saw smoke coming out of the windows and doors. The teacher was in a fit, tryin' to douse the fire she'd started in the wood stove to warm the room before any of the kids arrived. As soon as I saw the smoke, I remembered that some of the older boys had joked about stuffing the top of the chimney. So I dashed in to help, telling her that putting the fire out had only made more smoke. Then I told her the flue was probably stuffed. Using a ladder I climbed to the lowest branch of the red maple beside the school, and I managed to get the cloth out of the flue. But on the way back down the tree, I fell."

They stepped through the narrow entryway into the storage room. It was lined from ceiling to floor with shelves filled with various sizes of jars filled with honey.

"I stayed at the school while the teacher went to the Bylers' and got someone to substitute for her. She took me to the doc's, then brought me here and made me lunch."

"Really?" Hannah said, impressed with the personal attention this woman had shown. "Who is the teacher this year?"

Matthew shuffled around on his wooden supports until he was facing her. His eyes beamed. "The girl I told ya about. I told her this injury totally messed with my plan of going to the singing that next Sunday. She agreed to come get me if I didn't make her be the chauffeur and then invite some other girl to join us. Of course I agreed to that. So she came by and picked me up." Matthew laughed. "We had the most wonderful time you can imagine. We made the same arrangement for the next singing."

Hannah was so excited for him her skin tingled. "That's the best news I've heard in forever. I'm really happy for you, Matthew. But…" She closed the glass-and-wood door to the main house. "Matthew, we need to talk."

His smile faded slightly. *"Was iss es?"*

"Sarah saw us on the midnight ride."

Matthew chortled. "Ya take things too seriously, Hannah. The bishop won't eat ya, only admonish us for our own good. We did nothin' wrong during the world's shortest buggy ride."

Shaking her head, Hannah grabbed a plastic grocery bag from the shelf. *"Du muscht verschteh."*

Using his arms to balance his weight on the crutches, Matthew lifted both feet off the floor, showing off his stability. "Then explain it to me and maybe I'll understand."

Hannah took a large jar of honey off the shelf and put it in the bag. "She says we were gone a really long time."

He shrugged. "So, who cares?"

"Matthew, the bishop already thinks right poorly of me. My father doesn't know what to think of his eldest daughter lately. Luke blames me for his and Mary's accident."

Putting his uninjured foot on the ground, Matthew's brows scrunched. "That's not fair."

"*Ach,* it's ridiculous." The words came out bitter as resentment stirred a little deeper within her, each swirl eroding a bit more her desire to do what was right. "Sarah doesn't know it was you driving the buggy that night. Please, for your sake, don't tell anyone."

Matthew squeezed the handles of his crutches. "I can help get this straight, Hannah. We can go to your father and the bishop together and tell them the truth."

"No, Matthew. There's more to the gossip than what I just said."

"More?"

"Quite a bit more." Hannah placed another jar of honey into the bag.

"Has Sarah been saying other stuff too?"

"I...I don't think so."

Matthew held out his hand for the bag. As she hooked the handle of the heavy bag over his hand, he toppled forward. He grabbed on to the freestanding unit of shelves. It tilted forward. The jars rattled. Matthew tried to steady it while getting his balance. One of the crutches plunked to the floor, and the other fell against the shelf. "Whoa." Matthew wobbled on one foot. "If we knock over *Mamm's* whole shelf of honey, we'll never have to worry about another rumor—or anything else—ever again."

Hannah slid her shoulder under his arm and reached around him to take the bag from his hand. "The weight of the bag in the very hand that's trying to set the shelves steady is pulling them forward."

"You'll have to wriggle the handle loose. It's pinned between my hand and the shelf. If I move it, the shelves will topple."

With her shoulder steadying Matthew's left side and her trying to loosen the bag from his right hand, Hannah wondered if they'd get out of this mess without the shelves falling on top of them—or at least the jars of honey. When the doorknob rattled, Hannah was hopeful someone had arrived to help. Glancing in that direction, Hannah saw a beautiful young woman through the window. Her expression went from expectant to crestfallen within a split second.

"Elle," Matthew whispered.

Hearing the desperation in Matthew's voice, Hannah knew this was the young woman he so hoped to share a future with.

20

Paul paced to Mr. Yoder's barn again, watching for signs of Hannah. He'd spent days getting this trip all lined up, hoping, at the very least, to pass Hannah the letter that was in his pocket.

Come on, Hannah.

His grandmother was inside with Mrs. Yoder, visiting while Mary slept. It had taken him weeks to talk Gram into coming here; she probably wouldn't stay long.

He jammed his hands into his pockets and sighed. This wasn't the way it was supposed to go. Not after all the planning and scheming he'd done to get here today. If he and Hannah stood a chance of seeing each other on the eve of Thanksgiving, he had to get this letter to her today.

Surprisingly, Gram had readily agreed to his plan, which included her asking Hannah to come to work for her the day before Thanksgiving while he was off from school. He wrote Hannah the letter, telling her how important it was for her to get her parents' permission to accept Gram's invitation to work that day so they could spend some time together. Determined to put the letter in Hannah's hands personally, he'd told Gram they should visit the Yoders to check on Mary, never for a second anticipating that Hannah might not be there when he arrived.

When they knocked on the door where Mary was living during her recuperation, Mary's mother, Mrs. Yoder, greeted Katie Waddell warmly, and Gram introduced her grandson to her. Gram asked about Hannah, and Mrs. Yoder informed them that she was at Naomi Esh's place getting some honey.

Paul had excused himself and gone outside. He'd been pacing out here ever since. Rubbing the back of his neck, Paul's attention never left the horizon. His muscles tightened more with every minute that passed. He couldn't leave the letter with Mrs. Yoder or even Mary for that matter. If he did, it would probably cause quite an uproar.

He picked up a rock and threw it as far as he could. He'd missed his last class today and his work shift tonight to get this visit in, and now she wasn't here. He scanned the ridge, fairly sure he was looking at the property Mrs. Yoder had said was Esh land.

He strode in that direction. Maybe she'd be right across the hill, dawdling time away while Mary slept.

Through the window, Hannah saw the dejected young woman turn to go. Matthew let go of Hannah.

"Elle." He lurched for the door and stumbled. The shelves started tipping forward again. Hannah grabbed the shelf, and Matthew grabbed her. Several empty jars crashed to the floor.

The noise caused Elle to turn back, a look of concern in her eyes. She entered the room and grasped Matthew under his arm. He wavered awkwardly on one foot, still trying to get upright and balanced. Hannah put her strength under his other arm. Between the two females, they soon had Matthew balanced.

Hannah kicked the crutches out of their way. "Let's get him to a chair in the kitchen." Elle nodded, and together they escorted Matthew down the hall.

Except for her traditional clothing, Elle didn't look like any Amish person Hannah had ever seen. She had strawberry blond hair, some of which was dangling about her face in spite of the traditional bun and

Kapp. Her skin was as smooth and white as rich cream. Hannah could certainly see why Matthew was smitten with her.

When they reached the kitchen, he sat down. Elle shifted an adjacent chair and motioned for him to place his hurt foot on it. Then she whisked out of the kitchen and toward the living room. Matthew moaned and laughed as he placed his foot on the chair, calling out to her as she moved about. "It seems I'm destined to fall each time you're near."

"Oh, so it's my fault you're clumsy," Elle shot over her shoulder as she walked into the living room. "Just like it was my fault the flue at school was stuffed."

Matthew shrugged, but the playful delight had returned to his eyes. "She hasn't decided if I'm guilty of the wood-stove incident or not."

Hannah's interest moved from Matthew back to Elle as the girl reentered the kitchen, carrying a pillow. She was mesmerizing in an unusual way, with dainty features, long brown lashes in spite of her hair color, and pale freckles across the bridge of her nose. Elle looked briefly at Hannah. Her eyes were a color Hannah had never seen before. A light lavender mixed with blue. Absolutely stunning.

She'd never heard of an Amish woman named Elle, but the newer generation challenged the older one on all fronts, and names were just one area that people were stepping out in. Not every child's name was biblical anymore.

"Hannah Lapp, this is Elle Leggett."

Leggett? That wasn't an Amish last name, was it?

The girl held out her hand. As Hannah shook it, she noted this girl had an air of confidence that Hannah could only dream of.

Elle paused beside Matthew's chair, waiting for him to raise his foot so she could place the pillow under it.

Hannah turned the knob on the kerosene lamp in the middle of the kitchen table, making the room a bit brighter.

Elle gave the pillow that held Matthew's leg one last dusting with the palm of her hand. "I…I didn't mean to interrupt you." Her eyes flicked over Hannah. "I saw Matthew's mother heading for the barn. She said he was in the storage room and I should go on in. She didn't say he had company."

The concern that registered in Matthew's eyes was distressing, and Hannah knew he was beginning to see what she had tried to explain. Hannah's reputation was being tarnished by her own sister, and Matthew's newfound friendship with Elle could be ripped up by the roots before it had time to grow strong.

Elle held out her hand. "Hannah, it was nice to meet you. Samuel is awful proud of his oldest sister. He speaks of you often at school." She smiled. Elle's features held no malice or petty jealousy but plenty of disappointment. She nodded at Matthew and turned to leave.

"No." Matthew lightly smacked the table. "Don't go."

Elle looked from him to Hannah.

"Please stay." Hannah eased into a kitchen chair and shoved one out for Elle. "So, you teach in our district?"

Matthew rolled his eyes, playfully mocking Hannah. "She's been out of touch, bein' at the hospital with Luke and Mary for weeks and now chained to the Yoder place while Mary mends."

Inquisitiveness crossed Elle's features. "And you're here now because…"

Hannah stole a glance at Matthew. She liked this girl. Her direct but polite approach left no doubt what she wanted to know. "I…I sort of came for honey." Her cheeks burned. *Sort of?* She hadn't meant to word it like that, and now there was no backing up.

Matthew leaned forward. "Her real reason for coming here was to see me and talk. We're friends, Elle."

Elle eased into the chair Hannah had pushed her way.

Hannah noticed the same high spirits in Elle's eyes that Matthew had, but there was something else, something harder, more assertive.

Elle leaned forward in her chair. "If someone doesn't either clear the air or let me leave with my pride intact, you're going to need another trip to the doc's, Matthew Esh, and I'll not be accompanying you this time."

Matthew cocked his head. "There's no more between Hannah and me than there is between you and her brother Samuel."

Elle studied her.

Hannah searched her mind for something friendly to say. "I've never heard the name Elle among our people before. It's beautiful."

The girl stole a look at Matthew. "I was born in Pennsylvania, but I wasn't born Amish."

Trying to hide her surprise, Hannah stammered. "B-but you're Amish now? How is that possible?"

Elle leaned back in the chair a bit and let her hands rest in her lap. "When I was ten, my mother became very ill. Abigail Zook, my mother's best friend and a very loving Amish woman, began taking care of me. Not long after my mother died, my father left…and has never returned. To keep me out of the foster-care system, Abigail and her husband, Hezekiah, took me in while a search was made for any relatives I might have. None were found." Elle dispensed the information like memorized lines from a book rather than a past filled with heartache and hope. She possessed an inner strength that Hannah found inspiring.

Matthew's eyes were glued to Elle as he spoke to Hannah. "Abigail and Hezekiah have been married about fifteen years, but they were never blessed with children of their own. They only have Elle, and now she plans on joining our faith when the bishop says she can."

The looks that ran between Elle and Matthew left little doubt that she was as interested in him as he was in her.

Matthew had told her right. It was the strangest thing she'd ever heard tell of among the Amish. But Hannah couldn't let this go without making sure the girl had thought this through. "It's hard to live without electricity once you've had it."

Elle's eyes widened as she nodded in agreement. "No doubt. But Kiah—that's what I call Hezekiah—allows for bending a few rules." She pulled a cell phone out of her hidden pocket. "What he's not willing to bend rules on, I can live without."

Hannah stared at her. "How can you be so sure?"

Elle laughed. "Life is filled with sacrifices of one type or another. I've seen both sides of life, the fancy way and the plain way. I choose plain. Not because it will save me, because it won't. Just because it's where my life is, with Kiah and Abigail. When I have kids, I'd like Abigail to get to hold my babies and know they're her grandchildren, although she'll still be young enough to have a baby of her own if she could have children."

Hannah gave a slight nod, as if she understood the deep connection Elle felt to Abigail and Hezekiah. But she wasn't sure she did.

Matthew ran the palms of his hands across the tabletop. "She drives a horse and buggy around the district to make visits to her students' homes and such, but because she lives so far from here, she leaves the horse and buggy at the Bylers', and a driver takes her home."

Elle laughed. "More like the horse and buggy drives me. Can't say I've gotten the hang of making the horse do my bidding."

"I think the Bylers need to own a better-trained horse. I got one I'm working with that'll be up for sale in a few weeks if they're interested." Matthew leaned forward, catching a glimpse of the clock. "Ya better go or the driver will leave, and you'll be sleeping at the Bylers' for the night."

Elle stood. "Yeah, I'd better go. Hannah, it was nice to meet you. Samuel will like that I finally met you."

"I'm glad we had this snippet of time, Elle." Hannah rose. "I need to get the honey and go too. But I'll clean up the mess in the storage room first." She grabbed the broom and dustpan and walked out of the kitchen, giving Matthew and Elle a moment alone.

As she picked up the fallen crutches, Hannah heard thunder rumble softly in the distance. She leaned the crutches against the shelf. Sweeping the broken glass into the pan, she dreaded walking home. She hadn't been on a walk alone since her attack, except from the house to the barn. Her palms were sweaty with the thought.

After putting the broom and dustpan in a corner, she grabbed the bag containing the jars of honey. The heavy jars could be used as a weapon if need be.

When she stepped onto the porch, Elle was in her gig, pulling out of the driveway.

Naomi came across the yard, leading a horse-drawn cart. "Someone needs to take Hannah home before the rains get here. Since you're useless around the house these days, I chose you."

Relief as well as humor washing over her, Hannah laughed.

Matthew growled playfully. "Thanks, *Mamm.*" He made his slow descent down the porch stairs.

With a smile plastered on her face, Naomi motioned to the small rig. "I hitched the pony cart up for you so you can easily climb in and out of this low-to-the-ground thing." She winked at Hannah. "Now, go, Son. And if the rains catch you, stay at John Yoder's for the night."

"Gosh, *Mamm,* are you trying to get rid of me?"

Naomi chortled and turned to go inside.

Grateful for an escort, Hannah climbed into the weathered wooden rig. After settling on the bench, Matthew laid his crutches between him and Hannah. He took the reins and slapped them against the horse's back. Hannah set the bag of honey in the seat, feeling nervous about being gone so long.

The pony trotted across the top of the ridge and into the Yoders' barnyard before Matthew brought the rig to a stop. "I'm glad you got to meet Elle."

Hannah climbed out of the cart. "Me too. But remember what I said about that midnight ride. Just don't tell anyone it was you, and your relationship with Elle won't feel any strain from the rumors."

Matthew shrugged as he scanned the yards. "Looks like Mary had more *Englischers* come visit."

Paul was backing Gram's car out of the driveway.

Hannah's heart jerked inside her chest.

21

Paul pulled onto the paved road, disappointment so thick he couldn't think. Maybe it would be better if Gram drove, since he was almost blind with disappointment. All his weeks of planning ruined, and because he hadn't seen her today, he probably wouldn't have the chance to see her over Thanksgiving either. He doubted he could change his dad's mind about leaving the state for the Christmas holidays. After disappointing his father with how little he'd been home over the past few years, he couldn't refuse his father's gift of a family vacation at the beach. Besides being rude, it would cause a rift between them, and he needed his father on his side during the lengthy spell to win the approval of Hannah's family.

Paul sighed. He didn't know when he'd been more aggravated. Now he might not see Hannah until May. Would she continue to wait for him through all these unforeseen obstacles? Another angry sigh escaped his lips. May was too far away. Something had to be done.

He glanced at his grandmother. "Gram, you've got to help me get a letter to Hannah."

Gram's soft wrinkles seemed to droop more than normal these days. He figured she was missing Hannah as much as he was. Hannah was one of the few people who managed to ignore his grandmother's curtness and stubbornness. Gram could hire laborers left and right, but she couldn't pay someone to truly care. Hannah always cared.

Gram harrumphed. "I can't, Paul. I came here today. That will have to be enough."

He squeezed the steering wheel. "Please, Gram. Surely you can pass her one letter."

She shook her head. "I promised..." Gram dropped her sentence, squirming uncomfortably against the bucket seat.

Paul stopped the car, not caring that he was in the middle of the road. "Go on."

The lines on Gram's face stiffened. "You two will be fine...if you're supposed to be. That's all there is to it."

"Who did you promise that you wouldn't pass letters to Hannah?" Paul stage-whispered the words in an effort to remain gentle and respectful with his grandmother. There were only a few people who would ask for a promise like this from his grandmother: Hannah's father, her mother, or one of her older brothers. Paul decided to go with the most likely person. "Did her father come to see you?"

Gram didn't move a muscle. "She is his daughter, Paul. And whether you believe this or not, he has more rights over Hannah's life than you."

A deep disappointment stabbed him in the center of his chest. Mr. Lapp wasn't supposed to know, not yet. Not until Hannah was legally an adult so she couldn't get into too much trouble with her father. "What did he say?"

The sternness on her face softened as her eyes glistened with tears. Paul realized he'd been putting her in a tug of war for months by wanting one thing from her while Hannah's father demanded another.

She pulled a handkerchief out of her purse and dabbed at her eyes. "It came to his attention that Hannah had been waiting on letters to come to my house for her. Her father suspects there's an *Englischer* or Mennonite working for me who is tempting his daughter away from where God has placed her. He didn't ask for specific information, and I offered none. I did, however, agree not to allow any more letters." She shoved the hanky back into her purse. "Paul, I'm sorry, but the man has good points. She's his daughter, and by English laws she's a minor." She clapped her hands and motioned for Paul to get the car moving.

He eased his foot onto the gas pedal, driving without noticing much of anything. "How did he learn of the letters?"

"I think Sarah told him."

So even her sister was against him and Hannah being together. The magnitude of all that was against them settled heavily onto his shoulders.

Gram rubbed her forehead. "When Hannah got sick right after you left, Sarah started coming in her stead. She asked me if I had any letters for Hannah. My guess is that Hannah must have asked her to pick up anything that came to me for her."

Coming to a stop sign, Paul brought the car to a halt. "So her father is going behind her back to end things. This isn't good. I wanted a chance to earn his respect."

Gram glowered at him. "Kinda hard to earn respect when you're sneaking around behind the man's back."

Paul accelerated too quickly, causing the tires to squeal. "I don't know what else to do, Gram. Let her go when that's not what either of us wants? I mean, if God's Word said something against two people who love Him falling in love, then I'd back off."

Hannah stood by the side of the road, watching Gram's car disappear around a curve. She was so tired of life not being fair that she could crawl in a hole and stay there. She waited, hoping Paul would spot her in the rearview mirror. But as the car disappeared around a bend, her heart sank. She turned and trudged back up the driveway.

She heard a horse exhale and looked up. Matthew had ridden from the barnyard and down the driveway.

He stood beside the buggy, holding up the sack containing the honey jars. "You forgot the honey."

She reached for the bag. "Thanks." Holding the honey against her chest, she faced into the wind and took a deep breath, trying desperately to get a hold on her emotions.

Matthew motioned toward the paved road. "I take it whoever was in that car is the reason you don't mess with singings."

Hannah closed her eyes, weary of secrets, half truths, and slinking through life as if she was a sinner. Even Matthew didn't understand. She saw it in his eyes. In spite of Elle's background, he didn't understand that all she wanted was a life with Paul. That's all.

The wind thrashed against her cheeks as thunder rumbled and a streak of lightning shot across the sky. She wished it were possible for the wind to snatch her up and land her in a place where life wasn't a constant choosing of sides.

"You'd better go on in, Matthew. The rains will be here before you get to the edge of the field." Hannah took the pony by the harness. "Go on in. I'll put the rig in the barn and the pony in a stall. When the storm blows over, you can go home."

Matthew surveyed the skies while grabbing his crutches and getting out of the wagon.

Before he could say another word, Hannah led the pony into the barn. As she unhitched the animal from the carriage, a delicious new thought danced into her mind. Maybe, just maybe she could use the Yoders' phone to call Paul. She had no idea why she hadn't thought of it before. Maybe because using the phone for the first time earlier today had made her realize how easy it was to place a call. Excitement pulsed through her.

As she put the pony in a stall, another round of thunder clapped, vibrating the air around her. The fast-paced clops of a horse heading in her direction made her quickly fasten the stall gate and rush to the door of the barn.

Luke.

Looking pale with worry, he came to a halt just outside the barn and slid off the horse. Holding the reins, he sprinted into the shelter. "How is Mary?"

"Still asleep as far as I know." *Becky would be calling for me if she weren't.*

He thrust the reins toward her. "Edna said she had some sort of spell today."

"A tiny one." Hannah took the leather straps, knowing he intended for her to walk the horse until it was cool and to rub the sweat-soaked creature down. "We just need to make sure she has less excitement and no hint of discord with anyone." She patted the horse's neck, feeling the sweat on the beast. "She's never been one to cope well with gossip, and a quilting is not the place for her right now."

Between his concern for Mary and the brewing storm, Hannah knew her brother would be staying the night. With Luke there, hopes of sneaking out long enough to call Paul faded. She grabbed a sackcloth and started drying the horse's neck.

Luke struck a match and lit a kerosene lamp. "That's why she didn't want to come to the farm without you the night of the accident; she was afraid it'd stir unfounded gossip about us."

"She didn't want to be the target of speculation where you were concerned." She hung the damp sack on the rail and grabbed a dry one.

"Ach," he growled. "So it's my fault?"

"That's not what I was trying to say. Luke, I…I'm sorry I didn't go with you that night. Really I am." Hannah could only take his word for how her decision to stay home had resulted in their accident.

"Bein' sorry doesn't fix a thing, now does it? She's your best friend, Hannah. You knew how she felt about being seen with me on our property without you there to make it look like friends spending time together. You knew!" Luke turned his back on her and dashed for the house.

Large drops of rain pelted the tin roof. Hannah swiped the cloth over the other side of the horse. Luke's words could only hurt her so deep this time. His resentment against her was ridiculous. He had told Mary he forgave the man driving the car that hit them. So why couldn't Luke forgive his own sister? She was fast becoming weary of her brother. He was too much like her father—pleasant to those he agreed with, angry and demanding with those he didn't.

Longing to talk to someone who truly knew her welled in her heart. She had to call Paul, regardless of Luke's presence. Maybe now was the best time, while they thought she was tending to the animals. Hannah hurried to finish this chore so she could steal around the back way to the phone. If only she could hear his voice, she could endure until Christmas.

As she tossed feed into a trough, she noticed John Yoder's horse penned up for the night. The men and boys of the Yoder family must have returned from their hunt and from school while she was at the Esh place. Her stomach growled. It was past time for supper, and she hadn't had lunch.

She turned off the kerosene lamp and shut the barn door behind her. Standing under the eaves of the barn, she plotted the best route to the phone without anyone seeing her. Having settled on a course that went behind trees and bushes, she took off running.

Shaking from apprehension as well as the cold rain, Hannah yanked open the shanty door. She dialed 411 and asked for the phone number of Edgar Waddell, Gram's late husband. Using the paper and pen that lay beside the phone, Hannah soon had the number in hand. There was no way to deny that there were things about the modern world she liked. Feeling triumphant for the first time in forever, she dialed Gram's number.

When the phone was picked up quickly, she was sure it would be Paul.

"Hello," Gram said.

It was good to hear the woman's voice. "Hi, Gram. This is Hannah. The Yoders got a phone shanty, and…is…is Paul there?"

"No, dear. I guess Becky told you we came by her place, but he left as soon as he dropped me off. How are you feeling these days?"

Groping to find her voice, Hannah murmured a few niceties in order to answer her and hung up the phone.

She leaned her head against a wall of the tiny booth, aching to hear Paul's voice.

Between her miserable sorrow and the wet clothes that clung to her, Hannah shivered hard. She closed the shanty door behind her and headed around the back side of the house. The downpour had ceased, leaving only a light mist.

Her body ached from the day's events, and the hopelessness in her heart only added to her discomforts. As the wet clothes clung to her physical body, the aches and pains of the past few months clung to her soul, dragging her into ever-deeper waters.

She heard an automobile rumble on the paved road some twenty feet away. Hannah scurried into the shadows. A horn gave a short toot, and lights flashed. She turned. Through the misting night, she saw an old, midnight blue truck. The door opened, and Paul jumped out. He hustled toward her as if he'd caught a glimpse of her before she had retreated to the shadows. The sight of him in blue jeans and a button-down shirt running toward her was almost more than her knees could take. She ran down the hill and threw her arms around his neck. His strong grip lifted her off the ground and held her.

He nuzzled against her neck, even planting a kiss on her cold, damp skin. Her arms tightened. *Oh, please, tell me I'm not dreaming.*

He set her feet on the ground. His hands moved to her face, cradling it. She gazed at him intently, expecting him to speak. Slowly a smile eased his tense features, and she heard him draw a heavy breath. He lowered his face until his lips touched hers. Warmth and power swept through her. She had no idea a kiss felt like this. Desperate to bury all the pain her family had heaped on her, she reveled in the magnitude of Paul's touch. She kissed him, not wanting to ever stop.

Astonishment jolted her, and she pulled him closer, running her hand over the back of his head. His soft, warm, gentle lips moved over hers, and she returned the favor, until Hannah thought they might both take flight right then and there. Finally desperate for air, they parted.

Paul rested his hand on his chest. "Wow." He gulped in air. "I needed that so badly." His eyes bored into her. He smiled. "Hi."

Hannah bit her bottom lip, too thrilled and embarrassed to maintain eye contact. "I called Gram's. She said you were gone."

He reached into his back pocket. "I couldn't leave without trying one last time to get this to you." He passed her a letter. "It explains all sorts of things. I…I'm sorry, but I can't be here for Christmas. But I'll be at Gram's the day before Thanksgiving. It'd be our only time until this spring. Please tell me you can get away."

She took the letter from his hand, then tucked it inside the bib of her apron. She reached for Paul's hand. "I'll find a way."

His lips met hers again and again, and she finally understood the desire of a woman to yield herself to the marriage bed.

"I miss you so badly, Hannah. You can't imagine." He whispered the words as he kissed down her neck.

"Hannah?" a deep voice called through the low rumble of thunder.

Hannah jumped, turning her head toward the sound of Matthew's voice. She didn't see him, which probably meant he hadn't seen her. She cuddled against Paul's chest for a moment, then took a step back. "That's Matthew," she whispered. "Mary must be asking for me. I have to go."

Frustration seemed to pass through Paul's eyes.

"Hannah!" Matthew called again.

"Go," Paul whispered, nudging his head toward the *Daadi Haus.* "I love you."

"Always and forever, Paul," Hannah whispered. "Always and forever." She tilted her chin slightly as strength returned to her. Biting her bottom lip, she winked before trudging up the soggy hill.

Paul climbed into the truck, damp but ecstatic. His heart thumped against his chest. All he wanted to do was close his eyes and enjoy the exhilaration of what had just taken place. He ran his thumb over his lips.

Wow.

That encounter was not something he would have ever dreamed possible, unless he was dreaming of their wedding night. But even then, he hadn't considered that kind of uninhibited passion from Hannah.

Refusing to pass in front of the Yoder house, he cranked the truck and put it in reverse. Finally all his weeks of planning had meant something. Just about the time he was ready to explode in frustration, the most amazing encounter of his life occurred. Paul drew in a deep breath, determined to remember those few moments anytime discouragement tried to eat away at his confidence in their future. Reveling in the incident, he backed the truck onto a road to his left, then pulled forward.

Whenever he'd thought about seeing Hannah over the Thanksgiving weekend, he'd hoped to at least get a kiss on the cheek, maybe even a brush of their lips. But what had just taken place— That reunion was a million times better than the teary, discombobulating scene at the hospital. Funny, he'd gone to the hospital expecting a warm welcome only to find her an overstressed, teary-eyed mess. Earlier today he'd looked forward to slipping her the letter and gazing into her eyes from across the room. He'd been bitterly disappointed then too. But tonight he'd come by simply hoping to find a way to pass her his note or get a glimpse of her through a window. What he got was far, far more than he'd known to hope for.

Life—it's strange.

Now, if Hannah could manage to come to Gram's next week, they could have all day together before they were separated until his spring break or maybe until he graduated.

Paul mulled over the situation with Hannah's father. No parent liked the idea of his child, especially his daughter, choosing something aside from what the father had in mind. But surely Mr. Lapp could adjust.

22

Hannah stuck her sewing needle in the small tomato cushion and shook her hands, trying to get the blood flowing again. Laying Samuel's shirt on the finished pile, she mused over all the work she'd gotten done for her family while living at Mary's grandmother's place. She had worked extra hard since Paul had made his brief appearance. She'd baked goods and sent them home with Luke. He in turn had brought her mounds of mending, and she'd worked on it every spare moment. Getting up well before dawn, she'd done everything the Yoders needed before they needed it, determined to earn the right to go to Mrs. Waddell's for the eve of Thanksgiving.

Today was the day to ask permission to go. Her parents, with all the children in tow, were coming here to Mary's house after church.

With only the aid of a quad cane, Mary trekked into the room. Her gait was slow and a bit unsteady. Her eyes narrowed as she pointed to the sewing basket and stack of clothes. "On a Sunday?"

Hannah felt little remorse. "With everyone at church but us, it was a good time to get this done. My feet were propped up, and I was stress free."

Mary chuckled. "You, relaxed? Are you capable of taking things easy?"

The sounds of buggies and voices signaled that the families had arrived home from church. Hannah grabbed her scissors and pincushion and stuffed them into the sewing basket. She stacked the mended clothes on top and dashed for the bedroom, where she hid the evidence in a corner.

When her parents entered Annie Yoder's home, they told her that Sarah had ridden home from church with Edna. She was the only Lapp who hadn't come to Mary's today. At least the girl was showing some good sense. Unless she intended to apologize and take back the gossip she was spreading, Hannah knew Mary did not want anything to do with her.

After lunch had been eaten and the table cleared, Hannah found herself alone in the kitchen with her parents. This rare moment of solitude was the opportunity she'd been hoping for. *Daed* was lingering over a cup of coffee, *Mamm* watching him. The rest of the clan were playing board games in the living room. Hannah slid the last of the dishes into the warm, sudsy water, knowing her father wouldn't want her washing them until after sundown.

When she turned around, her parents had their heads together whispering back and forth. She wondered if they were discussing Aunt Zabeth. Maybe they thought Hannah was old enough to hear about the aunt she'd discovered months ago.

Their conversation stopped when they saw she was looking at them. They each gave a slight shake of the head, assuring her she was to ask no questions. Just as well. She had her own things she needed to talk about.

She dried her hands on a towel and drew a deep breath. "*Mamm, Daed,* I was wondering... See, I always help Mrs. Waddell cook before Thanksgiving. She packs everything in coolers and goes to her son's house in Maryland early Thanksgiving Day." She held her breath, waiting for their reaction. Hannah's explanation of Mrs. Waddell's Thanksgiving tradition wasn't the complete truth, but it was close enough. If they knew that for the past two Thanksgivings, Paul had worked beside her and then had driven his grandmother to his home in Maryland for the rest of the Thanksgiving weekend, they wouldn't consider this request.

A look of triumph and surprise crossed their eyes, giving Hannah the uneasy feeling that she'd just walked into a trap. Her mother gave a slight nod to her father. He turned the coffee cup in his hand, squeezing it firmly. "If...if you'll do something for your mother first, we'll allow it."

She moved to a chair. "*Was iss es?*"

Daed pushed the cup away from him. "We want you to come by the house on your way to Mrs. Waddell's." His eyes moved to his wife's. Uneasy looks in her parents' eyes replaced the victorious expressions of moments earlier.

"Okay." The word came out long and slow. "But why?"

Her father shrugged, his eyes focused on the table. "Could you do as we've asked without pestering us with questions?"

Hannah looked to her mother, who was staring a hole in the center of the table. What did they want? Whatever it was, they didn't desire to discuss it here with family and friends in the other room. By their responses, it was something they knew she would be against. Most likely they had heard about the rift between her and Sarah and intended to force her to put an end to it.

But it didn't really matter what their plan was. They were her parents, and she'd end up complying no matter what they wanted; otherwise, she wouldn't get a day at Gram's with Paul.

Samuel ran into the room with Mary's seven-year-old brother, Robert, hot on his trail. Nine-year-old Jesse followed, teasing them both by dangling a spit-up towel from their oldest brother's infant. The volume in the room grew by the moment.

Hannah rose from her chair, her parents watching her every move. The uneasiness of their request sat hard on her lungs. But no matter what they had in mind for her, no price was too high to pay to see Paul again.

Hannah's eyes bolted open. She tossed the covers back and jumped out of bed. Today she'd see Paul. Scurrying through the dark, cold room, she got ready for the day as quietly as possible. Leaving Mary asleep, Hannah slipped out the front door and headed for the barn.

The day before Thanksgiving dawned cold and cloudy. By the time the skies gave way to dreary light, Hannah had hitched John Yoder's horse to a buggy. After a quick stop at home, she would finally be on her way to Mrs. Waddell's. With her treasured anatomy book beside her so she could show it to Paul, she gave a light slap of the reins against the horse.

Before she'd even left the Yoders' barn, she spotted Matthew Esh rounding up stray cows. When she hollered, asking him what was going on, he said one of his brothers had left the gate open. Loose cows were a hazard for motorists. Hannah unhitched the buggy. She put the horse in its stall and then helped chase the roaming cows back toward Esh land.

Soon Mary's father, four of her brothers, and Matthew's two brothers joined them, and they managed to get the daft cows back where they belonged. After she and Matthew rounded up the last two cows, they stopped by his house for a drink. Matthew apologized for interrupting her morning, then he heated bricks for her feet while he hitched his warmest buggy to a horse for her. When she said she needed her book from the other buggy, he sent Peter to get it.

By the time Peter returned, Hannah was flustered at how much time had passed. But neither the late start nor the overcast sky could cool Hannah's spirits. She slapped the reins against the horse's back, spurring it to go faster. Though still unaware of what her parents wanted, Hannah was determined to do their bidding quickly—even if she had to apologize to Sarah for things that weren't her fault.

The horse's pace was entirely too slow for Hannah. She laid her hand on the cover of the anatomy book on the seat beside her, looking forward to studying it with Paul throughout the day as time allowed. She understood so much more now than last summer, when he had taught her a few things through his textbooks.

As Hannah neared her house, she was surprised to see her mother standing by the side of the road. She pulled the buggy to a stop and opened the carriage door. "A bit cold to be out here, no?"

Mamm patted something inside the bib of her apron and walked around to the passenger's side of the buggy without saying a word. Choosing not to give her mother any cause to begin a debate, Hannah slid the book under the seat of the carriage.

Mamm climbed in and wrapped her shawl more tightly around herself. "I need to ask you a question."

Hannah clicked her tongue, and the horse trudged forward. "*Was?*"

"Something's been weighing on my mind. I dreamed about it last week, and, well, Hannah, have you had a woman's time since the incident?"

Hannah's throat constricted. She didn't want to think about this, not ever, but especially not today. She shook her head. "But Mary hasn't had one since her accident. Dr. Greenfield said trauma can do that to a female."

Reaching into her bib, *Mamm* pulled out a small, rectangular-shaped box. "Follow the instructions on the back of the box."

"What is that?"

She drew a deep breath. "It's a pregnancy test."

Hannah's eyes blurred with tears as she pulled into the driveway. "*Mamm,* no. I'm not...I'm not."

"It's been three months, child. It's time to find out."

Feeling alarm at the very idea, Hannah said nothing.

Daed stepped out of the house, looking troubled. He walked to the buggy and opened Hannah's door. They had her cornered. She had to comply in order to see Paul today, but if the test was positive, she couldn't face him. No wonder their eyes had lit up at her request to go to Gram's. It meant she wouldn't argue about taking the test.

Powerlessness churned in her. Even if the test came back positive, she couldn't break her word to Gram and not show up for the workday. Her parents had to be banking on that.

Hannah folded her arms over her waist, rebellion rearing its ugly head. She wanted to rail against them, make them admit how calculating they were being.

"This is ridiculous," Hannah spat, not caring that she was talking back. But the frightening thing was, their request wasn't ridiculous at all. As much as she wanted to deny that she might be expecting, her body was changing in ways she'd never experienced. Her chin tilted upward, and her shoulders stiffened.

Mamm held the box toward her. "Take it."

Hannah obeyed. "I'm not pregnant."

Her father held the door open and motioned for Hannah to exit the carriage. "Come on. Let's go for a walk." His voice was the gentle, loving one she remembered from childhood.

Holding the rectangular box in her hand, Hannah followed him up the hill to the same bench they'd gone to after her attack. The same angry and confused feelings washed over her. *Daed* sat on the bench and patted the spot beside him. She sat. He took her hand. "Hannah, you're my daughter. No matter what comes, I'll take care of you."

Oh, God, I don't want to be pregnant. Please.

She chafed at the prayer. Either she was pregnant or she wasn't. Moaning to God wasn't going to change that. Neither would ignoring the possibility. But she didn't want to know, not today. Not on her last day with Paul until spring.

She blinked, trying to clear her vision and read the instructions on the home pregnancy test. "I'll do it," she said through gritted teeth. "But I'm not staying to read the outcome."

Pulling back on the reins, Hannah made the horse move at a snail's pace, biding her time so she could control her trembling. When Gram's farm came into view, Hannah spotted Paul's truck parked in the driveway.

She tugged at the right rein, pulling in behind it. Paul stepped outside before he could possibly have heard the buggy. He waved. His face beamed.

Inside her, a roar of determination exploded. She wasn't going to sink into a heap, not today. When she returned home, she was certain she would discover that the test proved she wasn't pregnant.

As she pulled the buggy closer to the barn, Paul fell in step beside it. Once inside, she pulled the reins and yanked the brake. Paul opened the buggy door and held out his hand. "I was getting worried that you couldn't get away."

She grabbed the book from under the seat and took his hand. "The Eshes' cows got out."

As soon as her feet landed on the ground, Paul engulfed her in a hug. "You're shaking." He released her, compassion in his eyes. "Go in and warm up. I'll tend to the horse. Maybe we'll get some time to talk alone if Gram takes a nap."

Hannah angled the book toward him. "A doctor at the hospital gave me this. I can't wait to show it to you."

Paul chuckled. "You and your love of science books."

She looked through the open barn door, studying the gray sky. "The air smells of snow, no?"

Paul loosened the leads on the horse from the buggy. "Hard to believe it'd snow this early in the season, but there's a chance of it today." He motioned toward the house. "Go on."

In spite of wanting to get out of the cold and into a warm house as quickly as possible, Hannah had no energy for hurrying across the yard.

She opened the back door to let herself in as she always did. Gram stood at the kitchen stove, stirring a pot of something. From the many wonderful aromas, Hannah could tell Gram had already begun cooking for tomorrow's feast.

"Hannah." Gram tapped the wooden spoon on the side of the pan, freeing it of dripping oatmeal before laying it on a small plate.

Hannah laid the anatomy book on the oak table, crossed the kitchen, and wrapped Gram in a hug. Hannah's arms hadn't felt this full in a long time. She'd missed Gram so badly—not as much as she'd missed Paul, but the emptiness had been painful.

Paul had always been so tied into Hannah's feelings about coming to Gram's that Hannah hadn't realized how much she loved this woman. Even in the long winters, when Paul couldn't visit very often, Hannah came to Gram's with the expectation of receiving and passing letters. But now, as she and Gram stood locked in an embrace that erased months of separation, Hannah realized her love for Gram stood on its own, regardless of Paul.

"You shake like a leaf, my girl." Gram released her. "Paul has built you a roaring fire, and I have fresh coffee."

Hannah turned toward the large stone fireplace. "No coffee for me, Gram, but thanks." The living room glowed in shifting amber and tawny colors from the reflection of dancing flames, dispelling the shadowy fears that made her shake. She loved a blazing fire in an open hearth. It warmed a home in so many more ways than a gas furnace, kerosene heater, or wood stove. Walking toward the dancing blaze, she remembered years of work, games, and bonding with Paul and Gram that had taken place in this very room.

Soon they'd begin a life together, and nothing would separate them. Perhaps after she and Paul married, they could build a small home right on this property. That way she could always be here for Gram.

Hearing a board creak, she turned. Her breath caught in her throat.

Paul.

With his shoulder against the doorframe, he smiled, looking relaxed and confident. She didn't know how long he'd been standing there while she reminisced over their past and dreamed of their future. As they stood across the room staring at each other, dreams of their future grew within her. A warm home, children, aromas of upcoming feasts, and love so strong it could give a backbone to a jellyfish—that was their future.

He held a steaming mug toward her. "Gram said you're not drinking coffee this morning."

"Dr. Greenfield, the man who gave me the book I brought, said I'm too young to be drinking coffee."

"Oh." Paul shrugged, taking a sip of the steaming drink. "I think if he knew how hard you always work and how good a cup of coffee is on cold mornings, he'd change his tune." He rubbed his chin. "There were bricks in the floorboard of the buggy. Am I missing something?"

Hannah untied her winter coat and slipped it off. "I thought you had Old Order Mennonite in your blood. How can ya not know what warming bricks are?" As she waltzed into the kitchen, Hannah playfully pushed against his shoulder.

Gram pulled a few green apples from the cupboard. "She's got a point, Paul."

Paul shook his head. "Any Old Order Mennonite in my blood is so far up the line it would take a genealogist to find the connection."

"The bricks hold heat and help keep the feet warm. Matthew put the bricks in the buggy when he hitched the horse for me." Hannah set a kettle of water on the stove. "Gram, you got a list of what all we're cooking today?"

Gram pulled a long, thin piece of paper from her apron pocket.

"Matthew?" Paul grumbled. "How come he fits into every conversation lately?"

Hannah took the list and read over it. "I didn't realize he had. Gram, is this a three or a five beside the butternut squash pies?"

Gram set a sack of flour on the table. "Five. Hazel, Paul's mom, is having extra family in for Thanksgiving. And the Millers too." Gram turned to stir a pot of broth on the stove. "I'm sure Paul's told you about the Millers. He and Dorcas are pretty close."

Hannah looked to Paul, and he rolled his eyes. "The Millers are close with my parents. Dorcas is one of their daughters."

The odd fluttery feeling around Hannah's heart returned but something else too. A burning sensation like resentment rose. It wasn't that he was friends with some girl that bothered her. What irked her was the realization that she never got to see him in his day-to-day life—while Dorcas did.

23

Paul flipped through the pages of the anatomy book Hannah had brought, not noticing much of anything but the long list of phone numbers the doctor had written on the inside cover. It seemed a bit odd, but the doctor must have figured the book was the best place to write numbers that Hannah would need if she ever had to make a call on Mary's behalf. He heard Hannah creeping down the steps. He closed the book. If his grandmother took that nap she'd agreed to, he and Hannah would have a couple of hours to themselves. Hannah tiptoed into the kitchen.

Paul stood. "Is she sleeping?"

Hannah moved to the stove to check on a pecan pie. "Close. She wanted to hear all about Luke and Mary's accident and recuperation. We talked for a long time before she felt sleepy."

He passed her a set of potholders. "Hannah, about Gram's remark. Dorcas is a friend of the family because her mother and my mother are best friends. End of story."

Placing the pie onto the cooling tray, Hannah's brown eyes gazed deeply into his. "I never thought otherwise. The girls at your campus have made me a bit jittery over the years but"—she grabbed cold cuts out of the refrigerator—"that's to be expected, I suppose." She opened a loaf of bread and began making two sandwiches.

Paul opened the game cabinet and pulled out Scrabble. He loved playing board games with her more than anything else...except the kisses they'd shared a week ago. That was amazing, and he wouldn't mind a repeat performance. But during games they talked about bits and pieces of everything until their connection was tighter than before and the bond between them had a sweetness that he craved when they weren't together.

He hated to admit it, but his need for long conversations was stronger than Hannah's. From what he understood, the desire for long, open talks didn't fit the household Hannah had been brought up in. Whether because of her upbringing or not, Hannah had a quiet restraint that buried life's events rather than shared them. Each time they got together, he had to patiently draw her out until she was sharing all the goings-on in her life and thoughts. An afternoon of talking heart to heart with her strengthened him for months.

She passed him a plate with a sandwich and a bowl of sliced bananas and strawberries. She set a can of pressurized whipped cream on the kitchen table near the Scrabble board. He squirted some fluffy cream onto his fruit. While lining up two letters, he briefly wondered if such a short word was allowed, but he decided it didn't matter since they played by their own rules anyway.

She frowned. "Yo?"

He took a bite of strawberries and whipped cream. After swallowing he answered, "It's a word." He leaned over to look at the numbers on the bottoms of the square wooden pieces. "Worth five points."

Her eyes danced with amusement. "Why, Paul Waddell. What's next? YoMama?"

Paul laughed. "That's not one word, and where did *you* hear such a saying?"

"At yohospital on yoTV." She looked at the seven letters he'd doled out to her. She sighed. "Are you rigging the game again?"

"Hannah," he chided.

She moved the letters around, frowning at them. "Yeah, I know, I know, you don't need to rig it to lose; you can lose all by yourself."

Paul burst into laughter. "I think you said that wrong."

Hannah cocked an eyebrow. "I think I said it perfectly right for the very first time, no?" She shook her head. "Now, let's see, H, E, E, A, E, A, P. What are the chances of me getting this many vowels on the first deal?"

"Obviously pretty good, or else you're just lucky."

She placed an A below the Y and her H after the A. "That's nine points, genius."

"That's not a word."

"*Yah.* It's a fine word."

He shook his head. "That's zero points for you, dear woman."

"You mean *liewe Fraa.*"

"Excuse me?"

" 'Dear woman' in Pennsylvania Dutch is *liewe Fraa.* Of course *Fraa* also means 'wife,' but..."

"Ah, so *yah* is a Pennsylvania Dutch word. But you pronounce it 'jah.' "

"If you'll cooperate, I'll start saying *yah.*"

"Oh, I see, my *liewe Fraa.*"

"Ya, liewe Dummkopp Buhnesupp."

"Hey, I heard the word *dumb* in that phrase."

Hannah covered her mouth, laughter shining bright in her eyes. "It doesn't have to mean 'dumb.' It could mean 'blockhead' or 'dunce.' "

He tried to glare at her, but her eyes, holding such joy, made even mock anger impossible. "I have no idea why I think I can win at this game. So, what did the other word you said mean?"

"You mean *Buhnesupp*?"

"That'd be the one."

"Bean soup."

"So you called me your dear dumb bean soup?" He fought to keep a straight face while watching her laugh so hard she covered her face. He studied his letters, trying to think of something that might make her laugh even harder. He placed two O's after her *yah* word.

She frowned. "Yahoo?"

"It's a search engine, e-mail, chat room. Yahoo covers all sorts of things on the Internet."

She patted his hand condescendingly. "The Internet. Didn't we decide that's your make-believe friend that you say carries answers for research, mails letters with no paper, and can send pictures without film?"

He removed his hand from under hers and patted her hand in the same manner. "You're gonna have to trust me on this one."

"I know it's a word. I think you yelled it out into the evening sky about a week ago, no?"

He was surprised she brought up the kisses, even in a roundabout way. He was beginning to realize this girl had a lot of surprises in her.

Paul leaned forward. "I don't remember actually yelling…or even whispering it. But if you could oblige me again, I'll be glad to oblige you and shout *yahoo.*"

Her cheeks turned a beautiful shade of pink. She lifted the pressurized can of whipped cream.

He chuckled. "First you threaten to pelt me with eggs and now with whipped cream. You may tease, but I know you won't follow—"

Cold whipped cream smacked him in the face. He gasped and reached across the table for her. She leaped up and ran out the back door. He grabbed the can and pursued her.

She bounded down the steps and across the side yard. When she turned, he saw surprise reflected on her face. "Snow!" She held her hands toward the skies as dainty white flakes drifted down.

"Whipped cream," Paul retorted. He took off after her.

She screamed and ran. He caught her around the waist from behind.

She laughed and squealed at the same time. Paul's heart thumped against his chest. They were made for each other. No doubt. "Apologize, Hannah."

She nodded. "Okay. Okay."

With her back against his chest, he lifted her off her feet and nuzzled her neck before planting a kiss.

"Paul, please." She squirmed against him.

He let her go, shook the can of whipped cream, and held the nozzle toward her. "Say it."

Her smile faded. She lowered her head while smoothing her skirts with the palms of her hands. Her demeanor was suddenly total meekness.

"Mock submissiveness is never a good thing, not for me." He grabbed her wrist.

Her face radiated innocence. "But I'm not mocking. I'm serious." She took a deep breath. *"Du kannscht net verschteh, Sitzschtupp Bobbeli."* She lifted her head, looking completely repentant.

Paul lowered the can, studying her. She meant her words, whatever they were. He passed her the can. "You win."

"Dankes." She curtsied.

"So, what did you say?"

She broke into laughter, squirted him with whipped cream, and took off running.

In less than ten seconds he grabbed her arm and stole the whipped cream. But he didn't dare squirt her. She didn't have a change of clothes here. "I can't believe I fell for that. You've become tricky since I left, no?" He used his best Amish accent.

She slipped on the snow and fell to her knees laughing.

He helped her stand, pulling her against him. "What did you say to me, Hannah Lapp?"

She gazed boldly into his eyes, once again surprising him. "I said, 'You can't understand, you living-room baby.' "

"You called me a living-room baby? And I thought you said, 'Forgive me.' No fair."

She smiled, a flame of desire shining in her eyes.

"Is that a common insult among the Amish?"

She grinned and raised one eyebrow up and down quickly. "I just made it up, because it fits."

Paul laughed. "Thanks."

He wrapped his arms around her, watching snow fall on her face. Slowly he bent and brushed her lips with a kiss. "You're incredible, Hannah. Every time I get to spend a smidgen of time with you, I'm reminded all over again how amazing you are." He coddled her face, gazing into her soul.

Her eyes grew distant. "I'd die without you, Paul."

He pulled her closer. "I feel the same way about you."

She ran her fingers behind his head, pulling his face to hers. Snow swirled around them as memories of this moment forged in his brain. They kissed until steam rose from their faces and formed a corona of vapor. This was the only woman for him. He'd never forget the joys of today—even when he was so sick of school he didn't think he could show up for class one more time.

They could make this work, whether they lived in Owl's Perch or Maryland. All they needed was each other and a chance. His lips moved over the cool skin of her cheeks, feeling the dampness from a few melted snowflakes.

Leaning back enough to look her in the eyes, Paul cradled a loose strand of wavy hair in his palm. "I didn't know your hair was this..."

She cocked an eyebrow. "*Uncontrollable* is the word you're searching for, and it's a hassle to keep confined."

Paul wound the soft curls around his finger. "Like the girl it belongs to?"

She shrugged, lowering her gaze, but not before Paul saw defiance spark in her eyes. She was an oxymoron in so many ways: yielding but defiant, caring but detached, belonging with him and yet...not. Sometimes, when the night was long and quiet, he worried that her undeniable beauty and deep naiveté would pull her into life with one of the young men in her community, leaving him empty ever after.

"Hannah." He released her hair and put his hands on her shoulders, looking her straight in the eye. "Be careful while I'm gone. There will be no end to the number of men wanting you." He ran his palms down her arms and clutched her hands. "Like this Matthew guy who keeps popping up everywhere you are."

She shook her head. "It's not like that with Matthew."

Paul squeezed her hands and forced a smile. He couldn't imagine any man not being drawn to her. "I trust your heart. That's not the problem. It's just...I'd go crazy if someone came between us. You need to be careful with the Matthews of your world. They hang around waiting for..." Paul drew her hands to his lips. By the look in her eyes, he could tell he was confusing her. "I don't want any part of you shared with someone else, not your heart, your dreams, or...your lips."

"Ach, Du bischt hatt."

Paul chuckled. "I know I've pushed too far when you fall into speaking your native tongue at me in frustration. I just want to shield you...us. And wisdom is the best protection against mistakes." He cocked his head, trying to read what she was thinking.

He saw deep pain reflected in her eyes, but why? They were clearing the air, making sure she understood the ways of men, preparing her for what was sure to come when she turned eighteen, confined in a way of life that pushed, like no other, for single people to find a mate quickly and among their own people. And he'd be months from returning to her.

He leaned to brush her lips with his, but she turned her head. "Tell me you understand what I'm saying."

"I understand." She cleared her throat. "You said you'll have nothing to do with me if I get tricked into sharing so much as a kiss with someone."

He kissed her forehead, ready to drop this subject before he ruined their time together. "Yeah, that about sums it up." He gave the line his best comedic voice.

She stiffened and pulled from his embrace, searching the horizon in every direction.

Paul followed her gaze. "What?"

Rubbing the back of her neck, she shook her head. "I...got the feeling we were being watched."

Concern ran hot through Paul. He looked across the vast fields. Gram's farm sat so far off from the main road in front of it and the dirt road behind it that it would be nearly impossible for anyone to see them. The only visible building was Luke's new harness shop, but no one was there today. He hoped. He studied the shop off in the distance. "It'd be hard for anyone to see through the swirling snow. But let's go inside. I need time to win this game of Scrabble, *ya*?"

Hannah searched the fields as she walked. "*Ya*."

Walking close behind her, with his hands on her shoulders, Paul gave her time to work through her thoughts and feelings. She'd been quite emotional since they'd become engaged. But he couldn't blame her. They were in a difficult position with all the time apart and the unknowns concerning how her family would take the news. He'd decided years ago, back when they were only friends, that he needed to do what he could to free her of the rigid repression by always giving her space to think and feel from deep within her soul. Hannah's becoming emotional so easily now was startling. Then again, a woman who had a tenacity for life like his Hannah had to feel intensely about many things. He was just glad she felt so strongly about him.

They climbed the short flight of steps leading to Gram's porch. When

Hannah took a deep breath and the muscles under his palms relaxed, he decided it was time to try to bring her some laughter. But how? They crossed the covered veranda, Paul right behind her with his hands still on her shoulders.

Yahoo.

That was it. Paul squeezed her shoulder, then spun out the porch door and onto the snowy steps. "Yahooooooo." He whispered it softly to the white flurried heavens.

He felt Hannah's boot on his backside. She pushed. With great theatrics, he stumbled down the few steps and landed on his knees. "Yahoo?"

She rolled her eyes and shook her head, but laughter erupted.

He sucked in a deep breath, as if he were about to scream at the top of his lungs. He saw Gram behind Hannah one second before the old woman called his name. He exhaled, pretending to choke. Hannah chortled.

Gram tapped her cane on the wooden porch. "Paul Waddell, what are you doing?"

He stood and bowed. "I'm sharing my great joy with the heavens, Gram."

"Well, stop it and get inside." She turned and, with her therapeutic shoes and walking stick, clunked her way into the kitchen.

Hannah was still snickering when she turned to follow Gram. Paul bolted up the steps, wrapped his fingers about Hannah's waist, and whispered against her neck, "Yahoo."

Hannah burst into giggles as they entered the kitchen. Paul moved to the counter and leaned against it. He shrugged innocently at Gram and winked at Hannah. Hannah bit her bottom lip and dipped her head.

Paul pulled out a straight-backed chair and turned it around, straddling it. "Gram, did you tell Hannah what we've discussed for my Christmas present this year?"

His grandmother took a glass from the cabinet and filled it with tap water. "I've agreed to give him the gift of talking to you. You'll come here the day after Christmas. Paul will be with his family in Florida, but I'll be home. I'll have a number where you can call him, and you two can talk for hours." She scrunched her face. "I hope I'm doing the right thing here. But I never promised not to allow phone calls, only letters."

Hannah's eyes narrowed, but she didn't ask who Gram had promised not to allow letters. Right then, Paul knew Hannah understood more than she voiced to him.

She drew Gram into an embrace. "A long conversation would be a wonderful Christmas present, Gram. Thank you."

He gave a nod toward the Scrabble board. "We have a game to finish."

Placing O-G-L-E after one of the O's in YAHOO, Paul straightened his shoulders in triumph. "If I had another G, I could do GOOGLE."

Hannah wagged her finger at him. "You know, these make-believe friends have got to go."

Paul shrugged. "We'll never know who won if we each keep using words and phrases the other one can't verify as real."

Hannah looked up at him through her lashes. "Winning the game isn't the point, is it?"

Paul winked and shook his head.

He followed Hannah's buggy in his truck, staying some thirty feet behind her. He wasn't sure if Hannah's request for him to follow her was because of the maniac who'd run her off the road in his car or because she still thought someone was watching them. No doubt a buggy wasn't much protection against weather or mean people. But it was better than her being on foot. After the car incident, he didn't want her walking back and forth to Gram's ever again.

When they arrived at the last bend in the road before her house, he stopped the truck and watched her buggy disappear into a fog of white haze. Her driveway was only a few feet ahead of her.

What a fantastic day they'd had. He said a quick prayer over her and put the truck in reverse.

By the time he returned, Gram's car was packed, and she was ready to go to Maryland.

24

As Hannah pulled the buggy into the driveway, optimistic energy bounded through her. Paul was amazing, and by the end of May he'd be living just a mile from her home. She hopped out of the buggy and flung open the barn doors. If she'd ever doubted it before, she knew now that she could never tell Paul her secret. He couldn't handle it.

Tugging at the harness, she led the horse into the barn. She would return it to Matthew tomorrow. As she unhitched the buggy, movement near her home caught her eye. She glanced up and saw her parents walking up the driveway toward her. If they were both coming to see her…

Her heart screamed in pain.

She looked down and continued to loosen the leather bindings, her hands trembling. In an attempt to calm herself, she began singing a song she'd learned in church. *"Herr Jesu Christ, er führt mich."*

"Hannah." Her father's voice faltered.

Without looking up, she sang the same lyrics, louder and in English. "Lord Jesus Christ, He leads me. He leads me." She clung desperately to the hope that she wasn't pregnant, that she and Paul could marry and raise children, and—

"You must listen to us, child," her father said over her singing. He placed his hand on hers.

She jerked away from him and turned to face him squarely. "No. Do you hear me? I said no!"

He nodded. "It is what it is, Hannah. We will take care of you." His shoulders slumped, and he looked old and weak. "But you must go to the bishop right away and tell him you are with child and how it happened."

"No!" She stomped her foot. "I won't. You can't make me."

Grasping his suspenders, her father drew a deep breath. "This is hard. I know it is, Hannah. But from our best figuring, you have until the middle of May before the baby will be born. You'll adjust by then."

Confusing thoughts screamed at her to run. *May? Paul's coming to Owl's Perch to live starting in mid-May.*

Could she keep this a secret from him if she were still pregnant and he was living a mile down the road?

"Hannah?" Her mother's shaky voice interrupted her thoughts.

Hannah lifted her chin. "I'll not go to the bishop."

Her father's demeanor changed from one of compassion to one of fury. "I am still your father, and you'll do as I say."

"Then you do as you say and tell him yourself." Hannah couldn't believe the defiance that rose within her.

Her father's face drained of all emotion. "I'll not. We've waited too long for me to be the one who tells him. He'll accuse me of hiding your sins for you, and then our whole house will pay for the secret that's been kept." *Daed* began pacing. "I should have never let you go back and forth to Mrs. Waddell's. Then this would never have happened." He stopped pacing and turned to her. "I forbid you and your sister to go ever again."

"What?" Disbelief churned within her, making her feel too powerless to even breathe.

"I'll not take a black eye in our church over this, Hannah. You will go to the bishop with this, or you will not be welcomed back under my roof." He turned and walked out of the barn.

Hannah's mother stood near the barn entrance, her eyes filled with sadness. "This is difficult. Believe me, I understand."

Hannah snatched a harness off the barn wall, put it on Matthew's horse, and mounted it bareback. "You understand nothing!" Hannah spurred the horse and flew past her mother. Unsure where she was heading,

Hannah urged the horse to go faster and faster, hoping to somehow outrun the shroud of reality that chased her.

Pregnant.

Through the powdery dusting of snow, Hannah galloped through field after field. Crying too hard to care where she was going, she released the reins and allowed the horse to choose its own path. Her mind tortured her with thousands of questions as horrid thoughts of what might happen to her and Paul played out before her. How could she possibly keep this pregnancy concealed from him?

Purplish evening skies loomed overhead by the time the horse stopped. Wiping the tears from her face, she glanced about the property. The poor creature had gone home and taken her with him. She slid off the weary animal and removed its harness. It ambled into the barn.

Frantic for time alone, she looked around for somewhere she might hide. Through blurry eyes she spotted Matthew's buggy workshop a thousand feet away from any other building on Esh property.

She ran to it, entered through the narrow back door, and climbed the wooden ladder to the storage loft. She stumbled to the far corner. Huddling behind crates and broken buggy pieces, she sobbed.

It couldn't be true; it just couldn't.

Her father had said he'd take care of her, but she knew him. When her stomach started rising like bread dough, he wouldn't even be able to look her in the eyes. As horrid and lonely as that would feel, it didn't begin to compare to what would happen if Paul discovered she was carrying a child that belonged to someone else. She buried her face in her apron and cried until she could cry no more.

Her head throbbing, she closed her eyes. She imagined herself existing in another place and time, before the rape. If only she could find her way back there.

"Hannah!" In the distance a young man's voice called to her.

She jolted, realizing she'd fallen asleep. She rose, her joints aching and sore. As she peeked through the attic vent, she saw two people with lanterns plodding through the snow, calling for her.

Oh no.

Closing her eyes and wishing she could disappear, Hannah waited. When she opened her eyes, the soft glow of lanterns still dotted the otherwise dark fields. No amount of wishing altered her reality.

It had to be almost daylight. No wonder her father had sent people to look for her. As she worked her way through the dark room toward the ladder, beams of light came through the opening, followed by the top of an Amish man's black hat.

Hannah stood stock still.

The black hat tilted back, and she saw Jacob Yoder. "Hannah, do you have any idea how many people are searching for you? What are you doing up there?"

"I…I fell asleep."

He set the kerosene lamp on the floor, but he didn't climb the ladder any higher. "Well, I figured you had to be somewhere out of the cold. Since midnight a group of men have been checking every building we could think of." He picked up the lantern. "You best come on."

As she climbed down the wooden ladder, she tried to brace herself for the day ahead.

By the time she placed her feet on the floor, Jacob was sitting on a wooden crate. "What's going on with you, Hannah?"

She shook her head. "I just needed time alone to think and…"

"Yeah, you fell asleep. I heard." He shook his head, his eyes scanning her from head to toe. "You stayed out all night, and the whole community knows it. Don't you realize what that will do to your reputation? I mean, men like a little spunk, Hannah Lapp, but you sure know how to push every limit that's been set."

"I don't need your approval, Jacob."

He stood there with his arms folded, staring at her. "Sarah's right. Tornadoes are more predictable than you." He nodded toward the door. "We need to let others know you're safe."

Jacob walked to her and held out the lantern. "I wouldn't want to be in your position when you face your father. Rumors about you and last night are already running wild."

The shed door opened, and Matthew's younger brothers stepped inside, each carrying a lantern. David and Peter gawked at her and then looked at each other.

David lowered his lantern. "People are looking for you, Hannah." His attention shifted to Jacob. "Your *Mamm* and *Daed* said you'd been out since midnight and if we spotted you to say it's time you came on home."

Jacob opened his mouth to speak, but no words came out.

"He just found me... I came in here last night and fell asleep... and..." Hannah's words trailed off. She knew how children of David's and Peter's ages liked to tell stories at school, the more scandalous the better.

David rolled his eyes. "Save it for the bishop and your father..."

Hannah felt sick at how powerless she was to stop the tongue wagging that was about to bury her alive. Without any doubt, word would quickly spread about her being found with Jacob. And Sarah would hate her forever after this.

Suddenly Mary came to mind.

Hannah turned to Jacob. "Does Mary know I'm missing?"

"She thinks you spent the night at your house."

"I've got to get back to Mary. Tell the others you found me."

The ties to her *Kapp* blew in the wind, slapping her in the face as she scurried across the fields. She pulled out the pins that held her prayer bonnet in place, jerked it off, and shoved it into the pocket of her apron. She had no intention of ever praying again, so she would never need it.

25

Lying in bed, staring at the ceiling through the darkness, Hannah moved her hand to her slightly protruding stomach. A tiny ball formed under the warmth of her palm, as if the child inside were begging for a bit of love from her.

Since Thanksgiving Day and right on through Christmas and New Year's, revolting reports had circulated about Hannah, saying that she'd tried to win Matthew away from Elle and that she was out all night with Jacob. But worse were the rumors that Hannah had been a gadabout while staying at the hospital and had been seen in the arms of a doctor.

In his arms. How ridiculous.

Others whispered about some English man whose identity no one knew, but he had picked her up in a horse and buggy after midnight. But none of the rumors mentioned that she was with child. Thankfully that secret had been kept between her and her parents.

After a while, the rumors died down, though Hannah was certain that mistrust toward her remained locked in people's minds.

Because Hannah couldn't ask anyone without it sounding wrong, she didn't know how Elle and Matthew were faring. Worst of all, Christmas had come and gone without any contact with Paul. Since she'd been denied the right to return to his grandmother's house, she wasn't able to call Paul the day after Christmas. Torture over what Paul must be thinking about her absence was constant.

She'd tried to use the Yoders' phone to call him, aching to hear his voice telling her about his plans for their future. But John Yoder had put a padlock on the door of the phone shanty. He'd even boarded up the glass so no one could break in. Hannah didn't ask why. She figured either her father had requested that or John had heard the rumors about her and had taken it upon himself.

Hopes of a future with Paul were about all that kept her tied to this place—that and Mary. Throughout the day ideas of going to Ohio and finding the aunt she'd never met floated in and out of her daydreams. Zabeth would understand the misery of being looked down on by everyone.

Aside from the fantasies, Hannah lived in a fog of ache.

She pulled the covers off, careful not to wake Mary, who was sleeping beside her. Slowly she sat upright. Trying to shake the ever-tightening trapped feeling, Hannah stood and tucked the covers around Mary. At least Mary was none the wiser about her pregnancy. But how much longer could Hannah keep it a secret? Her stomach was growing at a remarkable rate these days.

With Mary almost recovered, their sabbatical from church gatherings was drawing to a close. Starting the first church Sunday of March, they were both to return. That meant she and Mary had a little more than two weeks to find the strength to return to the meetings.

Hannah trudged into the bathroom to change.

Paul was never far from her mind. She thought she'd seen him drive by one Monday afternoon in early January as she and Becky Yoder hung nearly frozen laundry on the line. If Hannah hadn't been pregnant, she'd have run to the truck, and if Paul really was inside it, she would have climbed into the passenger seat and never returned to Owl's Perch. Ever.

Considering the magnitude of the sins she was supposed to have committed, she found it surprising that the Yoders allowed her to stay with Mary. Undoubtedly she was being allowed to remain because Mary wanted her near, and she knew nothing of the night Hannah had disappeared into Matthew's workshop or of the rumors surrounding Hannah—except for the bits Sarah had shared.

Even with minimal contact, it was clear to Hannah that these days the community tolerated her, nothing more. She could see it in the faces and hear it in the tones of those who came to visit Mary.

The fact that she refused to wear a prayer *Kapp* only strengthened the force of the gossip. She couldn't say she didn't care about the ugliness going around about her. The gossip cut her to the quick. But that wasn't enough to force her to wear her *Kapp*. She pulled her hair into a bun and tried to secure it with hairpins.

On the positive side, Mary was doing remarkably well lately. The home-health provider had come to visit Mary on two occasions. But Hannah didn't need the nurse's confirmation to know Mary was gaining strength daily. A testament to the power of love and community support, Hannah figured.

She pinned her apron over her baggy dress, thankful the Amish garb hid her figure well, then slid her feet into the black stockings. Every visit her parents made to Mary's, they managed to needle Hannah behind Mary's back. They wanted Hannah to tell the bishop about her pregnancy before he found out on his own.

Over and over Hannah refused. Going to the bishop meant Paul would find out. Besides, that was too close to confessing, and Hannah had no sin to confess, except the hatred in her heart for the man who had done this to her.

But neither anger nor denial of what was happening carried any answers for her. Wriggling one foot and then the other into her boots, Hannah allowed thoughts to ramble around inside her head. What was she going to do with the baby once it was born?

Keeping it wasn't one of her choices; neither was giving it to anyone who lived in Owl's Perch, Amish or English. Elle came to mind, specifically the things she'd said about her guardians, Abigail and Hezekiah Zook. According to Elle, Abigail was young enough to be a new mother, but she was barren. Surely they'd cherish a newborn. They sounded balanced and lenient within the Old Ways. Abigail and Hezekiah were probably the best choice she could make even if she had a thousand couples to consider. And if she handled this with a little skill, no one would be the wiser concerning where the baby came from.

The baby was due in the middle of May. By the time Paul graduated and spent a few days at home, he'd probably be in Owl's Perch before June first. If she hadn't had the baby by the time he returned, she might need to spend a few weeks with the Zooks. Paul wouldn't be able to catch a glimpse of her in passing if she were there. Once the baby was no longer in her life, she intended to marry Paul, with or without her father's blessing. The community had nothing left for her but stoic politeness. Their behavior would remain that way unless she repented and joined the church. That wasn't going to happen. So she'd do just as well to leave and start fresh with Paul.

Hannah couldn't imagine moving back home anyway. Luke still believed the accident was her fault. Sarah had spread rumors all over the county, reaching far beyond their district.

Hannah stuck another hairpin into her bun. It was time to dry her eyes for the day.

A creak of floorboards let her know Mary was stirring. Hannah jumped up and rinsed her face. It was daylight, past time to be in control of her emotions.

Yesterday Luke had thrust three letters at her when Mary wasn't looking. To her deep disappointment, none were from Paul. The notes had come to her through the mail delivery at her parents' house. They were from various Amish families within the community, begging her to repent and join the faith. All of Owl's Perch seemed to think she was some kind of harlot. And her father wanted her to confess her pregnancy to them?

No way. Legal adulthood was hers the ninth of March. But she couldn't leave then. The baby wouldn't be born until mid-May, and then she'd be free to go to Paul.

"Hannah, *kumm uff.*" Mary's voice carried through the wooden door.

"I'm coming." Hannah splashed another handful of cool water on her face. Mary thought Hannah's sadness was due to the rumors Sarah had started. If only her problems were that small. Hannah plodded out of the bathroom and into the bedroom. "Sleep well?" She grabbed some hairpins and added them to her bun, trying to keep her hair under control.

"*Ya.* If we get all the laundry done early, we could take Luke a lunch at the shop." Mary's eyebrows jumped up and down conspiratorially.

Hannah had no desire to go to the harness shop, but she couldn't tell Mary that. She would continue to pretend she didn't mind and to hope Mary didn't notice. Hannah grabbed a basket of dirty clothes. "Oh, good, we get to do my favorite chore: laundry."

Mary laughed and grabbed her hand. "While you were in the bathroom, *Mammi* Annie came to tell us that my aunt called yesterday. The doctor thinks the babies will be born this week. So *Mamm* and *Daed* are making plans to take everyone but us to Ohio." Mary shrugged. "*Daed* says I can't go this time. He's afraid it'd be too much stress, but he says he'll make it up to me somehow. I like the sound of that." Mary gave Hannah a huge smile. "Why don't you come eat with the family today? It might be the last chance you get before their trip. After breakfast we'll collect their dirty clothes and get started."

Hannah crinkled her nose, trying to keep things lighthearted. "I'm not hungry. You go ahead, and I'll work on laundry." She hoped Mary didn't hear her growling stomach.

She hadn't sat at the Yoders' table in weeks, and there was no way she was going to start today. They didn't welcome her anymore. The love that once shone in Becky's eyes had faded and been replaced by skepticism. Luke seemed to have turned Mary's brothers Jacob and Gerald against

Hannah as well, although she didn't know exactly what he'd told them. None of the Yoders were ever rude, but the scorn in their eyes was more than she could bear. So time after time, when Mary asked her to eat with them, Hannah made excuses to stay in the *Daadi Haus* instead.

While Mary ate breakfast with her family, Hannah washed and wrung out three loads of laundry. While dunking a shirt into the rinse water again and again, she heard a rustling noise behind her that drew her attention. When she looked up, she saw Mary holding the three letters Hannah had received yesterday.

Concern flashed in Mary's eyes. "I found these when I was removing the sheets."

Hannah dunked the shirt again. "If I'd realized you were going to do sheets today—"

"Hannah, stop this. I'm not that weak girl of a few months ago. What's going on? I know you've been miserable lately." She shook the letters in Hannah's face. "Talk to me."

Hannah cleared her throat, trying to gain control over her emotions. No matter how badly she wanted to tell Mary, her friend simply wasn't capable of handling the whole ugly truth. But Hannah had to tell her something. "What do you want to know?"

"You could begin by telling me about this doctor you were caught with."

Hannah ran the shirt through the wringer. "I was with him in midday, having a conversation. Nothing more."

"And the *Englischer* the rumors say you've been seen running off with?"

She shook out the shirt and laid it in the pile to be hung out to dry. "One ride for five minutes. It was foolish, I know. I had on my nightgown while I was standing on the front porch waiting for Luke to come home. A...a friend came by with a fast-moving horse and buggy. I rode with him." Hannah grabbed a soapy dress that had been through the wringer and began dipping it into the rinse water.

"If it's all so innocent, let's set the record straight."

Hannah lowered the dress into the water, refusing to turn toward Mary. *If it's all innocent?* Hannah's heart sank. Did Mary believe the rumors too? "How do you suggest we do that?"

Mary ripped the letters in half. "For one thing, you need to be at church, showing them where your heart is by being faithful and upright. I may not be up to a full service yet, but I'm well enough to be left here alone while you're gone."

Hannah lifted the dress out of the water and dunked it again. "And why do you think I haven't set things straight already, Mary?"

"I…I'm not sure."

Hannah turned to face her. "The only reason a person wouldn't try to straighten out the gossip is if, buried under the lies, there was a truth that was more dreadful than any rumor." She wiped her hands on her apron, anger and bitterness rising to the surface so fast she couldn't stop them. "Put that in your pot of *if*s and let it stew for a while."

Mary took Hannah by the shoulders. Determination and love shone in her features. "I have no *if*s, Hannah. I'm strong enough to hear the truth. Are you strong enough to tell me?"

Hannah paused, considering what to do. Stepping around Mary, she walked to the laundry room door and closed it. "It's an awful nightmare, and there's no waking up from it. If I tell you, it'll be your nightmare too."

Mary's greenish blue eyes stared at Hannah, filled with earnestness. "I only pray that I may be as good to you in your trials as you've been to me. I promise you loyalty and silence, Hannah. I promise it even from Luke, if that's what you want."

A craving so severe it caught Hannah completely off guard gnawed at her insides. She was withering inside from keeping it all to herself. She motioned to the wringer. They turned it on, blocking out their voices if anyone came near the doorway. Then they sat on the floor in a far corner, and Hannah spoke the truth—the complete, hideous, unbelievable truth. For the first time since summer, the weight lifted off Hannah's shoulders as she told Mary of her deep love for Paul, her hopes, her fears, even her rape and pregnancy.

As the words poured forth, Hannah worried that Mary wouldn't understand, that she might even turn and walk away. She hungered for Mary to still love her. But no matter how she responded when it was all laid before her, Hannah felt relief. She had finally told someone.

As breakfast ended, Sarah poured the last drops of coffee in her *Daed's* cup. In spite of the unbearable irritability that grated her insides, she kept her movements controlled. To let her father see an emotion outside the few he could cope with would be a huge mistake, one her big sister had taught her to avoid. Sarah coughed, hiding the sounds of disgust that naturally spewed from her at the very thought of Hannah. Her sister had crossed too many lines of late—even being seen with Jacob after staying out all night. But Jacob discounted that rumor right to Sarah's face. He said he'd had nothing to do with Hannah, and if he got his way, he'd never have to see her again. Sarah wasn't sure what to think about Hannah's motives toward Jacob. But Sarah longed to believe Jacob, to believe that everything between him and her sister was as innocent as he had made it sound.

After returning the pot to the stove, Sarah put the bacon and scrapple back in the refrigerator. As she began removing the breakfast plates from the table, her family went on to the next phase of their day, leaving Sarah in the kitchen alone. Except for the two youngest children, only a few mumbled words had been spoken all morning. Awkward silence had become a staple over the last few months, growing worse with each passing week. Sarah had no clue why her family moped around wordlessly. But the dark mood threatened to drive her mad.

After slipping into winter attire, *Daed,* Luke, and Levi headed outside to continue the endless chores of owning a small dairy herd. Samuel had to go to school in a little while, but first he needed to gather firewood from the lean-to and move it to the back porch. Esther, who would soon turn thirteen, wasn't going to school today. It was her last year to attend, and *Daed* had decided she could miss a few days here and there in order to help make up for Hannah's absence.

Mamm gave Esther and four-year-old Rebecca a few quiet instructions as they made their way upstairs to begin preparing their home for Sunday's meeting. It'd take the better part of the week to get their home as shiny clean as *Daed* and *Mamm* wanted it for a worship day. The rotation that scheduled church to be held on their property once a year had circled back to them.

She chucked another log into the potbellied stove and set the pressing iron facedown on top of it before turning to wash the last of the breakfast dishes. She'd been weary and cross of late. Both sleep and peace had seemed impossible. For months, a recurring nightmare had chased her. The unseen image tracked her, wreaking terror at night. And its memory haunted her during the day.

As her thoughts meandered in every direction, Sarah continued moving through the kitchen chores. She put jars of garden-canned kale and whole-kernel corn on the counter before placing the kettle on the back of the wood stove. In the five months that Hannah had been living under Annie Yoder's roof as Mary's nursemaid, the Lapp household had learned to run quite smoothly without her.

Sarah went to the cupboard, where freshly canned deer meat was stored. Things were better than just running smoothly. In spite of Hannah being trained in some medical knowledge, she no longer held a place of great respect within the community. Actually, due to a few rumors, Hannah's lofty position had plummeted. Her sister being on the outs with *Daed, Mamm,* and Luke felt even better than Sarah had imagined it would. When a snicker erupted from Sarah, guilt rose. She didn't mean to feel so giddy about Hannah's misfortune.

But the idea of spending another quiet, clammed-up day inside the house stole her fleeting delight in the dethroning of her sister. Sarah grabbed two Mason jars filled with meat. Setting both jars on the counter, Sarah sighed. What difference did it make if Sarah had told the bishop about that night? Sarah had kept tons of secrets for Hannah.

But her sister had done plenty of good deeds toward her too. Hannah had been a shield for her hundreds of times, like when *Daed* caught her dawdling away precious work time as she daydreamed. Hannah had stepped in between *Daed* and Sarah regularly, making all kinds of excuses until he stormed off without taking Sarah to the woodshed.

No matter. It was Hannah's own fault that rumors were ripping through the community. If she hadn't been doing something wrong to begin with, Sarah would have had nothing to tell. And if Hannah hadn't been so deceitful as to make herself look better than she really was to everyone, including Jacob, Sarah wouldn't have had cause to put Hannah in her rightful place by telling people what she was really like.

But Sarah's thoughts often stole her sense of time. Was it possible that Hannah had only been gone a few minutes that night?

If Hannah was telling the truth about that...

Stark terror ran down Sarah's spine. If *Daed* ever found out that she was the one who'd told the bishop about that ride, he might beat her until she had no tomorrow.

Fresh hatred for Hannah rose within her.

26

Paul turned out the last of the lights in the tire store and set the security system. His new title of assistant manager came with longer hours and more responsibilities, but it also came with a much-appreciated raise. The February wind slapped against him, sliding down the nape of his neck and back as he curved his body to lock the double glass doors. The lock clicked into place, and he shook the door to verify it was bolted. He stood straight, pulling his jacket tighter and shoving his paycheck deeper into his coat pocket. Paul waited by the door, making sure each employee's car started on this cold winter night.

Across the lot, he saw Jack climbing into his 2000 Honda Accord. The man should have received the promotion Paul had gotten, and he would get the position when Paul left in May...if Jack could pull his life together by then. Jack was in the middle of a divorce, and the word *depression* didn't begin to describe what he was going through. Jack's situation made Paul's blood boil.

Jack was a good and decent man who worked hard in every avenue of life. He'd had good reasons to be suspicious of his wife's faithfulness long before the ugly truth became clear. While he worked two jobs to support his family, Melanie was running around on him. Paul didn't know why it had taken Jack so long to see it. Having been around Melanie some, Paul had considered her capable of every bit of the buzz that was going around about her. But Jack, the poor sap, had refused to believe anything but what his wife said. He'd been a fool and had ignored all the signs while hoping for the best until the truth could no longer be denied.

While Jack was getting help from a therapist, Paul stepped into the position of temporary assistant manager so the company wouldn't hire a permanent employee in Jack's place. Paul had been so upset about Jack's situation that he ended up venting to Dorcas about it. Of course he'd also talked to her about his hopes and plans of a life with Hannah. He couldn't help but talk about that since Dorcas was one of only three people who knew about her.

Dorcas couldn't stop talking about a guy she'd begun dating a few weeks ago. Paul hoped the four of them could enjoy spending some time together, maybe playing board games at Gram's. His grandmother's place was Hannah's best chance of getting to be part of a double date.

As the last employee pulled out of the lot, Paul trotted around the back of the building, heading toward his car. In three months he would be in Owl's Perch with Hannah. Man, he was looking forward to that. As he came closer to his truck, he recognized the red Ford Taurus parked beside it. The driver's-side door opened, and Dorcas climbed out.

She batted her eyes against the strong wind. "We need to talk."

He stood motionless. He couldn't imagine what would make her drive all the way from Maryland to talk rather than using a phone.

She ran her fingers back and forth over her chin. "A few hours ago my mom and I got back from visiting Jeanie, my mother's cousin who lives in Owl's Perch."

Paul's heart lurched. "Is something wrong?"

She held up an envelope. "This is a duplicate of a letter that was sent to Hannah."

He closed the distance between them. "Sent by whom?"

She shrugged. "It's not signed." Dorcas stroked the edge of the envelope. "But Jeanie got it from the person who wrote it."

Paul studied the envelope in her hand. It was addressed to Hannah, but the seal had been ripped open. It had a stamp on it but no postmark across it, as if after preparing to mail the letter, someone changed their mind—maybe had even snatched it back from the mailbox before the mailman had a chance to pick it up.

Dorcas tapped the envelope against the palm of her hand. "There are things in this letter you need to know about." She lowered her head. "I'm sorry."

Indignation ran through him. "What kind of things?"

Dorcas pointed to the passenger door of her car. "If you want to know all I've been told, get in."

Paul ducked into the car, slamming the door behind him. "Make it quick because I'm going there to check on her as soon as we're finished." He pounded his fists on the dashboard. "Regardless of her father's or anyone else's wishes."

Paul's old truck knocked along the back roads as he burned rubber getting to Owl's Perch. Forget studying, tomorrow's classes, and work. Him and all his plans, always putting Hannah second. He sighed. *Idiot.*

He raked his hands through his hair. The whole community was buzzing ugly things against Hannah because they'd shared a kiss. The poor girl.

No one had a right to say Hannah was a sinner and needed to repent. He sped down the road, fuming at the injustice of it all.

Matthew Esh. The name dug its way past his anger at Hannah's accusers. Was there something to all these rumors? Dorcas had said Matthew's name a dozen times in all the gossip. But surely the community wouldn't be angry with her and write letters of correction if being alone with Matthew was the only "misdeed" she was accused of. They wouldn't hold it against her to this degree even if she did stay out all night with him...or was it Jacob Yoder that she was supposed to have stayed out all night with? She might get some mean-looking frowns, even a few murmurs or cold shoulders, but not letters and the community wagging their tongues freely about her. Something more than Matthew…or Jacob…was going on.

Was it possible she'd gotten caught up in a relationship with that English guy at the hospital that Dorcas mentioned? The rumors said she had, and she'd acted weird the night he'd showed up.

"That's ridiculous!" Paul railed against himself, smacking the steering wheel with the palm of his hand. "Are you going to join in and accuse her?"

The rumors were based on lies. He had no doubts about his Hannah. The truck jolted as he hit a pothole.

Well, okay, he had a few doubts. He'd witnessed firsthand how friendly Hannah was with Matthew. No big surprise that half the rumors involved him. The other half involved some nameless English person and that doctor Hannah quoted from time to time. One or two of the rumors had Jacob Yoder's name attached to them. Dorcas said Jacob was one of Mary's brothers. Heat ran through his body.

She wasn't guilty. No way. He knew her. She was simply naive and didn't always think about how things might look.

Dorcas had told him that, according to her mother's cousin, Hannah was still living at the Yoders' *Daadi Haus* with Mary. He intended to knock on the door and insist he be allowed to talk to Hannah. He had to make sure she was okay.

She might even be willing to leave Owl's Perch and go with him. She would turn eighteen in a little over two weeks. They could hide out somewhere until then if need be.

If she wanted out, he'd get her out.

The letter Dorcas had shown him, which was a duplicate of one sent to Hannah, had quoted Scripture about dressing modestly and being honest. He growled. Ridiculous hyperbole. Hannah was no more capable of sneaking out to be with a man in her undergarments than Paul was of flying.

Let's see them send those letters when they don't know where you live, Hannah.

As Paul pulled into the Yoders' driveway, he noticed there were no lights on in the house. He drove farther into the driveway, stopping in front of the *Daadi Haus.* He saw a light on in the living room. Maybe Hannah and Mary were still awake.

Paul knocked on the door. He didn't care if the whole neighborhood heard him. He was tired of sneaking around as if he and Hannah were sinners.

A girl with greenish blue eyes and blond hair covered by a white prayer *Kapp* came to the door dressed in a flannel gown and housecoat. He assumed it was Mary, though he'd never met her, since she'd been asleep the day he came to her house for a visit with Hannah. "Mary?" he asked.

She nodded.

"I'm Paul Waddell. I need to speak to Hannah. Is she here?"

She nodded and opened the door. "Hannah went to bed with complaints of aches. She's asleep now, and I'd hate to wake her."

Physical pains brought on by the emotional weight of the rumors, Paul figured. "I'm not leaving until I speak with her, even if every member of this district learns that I'm here."

Mary tilted her head, considering his words. Finally a smile crossed her face. "I suppose I'll be the one in pain if I don't wake her. I'll be right back."

Paul paced, much as he'd done when he'd come to visit her in November. She'd been out that day, and by her own admission she'd been with Matthew.

Hannah came to the living room door, her long hair loosely pulled into a bun with wisps breaking free everywhere. She had a shawl wrapped over her day clothes, but she didn't have her *Kapp* on. She looked a bit addled, as if she'd been sound asleep.

Paul bolted to her, clasping his hands over hers. "Are you all right? I heard..."

She stared at him, but she didn't ask why he was here or suggest he hide his truck. He rubbed his head, feeling confused.

Mary came up behind Hannah and whispered something in her ear in Pennsylvania Dutch. She held Hannah's head covering out to her.

"Ich kann net." Hannah shook her head, refusing to take it.

Paul would have found Hannah's refusal to wear her prayer *Kapp* disturbing enough even without any rumors flying on the winds. Doubts concerning her began nibbling at him. All the women from his sect of Mennonites wore *Kapps.* Where was her submission to the ways they'd agreed on as right?

As he tried to decipher what the two were whispering about, he'd never felt so out of place. Mary said something about calling for a doctor. Hannah reacted angrily. Did Mary need a doctor? Surely Mary didn't think Hannah needed one just because she'd gone to bed achy.

Mary grabbed Hannah's coat and helped her put it on, still whispering. *"Grossmammi iss do. Du kannscht net im Haus schwetze."*

"Ya, gut." Hannah nodded.

Yes and *good*—that he understood.

Hannah fastened her coat. "Mary's grandmother has moved back into her bedroom upstairs. We need to find a quiet place outside to talk."

Without a word, Paul followed her out the door, up the hill, and past the barn. When they came to a huge oak, she stopped.

She played with the bark of the tree, barely turning to look at him. "I didn't expect to see you until May."

"Dorcas came to see me. She said you're being treated poorly, almost being shunned among your people. I came to see if you're okay."

Looking wearier than he could ever have imagined, she shrugged. "There are rumors and displeasure among the People. But any mention of shunning is absurd. That's not done lightly and never to an unbaptized member. There's some pressure, but I'm fine."

She didn't look fine. She looked miserable. Whatever else was going on, she didn't seem the least bit glad to see him. "Have we made a mistake, Hannah?"

She turned, mumbling something in Pennsylvania Dutch. Then she seemed to realize her lapse and repeated her words. "If you don't know, I can't tell you."

He studied her. She'd changed. In a thousand ways he couldn't even define. "Tell me what's going on, Hannah. I'm always gone, always trying to build a life for us. I don't understand what's happening."

She stepped away from him. "When you graduate, will you still want me?"

He jammed his hands into his pockets, feeling the letter in one and his paycheck in the other. "Yes, absolutely."

Clearing her throat, she lifted her chin and nodded. "Then I'll be here."

Paul clutched the letter in his hand, pulling it from his pocket. "But, Hannah, where have all these rumors come from? What's going on?"

She glanced at the paper in his hands, but she didn't ask about it. "I'm tired. That's all."

He stepped closer to her, trying to look her in the eye. "That answer doesn't address my question about the rumors. Were you out for a ride in your nightgown with some guy?"

She returned to playing with the bark on the tree. "I want to answer you, Paul, but you've got to hear me out. Okay?"

He shoved the letter back into his pocket. "All right."

She spoke without looking up from her fascination with the tree bark. "Almost every rumor you've heard has a piece of truth in it."

Doubts and questions came in on all sides. "Go on." He moved in closer until he was directly behind her as she faced the tree.

Hannah sidestepped, moving out into the open. "I did go for a ride in my nightgown. It was the night of Luke and Mary's accident. My family had gone to bed. I hadn't felt well for weeks and was restless. Luke and I had argued earlier that day. I wanted to talk to him as soon as he got home. So I waited on the porch in my gown. Matthew drove up with a new horse and buggy. When he offered me a ride, I took it. We were only gone for a few minutes."

Matthew Esh again. Paul simmered quietly.

She brushed wisps of curly hair from her face. "I've paid dearly for those five minutes, Paul."

"And is Matthew paying too?"

She shrugged. "As far as I know, we've kept his name out of that particular rumor mill."

Paul propped one hand against the tree and kicked at a patch of snow. "And the gossip about you and that doctor?"

Paul listened as she explained rumor after rumor. He was disappointed in his bride-to-be. She should have handled herself more carefully than to have been in the hayloft with Matthew. To Paul, the fact that the bishop caught them was beside the point. And there was no way she could justify staying out all night just because she was upset. The thing with the doctor didn't seem as inappropriate as the other issues. But the longer he listened, the angrier he became. Her carefully worded explanations were beginning to sound like fabricated stories.

The night he went to the hospital, he'd heard Matthew mockingly call her a liar, teasing her that he knew her better than anyone and that she lied really well but not well enough to trick him. Was she really a liar? According to what Dorcas said, even the church leaders thought she was being deceptive.

Had he allowed himself to be blind, like Jack? Paul was only in Owl's Perch sporadically, and even then he was confined to his world, waiting on her to come to him. Matthew had been with her the day Paul came to visit. Later that night Matthew had called her name, searching for her while she was secretly in Paul's arms. Matthew had warmed the bricks for Hannah's trip to Gram's, but he had no way of knowing Paul was waiting for her at the other end.

"You spent an entire night alone in Matthew's repair shop. And when you were found, Jacob Yoder was with you. But it's all perfectly innocent?"

"I fell asleep. When I woke up, Jacob had come into the shop looking for me." Tears rolled down her cheeks. "I'm telling you the truth, Paul."

Her crying addled him. "Okay, okay. But answer me this. Every piece of this puzzle is attached to one common thread." He paused, pity for her beginning to drain from him as indignation stirred. How many times had Melanie cried her way back into Jack's heart? "The common thread is you being too sick or too upset to go home. I understand why you were concerned about Luke not coming home the night of the accident. But why were you so upset that you ran to Matthew's repair shop? And what caused you to be so sick after I left that they burned your clothes and Sarah had to take your place at Gram's?"

She lowered her head. "You know enough about that day, Paul. There was the car…and…"

He grabbed her arm. "Hannah, what is it you're not telling me?"

She jerked against his hold. Determined to look into her eyes and finally understand, he pulled her toward him.

A firm, round belly pressed against him.

"No!" She placed a hand on his chest and pushed him away.

He held tight to her wrist, staring at her. As if in slow motion, he splayed his free hand and laid it on her stomach. It was as round and firm as if it held a basketball…or a baby.

His precious Hannah was pregnant.

Dear God, what a fool I've been.

A thousand thoughts ran through his mind within a few seconds. No wonder she'd been so evasive with him. She was carrying Matthew Esh's baby! Nothing but friends, indeed. But apparently he didn't want her and their child because Hannah had asked if he would still want her after graduation. Did she really expect him to raise another man's child as his own?

Great, racking sobs shook her body as she tried to pry his fingers off her stomach. "Paul, I-I can explain. I…"

He grabbed her by the shoulders. "You always have an explanation. Always! And I've always been fool enough to believe you. No more, Hannah. No more!" Pulling his keys from his pocket, he ran down the hill.

"Paul!" Her scream was haunting, but he refused to look back. "Paul, please! The unmentionable happened. Please don't leave me!"

He jumped in his truck and started the engine as her last words rang in his ears. "The unmentionable" meant either adultery or unmarried sex. How in the world could he forgive her?

He glanced up the hill. Hannah was on her knees, rocking back and forth and screaming for him to listen to her. Tears blurred his vision. He'd been such a fool. He threw the truck in reverse, with no intention of ever laying eyes on her again.

27

Barely aware of her surroundings, Hannah watched Paul back into the road, squealing his tires as he sped off. He was gone. It was over. The only thing she'd wanted out of life had just left, hating her. The cold, wet ground seeped through her clothing, making her shiver. The sobs jolting her body tore through the silence of the damp night air.

A pair of gentle hands covered Hannah's shoulders, helping her rise to her feet. "Sh, *Liewi.* It'll be okay. It'll all be okay." Mary steadied her as they walked back toward the *Daadi Haus.*

Human silhouettes formed in the driveway as Mary and Hannah made their way down the hill. Through her blurred vision, Hannah saw Mary's parents and two of her brothers. She had no idea how much they'd seen or heard. But what did it matter now? Paul knew the truth, and he'd made his choice. He thought she was a liar, and he'd left her. She knew he would never return.

A cool cloth pressed against Hannah's brow. She stirred, wondering how long she'd slept once she could weep no longer. Her pain had poured out as she huddled in the bed like a child, crying for hours. Each time she roused for a few moments, Mary had whispered reassuring words to her.

Drawing a deep breath, Hannah pulled her aching body to a sitting position. She hurt all over: her back, thighs, head, and across her stomach. Leaning back, Hannah rested against the headboard, waiting for some of the pains to subside. Her eyes closed; she took a few deep breaths. "What's the time?"

"It's ten in the morning."

The baby shifted. On impulse, Hannah reached for Mary's hand and placed it on her stomach.

Mary gasped. "That's so amazing."

Hannah hadn't ever thought so before, but maybe Mary was right. She opened her eyes and realized she still had on her day clothes from yesterday. The skirts were covered in mud, and to her horror she remembered kneeling on the ground begging Paul not to leave her. She groaned. A lot of good her begging had done.

Mary shifted her hand as the baby moved, following the slow, easy motion across Hannah's belly. "It's a *Bobbeli,* Hannah. A real *Bobbeli.*"

It kicked and Mary jumped. She laughed, but Hannah couldn't find any humor in the incident. It was a real baby, all right. One that belonged to a creep.

Mary placed the cloth from Hannah's brow in the bowl and walked to the dresser, where she set the basin down.

Hannah put her feet on the floor, rubbing her rounded, aching sides.

"I'll do the laundry; you rest." Picking up Hannah's pair of mud-caked stockings, Mary gave an exaggerated roll of her eyes. "*Mamm* set the tub of dirty clothes on the back porch. But my aunt gave birth to her twins during the night. My whole family left for Ohio before sunrise, and they'll be gone for the week to help my aunt with her young brood and the newborns. They left us a key to the phone shanty, saying they'd be calling some here and there." Mary dunked the stockings into the bowl of water, dipping them up and down.

Twins. The word conjured up images of Hannah's aunt who had been shunned. It was hard to imagine what Zabeth's life must be like after all these years without any family around her. Hannah wondered if Zabeth regretted doing whatever it was she did that caused her to be put under the ban.

Hannah dismissed those thoughts and gazed at Mary. "It's not laundry day, is it?"

"No, but we didn't do laundry Monday. We talked and cried."

Hannah supposed it was a good thing she'd told Mary everything a few days ago, or last night would have been even worse, if that were possible.

She rose. The room spun, and she grabbed the headboard to steady herself. "I need to take a shower."

Mary came to her. When Hannah turned around, Mary untied and unpinned her pinafore. "I don't think my family heard much of anything last night. If they had, they wouldn't have kept their plans and gone to visit my aunt. *Daed* said something about us not milling about the property at night while they're gone."

"It doesn't matter what they heard, not anymore." But Hannah knew it did. In a world where conforming was paramount, her parents could pay a high price for Hannah's defiance of the Old Ways. If the bishop decided she had to do things a certain way, and she refused, he could do little to her. But his power over her parents was another matter. They wouldn't be shunned, but they'd be ostracized, however politely.

"Pacifists," Hannah mumbled. "Passive aggressive is more accurate."

Brushing wisps of hair off Hannah's neck, Mary whispered, "My family didn't come outside until they heard Paul's tires squeal."

It took a few moments for Mary's words to sink in. Hannah slid her apron off and faced Mary. "Then they don't know about..." She touched her protruding stomach.

Mary laid her hand on Hannah's belly. "They don't know." Mary's warm, gentle hand caressed Hannah's stomach, and her face crumpled with sympathy. "We could surround the little thing with love, no?"

As Mary spoke the words, the infant fluttered in a new way, as if it had been waiting to hear a caring word, causing Hannah's soul to stir with an inkling of an emotion that had never been a part of her before. Hannah felt sorry for the tiny being. It seemed so desperate to be loved.

As she headed for the shower, Hannah noticed their half-sewn "Past and Future" quilt on the side table. The women of Owl's Perch had donated so many scraps of material for the future side of the quilt, there'd been plenty left over to make baby blankets for the children Luke and Mary would have. Running her fingers across the basting that held the two sides together, Hannah dismissed the pity she'd felt moments earlier. "No, I can't love this child, but someone else can."

Mary grabbed a clean apron and dress off a peg and passed them to Hannah. Taking the clean clothes, Hannah padded into the bathroom. A vision of the monster who had fathered the baby jolted Hannah, and she bristled against Mary's suggestion.

Talking from the other room, Mary changed the topic. "You'll miss our shower when you move back home."

Tuning out Mary's effort at general niceties, Hannah closed the bathroom door and leaned her forehead against it. She and Mary were long overdue for returning to normal life. But when the news of her pregnancy spread, she would no longer be welcomed at the Yoders'. And her father wasn't going to let her move back home unless she set things right with the church leaders.

What am I going to do?

Her future with Paul was destroyed. The pain of that was so deep it hurt to breathe. She'd known all along if he knew the truth, it would end everything. Her best efforts at concealing the pregnancy had failed.

She finally moved to the tub and flicked on the water. The only thing left to do was to make plans for the baby. Hannah's life was over, but a new life was growing inside her, preparing to embark on its own journey on this planet.

She sat on the side of the tub, moving her hands over her swollen stomach. The baby was still now, quieted for a nap, she supposed. Pulling the lever on the faucet, Hannah started the shower running. Amid all the heartache and embarrassment clinging to her, a new desire sprang forth. She eased to the bathroom door and listened. Mary had left the bedroom. Tiptoeing through the room to the dresser, Hannah kept her eye on the bedroom door. She opened the drawer with the stethoscope, wanting to hear the infant's heartbeat. But she didn't want Mary to see her. It was a private thing, something between a mother and her child.

As she grabbed the stethoscope, she shuddered. *A mother?*

Hurrying, she slid out of her dress, put the stethoscope in her ears, and began searching for a heartbeat. Unable to find it, she flicked the water off and listened again. After a minute of moving the stethoscope around, she heard a whooshing noise. That had to be it. It was rhythmic, like Mary's heartbeat, but much faster.

Chills covered her. *Like Mary's heartbeat?*

Oh, dear God, it's a real baby.

She had known that, hadn't she?

Listening to its blood flow through the tiny chambers of its heart, she had to admit the truth. She'd realized it was alive, but she'd wished over and over it wasn't. She'd known it was growing and that it had the power to ruin her and Paul. But never, not once, had she had a suspicion that it was as precious as Mary's heartbeat. She took the stethoscope out of her ears and dropped it on the floor.

Placing her hand over her belly again, the baby balled up under it, as if responding to its mother. Remorse entered Hannah's heart. "I'm sorry. I'm so, so sorry."

She took a deep breath and stepped into the shower. As the warm water soothed her taut, sore muscles, she tried to ignore the awful grief of losing Paul. She put her face under the showerhead and let the pelting water rinse away her tears. As she leaned against the shower wall, visions of Paul's angry face haunted her. He'd had no mercy for her, only judgment.

God, help me, please.

An image of a tan-skinned, young Jewish girl, about Hannah's age, formed a vision in her mind's eye. That girl had been pregnant before she was married too. The picture lasted less than a second, but suddenly Hannah didn't feel so alone. A sense that God had not abandoned her, and didn't intend to, strengthened her.

This sense of God was a welcomed one, and it wasn't completely new. She'd felt His closeness and acceptance after Luke had spewed his venom on her, before Matthew showed up at the Yoders' barn back in October. But within a month she learned she was pregnant, and from there most thoughts of God were far from her as she desperately tried to hide her pregnancy from Paul. Oddly, God didn't seem angry with her about it. He seemed more than willing to step in and comfort her. She propped her palms against the shower wall, muttering confessions of her weakness. Tears clouded her eyes, but they weren't from sorrow or self-pity. She'd tapped into joy, unbelievable as that was. As the thoughts gave her courage, she knew what had to be done. This infant and she were connected. It didn't belong to its father; it belonged to the Father. That's who Hannah would pray the child would take after: its heavenly Father.

As she got out of the shower and dressed, her thoughts spun with snippets of hope. But all traces of good feelings aside, her reality hadn't changed a bit. So now what? Pinning her wet hair into a bun, she searched for answers.

Although Mary wasn't in the room with her, the memory of her soft voice filtered through Hannah's soul. *We could surround the little thing with love, no?*

She ran her hand over her stomach. Suddenly another understanding poured into Hannah's mind. Love—real, God kind of love—gave the infant worthiness, because in life each being was both worthy and unworthy at the same time. A tiny bolt of laughter ran through Hannah. "Yes, Mary. Yes, we can surround this baby with love."

Mary listened without interrupting as Hannah paced the room, explaining her decision to keep the baby. Mary nodded. "We will cherish the babe because it is, simply because it is."

Going from one end of the room to the other, Hannah voiced her thoughts. "I have no money and a baby on the way. How will we do this?"

"*Ach,* Hannah, you'll have to get the support of your family and our community. I can see no other way. Our parents inherited their homes. Luke and I have a place because people donated money and their labor. You can't provide for a baby on your own."

A slow pain worked its way through Hannah's back and around her abdomen. It intensified, and she grabbed the back of the couch, waiting for it to ease. When the discomfort stopped, she took a breath.

Mary held up her index finger, telling Hannah to wait. She dashed into the bedroom and came back holding Hannah's *Kapp* in her hands. Mary had scrubbed it clean and, by the looks of it, had probably spent over an hour ironing it. "It's time for this, no?" Mary held it out to her.

Hannah closed her eyes, feeling the weight of joining the church bear down on her. She placed her hands under her round belly and stared at the ever-growing ball before she moved to the window. As she watched the barren trees sway in the winds, she wondered if she'd always feel this trapped.

"Hannah, I see no other choice. Your father will not help you if you don't come under the church's leadership, and he won't allow anyone else in the community to help you either…even if they would. Even my *Daed* is not going to allow us to remain close if your father is set against you."

Hannah leaned her forehead against the cold window. "Oh God, help me."

Mary placed her hand on Hannah's shoulder. "He is helping you, but to take the help He's provided, you must put this on."

Hannah turned and studied the sheer *Kapp*.

"I'll be behind you every step of the way."

Mary was right; it was the only way. "Yes, it's time to come under the leaders' say. But there isn't time to join the church before the baby is born."

Mary cupped her hand under Hannah's chin, tilting her face up. "The baby won't know it was born before instruction classes began or that it was several months old before you finished and then joined the church. The people won't tell, not once you're baptized. They will forget those things that are behind." Mary gave a sad but sweet smile. "And they won't speak of them again."

An undeniable need to settle the issue as soon as possible grew within Hannah. "I've dreamed for too long of a life that became impossible the moment I was attacked." Hannah took the *Kapp*. "Maybe before."

Mary wrapped Hannah in her arms. "Then we'll do this together."

Hannah hugged her, thankful for Mary and determined to be the kind of mother this child would be grateful for. "Make arrangements for the bishop, preachers, deacon, and *Daed* to all come here this afternoon, but I need to see Matthew first."

28

Paul pulled into the tire store, not quite sure how he'd gotten there. Although he'd shown up in class that morning, he didn't remember anything that was said and couldn't recall leaving campus. It was scary to be at work with no memory of having driven there.

Hannah wasn't going to win at this twisted game of hers. That's all there was to it. He'd keep to his routine and put every memory of her to rest. He sighed. It was going to be a long journey to healing. He hurt as if Hannah had gazed lovingly into his eyes while jamming his heart into a meat grinder. He was still so angry he couldn't quit shaking. Difficult as it was to understand, Hannah was just like Melanie. And he, just like Jack. He'd been a fool not to see it sooner. Finally he comprehended the unnamable thing that had stood between him and Hannah all these months. It was her unfaithfulness.

He clocked in and moved to his messy desk in a tiny, poorly lit back room. Sorting through papers that had been piled there while he was at school, he tried to think through the cloud of betrayal covering his mind. He pulled a new order from the stack and began jotting down information for a paper receipt.

"Hi." Carol's voice pulled him from the dozen different worlds colliding inside him.

He didn't look up. Undoubtedly, Dorcas had told her what was going on. Now she was here to check on him; he was sure of that. "I'm fine, Carol. Go home."

"I'm really sorry, Paul."

Paul crumpled the receipt he'd just messed up and grabbed another blank one from his desk drawer. "Yeah, I bet you are."

"Paul." She sounded wounded. "I never wanted you to get hurt."

He tossed his pen on the desk and looked at her, hoping she had some sort of answer for him. "How could I be so wrong?" His voice cracked, and he wished he hadn't started this conversation. Tears had choked him some during the night as he wrestled with memories and the realization of who Hannah really was, or rather who she'd become. But he wouldn't shed another tear over this. Not one.

Carol closed the door behind her and took a seat. "So I take it you confirmed the rumors about her…seeing other guys while you weren't around."

"Yeah." That was an understatement. But Paul wasn't going to tell anyone that Hannah was pregnant. If he'd only opened his eyes, it would have been obvious long before she conceived. When did she get pregnant anyway? Was it before or after she'd agreed to marry him? He huffed at himself. It didn't matter.

"Paul, I think it would help if you talked about things."

He picked up the pen, holding it in the middle and tapping each end back and forth on the desk. Talk? His sister probably couldn't handle hearing what he had to say right now. After studying the effects of drugs, alcohol, and unfaithfulness on families while dealing with Jack and Melanie, he'd grown quite cynical of people. He'd seen pessimism grow in him for a while, but he never thought he'd have cause to disrespect Hannah of all people.

Still, in the depth of his soul, he couldn't believe what was happening. He simply couldn't fathom Hannah giving herself like that to another man. He picked up a stack of folders and set them in front of him. There had always been things about Hannah that stunned him. Her ability to sneak off from home time after time without getting caught, the way she could hold secrets from everyone, her ability to attend church while planning to leave her faith, her warm openness with Matthew. Her friendliness must have included that doctor who gave her the really nice book with all his phone numbers in it. Hannah had become uncomfortable when Paul had mentioned the phone numbers.

If he'd been following the clues, this wouldn't have been such a shock. Flirting with Matthew at the hospital. Throwing herself into Paul's arms that night at the Yoder place. Kissing him like…like a woman who'd been kissed many, many times before.

He rose. "I've got work to do."

Carol gave him a hug that he didn't return. "At least no one knows about this but Dorcas and me. We won't tell anyone."

Paul eased out of her embrace and shuffled papers on his desk. "The silver lining: saving face." He opened his desk drawer, in search of what he didn't know. When Hannah's community learned of her pregnancy, there would be no saving of face for her, no place of refuge. What a mess she'd made, and what an awful price she would pay. In that moment he realized the heavy, unbearable grief that covered him was also for the suffering Hannah would go through. She'd been foolish, even deceitful, but the price she'd pay would cost her dearly for life.

A sharp pain shot across Hannah's back, stealing her breath as she trod across the pasture toward Matthew's house. "I have much to do today, God. Grant me the strength and wisdom." She whispered the words, knowing there was no perfect answer for her situation. Nothing she could do would set everything right. She would take her time of instruction this summer and join the faith in the fall. That way her father would be calmed and allow her to live in his home and keep her baby.

As she drew closer to the Esh yard, she heard a rhythmic tapping coming from the repair shop. She knocked on the door and opened it.

Matthew sat at his workbench, hammering a tiny nail into a frame holding a piece of glass. He glanced up, then returned his focus to his bench. Dread shuddered through her as she remembered Paul's reaction. She rubbed her thumb against the palm of her hand. "Matthew, I'm going to talk to the bishop today." She drew a breath. "But I need to see Elle first."

Matthew tossed his hammer onto the bench. "You slept in this shop all night, causing rumors about me as well as Jacob. Haven't you caused enough trouble between me and Elle?"

Hannah walked closer to him. "I'm sorry, truly I am."

Lifting a broken wheel to a different section of his workbench, Matthew nodded. "She's still wavering a bit about believing that I never saw you that night. She's been pressing the brakes on our relationship. It'd be best if you stayed away from me...and her."

Her throat stinging from tears she wouldn't let flow, she leaned against an exposed beam. "Matthew, I don't know how to say this, but surely you of all people know I'm not guilty of all that's being said of me."

Matthew captured her gaze and held it. "Yeah, I know that. But I can't let nothing about you destroy me and Elle. She needs me right now. That's possibly the reason she's hanging on to the hope that I'm telling her the truth about us. Her real father has written her a letter. He's meetin' her tonight at Kiah's place for the first time since he ran off. I can't tell ya how much it means to her that I be by her side for this. She says she'll see him, but she won't let him change her mind about joinin' the Amish faith."

Hannah prayed for strength. "I never intended to join our faith, not since I fell for someone who wasn't Amish. For years, Mrs. Waddell's grandson and I have been seeing each other every summer, sometimes during the school year." Hannah cleared her throat. "Last summer, the day he was leaving for his last year of college, he asked me to marry him. Even on that day I never shared a kiss with him, Matthew. I promise."

Matthew waved his hand toward the couch. "Ya look awful, like you need to sit."

Glad to get off her feet and hopeful it would ease her back and leg pain, Hannah moved to the sofa. Matthew sat on the far end of it.

She stared at the scars on the palms of her hands. "You heard that I had an incident with a vehicle. Well, that's not the whole truth. Matthew, I…I was forced to…to be with a man."

"What?" He jumped up. "No." He shook his head and walked away from her.

Hannah closed her eyes, hoping Matthew believed her. When she opened her eyes, he was facing her with hurt and anger mingled on his face.

"I'm so sorry." He eased onto the couch and took her hand.

Another pain shot down her sides. She squeezed his hand. "Thank you. At first, *Mamm* and *Daed* wanted to keep it a secret so that maybe I could still get a husband. I wanted to keep it a secret so Paul wouldn't find out, so he would still marry me."

"The beginning of September is when you started hiding out at home more than normal."

She nodded. "Yes. The buggy ride we took was the first ray of hope that had entered my world since I was…since that night."

"Our ride began a hard time of rumors for you. It's time we tell everyone the truth. It'll make things go easier for you."

"No," she snapped. Closing her eyes, Hannah blurted out, "Matthew, I'm pregnant."

Matthew looked as if he might keel over from the shock of her words. Finally he drew a deep breath. "What can I do to help?"

His kindness made it impossible for her to speak.

Matthew leaned forward, propping his forearms on his knees. "You said you wanted to see Elle. Do you think telling her about your"—he pointed to her belly—"is going to help?"

"When she hears I'm pregnant, you know what she'll think—that either you or Jacob is the father." A sob jolted from her throat, but she forced herself to regain control. "I know you're sorry you ever spent a moment with me, and if I could change things to protect you, I would. But I can't. I'm sorry."

Matthew's hand covered hers. "No." He squeezed. "I'm the one who's sorry. I should have come to see you, to make sure you were okay, to learn why you'd slept in the shop that night." He patted her hand. "Don't worry. We'll try to set this right. If things go awry, it's not your fault."

Her mouth hung open. This wasn't what she'd expected. He had no repulsion that she was pregnant by some maniac *Englischer*? He had no accusations that somehow all this was her fault?

"What will you do to clear Jacob's name?"

Hannah shook her head. "I'm not going to do anything to try to make Sarah's life easier. Besides, she'll believe Jacob easy enough. You and Elle are innocent bystanders in all this. I've got to try to make her believe the truth."

He rose, looking at the clock that sat on his workbench. "School's been out for a bit. But the driver won't pick Elle up for another hour. She always stays and grades papers and such. We could catch her. But maybe we should wait until after the stress of this meeting with her father. I'm going to the Bylers' tonight, and a driver is picking me up there so I can join Elle about an hour before her father arrives."

Hannah remained on the couch, thinking. To push forward seemed selfish, yet to wait was dangerous. She had to tell the church leaders that she was pregnant as soon as they arrived at Mary's *Daadi Haus*. "If we wait, the news might reach her before we talk to her."

He jerked his hat off and thrust his hand through his hair. "What should we do then?"

The hinges on the front door of the shop creaked. Ten-year-old Peter burst through the door, laughing. "Tell him I didn't do it, Matthew." He hid behind his big brother beside the couch.

Thirteen-year-old David ran into the room. "Tell him I'll get him anyways." David lunged at Peter.

"Easy, boys." Matthew spread out his arms, keeping them at bay from each other.

The teasing in the boys' voices made Hannah miss Samuel and little Rebecca, who she hadn't seen the past few months. They wouldn't recognize their eldest sister if she didn't start seeing them more often.

The door popped open for a third time. Elle entered. The smile on her face faded at the sight of Hannah.

Matthew glanced at Hannah. The decision of whether to wait had just been jerked from their hands.

29

Hannah trod across the lumpy, pothole-filled pasture. Her thighs burned and throbbed. The increasing pains in her sides made taking a deep breath impossible. Surely the discomforts she'd been suffering wouldn't keep growing throughout the pregnancy.

Her foot landed in a brown, grassy hole, and she stumbled. She'd never noticed before how difficult this field was to cross. The aches in her sides turned into sharp pains as she plodded through the barnyard and onto the Yoders' lane.

When she opened the door to the *Daadi Haus,* she heard low tones of men muttering to one another. Before Hannah had fully entered the home, Mary hurried to her side. "They've come to talk to you."

The horses and buggies must have been pulled into one of the barns, meaning the leaders knew they'd be here a while. Hannah didn't know whether the bishop and preachers had responded to the news so quickly because they were willing servants of the people, or if they were simply vultures swooping down on a fresh carcass.

Needing a few moments to compose herself, she stepped inside the enclosed back porch, leaned against a canned-goods pantry, and took a deep breath.

Elle had been visibly shaken upon hearing what Hannah had to say. But she responded that she had too much going on with her father to know what she thought of Hannah's confession. She seemed to want to believe Hannah's account but needed a little time before making a stand.

Hannah understood Matthew's desire for Elle. Unusual beauty was the least of the girl's attributes. She was so open and kind as they talked that Hannah found herself wishing she was more like her. Before leaving, Elle had caressed Matthew's face and smiled, saying they could remain friends no matter what. To his credit, Matthew didn't beg her to believe him or become angry with Hannah over her part in all this.

In the face of this upcoming meeting, Hannah could only hope the men would be half as gracious as Elle had been.

"Kumm." Mary put her arm around Hannah's shoulder and led her toward the living room, where the men waited. As they passed the bedroom, Hannah caught a glimpse of the "Past and Future" quilt, lying on the table beside the bed. Each half of the quilt was vital, that which had already happened and that which was yet to happen. A spark of hope danced across Hannah's heart. Soon enough what faced her today would be part of her yesterday.

The four men rose as she entered—not out of respect for her as a woman, she was certain, but because they thought she had summoned them in order to repent. She did intend to repent of any wrongdoing on her part, but she had no intention of repenting of things that weren't her fault. That's where things would get sticky.

She eased into a chair in front of the bishop. The men took their seats as tension mounted. Her father sat to her right, along with Preacher Nathaniel Miller. Preacher Ben Zook sat to her left. She'd known Nathaniel since before he became a preacher. Ben had been close to her grandfather when Hannah was just a girl and had spoken words over her grandfather when he died.

The deacon hadn't come. He was probably unable to drop everything and get here on the spur of the moment. There were organized ways of doing things—certain days and times set apart for such matters. But exceptions were always made to help those in need. Clearly, Hannah was in need.

The bishop laid his hat in his lap. *"Was iss letz?"* Bishop Eli Hostetler was the most intimidating man in the room. His weathered face and beady eyes made him look as old as Hannah imagined God to be—and just as displeased with her. Eli's knobby body was as thin as the rickety boards that were barely holding the old barn together.

Hannah tried to swallow, but her mouth was too dry. The bishop wanted her to get right to the point. But where should she begin?

She gazed at each man, wondering if she possessed the strength to say all that needed to be said. Nathaniel Miller was about her father's age, early forties, with small brown eyes and a large nose that didn't fit his face. Ben Zook was older than the bishop's fifty years by about a decade. He had deep scars over his face that Hannah had always assumed were from acne when he was younger. Slowly her eyes made their way to her father, who wouldn't even look at her.

She willed herself to begin. "At the beginning of this ordeal, my father asked me to come see you. He begged me over and over. But I didn't listen." She drew a ragged breath as another round of aches went through her back and thighs. If the ordeal was Hannah's pregnancy, then her statement was true.

From behind her, Mary passed her a glass of water and several handkerchiefs. As Hannah took a drink, she skimmed the men's faces. Her father's gray blue eyes had a sense of hesitancy about them, of what Hannah didn't know. Was he unsure of the bishop's reaction or unconvinced of his daughter's virtue? Had he fallen prey to the rumors?

She shifted her attention to the bishop.

Hannah started to lean forward to set the glass on the table, but Mary reached out and took it for her.

The bishop cleared his throat. "Mary, I think it would be best if you left us alone for a spell."

Mary nodded. "I'll be in my house if you need me."

As she rose to leave, the bishop glanced at Hannah's father. Hannah knew that what she'd begun might take weeks or even months to finish working out. No matter what the bishop decided, there would be families who disagreed. The families who believed the rumors would accept nothing but full disclosure and repentance on Hannah's part. The ones who chose to believe Hannah's confession today would be resentful until the one who began the gossip came clean.

If it weren't for Matthew and Elle's relationship, Hannah would welcome people learning all there was to know about the gossip. Matthew could probably set people straight, and Sarah would have to admit that she lied about how long Hannah was gone that night. Hannah would thoroughly enjoy seeing Sarah get put in her place.

When the back door closed behind Mary, Eli nodded at Hannah.

Averting her eyes so she didn't have to see the men, Hannah explained. "In the last days of August, I was on my way home from Mrs. Waddell's, our Mennonite neighbor..." With stammering and long pauses, Hannah described the attack the best way she knew how. When she finished, the room was silent for a long time.

The bishop turned to her father. "Zeb, do you believe this account?"

She would have been less startled if the men had held her at fault for walking along the road that day. She'd just revealed the most embarrassing event of her life to these men, and the response was to accuse her of being a liar?

Her father stared at the floor. "I...I was there when she came home. I have no doubt of the trauma that took place."

Eli arched an eyebrow at him, then turned his attention back to Hannah. "And the midnight ride in your nightgown?"

"It was only a few minutes. I never left sight of the house."

The bishop didn't look as though he believed her, but he said nothing.

Hannah's head throbbed, and her sides ached. Sarah's rumors had the bishop discounting everything Hannah said. But she didn't have the strength to drag her sister into this. Besides, it was quite clear that even if she tried to straighten things out by saying that Sarah was a liar, no one in this room was going to believe her.

The bishop continued. "Is it true that you exchanged letters with a Mennonite man against your father's wishes?"

She wished that was a lie, but she couldn't deny it. She nodded.

"Is it his child you carry?"

"No! I told you—"

The bishop interrupted her. "Is it true that the day before Thanksgiving you were in that man's arms, the one you were sending secret letters to, kissing him while your body carried another man's child?"

So, someone had been watching her that day, and they'd told the bishop. Or maybe he was the one who had seen her. She nodded.

"And is it true that Matthew Esh told you that you were a liar?"

Hannah covered her face with the handkerchief. She was buried too deep in mistakes to ever clear her name. What could she say? The bishop himself had heard Matthew say that. Hannah couldn't deny it. No wonder the man had kept silent about his discovery of them in the barn that day. He thought Matthew was correcting her, not playing. If she explained that it was a game, then the bishop's view of Matthew could change, causing even more rumors to run through the community about her and Matthew. If Sarah was ever going to be held accountable for the lies she'd told, Matthew had to be held in high esteem by the church leaders.

She nodded.

"Is it also true that you've snuck off from your home to be with this Mennonite man on many occasions over the years, using your work for Katie Waddell as an excuse?"

She lowered the handkerchief and stared at her lap. She couldn't look at her father. What must he think of her?

The bishop drilled Hannah over and over concerning the same rumors, trying to get her to expound on the reports. She could think of nothing that could open their eyes to the truth. Then again, almost every rumor was rooted in truth, only a twisted version of it. How could she untangle herself from it?

By the time the clock struck five, Hannah was so tired, so racked with physical and emotional exhaustion, she couldn't even lift her head.

"Look at me!" The bishop's voice thundered through the house.

Hannah lifted her face for the first time in over an hour.

"You will stay here alone tonight. Zeb, since Mary's family is visiting relatives quite a ways from here and can't easily return, I think the best place for Mary is with you. The community will accept our decision better if Mary stays with those who will become family members later this year." Bishop Eli folded his hands and stared at them for a spell before looking at Hannah. "Tomorrow we will return. I suggest you spend the night thinking on this account of 'rape.' Consider hard, Hannah, the path you are choosing. There can be no forgiveness without true repentance. We cannot allow you to join the church if you are covering your sin through lies." He rose, and the other men followed suit. "Perhaps a night alone will cause you to think more clearly. I'm concerned that Mary's devotion and her naiveté are serving your manipulation and lies, causing them to grow within you, but she won't be around tonight."

Without standing, Hannah looked up at her father. "Do you question me about the attack too, *Daed*?"

He stared at his daughter. "You have lied to me for years about Mrs. Waddell's grandson. What am I to think?"

Hannah was dumbfounded. How could he think that the brokenness he witnessed the night she came home with gashes in her hands and trauma to her body was somehow linked to her rebellious relationship with Paul?

In unison, the men turned their backs on her. It was a warning of what was to come if she kept to her story of rape. When the door slammed, Hannah buried her face in her hands, too drained to even cry.

30

The wall clock above the mantel ticked on persistently. An eeriness she had never experienced before filled the evening. She was truly alone for the first time in her life. This separation from human contact felt unruly—even boisterous. And the silence grew louder with each ticktock.

A howling wind interrupted the lull, pushing hard against the house and making it moan. Hannah rose and ambled to the window. Snow lay sparsely across the ground, but the heavy flakes that continued falling from the black sky said the land would be hidden under a blanket before long.

Thoughts of Ohio played across Hannah's mind. At the moment it sounded like a safe haven. She wondered if her aunt might appreciate getting a visit from her brother's eldest daughter.

She huffed at her silliness and placed her hand over her stomach. "We knew it would be a battle to get back in the good graces of *Daed* and the church, but it seems your mother has made things even worse than she realized." She patted her belly. "I'm sorry, little one."

Pulling the shade down, Hannah realized she'd drawn one thick curtain after another between her and her parents through years of deception concerning Paul. How foolish could she be?

Her stomach grumbled, reminding her she hadn't eaten since…dinner yesterday. Plodding into the kitchen, Hannah grabbed a kerosene lamp off a nearby table. As she struck a match and lit the wick, her hunger faded. She hurt all over, from her upper rib cage to her knees. She pulled a few ibuprofen tablets out of a bottle and swallowed them with a glass of water. The bottled medicine had to be better than the homegrown and ground lobelia her family used. On her way back into the living room, a muscle spasm forced her to grab on to a chair and wait.

While she took some deep, relaxing breaths, she wondered if these types of aches were normal. Another spasm hit her lower back and worked its way across her stomach. She moaned, long and low, waiting for the ache to stop. The odd, painful feeling lasted nearly a full minute. Something was wrong. It had to be. Panic jolted her. No one was around. The phone shanty was locked.

Stop worrying. You're fine. It's been a long, grueling day, and your body is weary, nothing more.

The terror leveled off as she assured herself the symptoms were due to the difficulty of the last twenty or so hours. Heartache over Paul lashed out at her. None of what was happening in her life was as painful as losing Paul. But he was gone, and right now her focus needed to be the infant inside her womb.

She shuffled into the bedroom and lay down, covering herself with a blanket. Surely a little rest, along with the pain reliever, would ease the tenseness across her lower back and stomach.

As soon as she laid her head down, sleep came. It was a restless, pain-filled sleep but ever so welcome. When a knock at the door thundered through the room, Hannah glanced at the clock. Eight. Surely the bishop's decree that she spend the night alone had made the rounds already. Who would dare come to her door?

Paul?

Hope stirred. Could it be possible that he came to believe her?

After tossing back the covers, Hannah waited for another long, hard spasm to abate.

The knock at the door came again. "Hannah? It's me, Matthew. Are you all right?"

She felt sick as her foolish anticipation fell to the floor with a thud.

Pushing against the bed, Hannah rose to her feet. She waddled through the rooms and opened the storm door. A blanket of snow covered the ground, and snowdrifts were stacked in various places as the wind danced across their cottony tops. "What are you doing here? Aren't you supposed to be with Elle?"

The wind slashed through the air, ripping the door out of Hannah's hand. Matthew grabbed the storm door, holding it tight. "Her father's plane ain't even landed in Baltimore yet, but I'm on my way to meet a driver just as soon as I make sure you're doin' all right."

Wishing they could enter the warm house, at least enough to close the door, Hannah grabbed a shawl off the nearby coatrack. "You heard about the bishop's edict?"

He nodded, pity showing in his eyes. "I wasn't going to come in. I just needed to check on you. His instructions didn't say someone couldn't check on you."

Hannah smiled in spite of herself. Matthew had always been one to obey while bending the rules when he disagreed with a decree. "I'll be fine, Matthew. I just need some rest." As she spoke the words, tightness sprang from nowhere, almost stealing her breath. Grabbing the doorframe, she panted. In response to his worried expression, she forced a laugh. "I'm fine. Really. I just overdid it today, and my body's having a fit about it."

Matthew stooped. "You sure?"

Determined to leave his life as uninterrupted as possible, Hannah pushed her fears aside and answered as lightheartedly as she could. "Yep. Go. Please, whatever you do, don't be late."

"I'll be back to check on you as soon as I can. It'll be after midnight for sure, maybe close to two before I return." He paused. "You don't look so good."

"Dankes." Hannah managed a tiny curtsy.

Matthew didn't chuckle. He pulled his hat down low and headed for his buggy.

She locked the storm door, still panting. The only things she needed were her bed and some rest. Matthew should not miss being with Elle because of that, especially not tonight. As the carriage disappeared through the haze of powdery snow, she closed the wooden door and went back to bed.

Between shooting pains and aching tightness, Hannah dozed. Suddenly she bolted upright. Her skirts were wet. She pulled herself out of bed, lit a kerosene lamp, and headed for the bathroom. A sharp pain stopped her cold. Trembling, she set the lamp on the table. Like lightning momentarily illuminating a dark sky, suddenly reality dawned on her. Her aches and pains weren't from the difficulty of the past day. She was in labor. From the best she could remember, she had been for more than twenty-four hours.

But the baby's not due until the middle of May.

As that realization settled over her, she wanted to cry out to God, but a sense of betrayal stole her words before they could form.

It was the third week of February. If the baby came now, it might not survive.

Sinking to her knees, she moaned as a long, hard contraction pulled downward on her stomach. Her mind whirled in a hundred directions. Feelings of utter stupidity flooded her. She should have realized hours ago that these weren't normal aches and pains, even though she'd never been through so much turmoil in her life.

When the tightness eased, she rose, using the bed for support.

As she gained her footing and her breath, ideas popped into her head left and right. Mary kept the key to the phone shanty in her pocket. That meant Hannah would have to go to the barn, grab an ax, then make her way to the phone shanty and try to break into it. But did she have the strength to do all that? The answer had to be yes. But she could barely claw her way to her feet with the aid of the bed.

The anatomy book.

Holding her belly with one hand, she scoured the dresser drawers, searching for the book. It had a section on birthing babies. It was only a few pages, and she had read them several times, but… She tossed clean clothing from the drawers onto the floor. Where did she have it last?

Under the mattress! That's where she'd put it. She eased her way back to the bed and ran her hands between the mattress and the box springs. Her fingers touched the smooth, silky cover, and she pulled it out. Breathing with difficulty she flipped the book open to the section on home delivery and began reading. With each word she read, she shook harder. She couldn't do this.

A knock at the door made her jump. Hope sparked—someone had come. She shuffled across the floor to the back door. As she lifted the shade to look out, both relief and dread flooded her.

Matthew.

Fighting within herself, she opened the door. "Matthew," she whispered, "why are you back here?" Placing her arm under her belly, she lifted some of the weight. She could feel her wet, cold skirts against her legs. Her breath came in short puffs as stabbing pains worked their way down her back.

Matthew put his foot over the threshold, making her back up to allow him entrance. He angled his head, trying to read her face. "I had to return." He frowned. "Hannah, are you holdin' a secret?"

She hesitated. If she told him, he'd stay, and nothing about his quiet life would remain intact. Self-hatred covered her, but it held no answer. Fear of being left alone squelched her concerns. "I need help. I think the baby's coming." A sob racked her body, causing her to stumble forward.

Matthew tucked his hand under her forearm, steadying her. He helped her to the bedroom. "I knew somethin' wasn't right. I just had this feeling..." He eased her onto the bed. "I'll call for help."

"The shanty is locked and boarded," Hannah sputtered.

Anger ran through Matthew's eyes. "Don't worry. I'll get in. You stay put."

As he ran for the door, a deep pressure grew in Hannah's body. "Matthew, wait." Her voice came out a mixture of a desperate whisper and a scream.

In a second he was by her side. Hannah pointed to the book. "I need scissors and string from the sewing kit by the dresser. And I need some clean sheets, towels, and...and the nasal aspirator from the medicine cabinet. Hurry."

Almost throwing the stuff at her, Matthew fulfilled her requests, then darted out the door.

Settling herself against the pillows piled at the headboard, the desire to push became so strong she almost couldn't stop herself. She panted through the next few contractions, silently begging herself not to push.

Outside she heard glass breaking and boards being beaten and ripped.

The desire to push grew stronger than her will, more powerful than anything she'd ever experienced. She took a deep breath, and her body took over, ignoring her mental commands to stop. She pushed and moaned. Pushed and panted. Pushed. Pushed. Pushed. Her brow became drenched with sweat. She begged her body to stop pushing, to give Matthew time to get an ambulance. But it wouldn't.

The back door banged and clattered, sounding as if a herd of cows had come in out of the foul weather. A moment later Matthew stood at the door of the bedroom, his face taut with worry. "I got in, but the lines are down. I'm going to fetch *Mamm.*"

Hannah raised her hand in the air, unable to speak. Matthew paused, rocking back and forth nervously on the balls of his feet. When the contraction eased, she relaxed against the pillow and drew a breath. "Don't leave me. Please."

"Hannah, you need help. I'll ride bareback across the fields and be back in less than ten minutes. My mother's no midwife, but she's helped deliver a few babies in her time. I…I can't keep you or the babe from dying."

Matthew was as pale as the sheets under her body. His legs carried him like a newborn calf trying to stand. Another contraction slowly built force. "Go," she whispered.

Matthew sprinted across the room, tripping over the sewing basket he'd left out earlier. She heard the back door slam shut.

Her body told her when to push, when to take deep breaths, when to rest. *Hurry, Matthew.* The minutes ticked by with only the sounds of the clock and the howling wind. Amid the pushing and resting, a small head appeared between her thighs.

It wailed in loud protest. Relief ran through Hannah, giving her fresh strength to take on the newest phase of this ordeal. Stacking pillows behind her for support, she leaned forward, holding the clean towels. The little body that issued from hers was tiny. Too tiny. She'd had baby dolls that fit inside her hidden apron pocket that were as large as this baby.

A closer look told her she had given birth to a girl. A daughter. Her child. She dried the infant, noticing even in the dim light of the kerosene lamp that the little one's coloring appeared more like that of a salamander than a baby. The skin was translucent, making the mapping of the veins evident.

Hannah drew the flailing girl into her arms. The book said warmth was paramount. Hannah wiped her off more and wrapped her in the soft sheet and then in the "Past and Future" quilt. The infant screamed, but her eyes didn't open.

Snuggling with her newborn, Hannah smiled down at her. Basking in the maternal feelings that were coursing through her, she cooed. "Rachel is a good name, no?" Her daughter opened her eyelids and seemed to focus on Hannah's face. Tears burned Hannah's eyes. "Hi," she whispered.

The infant blinked, then closed her eyes. Before Hannah drew her next breath, a catlike sound came from Rachel. A moment later a pitiful moan escaped her miniature body. Hannah pulled the wrappings away from the infant's chest, watching…for what, she wasn't sure.

Her daughter's chest caved inward. Hannah's heart thudded hard. Her baby was struggling for air.

The back door banged open, and Naomi rushed to Hannah's side, carrying a folded towel full of items. She laid the bundle on the bed and opened it.

Hannah broke into sobs. "She can't catch a breath. God, please, she's not breathing."

Naomi eased the quilt away from the infant's head and gasped. She met Hannah's stare and shook her head. Hannah didn't need words to know what Naomi was thinking. Rachel was too young, too premature to survive.

Naomi tied off the umbilical cord and cut it with the scissors she'd brought with her.

Sobbing, Hannah drew her convulsing daughter closer to her chest. "Forgive me."

Pitiful moans escaped the newborn as she fought for air. "Be stubborn, Rachel," Hannah cried. "Fight." Hannah hugged her close, willing her to live. She whispered to her in English, refusing the Pennsylvania Dutch of her forefathers.

Hannah sensed Naomi's movements about the bedside as she took care of her midwife tasks. But Hannah never once removed her focus from Rachel, even as the little girl's skin became deeper and deeper blue. After several minutes, her daughter stopped squirming, stopping moaning, stopped everything. Feeling the little girl's life slip away, Hannah wished she knew what those nurses at the hospital knew. Then she might be able to save her.

Rachel's body jerked and then stilled so completely that Hannah knew beyond a doubt her daughter had drifted into another world, one that Hannah probably wouldn't see for many decades. Guilt bore down on Hannah's soul, ripping her heart. She rocked her infant until she knew there was no way to revive her even if medics showed up in the next second.

Regret twisted her heart like a steel vise. If only she'd been up front with everyone about the rape from the start, maybe this wouldn't have happened. She studied the lifeless being in her arms as one word forced its way out of its hidden spot deep inside her. *Rape.* Chills ran up and down her body. "I was raped!" The words poured forth with strength she didn't possess. "If only I'd told…if I'd confessed that to begin with…" The words died in her throat.

What was so horrible about owning up to the rape? Hannah closed her eyes, tuning out Naomi's movements and everything around her.

Resentment at the injustice of the attack rose, demanding to be heard. But as she allowed that thought, a thousand others flooded her: reflections of the bishop's harshness, Luke's bitterness against her, Sarah's backstabbing, the district's thirst for gossip, her father's constant wavering on every subject except his dislike of Mennonites and the unquestioning obedience of his children to his strict ways.

Resentment took hold of her, and she nurtured it as strongly as she would have nurtured her child if she'd been given the chance.

31

Her body still aching from giving birth less than eight hours earlier, Hannah stood by her infant's half-dug grave. The sickening hole in the ground that would hold her infant was under the large beech tree on Matthew's property. The air was unbearably cold, even with the sun shining brightly at eight o'clock in the morning. The fields were covered in a thick layer of snow.

The lines and creases of Matthew's face hinted at a multitude of emotions. He jammed the blade of the shovel into the frozen ground and dumped icy dirt next to the undersized hole. The frozen flecks of the broken sod glittered like shards of glass under the morning rays.

Matthew drove the shovel into the earth again. Digging deep in frozen turf was an arduous task. But his act of kindness had relieved Hannah's father of the need to decide whether he would allow an illegitimate infant of an unbaptized mother to be buried on his land.

Matthew had proven again what Hannah had known about him since they were young: that he was stalwart in his decisions and able to bear the weight of the *Ordnung* while carrying out its truths in his heart. Hannah knew Elle hadn't left his thoughts for a moment. Her name seemed to be etched across his worried brow. But he hadn't once mentioned her or shirked from helping Hannah in any way he could throughout this ordeal.

He'd missed being there for Elle last night during what was probably the most difficult event the yet-to-be-Amish girl had endured. Elle had been forced to face her father, the man who had turned to alcohol and then abandoned his daughter not long after her mother died. And poor Elle had to do it without Matthew by her side. That had to be eating at Matthew.

Keeping him from Elle was another rock in the burlap bag that was tied around Hannah's neck and another incident she could do nothing about.

When the hole was dug, Matthew leaned the shovel against the nearby tree. The sounds of a horse and buggy made him turn and peer in that direction. Hannah didn't bother to look. She was too tired, too numb to care who'd come. But even through the haze of trauma and exhaustion, she understood that anyone's arrival at this secluded spot meant all of Owl's Perch knew of last night's events. She could only assume that Naomi Esh had gone home before sunrise and had spread news of the scandalous events to people desperate for Hannah's correction from God.

Hannah felt a gentle hand come under her forearm, steadying her.

"I'm so sorry, Hannah." Mary's voice cracked.

Mary's embrace was warm. But Hannah didn't speak. She didn't even weep. No amount of crying could change what had happened.

Mamm, Daed, and Luke filled in beside Mary. There they all stood, about to bury a child no one but Hannah knew the name of. Matthew stretched two long pieces of rope across the open hole. Luke stepped forward and grasped the two ropes on one end while Matthew trod to the buggy and easily lifted out the foot-long pine box that carried Rachel. He had done everything he could to help Hannah while possibly laying an ax to his own life in the process. Grabbing the ropes on the end opposite Luke, Matthew pinned them under his boots on his side of the grave and then leaned over to place the wooden box on top of the ropes. He stood.

Six grief-stricken faces stared at the handmade coffin and freshly dug grave. The chestnut horses stomped the cold, hard ground, causing the black buggies attached to them to rattle and creak. Luke and Matthew, positioned opposite each other, held the ropes that looped under the casket. They carefully lowered the wooden box into the ground.

Mamm wept quietly. Hannah's father spoke words of forgiveness. But Hannah couldn't accept his words. Her heart was being consumed with a brutal rage. How could her daughter be dead, without ever getting the chance to live? The tiny thing had never even felt her mother's love, because Hannah had never had any, not until it was too late. A sob broke from her throat, piercing the frigid air that surrounded the group.

Hannah thought of how much the Amish had given to support Luke and Mary in the wake of their accident. Yet those same people had devoured the rumors about her. The bishop and preachers had treated her worse than a leper. Her own father had wavered under the bishop's questioning and had abandoned his daughter in the process.

Matthew prayed aloud, but Hannah heard little of what he said.

A cold wind flapped against their bodies as Luke shoveled frozen soil over the wooden box. His face was as rigid as stone, his movements those of a detached gravedigger.

Mary tugged at Hannah's arm, trying to lead her to a buggy. Hannah's feet seemed rooted in place.

Her mother started walking toward her, but Hannah's father stepped forward and wrapped his hand around his wife's arm. He stared at the ground, mumbling, "Your daughter grieves severely for an infant conceived by rape, no?" His eyes lifted to meet Hannah's, accusing her of things she couldn't disprove. Her mother lowered her head and took her place beside her husband as they walked away from Hannah and back to their buggy.

Hannah's heart froze a little harder. Would this be her lot forever—to live among a people who condemned her for things she hadn't done?

She studied the white fields with barren trees lining the horizon and scattered in small patches around cleared pastures. Her vision blurred, and she couldn't see anything but gray light. Finally she turned to follow Mary's gentle nudging toward the buggy.

"Hannah."

She stopped. It was a whisper from somewhere. Scanning the fields, she looked for signs of mockers, but there were none.

Mary squeezed her arm. "What is it?"

"Did you hear that?"

Worry creased Mary's face. She shook her head. "I didn't hear anything."

Hannah stared at the faces of those who surrounded her. Obviously, no one else had heard the voice. She trudged toward the buggy, snow crunching beneath her feet.

"Hannah." This time the two syllables of her name were drawn out, like the echoes inside an empty barn.

She stopped and turned. "I'm listening." She said it aloud, not caring what anyone thought.

"Kumm raus."

"Come out to where?" She made a complete circle, listening for an answer, but she heard none. When her gaze landed upon Mary, she saw that the girl had gone pale.

Matthew came beside Hannah and led her into the buggy. "You need sleep. It's over now. It's time to rest."

That was it. She needed sleep. With the aid of the portable wooden steps that Matthew placed on the ground, Hannah climbed into the buggy.

"Hannah." The familiar voice returned. Afraid of what responding to the voice would do to Mary, Hannah didn't dare answer.

As the buggy plodded across the field to the Yoders' *Daadi Haus,* the wind whispered her name over and over, begging her to *kumm raus.*

Hannah would be glad to go, if she only knew where.

Through the murky sleep of grief-filled nightmares, Paul's own groaning woke him. "Hannah, *kumm raus!*" The cry resonated in his head.

He sighed and sat upright, placing his feet on the floor and his head in his hands. Streams of sunlight poured in around the white shades hanging over the windows. He glanced at the clock. Eight o'clock. Just two and a half days ago he'd discovered Hannah's pregnancy. How would he ever get over that?

The door to his shared bedroom popped open. Paul leaned back, determined to act as if he were fine.

Marcus strode in with a towel tied around his hips and water covering his upper body. "Man, Waddell, you look like death warmed over. It's no wonder. You must've called for that Hannah girl a hundred times, whoever she is."

Paul grabbed his pants from the foot of the bed and jerked them on. *Yeah, whoever she is.*

Sifting through dirty clothes, Marcus picked out a pair of pants and a shirt. "The snowplows have cleaned up the mess from the storm night before last. But last night's winds knocked out the electricity to most of the campus. All classes are canceled."

Jerking open a drawer, Paul seized a fleece shirt and put it on. No matter how angry and hurt he was with Hannah, his heart kept calling to her, in Pennsylvania Dutch no less.

Marcus pulled on his baggy jeans. "So, I figure this Hannah girl must be what's kept you from dating anyone else or even looking, for that matter, right?"

Paul didn't answer. Hannah meant so much more than that to him. She was the lion that roared in his soul.

And the girl who's carrying another man's baby.

Pain thudded against his chest.

Marcus poked his still-damp arms through the sleeves of a dirty sweatshirt. "So, what does 'come ros' mean?"

Paul had heard Hannah use the phrase many times. "I'm pretty sure it means to come out."

In spite of the different worlds that sometimes made it hard to understand each other's lives, there was always a force within both of them that drew them together. Over the years her sweet innocence and wild sense of humor had clashed with her unwavering sense of propriety, and he'd always understood that.

Clouds of jealousy parted momentarily, and for the first time since he'd confronted her, Paul saw something besides the green-eyed monster. Was it possible that the wedge between them wasn't Matthew or Dr. Greenfield or any other man the rumors conjured up? Could the chasm he'd sensed from their first contact after they were engaged be caused by Hannah withholding some other secret?

"The unmentionable." He mumbled the words, pacing the undersized room.

Marcus's face registered confusion. "Uh, yeah, you've obviously spent years not mentioning her."

Paul frowned, refusing to get sidetracked. "No. She used the word *unmentionable*..." Paul raked his hands through the knots in his hair. "You know the Amish a little. One word often means several things. What do you think they would use that word for?"

Marcus sat on his unmade bed, smiling at Paul. "Ah, so she's Amish. That explains a lot. The way you've kept it under wraps, I thought maybe you'd fallen for an older divorcée with a passel of kids."

Paul scowled. "Stop joking around and stick to the subject. This is serious."

Marcus nodded, but the grin didn't leave his face. "Okay, okay. Let's see, I've heard my aunt use that word. She lives among the Amish in Lancaster. The only time I've heard it used is when they're talking about adultery."

"I know that." Paul shoved his hands into his pockets. There had to be something he was missing.

The smile disappeared from Marcus's face, and he sat up straighter. "I think they use that word to describe anything to do with sex. So I guess it would include premarital relations, probably even rape."

Dumbstruck, Paul couldn't respond. Rape? That wasn't the answer he was searching for. Wasn't there something between Hannah giving herself to someone and rape? Both ideas were incomprehensible. Totally unacceptable. Confusion and anger fought for control of his body.

Marcus broke through his thoughts. "For that matter, *unmentionable* would probably be used instead of adjectives like *pleasure, gratifying,* or *desire.*"

Paul bristled, looking at the floor. "Keep the unnecessary annotations to yourself, okay?"

Marcus leaned forward. "I didn't mean…"

Paul sighed. He had left the subject of sex out of every conversation with Hannah, telling himself it was inappropriate. Maybe it was, or maybe he wasn't any more comfortable discussing that subject than she would have been.

Paul opened his nightstand and looked in his bowl of change to see if he'd dropped his keys in there when emptying his pockets. If sex was a topic even he was uncomfortable talking about, there was no way Hannah would have brought it up with him. "Especially if she thought I'd think less of her."

"What?"

Paul sat on his bed and put his elbows on his thighs. He buried his head in his hands. "Never mind. Listen, you date different girls regularly. Have you ever thought one of them was seeing someone behind your back?"

"Hey, I spend my time with quality women—Bible-believing, God-honoring, denying-their-darker-side women. Besides, I think most girls would rather handle things relatively honestly."

Paul sighed, trying to remember the exact words Hannah had said. "Relatively?"

Marcus shifted on the bed, making it creak. "They'd rather dump a guy than cheat on him, even if it means fudging a little on why they don't want to be with him. So, is this Hannah the kind of girl who would be relatively honest, or would she be more likely to run around behind your back?"

Paul lowered his hands, making eye contact with Marcus. "She did make a few remarks recently about me not wanting to do all that it would take to wait for her. She never talked like that before we became engaged—"

"Engaged?" Marcus interrupted.

Paul stood. "I… We…were… I don't know." He paced the small room as his mind conjured up images from years of friendship with Hannah. His need to build a foundation that went deeper than just friendship had begun when he'd returned to Gram's two summers ago. Hannah's beauty had blossomed strikingly, and he knew she would attract every single man around. The night he went to the hospital to see her, her friendliness with Matthew watered the seeds of jealousy that had been planted long before. When her reaction to his visit was less than enthusiastic, his lack of confidence turned into festering envy.

"Paul?"

He stopped pacing and sat on the bed again. "I went to see her the night before the snowstorm. We argued and I left." Paul punched the mattress below him. "What happened to us?"

Marcus shrugged. "I have no idea, my friend. You haven't told me anything about this girl, you know."

Neither Paul nor Hannah had anything to lose at this point, so Paul told Marcus all about her. As he talked, he realized he should have done this with Marcus years ago. Just airing everything cleared his mind and made all sorts of things make sense. As he retraced their relationship, doubts he'd had about Hannah's faithfulness began to shrink.

Marcus's eyes shifted back and forth, studying Paul's face. "She's pregnant?"

He nodded, all doubt of Hannah's innocence completely gone. His insecurity and jealousy had blinded him for a few days. "You can't mutter a word of this to anyone."

"Come on, Waddell. You know I won't."

"It's just that I've spent years trying to protect her, not letting anyone know about us so her father wouldn't find out and punish her." Guilt at leaving her there, begging him to listen to her, hounded him. "Dear Father, what have I done?"

Paul grabbed his shoes and yanked them on. "I've got to go to her and make this right. She'll be eighteen in two weeks. I'll need to hide her until her birthday, but after that her father can't legally make her return home. I bet the reason she's not living under his roof anymore is because he won't let her." He lunged toward the door.

Marcus stepped in front of him. "Wait. Just take a few minutes and think about this. You're talking about some serious baggage. Maybe rape and a baby?"

Paul stopped, horrified at the words that had just come out of his friend's mouth. "And I can only hope she needs me enough to forgive me."

As Paul strode toward the door, Marcus followed him. "The winds have caused snowdrifts across some of the roads. I doubt if the snowplows have gotten to the back roads of Owl's Perch yet. Let me go with you. I might be able to help."

Paul grabbed his coat off a chair. "In spite of the complete idiot that I am, I'm fine on my own."

"Look, I'm sorry about the baggage comment. If this is what you want, I'll back you. But you need to give me a break here, not to mention yourself. Your reaction wasn't what you wish it was, but you got sideswiped. You can't hold it against yourself because you needed time to think and process. That's just part of being a human."

Paul's heart lurched. "Sideswiped!" What an idiot he'd been. He grabbed a kitchen chair and squeezed the wooden spindles as hard as he could, rage building inside him. "That's when she stopped going to Gram's. That's when she started acting weird. The unmentionable must have happened..." It all fell into place. He couldn't bear to think of what had happened to her...and what he'd done to make matters even worse.

Unable to take any more, he lifted the kitchen chair into the air and smacked it over the table, wishing he could find the man who had dared to hurt his sweet Hannah. He brought it down again and again until he held only spindles.

He turned to Marcus. "We waited years, were willing to wait years longer to win her father's approval, and some idiot took advantage of a girl weaker than himself." Paul's peripheral vision turned red and began closing in around him.

Marcus had backed away as Paul destroyed the chair, but now he stepped forward. "Paul, you're wasting time. Hannah needs you. Come on, I'll drive. My car has better traction in the snow than your truck."

Paul dropped the pieces of wood. How would he and Hannah ever find their way back to who they once were?

Marcus grabbed his keys off the hook beside the front door.

Climbing into the passenger seat of Marcus's Ford Escort, Paul wrestled with guilt and a sense of urgency.

As they traveled north on 283, Paul rapped his nervous fingers on his leg. "What's with all the brake lights?"

Marcus shifted into second gear. "I don't know, but it doesn't look good."

32

After burying her daughter, Hannah slept fitfully for hours in Mary's *Daadi Haus.* But the high winds that screeched all night made rest nearly impossible.

When morning broke and she heard familiar voices, she almost felt sane. She sat up, listening to the Pennsylvania Dutch words fly back and forth between Luke and Mary. Since it was barely daylight, Hannah figured Luke must have stayed the night at the Yoders' main house. Hannah eased her body upright, every part of her painfully aware that she'd given birth just two nights ago.

"You can't believe she doesn't know who the father of her child is, Mary. That's ridiculous. If you want to forgive her, fine. But at least make her be honest about her situation."

"You're wrong to hold such bitterness against her, Luke. Why do you hate her so?"

"I've got my reasons. And you'd do well to take more stock in what Sarah says and less in what Hannah says."

Hannah swallowed. Part of her wanted to step out and not eavesdrop. The other part wanted to stay put.

"I want to know what you have against Hannah." Mary's voice was different than Hannah had ever heard it.

"Fine. I'll tell ya. If she'd agreed to go with us the night I was gonna propose, we wouldn't have been out at the Knepps' place."

"What? You think you would've proposed with Hannah around? Just who are you foolin'? And if you want to blame someone for that night, blame me. I'm the one who was supposed to be driving. I'm the one who twisted the horse's reins around the stob. I'm the one who didn't want Sarah blabbing to the whole community about us being a couple when I didn't know how you felt."

"I...I... Hannah's the one who's been running around seeing that Mennonite behind everyone's back."

"And just who did you see behind everyone's back during your *rumschpringe,* Luke Lapp?"

"You're...you're seeing this all from Hannah's side."

Luke sounded rattled, and Hannah was glad. She didn't possess the strength to step into the room and argue with Luke. Besides, Mary was making headway—opening Luke's eyes. Hannah was sure of it.

"This argument has gone on way too long," Mary said.

Through the open bedroom door, Hannah saw Mary cross from the kitchen into the living room. Shaking, Hannah hid behind the doorframe and watched.

Mary thrust Luke's coat and hat toward him. "If that's how you feel about your sister, it's time you left." She opened the front door. "And ya need not bother returning."

Luke scowled. "Will she fool you your whole life, Mary?"

Mary pointed out the door. Luke took his coat and hat and stormed out. Mary sat on the couch and started crying.

Hannah rested her head on the doorframe. Causing trouble seemed to be her gift, her destiny. She didn't mean to. Sarah was right; Hannah was a tornado. Hannah had caused divisions in her own household and between Matthew and Elle and probably in every home within her district and beyond. She couldn't take it any longer. There had to be something she could do.

"Hannah. Kumm raus."

Chills ran up her back. That whisper was calling to her again. The voice sounded familiar, but she couldn't place it. The tone was soft and pleading.

The cold floor made her sore, achy body hurt even more. She returned to her bed and crawled beneath the blankets. As she closed her eyes, her mind danced to a place where no one knew her, a place filled with people who accepted her as if she'd never worn a scarlet letter that she didn't deserve.

Ohio came to mind again, and a half smile tugged at Hannah's lips. Wouldn't that be something—to leave all this behind? She could look up her Aunt Zabeth and maybe begin life anew.

The idea of leaving brought more than just hope of finding respect outside Owl's Perch and of ending the wars that had begun between people she cared about. The dream seemed to open her heart to the possibility of forgiving those who'd wronged her and letting go of her bitterness. With each moment of reflection, the hateful anger that raged within her began to quiet.

If she left, Mary and Luke would come to a we-agree-to-disagree resolution of some type. They loved each other too much not to. Her father wouldn't have to decide what to do with or about Hannah. She wouldn't have to spend a lifetime facing people who believed the rumors or at least pondered the truth of them.

Some people in the district would disrespect Hannah for the rest of her life. From what she saw at the graveside, she had even come between *Mamm* and *Daed*—*Mamm* wanting to comfort her, *Daed* treating her like an unrepentant adulteress.

Mary and Luke, Matthew and Elle were paying a ridiculous price on her behalf, being divided because there was no proof of her innocence, only evidence of sin—the child she carried, the men she'd been seen with, the lies she'd told her parents over the years. Hannah sighed. That was only part of the problem she'd cause over the next few years.

But if she left… The thought pulled at her imagination.

Where would she get the cash to travel? She had very little money… except the funds she and Paul had in an account together. She didn't have the bankbook, but Paul said she didn't need it to make withdrawals or deposits. Nine hundred dollars of the money in that joint account was hers. That should be enough for all her needs until she found a job.

Maybe she could go to Ohio and find her Aunt Zabeth after all.

She would need to call the bank and see if she could withdraw money using her pictureless identification card. She only wanted to take what was hers. There was no way she'd ever touch Paul's money.

The fanciful idea grew quickly. Dreaming of the possibilities, but too sore and tired to think anymore, Hannah dozed off.

She woke less than an hour later, feeling a bit of physical strength in spite of the emotional agony. Even before she opened her eyes, thoughts of leaving sailed across her soul, leaving some hope in their wake. The desire to leave this disgusting mess behind was stronger than anything she'd felt in her life.

Ohio.

The compelling thought caused hope to stir within her.

She smelled coffee and eased out of bed.

As she took a shower and dressed, an even stronger thought entered her mind. The voice that had been whispering her name had carried a captivating message: *kumm raus.* Those words formed images of her packing and landing in a new place.

Was that really possible?

Titillating desire mixed with nervousness made her feel like the Hannah of old, the one she'd been before the attack. The world beyond Owl's Perch was a big one, filled with good and bad people, to be sure. But she'd already encountered the worst life had to dish out, hadn't she?

Maybe there was something better. Maybe there wasn't. Either way, she was tired of life in Owl's Perch. She'd tried to please everyone, especially Paul. Those nurses at Hershey Medical Center didn't hang on what men thought or wanted, not like she had.

She slipped out of the bathroom and tiptoed to the bedroom window and gazed across the snow-covered fields. As she watched the sun dance off the white blanket that covered the tree limbs, she saw some Amish children sledding in the distance. If only she were young... The whispers of yesteryear rang in her head. But even that didn't beckon to her like the dream of leaving.

Hannah closed the bedroom door and pulled a stack of paper from a drawer. Before she left, she had to do what she could do to repair some of the damage.

She wrote a long letter to Elle, praying she would accept her explanation and forgive Matthew for not being with her the night she'd had to face her father—the night Hannah needed Matthew. Elle would lose a good man who loved her dearly if she didn't forgive Matthew his only fault, which was an overriding loyalty to the needy. Hannah had needed him more that night than Elle. Matthew knew that, and he'd acted on it. Surely Elle could see that if the child had been Matthew's, he would never have begun a relationship with Elle. Elle was smart. She could see past the lies to the truth, especially if Hannah bared her heart on paper.

She wrote a letter of thanks to Matthew, the only male friend she had left and someone she would pray for the rest of her life. Pray for? Hannah smiled. Yes, she concluded as she shook the dust of this place off her feet. She would pray in her new life. She would.

She wrote to Luke, hoping he could find it in himself to stop blaming her for Mary's injuries.

Weaving words of hope and forgiveness into the letter to her parents was the most difficult. She begged her *Daed* to understand that she needed to leave. There was no doubt in her mind that her decision to depart the

Lapp household and separate herself from the community here was for the best. Then her shame would be counted as hers alone and not as a reflection on her family.

As she filled page after page with words of her new decision, the force of life slowly flowed back to her. The idea of leaving was terrifying. But staying would be slow death.

I'm not eighteen yet.

That bit of realization stole her breath. It was thirteen days before she turned eighteen. For a moment she considered staying until her birthday. Hope drained from her. A sensation of losing her mind washed over her, and she knew without any doubt she couldn't stay—not even until she became a legal adult.

The two people who would be the saddest would be her mother and her dear friend Mary. They would understand her plans, but Hannah wasn't naive enough to think that they'd agree with her decision. They were too afraid of angering God, of severing ties, of Hannah getting hurt.

Hannah closed her eyes, contemplating whether *Mamm's* and Mary's future concerns for her were well-founded or not. She had no desire to make things worse by leaving without giving thought to what their reservations would be.

Hannah played out conversations in her mind, careful to hear every bit of apprehension her mother and Mary would share. But after considering all possible arguments either one would present, she decided fear was the only sound reason they'd have—fear of the unknown, of what might happen, of what might not happen.

The imagined conversation had brought up valid points. She might run into danger, might not get a job, might...might...might. The torments of what could happen frightened her. As Hannah burrowed deeper into her own thoughts, looking for answers, a startling revelation sprang forth. Fear might be her traveling companion, but she didn't have to let it stop her. Perhaps she'd have to carry it with her, unable to get free of it. But she didn't have to become immobilized by it. *That* was within her power to decide.

Excitement at that understanding grew, and desire to move forward became a part of her. With stacks of triple-folded letters all around her, Hannah took pen in hand to write the last letter before making her final plans to leave.

Hannah stacked the letters together and laid them inside the book Dr. Greenfield had given her. With trepidation she eased out to the kitchen to tell Mary of her plans. Hannah was surprised to see Matthew sitting at the kitchen table with Mary.

They turned to look at her. Relieved smiles erased the misery on their faces.

Matthew rose and pulled out a chair for her. "Good morning. Come sit."

Glad to get off her feet, Hannah eased into the chair. "How are things with Elle?"

Matthew shrugged. "I heard from the Bylers that her father didn't arrive that night due to the weather. She hired a driver the next day and went to meet him in Baltimore and spend a few days there. Other than that, I don't know."

Matthew poured a cup of coffee and passed it to Hannah. Mary dished out a gigantic cinnamon bun from a pan in the center of the table and placed it beside the cup. Deciding she was no longer too young for coffee, Hannah took a sip of the warm, brown liquid. She played with the metal cup in her hand, praying that Mary and Matthew would support her resolution. "I'm glad you're both here," she said, her voice sounding even more resolved than she felt. "I need to talk to you about some decisions I've made."

33

The sun warmed the snow-covered earth as Hannah stood in John Yoder's beaten and damaged phone shanty, waiting for the woman at the bank to complete her verification. Mary and Matthew stood nearby, talking in low tones.

"I'm sorry," the woman said, coming back on the line, "but that account has been closed."

"What?" Hannah barely breathed.

"All the money has been withdrawn from it." The woman ended the conversation with another apology, and Hannah hung up the phone.

She couldn't believe this. How could the account be closed?

Hannah lowered her forehead against the receiver, which rested in its cradle on the wall. The disappointment and betrayal were too great for her to bear. Was Paul not at all the man she'd thought him to be?

Mary took the few steps to the shanty's doorway. "What'd you find out?"

Hannah closed her eyes and gave a long, slow shrug. "The account is empty. I...I guess Paul took the money."

Mary wrapped her arms around Hannah. "I'm sure he's just not thinking straight, Hannah. He'll come around. Maybe you should contact him."

As they walked to Mary's front porch, Hannah squelched that burning desire. She hated to admit it to herself, but she ached to call him, to hear his voice one last time, to at least say good-bye.

Hannah sat on the top step. "I've got a little money from the summer's produce. I guess it'll get me somewhere."

Matthew sat beside her. "I think—"

The phone rang, and Mary ran across the yard to answer it.

Hannah smiled. "Her strength is back, no?"

"*Ya.* She does well, thanks to you." Matthew leaned his forearm on his thighs. Neither of them spoke for several minutes. "Hannah, are you sure about leaving?"

Before Hannah had time to answer, Mary strode back to them, hurt showing in her face. "That was my parents. They are returning today and..."

Hannah didn't need to be told what that call was about. She patted the step beside her. "I'm to be off their property before they arrive."

Mary sat. "I'm sorry."

Hannah placed her arm around Mary and rubbed her shoulder. "I'm sure my own mother feels much the same way. I know *Daed* is angry and telling her not to come, but he couldn't keep her from coming to me if she had a mind to."

Matthew tugged his hat lower on his head. "I've got some money."

"That money is for you and Elle to start a home with."

He stood. "Don't deny me the right to do what I think is right. I've spent too many months trying to stay out of hot water when I should have been trying to be a friend." He shrugged. "Either Elle gets that or she doesn't."

Hannah reached out and clutched his fingers, overwhelmed with his generous spirit. "I'll send the money back as soon as I can, after I get a job and get settled."

Matthew gave her hand a warm, reassuring squeeze. "Don't worry about trying to pay me back. Just let us know you're okay every so often."

Mary hugged Hannah, tears brimming in her eyes. "*Ya,* write to us."

"I will." Laying her head on Mary's shoulder, Hannah said, "Let's call the train station and arrange for a driver."

Matthew helped her to her feet. "Call Russ Braden. He's the easiest driver to reach on such short notice. While you do that, I'll run over to the safe in my shop." He studied her. Then without a word he took off to fetch the money.

Paul was glad they'd taken Marcus's car since it had a radio. He flipped on a news station, listening for a traffic report. A minute later he heard about a bad accident somewhere ahead of them that would have traffic backed up for a long time.

Paul took a deep breath to keep himself from hitting the dashboard. "How could I do that to her?"

Marcus turned the radio to an instrumental music station. "Personally, I think you were justified in walking out on her. But let's just say you blew it by handling the whole thing wrong. We all blow it, Paul. Hannah's got some responsibility in this too. Right?"

Paul shook his head. "I should've known better. The ridiculous thing is, aside from my uncontrollable jealousy, I did know better. She's so amazing, Marcus. When you get to know her, you'll agree."

As they sat in stand-still traffic, Marcus had the car in neutral with the handle of the emergency brake raised. "She must be special to have grabbed your attention and kept it all this time. How'd you meet her?"

"She was Gram's helper when I went home to supervise those guys we hired to replace Gram's roof and repair the barn and fences. She was fascinating: quiet, a hard worker. But when she spoke, she had a dry sense of humor. Weeks later when I went back for a family gathering at Gram's, I was sure she'd be happy to see me. She didn't even seem to notice my presence. So I hung out in the kitchen, giving her time to realize I existed. She passed me a chef's apron. To her I was either helpful or in the way." He chuckled. "I was hooked right then. There's no figuring her out, but there's pure pleasure in being with her."

Marcus smiled wryly. "Okay, so maybe I should have been glad you weren't able to talk about her all this time."

"Get us out of this traffic, and I'll never bore you again."

"Promise?" Marcus revved his engine as if he could take off somewhere.

Paul leaned his head against the headrest and growled in frustration.

Hannah gazed at the prayer *Kapp* in her hand. Mary stood behind her, pinning Hannah's apron to her dress. Traveling regulations dictated that she either have a photo ID or wear full Amish garb with her pictureless ID. Though ready to be free of everything Amish, Hannah placed the covering on her head and attached it to her hair using straight pins. She turned and faced Mary.

Mary brushed a piece of lint from Hannah's dress. "Are you sure about this?"

She nodded, unable to speak. She took Mary by the hand, and they walked outside, where the driver was waiting.

Matthew loaded Hannah's bag into the trunk of the hired car. As he shut the trunk, a buggy pulled into the driveway. Matthew turned. "Elle."

The cool nod she gave him could have come from an aristocrat sitting in a fine carriage rather than an Amish girl in an open wagon.

"I thought you were in Baltimore." He stepped toward her buggy. "I'm sorry about the other night. Are you—"

Elle interrupted him. "You don't seem to ever lack for info about what's happening in Hannah's life." Her eyes moved to Hannah. "What's going on?"

Hannah stepped off the porch. "I'm leaving."

Elle's jaw was set, her cheeks flaming red from the cold wind. "Then at least some of what I've heard is true."

"Very little, I'm sure." Mary's voice wavered.

Elle shot an angry look at Matthew. "Did you disobey the bishop's decree concerning Hannah? Did you go to her when I asked you to be with me that night?"

"It's a long story, Elle, but now isn't the time."

Hannah pulled Mary into a hug. After a long, teary embrace, Hannah released her. Then she stood there, fidgeting with her apron, wanting to clutch Matthew and tell him how thankful she was for his kind, understanding spirit. But to do so might cause even more trouble between him and Elle.

A look of determination passed through Matthew's eyes. "I'm goin' with ya. When you're settled on the train, I'll return to Owl's Perch."

"That's ridiculous." Elle raised her body slightly off the bench seat, making the horse step forward. "What do you expect me to think of this?"

Matthew took Elle's horse by the harness, stopping it from moving any farther. "Her train don't leave until early afternoon tomorrow. Mary can't go; her parents have made their stand clear. Hannah's my friend, Elle. I won't leave her in Harrisburg to stay overnight at some hotel by herself."

Elle scowled, clearly getting angrier by the second. "If you don't care at all what I think, why don't you just say it outright, Matthew Esh? You've pretty much just told me you plan to stay at a hotel with her. If you do that, you're sure to get in trouble with the church leaders. You'll be disciplined by the bishop. You know you will."

Matthew released his grip on the horse and walked closer to the buggy. He placed a foot on the spindle of the front wheel. "I know. But they're wrong about Hannah. And friends should stick by each other, even when it costs them."

Elle cocked an eyebrow. She stared at Matthew for nearly a full minute. He watched her face, looking neither worried nor apologetic. Hannah struggled to breathe, guilt heavy on her heart.

Tugging the reins low, Elle caused the horse to back up. Matthew removed his foot, acceptance in his features. Elle's beautiful eyes never left his face as the horse continued backing up.

She stopped the buggy, her brows knitted, her gaze still fixed on Matthew. "Regardless of where we end up in all this, it still seems best that someone go with you, Matthew, to keep things looking respectable before the People and the church leaders." She looked to Hannah. "You have to know that's true."

"Yeah, absolutely. But there's no one else."

"I'll go."

Hannah was startled by the woman's voice behind them. She turned and saw Naomi Esh standing near the car with her hands on her hips.

"I was there the night Hannah's baby died." Naomi gave a weak and humble smile at Hannah, then turned to face Elle. "I believe her account of how she came to be with child. But I'll not have my son's reputation ruined, and clearly he's determined to go with her."

Elle shrugged. "I guess your mother chaperoning will count for something when the church leaders hear of what you've done."

Matthew pulled a letter from his pocket. "Hannah wrote this to you. Maybe it'll help ya understand." He gave a nod to Hannah and motioned for her to get in the car.

Hannah turned to embrace Mary one more time. Her friend broke into sobs.

"It's okay, Mary. I'm going to be fine." Hannah placed her hands on

Mary's shoulders and put some distance between them. "You'll be fine too. Make amends with Luke. He'll come around concerning me as time goes by."

"Mary," Elle said.

Hannah paused as Matthew held the car door open for her.

Elle smiled at Mary. "I'm staying with the Bylers tonight. Esther Byler is helping me with some projects for the kids at the school where I teach. Would you care to join us? We certainly could use your help."

The grief in Mary's face, as well as the lost look in her eyes, faded a bit.

Remorse as well as thankfulness entered Hannah as she considered that if she left, Elle would likely become Mary's closest friend.

"Hannah." The whispery voice floated across the fields, seemingly coming from all directions.

Instantly Hannah's resolve was renewed. She climbed into the backseat of the waiting car. Hope in the future lifted her spirits.

34

About the time Paul couldn't take one more minute of waiting, traffic finally started moving again. He drummed his fingers on the dashboard. He had to get to Hannah and offer to take care of her and her baby. Maybe, eventually, she'd come to trust and love him again and they could marry.

As they finally entered Owl's Perch, he gave Marcus directions to the Yoder place.

Marcus pulled into the driveway. Paul jumped out of the car and banged on the front door of the *Daadi Haus.*

Come on, Hannah. Answer.

No sound came from inside; he saw no flickers of light from a kerosene lamp. He knocked longer and louder. Still no response. Disappointment and concern threatened to swallow him.

Paul climbed into the car. "We're going to the Lapp place." He gave Marcus directions.

As they pulled into the driveway, Mr. Lapp stepped out of his house. Paul got out and spoke to Mr. Lapp from across the roof of the car. "I'm looking for Hannah."

He waved Paul away and marched off toward the barn.

Paul caught up to him. "Mr. Lapp, please. I need to speak with her."

Mr. Lapp sighed. "She doesn't live here anymore. I did my best to protect her. But her sneaking around did more damage than a father can stop." He paused and looked at Paul. "It's you, isn't it? You're the one she wrote letters to and snuck out to visit."

There was no easy way to explain his relationship with Hannah. He loved her, to be sure. But that wasn't what Mr. Lapp wanted to hear. "I'm Katie Waddell's grandson, Paul."

Mr. Lapp studied him. "It didn't have to end this way. If she hadn't been so stubborn about going to the bishop—"

"Where can I find her?"

He frowned. "She's staying at the Yoder place."

"I went there. No one's home."

The look on Mr. Lapp's face told Paul that was news to him. "It seems I've spent far too much time not knowing where my daughter was or what she was up to." Mr. Lapp stalked off, grumbling as he went. "Please leave. Just go, and let me forget for a while the devastation you've brought to us."

Paul hated the way Mr. Lapp perceived the events, but it would take a lifetime to change the man's opinions, if it could be done at all. Paul climbed in the car and slammed the door. "How can he just turn his back on his own daughter like that?" Guilt rose within Paul, choking him. He had turned his back on Hannah too.

Marcus shrugged. "Where to now?" He backed down the driveway and stopped where the road met the lane.

"Let's go back to the Yoder farm. From there we'll try to find the Esh place. She and Matthew were friends. He should know where she is—not that he'll tell me." He looked at Marcus, desperate for some answers. "We have to find her."

"We will. Even if we have to cruise her district all day and night. But first, can we go by your grandmother's and get some food? I missed breakfast."

That was a brilliant idea. Maybe Gram knew where Hannah was. Maybe Hannah was even there. "Yes. Go there first."

Marcus pulled onto the main road.

"Do you have your cell with you?" Paul asked.

Marcus pulled the phone from his jeans pocket.

"If Gram doesn't know where Hannah is, I'll call my mother and tell her what to do if Hannah calls. Then I'll call Carol and Dorcas. One of them should be willing to go to our apartment and man the phone. Ryan or Taylor will let them in, but I don't trust our roommates not to leave for a food run or something, even if I ask them to stay by the phone for me. I'll make sure Gram stays near her phone too. If Hannah calls any of those places, I'll get the message right away." He held up Marcus's phone and waggled it.

Hannah lay on the bed, staring at the soft lighting of the electric floor lamp at the far end of the hotel room. The sun had gone down, but there was no need for matches or kerosene lamps.

She clutched her train tickets to her chest. Buying them was the first thing she and Matthew had done when they'd arrived in Harrisburg. He gave her the money for the one-way tickets, but he hadn't joined her when she talked to the man at the ticket window. The man patiently helped her decide what train she needed to take and where she needed to get off. Her final destination would be a little depot in Alliance, Ohio. That was the closest depot to where her aunt lived in Winding Creek.

Matthew and his mother were out getting supper. Hannah remained behind, desperate for some time alone. Matthew said he'd bring her back some food.

A phone sat on the table beside her, begging to be used. She desperately wanted to call Paul and have some type of friendly ending to their longstanding relationship. She sat upright and lifted the receiver from its cradle. At Thanksgiving Paul had given her the phone numbers for Gram, his parents, his apartment, and even his sister. She'd memorized them all.

Following the directions taped on the tabletop next to the phone, she pressed the button to get an outside line and then punched in the number to his apartment. Leaning back on the bed, she drew a deep breath. Her stomach ached with nervousness.

"Hello?" a young female voice answered.

"Uh, yes, this is Hannah Lapp. I'm trying to reach Paul Waddell."

Daylight peeped over the horizon as Paul continued to cruise Owl's Perch in Marcus's car. Gram had been no help, saying she hadn't heard from Hannah in months.

He'd left Marcus at his gram's house, thinking Marcus'd be better suited for reaching him than Gram if Hannah did call. He'd contacted his parents, his sister, and Dorcas, making sure every place Hannah might call was covered. His mother was baffled and stressed to learn of Paul's relationship with Zeb Lapp's daughter, but she said they'd do as he asked.

When he drove back to the Yoder place, he discovered that Mary's parents had arrived home at some point while he was riding around the district. When Paul knocked on the door and asked about Hannah, he learned that they didn't know where she was. The looks on their faces said they didn't much care either. When he asked to see Mary, he was told she wasn't at home, and they weren't going to reveal where she was. But he did learn that Mary's mother had gone to see Mary, wherever she was, and Hannah was not with her. They wanted it to stay that way.

As he continued driving, Paul studied the homes and yards of every Amish place, hoping for a glimpse of Hannah or Mary. Using Marcus's cell, Paul called his parents and Gram; no one had heard from her.

He dialed his apartment and waited for someone to pick up. After what he thought were too many rings, Dorcas answered.

"Hello."

"Hey, any news?" Paul expected a quick answer, but instead the line went silent. "Dorcas, did Hannah call?"

Dorcas stammered and stuttered, infuriating Paul. "Uh, well, there was a call...but, uh, it...well..."

"This is no time for incompetence, Dorcas. It's an easy question. Did Hannah call?"

There was a shuffling sound, and his sister came on the line. "Easy, Paul. You made her cry. This is a pretty miserable place to spend the night with Ryan and Taylor in and out at all hours. We've had to argue with them twice in order to keep them off the phone, and the best we've been able to do is doze on these horrid things you call couches. I was outside, getting something from the car, when the call she's talking about came in. Dorcas said a young woman called, saying something about a party coming up next Friday."

Disappointment flooded him. "That call would have been for Ryan or Taylor. Did anyone else call?'

"Not unless it came while I wasn't within earshot. Dorcas, did anyone else call?" There was a short pause. "No, no one else called."

"Carol, please stay close enough to hear the phones, okay?"

"Sure. I can do that."

He disconnected the call, concern growing with each passing moment. "Hannah, my Lion-heart, where are you?"

The argument Luke'd had with Mary yesterday kept repeating itself in his mind as he climbed into his buggy and took off down the road. He'd spent all night rehashing what she'd said. In the morning he woke feeling even more confused. He hadn't been able to shake the feeling even though he'd dared to spend this Sunday morning at his harness shop.

So he decided a good, brisk ride would clear his head. He flicked the whip, making the horse pick up speed. His sister had managed to come between him and Mary without so much as opening her mouth.

How was that possible?

He knew the answer. She'd done things she shouldn't, really bad things, and the rumors had caught up to her. Of course Mary thought she was innocent. Mary loved her. And he was sure his girl never saw or knew the things Hannah had done that caused the rumors. If Hannah ended up ruining him and Mary, he'd…he'd… Luke sighed. He didn't know what he'd do.

With thoughts of who was right and who was lying swirling through his mind, he rode farther and farther, ignoring the cold temperatures. It did seem odd for Hannah to have this many rumors about her when her worst behavior seemed to be her love of working for Mrs. Waddell. Hannah saw that grandson of Mrs. Waddell's during her visits, but he didn't hold that against her. As Mary had pointed out, he'd done similar stuff way back when.

Luke tugged on the right rein, guiding the horse onto the dirt road near the Knepps' place. The need to see the place where the accident took place had nagged at him long enough. Since Mary wasn't speaking to him, he had a little time for getting this ghost behind him. A tremor of nervousness made his chest constrict. Old Bess jerked her head into the air and whinnied.

"It's okay, ol' girl. It's okay."

He didn't find his words a bit comforting. He squeezed the reins in his hands as memories of that horrid night rushed at him. Bess became flighty as they approached the spot where she'd been injured. Luke pulled back on the reins and jumped out of the buggy. "Easy, Old Bess." He patted her neck and led her onto the small path that went by the old tree where he'd proposed to Mary. Once off the main dirt road, the horse settled a bit.

Drawing a deep breath, Luke rehashed parts of his argument with Mary. Before yesterday, he'd had no idea the girl could argue like that. Why, she said if he had to blame someone for the accident to blame her. Okay, so maybe he had been looking to blame someone, and maybe it wasn't his sister's fault. But that didn't clear her of all those rumors.

Luke tucked the reins under a heavy rock, knowing Old Bess would stay wherever he put her without much fight. He ambled back out to where the accident took place. Absorbing how different the fields looked with their thick layer of snow and patches of tall brown grass sticking through, Luke climbed the fence on the far side of the road. The leaves had been green when he and Mary were here last. Somehow this past fall he'd missed autumn's changing colors and the trees going bare. Stomping through the high snow to the area where he'd landed after being thrown from the buggy, he realized he'd sailed through the air quite a ways. But he had no memory of that.

What did happen that night?

As if waiting to be asked that question, memories of crying out to God came to him. When he'd prayed for help that night, he'd been engulfed in…something. Maybe compassion? The nightmare of trying to find Mary washed over Luke. The awful realization that he didn't know how to use a cell phone and that Mary might die because of his helplessness had left him square in need of—

Chills ran up Luke's arms. He looked skyward, watching billowy gray clouds roll and slide east.

Square in need of…

What was it that he needed so badly that night, the very thing that seemed to cover him with acceptance and strength at the same time?

He'd been injured and too weak to do anything on his own. What had taken place between him and God that night?

With questions churning inside him, Luke headed back to the buggy.

What was it, God?

Like an unexpected peal of thunder ripping across the sky, Luke knew. It hadn't been one understanding. It was a lot of things, all parts of God, which had forgiveness, strength, and hope rolled into it. Once the feeling touched him, things he shouldn't have been able to know, he knew. How to find Mary dawned on him instantly after he prayed. Strength he hadn't had before entered him. He never figured out how to use the cell phone, but the car horn idea came to him, and he knew how to do that. He'd been told that constant noise had caused someone to call the police.

A bolt of energy ran through him.

Oh, God, I see.

"There's a part of You that talks to people sometimes. That tells us something that isn't passed down by the church leaders…or *Daed.*"

Luke knelt on the cold snow, bowing his head. "Dear Father, thank You for saving Mary and me that night." He saw Hannah in his mind's eye. He lifted his face toward heaven. "God, what am I to think of her?"

No instantaneous ideas came to him. Luke remained on his knees, hoping wisdom would pour from heaven onto him. It didn't. He started to shake as the snow melted under him, causing his pants to soak up cold water.

He rose and made his way back to the buggy. As the horse plodded toward his harness shop, thoughts of his sister over the past six months ran through his mind. When his harness shop came into view, Luke saw a car parked in front of it.

A customer on a Sunday?

As Luke pulled the buggy to a stop, their milkman, Mr. Carlisle, stepped out of his car. "Luke,"—Mr. Carlisle closed his car door—"Russ Braden came to see me about an hour ago. Something was weighing on his mind, and now it's weighing on mine."

Luke couldn't imagine why Mr. Carlisle was telling him about Mr. Braden. "Yeah? What's that?"

Hannah sat in the train station clutching her tickets and ID, feeling as if she held her future in her hands. She'd had a restless night, hoping Paul would return her call. He hadn't. With fading hopes, she'd stayed at the hotel as long as possible, giving him time to change his mind and contact her.

Perhaps it was best that she not tell him good-bye. Temptation to reveal where she was going might have been too much if she'd spoken to him. It was important that no one know where she was heading. She wanted a fresh start, with no worry that someone might show up or send another horrid letter warning her of the wages of sin.

Drawing a deep breath, she gazed around the train depot. It wasn't particularly large. But the building was interesting and looked to be centuries old. She couldn't help but wonder how many people over the years had come through here to begin a new life elsewhere.

A thousand emotions vied for her attention: guilt over leaving, hope at what lay ahead, longing to find peace, desire to succeed, and overwhelming grief. She took a seat on a long wooden bench, waiting for Matthew to return. He'd gone to the ticket window to ask a few more questions concerning arrival times and such, but he'd promised that he wouldn't pry about her destination.

The overriding emotion seemed to be the misery of feeling that her body, mind, and spirit were disconnected from one another. As if her body was here but her mind and heart were suspended in some distant, fog-covered world. Perhaps if she took her body to a new place, a clear mind and a mended heart would join her…someday.

Matthew put her lone suitcase on the floor beside her and sat down. "I upgraded your accommodations. The train from here to Pittsburgh is coach only. But once you get on the train in Pittsburgh to wherever your final destination is, you'll ride first class in a roomette. Meals are free, and you'll have a berth to sleep in, private bathroom facilities, and a door that can lock."

Hannah crossed her arms over her waist. He shouldn't have paid extra money to upgrade; riding coach all the way would have been fine. "Matthew…"

"You need the rest, Hannah." Matthew was resolved, and he wasn't going to apologize. "In a few minutes a redcap will come by. He'll take you to the train platform by elevator to save you from clomping down a couple dozen fairly steep stairs." Since Matthew had traveled by train a few times, he explained to her about tipping the redcaps and the basics of life on a passenger train. When he finished, they sat in silence.

To Hannah's chagrin, he'd given her nearly two thousand dollars in cash, in addition to paying for her train tickets and everything else since they'd left Owl's Perch. If he could work things out with Elle, he'd need that money to set up a home. It would take him years to recover.

Matthew removed his hat and set it on the bench beside him. He rubbed his forehead. "Hannah, promise me you'll take care of yourself." He sighed. "You'll have no one to make sure you're eating or anything."

Hannah wrapped her hand over his. "I promise, Matthew. I'll eat whether I'm hungry or not. I'll rest and take good care of myself."

Mr. Carlisle turned down another narrow street. "When we get to the train station, you want me to wait in the truck or go with you?"

"I don't know." Luke's laced fingers tightened. "What if she's gone already?"

Stopping at a red light, Mr. Carlisle turned to his passenger, concern clouding his eyes. "We're cutting it close. Russ wasn't sure what time her train was leaving. He only knows what he overheard in the car after the train tickets had been purchased."

Luke tried to remember what Mr. Carlisle had told him less than an hour ago. All he could recall was that Carlisle's friend Russ, who worked as a driver for many of the Amish, had taken Matthew, his mother, and Hannah to the train station late yesterday, waited for them while they went inside, and then taken them to a hotel. Russ had heard them say that Hannah had purchased a one-way ticket, but he didn't know her destination. He did hear them plan to use the hotel's shuttle service to get Hannah back to the depot today around twelve thirty.

Mr. Carlisle checked his watch. "It's one fifteen now, so that was forty-five minutes ago. Russ thought they were planning to get to the station about an hour before their train leaves." He tapped the steering wheel. "If I got it figured right, that gives us a ten- to fifteen-minute window to catch her."

"If I hadn't been out riding this morning…"

The light changed, and Mr. Carlisle made a right turn. "And if Russ had told me what was going on yesterday after he dropped them off at the hotel rather than waiting until this morning to come see me, we wouldn't be in this fix."

"I'm glad ya came to tell me. I just hope we get there in time."

"When your father finds out I kept this from him, well, it won't go over too well. But I figure Hannah got a bad shake in this deal, and I'm not tattling on her. I'm just givin' you a chance to intervene. Maybe you can talk her into not leaving."

"I hope so."

Shifting gears, Mr. Carlisle turned left. "I don't know what's really going on with Hannah, but I've been hearing stuff for months. One thing I do know: Hannah doesn't deserve what's been happening to her. I don't give a rip how many of those rumors are true."

Luke nodded, realizing the full truth. If Mr. Carlisle could see it, why, as Hannah's brother, couldn't he have seen it sooner? He just hoped he wasn't too late to talk her into staying. With a few people on her side, she could weather this storm. He had to convince her of that.

When Mr. Carlisle pulled up in front of the train station, he nodded toward the depot. "I'll park and meet you out front. You go find your sister. When you're ready to leave, just come outside."

Luke opened the truck door and climbed out. "Thank you, Mr. Carlisle."

"You're welcome. Now, hurry."

Walking through the two sets of doors, Luke took in the large open area in a single glance. Hannah wasn't there. To his left was a small store. Through the shop windows, he saw a few people milling about; none of them was Hannah. In the far corner to his right, a small line of people waited at the ticket window. She wasn't there either.

He jogged through the next set of open doors, which led to another large room with wooden benches sitting end to end and back to back. Still no sign of Hannah.

God, please let me find my sister and take her home.

Suddenly he saw her and Matthew sitting on one of the benches. A small suitcase sat at his sister's feet. "Hannah!"

When she turned and saw Luke, shock covered her face. She rose from the bench.

Luke rushed to her. He studied her pale face. Only one thought filled his mind. "I'm sorry. I'm so very sorry." Without waiting for her to respond, he hugged her tight. She didn't push him away, but she didn't return the hug. "Please come home, Hannah. What happened to you is awful, and you ain't been done right, but don't leave."

Hannah took a step back. "That's what you say today. What about tomorrow?"

Luke took her hands in his. "I've been mean and difficult, and I'm really sorry for all of it. Give me a chance to make it up to you."

She eased back onto the bench and stared at her lap.

Luke bent closer. "Mary and I will take care of you. You can live in the apartment over my harness shop."

Hannah lifted her chin and looked at him. "*Ach,* Luke, you're not thinking. With the bishop set against me like he is, you could get shunned for such a thing. And for sure it'd ruin your good standing with the church." Hannah took a deep breath. "I've been branded, Luke, and that will never go away."

"But what about that...guy?"

"Paul? He fled the moment he discovered I was pregnant. I knew he would."

"You ain't exactly given him time to adjust."

She rose. "I'm not living every day of my life hoping he'll come back. I couldn't stand that. Even if he comes to realize I'm innocent, what's he going to do—still want to marry me? Besides, he's not coming back, and I don't want to live in a lonely world with no hope of a future, barely being tolerated among our community, while Paul finds a new love, gets married, and has children." Her body trembled, but her eyes blazed with determination. She'd obviously thought this through.

A uniformed man strode by. "Train for Pittsburgh will begin boarding in two minutes," he called out. "Please have your tickets ready."

Luke felt panicky. He had to change her mind. "So you have some things to work through. It's the hand you were dealt, Hannah, but Mary and Matthew and I will help you. We'll set things right with the church. It may take some time, but…"

A man wearing a red cap stopped in front of them. "If you wish to ride the elevator to the platform, I'm heading that way in just a minute."

Hannah drew a deep breath and stared at Luke. "Think, Luke, just really think about this. Would you want to stay if you had to face what I'll have to face for the rest of my life?"

Luke searched his sister's face. She'd borne so much grief and condemnation that she was no longer the girl he'd known only six months ago.

God, help me. What do I say?

No one spoke as he waited to get some inkling, some word of wisdom.

Let her go.

His heart sank. He wanted the chance to do things right, but this wasn't about him. "You will write to us or call Mary and let us know when you're settled?"

"I will," she said, her eyes misting. "I promise."

The redcap returned, pulling a long flatbed dolly behind him. Matthew stood and passed the man Hannah's bag and a ten-dollar bill. "Make sure to carry this bag onto the train for her and get her a seat."

"Absolutely, sir." The man grabbed her suitcase and placed it on the dolly. He then turned to collect some of the other passengers' bags.

Matthew gently placed his hands on Hannah's shoulders. "You're sure about this?"

She stroked the two tickets in her hands. "Yes." She hugged him tight. "Good-bye, Matthew."

He squeezed her gently. "Bye, Hannah. You take care and write to us."

She backed away. "I will." She turned to Luke. "I'm going to be fine."

Luke swallowed hard. "Can you at least tell me where you're going?"

She shook her head. "It's best that no one knows."

Luke hugged her, wondering if he would ever see his sister again. "You're probably right."

When he let her go, she looked at him for a long moment. "Thank you." She grabbed one of Luke's hands and one of Matthew's. "Both of you."

The redcap paused in front of Hannah. "You ready, ma'am?"

She let go of their hands. Matthew's returned to his side, but Luke held on to his sister. A shadow of insecurity came over her face.

Luke released her hand and turned to the redcap. "She's ready."

Hannah glanced at her boarding passes, one for the first leg of the trip to Pittsburgh and the other for the Amtrak passenger train that would take her to Alliance. Gripping her tickets as well as her ID, she felt her resolve weaken. At the moment, hope only slightly outweighed her anxiety.

Grateful Luke had come and shared his feelings, Hannah fell into step with the small group of people following the redcap as he pushed the dolly filled with luggage. After twenty or so steps a hallway came into view on her left. The beauty of the Harrisburg Train Depot ended abruptly as gray concrete seemed to cover everything except the dingy-looking elevator doors.

She turned and waved at Matthew and Luke. They both waved back, looking torn between supporting her decision to leave and wanting to keep her near. Pulling her attention away from them, she walked to the elevator and squeezed in with the few others who weren't using the stairs.

The redcap pushed a button. As the doors began to close, realization of what she was doing hit Hannah like an ice storm. A voice inside her head screamed at her to grab a piece of luggage off the dolly and shove it between the doors. Was she making the worst mistake of her life? How could she leave everything familiar behind? Could the pain of knowing that her daughter might have lived if she'd handled things right have caused her to imagine God was leading her away from the source of her pain?

She fought to get control of her fears. How could she, a girl with an eighth-grade education who'd just given birth and buried her child, move to some foreign place and start over?

Closing her eyes, she remembered the whispery voice, and her fears calmed a bit.

35

As the sun went down for the second day, Paul made another round through Owl's Perch. He'd known the Amish community could keep its silence, not even giving an impression of politeness if they thought an outsider was subversive, probing, or inappropriate. Regardless of who knew what, those he approached either turned away from him or closed a door on him without sharing a bit of information.

In spite of knocking on Matthew Esh's and Mary Yoder's doors, he hadn't convinced anyone to share more than a hard countenance and an unwillingness even to hint where Hannah might be. Mr. Esh had informed Paul that Matthew and his mother were gone for the night. When Matthew returned, Paul could ask whatever questions he wanted. Matthew was a grown man, and he could decide for himself what he wanted to say on the subject of Hannah Lapp.

Her name seemed to be poison on the man's lips. "Ya don't need to knock on the door again, asking for him. When he gets home, someone will hang a towel on the front railing." During the curt, brief conversation with Mr. Esh, Paul got the feeling that Matthew's being gone was in some way related to Hannah. Maybe he'd taken her somewhere to hide while the community calmed down.

With nowhere else to turn, Paul had gone to Gram's the night before and had slept a few hours before beginning his search again. He'd straight-lined it for the Esh place, but there was no towel hanging out. As he drove on, going through the community again and again, he had to face that his willingness to accept Hannah's reality might be too late. She'd gone into hiding somewhere, and unless Matthew helped him locate her…

His heartbeat quickened when he spotted what looked like an Amish woman riding in a van, sitting next to a driver, with an Amish man in the backseat. Paul's fatigue fell to the wayside as the car drove into the Eshes' driveway. He pulled up beside the other vehicle and jumped out. The woman barely looked at him as she closed the car door and trudged toward the house. When the man climbed out of the backseat, Paul immediately recognized him.

"Matthew," he called.

Matthew glanced up before turning back to pay the driver. The driver shook his head, refusing the money and drove off.

"I'm Paul Waddell. I'm looking for Hannah."

Matthew looked at him with eyes that were every bit as unfriendly as Mary's and Hannah's father's had been. "She's gone. My mother and I took her to the train station."

Paul's heart seemed to stop beating. "Where did she go? How can I contact her?"

Matthew shook his head. "She didn't say. She doesn't want anyone to know where she's going."

Paul struggled to stay standing.

Matthew stepped forward, his features changing from coldness to puzzlement. "Why did ya take her money?"

As if a second fist had hit Paul in the chest, he gasped. "What?"

"The money in the account that belonged to both of you. Why did ya take her part of it?"

"I never… It's gone?"

Matthew nodded.

Paul's chest constricted as he carried on a conversation that had nothing to do with helping him find Hannah. "I only use that account twice a year, putting money into it after all expenses have been paid out for a six-month period. But…is it possible that Hannah lost the bankbook the day I gave it to her, the day she was raped?" Paul rubbed his forehead, feeling unbearably dizzy. "If her attacker got his hands on the bankbook and emptied the account, then maybe the police will have a lead to find her attacker. Will you go with me and tell them what you know about it?"

Matthew dipped his head and sighed. "I don't know. I disobeyed the bishop on some things concerning Hannah, and I'm in a lot of hot water with him...and my girlfriend."

"I...I didn't realize you had a girlfriend."

"I did..." Matthew shrugged before he reached into his pocket and pulled out a letter. He handed it to Paul. "Hannah said you'd come looking for her at some point."

Paul snatched the letter as if he'd been thrown a lifeline. He tore it open, hoping it would tell him where to find her.

Paul,

If you're reading this note, then you've come in search of answers, perhaps in search of me. I have no way of telling how much time has passed. Maybe you have a family of your own by now.

I'm not sure how much help I can offer you, but I had to go. It seems that no one believes my account of how I conceived a child. The injustice of this is more than I'm willing to bear. I need to get away, to start fresh. I had to put everything behind me and begin anew, like putting new wine into new wineskins, ya?

I hope you find peace, Paul. I don't hold you responsible for your reaction. I hope you don't hold resentment against me for mine. I wish you well.

Hannah

Feeling as if he'd been thrown into a deep pit with no way out, Paul held tight to the letter. "How will she support herself and a baby?"

Matthew didn't answer.

Paul searched Matthew's eyes, looking for hints of things he wasn't saying. "Does she have a plan? Is she going someplace where they'll help her and the child?"

Matthew folded his arms across his chest. "Hannah went into labor a couple of days ago. The baby died."

A loud, unstoppable groan left Paul. Unable to stand on his own, he placed the palms of his hands against the roof of Marcus's car. She'd given birth since he'd seen her a few days ago?

God, how can anyone survive all this alone?

"She'll get a job," Matthew went on.

Paul drew several deep breaths, needing the cold air to keep him from turning into a raving maniac. "But if she has no money..."

"She didn't leave empty-handed. She has enough to take care of herself in any way she needs until she's on her feet. I...I made sure of that."

Paul lowered his head into his hands, too hurt and tired to know what to think.

Matthew placed his hand on Paul's shoulder. "She needed to go. Trust God with that."

God wasn't the issue here. It was Hannah, who'd chosen to run off while Paul had spent nearly two days and most of a night looking for her. Why did she have to keep the pregnancy such a secret? Couldn't she have found a way to tell him months ago so they at least had a chance of working through all this? Who would she go to for help now?

Frustrations and fears melted together until Paul had no idea what he felt—or what he should feel.

"Paul, trust that Hannah figured out what she needed and that she's doing it."

Paul lifted his head and gazed into Matthew's eyes, seeing the same kindness and understanding Hannah must have seen. Matthew lowered his hand as Paul began to reread the letter.

Hannah wanted a fresh start. As he read, the frustration of nearly thirty hours of riding through her community searching for her released its grip on him. The phrase "new wine into new wineskins" was biblical symbolism he'd shared with Hannah on several occasions. Despite his anguish, a gentle peace slowly eased over him. The young woman he'd always thought had the heart of a lion had just broken free of her cage. A smile tugged at his lips.

Maybe Hannah and Matthew were right. Perhaps she did need a clean break from the scandal and grief that the rape had caused. But he wanted to be with her.

"You say she has plenty of money and a plan?"

Matthew nodded. "She's safe, Paul, and probably enjoying the freedom to find her own path in this world."

Paul walked to the edge of the driveway and gazed across the snow-covered pasturelands to the distant hills. The view was almost a perfect image of the dreams that had haunted him night before last. "Two days back I dreamed throughout the night that a voice was calling to Hannah from across the lands to *kumm raus.*"

"Paul." Matthew's voice broke with emotion, and Paul turned to look at him. Matthew's brows knitted tightly, and shock covered his face. "She heard the same words call to her as we stood near her infant's grave site. She even answered it aloud."

Paul couldn't budge as Matthew's words worked their way into his understanding. He studied the horizon, mystified at this assurance of Hannah's departure.

Confusion and heartache lifted somewhat as optimism surrounded him. Confidence that she would return one day took root. He would hold on to that hope and continue to pray that the Lord would heal her and complete the work He had begun in her—in both of them.

Godspeed, Lion-heart. Godspeed.

After stepping off the elevator and onto the train platform, the redcap asked Hannah to wait on a bench while he boarded the others first. He reassured her that he'd reserve a seat for her that had room for her carry-on. As she waited, her thoughts turned up the heat on worry.

Her community and other family members besides Luke had to know by now that she'd left Owl's Perch. The Yoders and even her own parents didn't want her living under their roofs, but that didn't mean they would accept her leaving. The faster she could put more distance between her and her people, the better.

For them and for her.

The minutes seemed to drag by, and her heart palpitated several times before the redcap returned. He led the way as they followed the yellow line, passing several cars in the process.

He came to a stop. "This is your car, ma'am." Without leaving the platform, he passed her bag and ticket to a uniformed man on the train, who seemed to be expecting her.

Before she'd decided whether she should tip the redcap again or not, he'd disappeared.

With the porter leading the way, Hannah strode down the aisle. He motioned to a seat near where baggage was being kept. "I'll put your bag right here in front of you. If you need anything, let me know."

She eased onto the thick blue chair, glad she had the whole row to herself. Through the train window, she could see people on the upper level of the building she'd left minutes earlier. People young and old were gazing through the glass from inside the building, waving their good-byes to loved ones. Neither Matthew nor Luke was anywhere to be seen, and she wondered if they'd already headed home.

Doubts tumbled through her mind while grief and uncertainty assaulted her emotions. Maybe the voice that had called her to *kumm raus* was simply her mind playing tricks on her and she'd been foolish enough to follow it. She closed her eyes and leaned her head back, wondering how she could plan a future based on a nondescript, unspecific voice.

The train shifted forward smoothly, and her misgivings quieted some. As it began swaying and picking up speed, Hannah's hope stirred again. Soon she began to feel as if she were soaring like an eagle rather than gliding and jolting along on train tracks. She was beginning a journey between her and God. It had to be worth taking.

As the hours passed, Hannah watched the ever-changing scenery outside her window. Every time the train stopped and then pulled out from another depot, she sensed she was leaving behind a bit more of her overwhelming sense of powerlessness. It became easier and easier to breathe as the train moved northwestward. She hadn't expected that.

As she stared through the window, a soft whisper crossed her soul.

Nevertheless.

It was an odd word coming to her at an odd time, but it kept circling through her mind, whispering hope. Life hurt. Nevertheless, it was a gift worthy of honoring.

Nevertheless.

The word came stronger this time, immediately lifting her spirits and causing sprigs of new faith to grow.

Her infant had died. Nevertheless, Rachel was now with God.

Hannah's relationship with Paul was over. Nevertheless, God's strength would pull her through.

If everything ended with God, then those who were in Him had a good ending—eventually.

A deep warmth comforted her.

If she already felt this much healing before she'd even gotten on the second train, what healings lay ahead as she learned about life and God over the next few months or years?

She closed her eyes and basked in the warmth of her renewed faith in the God who loves His children.

She'd find her aunt and make plans from there. For now, that's all she knew. And for now, that was enough.

A desire to write to Paul swept over her. He needed to know about *nevertheless.* Regardless of the way things turned out between them, God had a plan.

Glossary

ach—oh
alt—old
Ausbund—a hymnal
begreiflich—easy
Bobbeli—baby
Buhnesupp—bean soup
Christenpflicht—a book of prayers
dabber schpring—run quick
Daadi—grandfather
Daadi Haus—grandfather's house. Generally this refers to a house that is attached to or is near the main house and belongs to a grandparent. Many times the main house belonged to the grandparents when they were raising their family. The main house is usually passed down to a son, who takes over the responsibilities his parents once had. The grandparents then move into the smaller place and usually have fewer responsibilities.
Daed—dad or father
dankes—thanks
deerich—foolish
dich—yourself
die—the
do—here
Druwwel—trouble
du—you
du bischt—you are
du kannscht—you can
Dummkopp—blockhead or dunce
duscht—do
ehrlich—honest
Englischer—a non-Amish person. Some conservative Mennonite sects are not considered *Englischers.*
entsetzlich—awful
es—it
Fraa—wife or woman
Gaul—horse
Grossmammi—grandmother
gut—good
hatt—difficult

Haus—house

Herr Jesu Christ, er führt mich—Lord Jesus Christ, he leads me

ich—I

im—contraction meaning "in the"

iss—is

Kammer—bedroom

kann—can

Kapp—a prayer covering or cap

kumm—come

langsam—slow

letz—wrong

liewe—dear (adjective)

Liewi—darling; dear (noun)

Mamm—mom or mother

Mammi—shortened term of endearment for grandmothers, as in *Mammi* Annie

mei—my

muscht—must

net—not

Ordnung—The written and unwritten rules of the Amish. The regulations are passed down from generation to generation. Any new rules are agreed upon by the church leaders and endorsed by the members during special meetings. Most Amish know all the rules by heart.

Pennsylvania Dutch—Pennsylvania German. The word *Dutch* in this phrase has nothing to do with the Netherlands. The original word was *Deutsch,* which means "German." The Amish speak some High German (used in church services) and Pennsylvania German (Pennsylvania Dutch), and after a certain age, they are taught English.

raus—out

rei—in

rumschpringe—running around

saage—say

schick—behave

schwetze—speak or talk

Sitzschtupp—living room

uff—on

un—and

verschteh—understand

was—what

was denkscht?—what do you think?

wie—how

wunderbaar—wonderful

wunnerlich—strange

ya—yes

zerick—back